CROWN & CREED

The Shard of Elan, Book 3

Laura VanArendonk Baugh

Æclipse Press
Indianapolis, IN

For my creative online chat group,
who kept me sane in this insane year.

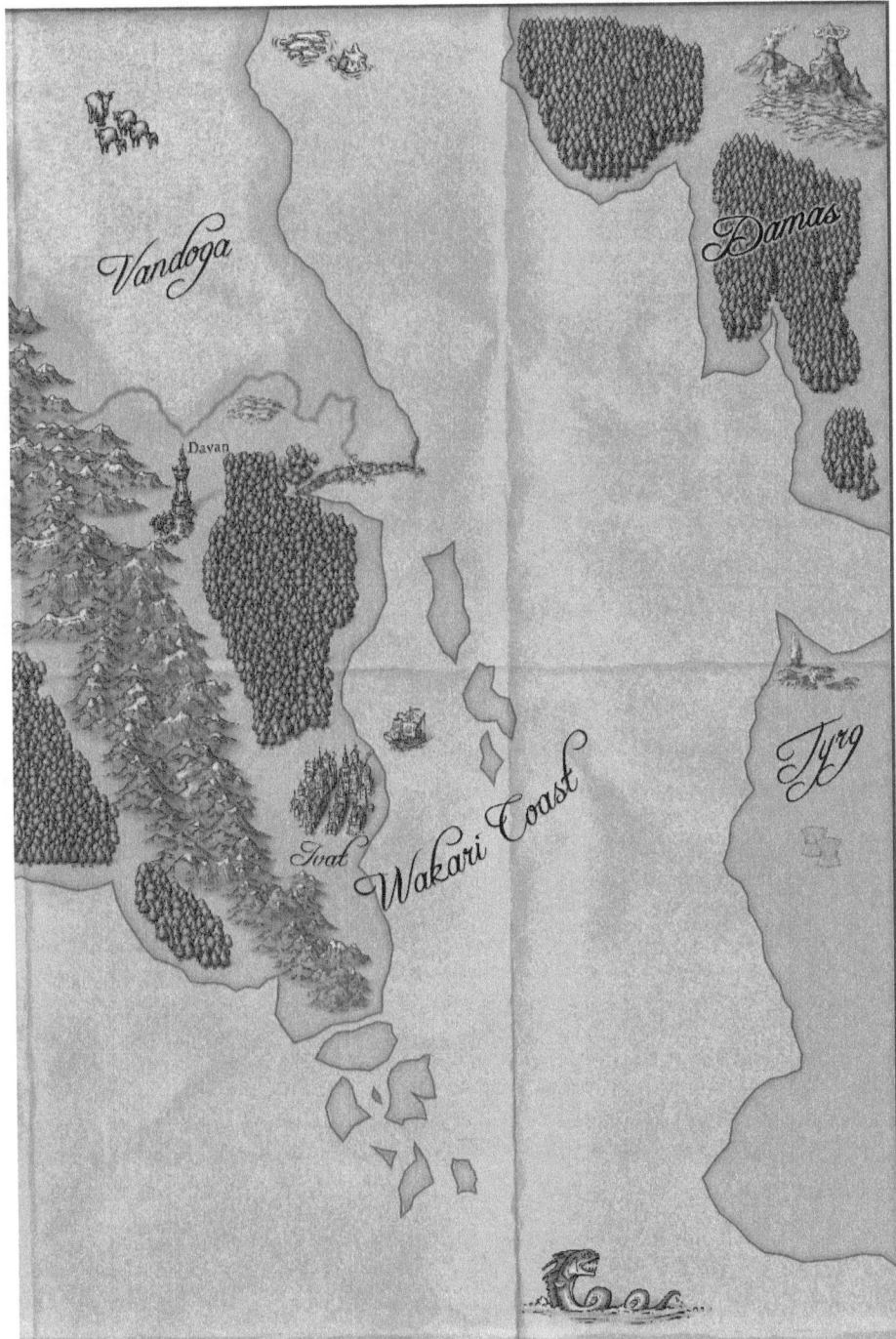

CHAPTER 1

Ariana dashed across the wintry courtyard, dodging soldiers and slaves, her breath tight in her chest in a way which had nothing to do with her frantic pace. Someone called after her, alarmed by the sight of a Mage of the Circle in a hurry, but she did not look back. She ran to Shianan Becknam's office and quarters.

She beat on the door with the heel of her fist, unreasonably afraid that what she had heard had been wrong, afraid the confused rumors that always circulated after battles until clearer reports arrived had led her to false hope and renewed despair.

The door opened, and a black-haired man looked at her, and her heart sank. Not Shianan. Someone else had his office now, of course, because Shianan had been struck down by magic in the cellar of the Wheel. The disjointed story she had heard about the injured prince-heir had been incorrect at least in part, and—

"My lady," the black-haired man said. He was a slave, she saw now, and she thought he looked faintly familiar. She must have seen him around the Naziar before he came to Shianan's old rooms.

"I'm sorry," she said breathlessly. "I have made a mistake. I'm sorry." She turned to go, choking on fresh grief.

"Luca," came a voice behind her, from within, and she froze. It sounded so like—

"Master," the slave said, stepping back from the door as Ariana looked back despite herself.

"What is it? What's happened?" And then Shianan was in the office, visible through the door, looking toward her.

He was bare-chested, braies and leggings tied about his waist, anxiety in his expression. He'd rushed from his room. He saw her, and he froze.

Ariana stared through the open door. "You're alive."

He looked back. "I am."

"I saw you die. I was there when he killed you. I—I didn't know you had survived, not until—not until I heard about the prince." She swallowed, her throat closing about her words. *Not dead*—!

Shianan cleared his throat. "Luca," he said without turning, "I'm sure there is something to occupy your attention."

Luca nodded and went toward the living quarters, and Ariana heard the door close behind him.

She didn't move. She should go into the office, step out of the courtyard, speak to him properly, and she could only struggle for air and words.

"Are you all right?" His eyes searched over her face. "I mean, you were taken there..."

"I'm fine. I'm fine. I was a guest there." She could feel the tears coming, long-suppressed grief finally working free in its negation. "I'm so glad you're alive."

His throat worked. "Ariana..."

They couldn't stand apart like this. She moved forward, gaining speed as she went, and embraced him. He reeled slightly, and an instant later his arms closed about her, sliding beneath her cloak.

"Shianan," she whispered, her voice failing. "I watched you die." His bare shoulder was warm beneath her cheek, and her first tears slid damp over it. "And I couldn't even mourn you."

He held her without speaking.

She turned so her face rested against his neck, the faint prickle of growth biting at her. "And the last thing I'd said to you—I'm so sorry."

His fingers convulsed on her back. "Ariana," he began softly. "I spent the whole of that day trying to find words to apologize. After the king—I ran away. I was a coward, and I ran. I couldn't face you, not when..."

She squeezed him. "It's all right."

"It's not all right." He gulped. "I cannot court you. And now that he knows, I won't even be able to—to do this. Even to speak to you."

He'd asked to court her. Surprise and delight and disbelief warred for supremacy even as the finality of his words cut at her. "Surely..."

"He's taking my title. It should have been done already, the battle put it off, but now it's only a matter of time. The prince-heir came to see me, while I was hiding and brooding. He—you won't know, I haven't had a chance to tell you, but His Highness—he's a good man. And he is..." He chuckled faintly. "He's like a brother to me."

She smiled despite herself. "Imagine that."

"And he came for me. But even the prince could find no hope for this. I can't risk this, Ariana. I can't risk you. Can you imagine if we were known? If the council and the court and the Circle and everyone knew you'd been admired by the bastard? Can you imagine what your position would be after that?" He released her and placed his hands on her arms. "I won't see them hurt you, Ariana." He pushed her gently backward.

She stared at him, her chest tightening. "But..."

"I'm sorry, Ariana. I'm sorry. I shouldn't have run, I should have told you directly. I shouldn't have let it come to this at all. I knew better. I'd hoped... But I'm sorry."

She shook her head, her vision blurring with hot, angry tears. "No! Not like this. Not after I thought you were—not after everything else." Her pent grief burst free at last, and she began to weep despite herself. "I don't care what anyone says—I'm not ashamed of you..."

"Oh, Ariana, don't cry. Please, please, don't cry. Of all the cheating, twisting, hamstringing... Please, don't." He stared at her helplessly, still holding her arms, and then he crumpled and pulled her close, cradling her head against his. "Oh, Ariana, I'm sorry. I'm so sorry." He was crying, too.

"Shianan—"

"I'll go. It will be easier that way. You're part of the Circle, you have to be here, but I'm a soldier, I can go anywhere, once the prince... It will be easier."

"No! I want you here."

"It can't be."

"But you saved the prince! Didn't you? They're saying you carried him to help. Surely if you saved the prince..."

"Did I?" He shuddered. "They won't even speak of his condition. I saw how he was wounded; I may not have saved him at all."

His words broke over her like icy water. "But—oh, Shianan, your friend. Your brother." She tried to lift her head.

He pulled her tighter, blocking her eyes. "It's—it will be all right." He swallowed hard against her. "I lived well enough before I had either of you."

She began to cry anew. "Don't—"

"We can't, Ariana. We can't." He detached himself and stepped back, pulling her black hood up over her hair. "Go now. It won't ever be simpler. Just go." He kissed her forehead, brief but longing. "By all that's holy, I love you, Ariana. Please believe that. But you have to go."

She stared at him, the floor unsteady beneath her feet. "We could—"

"We can't. You can't." He rubbed an arm savagely over his eyes and turned, leading her by the wrist. "You have done me a great honor, and your father has been most kind—but I'm the bastard. And I'm sorry for that, I truly am." He tugged once more at her hood, hiding her tears. "Go. I love you. Go."

She shook her head. "There has to—"

He opened the outer door and, almost gently, pushed her outside.

Shianan hooked the door with his foot and kicked it after Ariana's widening eyes. He slapped the bolt into place and leaned against the door, hearing his pulse wild in his ears and unable to breathe.

It was foolish to bolt the door against a Mage of the Circle. She would be inside in a moment, and he dreaded and longed for that entrance.

But his heart pounded on, and at last his chest loosened so that he could draw breath, and there was still no quivering explosion against his back. She did not return.

His throat spasmed and he slid to the floor, the door rough against his bare flesh, trembling with the bitterness of it. Ariana had been a real friend, not merely a fellow soldier or a slave who needed help, but someone who had liked him for himself even when he was a liability.

He could not stay here. He forced himself to his feet and went into his quarters to dress.

Opposite the door, Luca sat against the wall, knees to his chest and the heels of his palms deep in his eyes, silent.

"Why?" Shianan demanded, knowing anguish made him irrational but unable to check himself. "What's all this to you?"

Luca shot him an unexpectedly piercing glare. "Do you think you are the only one to lose someone?"

Shianan stared at him, startled and stung, and then hot anger shielded his hurt. "Get out." He was in no condition to speak now; some part of him still knew that. He wrenched his gaze from the slave and tried to soften his tone. "Get out."

Luca got to his feet and left, moving wide around him.

He clenched his fists, pushing away Luca's challenge and the awful, hideous void Ariana had left in his arms. He swallowed and ordered his mind as a soldier. There were tasks to be done, urgent tasks and many, and they would mercifully require the whole of his thought. He tore a shirt from the chest and jerked it over his head. He dressed quickly and sloppily, yanking his boots into place.

When he went into the office again, Luca had gone. Shianan felt a fresh pang; he should not have spilled his emotion onto Luca. One more person he'd made to suffer.

Shianan passed his hand over his eyes one last time and went out into the courtyard, starting for the warehouses of dead soldiers.

CHAPTER 2

"No, no, it was all the doing of Ariana Hazelrig." Mage Taev Callahan shook his head in overt regret at his own limited contributions. "She had asked me about dall sweetbud—I suspect now that's when she first realized the Ryuven had it—but I had nothing to do with its coming. I didn't even know of its existence until she brought the bushel to us; I suppose she thought I would know how best to prepare it for use. But no, all the praise should go to the Black Mage."

"My lord mage, will this herb truly counter the plague? How much is needed to heal a sick man so that he will not carry the plague to a healthy town?"

Mage Callahan smiled indulgently. "First, let me say that while this has been called a plague for some weeks, it is in fact merely a flux; most recover with treatment. And it seems that a single dose of dall sweetbud is enough to heal this particular flux, so those in line to buy should be patient, and those at the fore of the line should not be greedy."

"They say it cures all!"

"Well, in all my research I have not found any universal panacea. But dall sweetbud is certainly an excellent treatment for many things, and it cannot hurt to stock every physic kit with a packet or two." He paused, considered. "Yes, I would consider it vital for every goodwife and mother to purchase a small supply."

"So we do need the dall sweetbud?"

"Oh, yes." Callahan nodded, rubbing his thumb along his scar. "In my opinion, this bringing of dall sweetbud is one of the most urgently important accomplishments of this age."

"So could have Becknam!"

His name drew Shianan's attention to the soldiers across the yard. They were bunched close, facing inward. A bad sign.

"You rotting whoreson—take back your lies!"

"My word's my own—I don't take it back for bastards!"

The first punch struck squarely, and as half the cluster of soldiers leapt to separate the combatants, the other half leapt to join them. Sergeant Parr and Captain Torg rushed to join Shianan and they shouldered in, bellowing orders. Torg was not much use with his crushed arm, but Parr and Shianan pulled soldiers from the edge and threw them aside, shouting at them to stay clear, and waded to the center. The fight ended quickly as the soldiers recognized the officers.

"What's this about?" Shianan glared about the group, noting the differing yellow and green collars. "Oh, king's oats. Alham troops, across the yard. Reshire troops, back to your own warehouse. And all of you find something useful to occupy your time, or the slaves digging graves will have a rest."

Sullen silence indicated comprehension. A few men made as if to protest but thought better of it. Belligerent glares were exchanged, and shifting weight promised retribution at a later time.

"Did you not understand me?" Shianan demanded. "Move!"

Part of him wanted to punch a few more brawlers, just for the superficial satisfaction of it. But the soldiers obediently separated and moved apart, jaws jutted in defiance.

"Commander, you want—"

"Solve it yourself, Parr," Shianan snapped. "I have enough to do today."

Parr hesitated. "But, sir, it's only—"

"Sergeant!" Shianan checked himself. Alanz had not returned from Arakadamia, and Parr was struggling to adapt. He took a steadying breath. "'Soats, Parr, what is it?"

The sergeant hesitated. "I'll take care of it, sir."

"Good man." Shianan looked at Torg, who was adjusting his sling. "And do you need me for anything, or can I take care of other business for an hour or so?"

Torg's face was unnaturally expressionless. "Go on, sir. We'll hold it."

Shianan nodded and turned away, hating how everyone reacted to him. Hating that he was acting to bring such reactions.

His head pounded with every step. After Ariana's visit, he had overseen the claiming of the dead. That had grated his remaining presence of mind to ragged shreds. Every still body on the warehouse floor was another life lost under his command. Soldiers could not but die in such a battle—but some of them might have lived, had they trained differently, or longer, or for other scenarios...

He took too much upon himself in that regard; his first commanding officers had told him so from the beginning. But his sense of responsibility had never faded. "That's good," Rictman had commented seriously. "It makes you a thoughtful and fair officer."

Rictman had been a commander, amazingly unreachable when Shianan had first been made a sergeant. After a pack of leucrocutas had savaged his first little command, Rictman had come to him one evening. "It's good to consider your men as people, as valuable lives. They are not toys to be used and broken and discarded without consideration." He looked hard at Shianan, who flushed with hot shame. "But they are soldiers, and they will fight, and some of them will die. And if we hesitate to let them fight for fear of danger, we lose all they are and shame all they represent."

Still, Shianan could not conscience knowing so many of his own were dead. It had not been as devastating as Luenda, in the end, but it had been bloody enough.

He went to the kitchens. He had fallen asleep before Luca returned with his supper the night before, and the morning's business with Ariana had kept him from breakfast. One of the kitchen slaves gave him a thick slice of mutton pie, and he devoured it.

He brushed a couple of stray crumbs from his clothing, making sure he looked presentable after the scuffle, and entered the Naziar palace.

He had visited Soren's office, but never the royal quarters, though he knew where to find the wing. It did not surprise him to see two guards flanking the closed doors. They stiffened as he approached.

"Good afternoon," he began. His voice sounded steady enough, but he thought the unnecessary greeting betrayed his uncertainty. "I've come to visit His Highness."

"No one's permitted, your lordship," replied a guard promptly.

He had expected as much. That was their duty, and as an army commander he had no authority over the royal guard. "I understand. Could I at least have some word of him? I know there aren't any general announcements, but if I could just speak to someone..." He sounded too eager, too anxious. "I won't be long, I—"

"Not permitted, my lord," the guard repeated tightly. His fingers whitened on his polearm.

Something was wrong; while Shianan hadn't expected immediate admission, there was no reason for the guards to be this touchy. Was Soren already dead, the truth a secret for political reasons? His pulse quickened. "Look, I want to see someone about him. I'm the one who carried him for help, after all. There will be a healer in this wing, or a secretary, or your own captain, and I—"

"No, my lord." The guard exchanged a quick glance with his companion, and each of them shifted in place. "You're not permitted."

"Your lordship?" came a third voice. Shianan glanced over his shoulder and saw Ethan, Soren's personal servant, a few paces behind him. "Your lordship, there's a man who wants a word with you, if you please."

Ethan would be unlikely to have a message from the army or court—but he might have a message from Soren. Shianan nodded and turned back to the guards. "I'll return later, with permission," he said evenly. "Thank you for your attention to duty."

Ethan looked ill at ease. "This way, your lordship." He led Shianan down the corridor, around a corner, and into a storeroom of covered furniture. He closed the door behind them. "My lord, I'm sorry. But you can't be here."

"How is he?" Shianan asked quickly.

"He's—he's alive. He's not well, but he's alive. Thanks to your lordship, some say." Ethan looked unhappy. "But others... You aren't to be here, my lord. You've been banned."

Something chill formed within Shianan's chest. "What do you mean?"

Ethan looked miserable. "There's talk that you might—please, my lord, I didn't say this. I never said this."

"Of course you didn't. Now what wasn't said?"

"There's talk that you did this, that you were the one to wound him. That you weren't trying to save him when they found you."

Shianan could not comprehend. "What?! I—but I broke off the shaft, I carried him for miles! 'Soats, I faced Ryuven over his—"

"Yes, my lord, yes! But there's also that he was wounded with a spear, which isn't typically used by the Ryuven, and—it isn't thought you have much love for His Highness."

"I haven't—what?"

"Jealousy, my lord. They say you've always resented the princes, and—and that if you could kill first one, and then the other, you might hope to be raised to legitimacy yourself for a chance at the throne." Ethan seemed to shrink as he spoke; he did not like being the bearer of such news.

16

"That's ridiculous! I don't want the throne—'soats, no. And kill the prince? I've sworn myself to him, I wouldn't—"

"Have you, my lord?" Ethan actually wrung his hands. "Who witnessed it? Who can swear you're loyal to the prince?"

"Soren himself! And I—"

"My master cannot speak for you."

"What do you mean?"

"He's not awake often, and when he is—he isn't himself." Ethan swallowed. "He's barely holding to life, my lord, and some think you killed him."

Shianan stared at the slave for a long moment, wishing his mind would in mercy go blank. But it did not, and he considered that, in fact, he had carried the prince away from the camp in his search for escape. In fact, he had indeed long resented the princes. In fact, almost no one knew of his and Soren's recent friendship. He had been compelled under duress to swear reluctant allegiance to Alasdair; no one would believe he had also willingly sworn to Soren.

The soldiers' fight that morning took on new meaning. Such a rumor would spread like fire through oil.

He rubbed a hand over his forehead and uttered the foulest language he knew.

"He's not dead yet, my lord. If he—when he wakes to himself, he'll tell them. But until then, there are orders to keep you well out."

"Do they think I'll kill him right here in the palace?" demanded Shianan. "Do they believe I could have meant to kill a soft-muscled blueblood and somehow failed?" He stopped and blew out his breath. "I mean no disrespect to your master, but—"

"I know, your lordship."

Shianan clenched his fists, put one to his mouth, turned away from the slave. "How is he—really?"

Ethan's voice was brittle. "You were the last to see him truly alive."

The words went through Shianan like icy steel, shredding him. He stared at nothing, without words. At last he turned back, a long habit of iron control settling over his body. "Thank you for telling me."

Ethan licked his lips. "My lord, I must go. If I were... I'm sorry, my lord."

Shianan nodded. "It's not your doing." He shoved his hand through his hair, curling his fingers fiercely into his scalp. "Go. I'll wait a few moments and leave separately."

Ethan slipped through the door, and Shianan sank down upon a sheeted chair. It was impossible. He would not, could not have harmed Soren. And if they thought him capable of murdering the prince—!

There was no real evidence against him, but he'd learned how easily false witnesses could be found. At least he had expected to take the consequences of stealing the Shard; he had never intended harm to Soren.

At last he stood and went out into the corridor, moving numbly. He wanted to be someplace else, someplace far away, perhaps Fhure—but out of the palace would do for a start.

CHAPTER 3

Luca hesitated outside the painted door, unsure if he wanted to enter and more afraid of being seen lingering outside. Slaves did not loiter, and not outside of temples. He should feign an air of purpose, or he should return home to Shianan's office and quarters. He needed nothing here.

But guilt, or obligation, or a faint and stupid hope pricked at him, and after a quick suck of breath, he ducked his head and went into the dimmer building. He avoided the open central space, where guests talked or gathered for small ceremonies of worship or waited for priests, and slipped to one of the alcoves for private prayer and supplication. He chose a small one, with less decoration, one where no one would complain of a slave's use.

Safely arrived, he drew a breath and tried to decide why he'd come. He had pleaded for Shianan's safe return, and his gift had been refused. *One cannot bribe the One who created all things.* But once his prayer had been answered, he could bring an offering and speak gratitude.

Luca licked his lips. Desperation had helped him to pray before. Now he felt awkward speaking toward a wall, and to a god who had let him suffer so much.

"Good morning."

Luca jumped at the voice and turned toward the priest. As always, the not-quite-familiar robes made his stomach clench. The Gehrn had modeled their clothing after the priests of the Wakari Coast, not those of Chrenada, but there was enough similarity to make his heart quicken. "I beg your pardon, my lord."

"For what? You are welcome to pray here." The priest gestured. "I'm sorry, it seems I gave you a start."

Luca's face should have been more schooled at hiding his emotions. "No, my lord, I was—I was startled, yes."

"You thought I was someone else."

Luca could understand why some people trusted priests as messengers of the Holy One, if they regularly spoke with such uncanny insight. "Yes, my lord. I'm sorry."

The priest smiled away the second apology and then sobered. "How can I help you?"

Where were you when I needed help? Luca wanted to ask, but he shook his head. "Not now."

The priest nodded once. "You prayed before, for your master."

Luca hadn't recognized him, thinking more of the robes, but this was indeed the same priest who had spoken with him before. "My master's come back. He's safe." He lifted the small bag of coins he had brought, a wordless gesture of embarrassed gratitude.

Shianan, at least, had returned to him. Marla and Cole and the others... He prayed for them, too. He had written to Thir and Jarrick, and he had asked them to watch for them. It was a slim chance, but it was all he could do.

"How good to hear it!" The priest seemed to study Luca in the candlelight as he tipped the coins into a collection box. "You bring an offering in gratitude, but you don't seem pleased."

Luca shook his head tightly. "He's returned, and he's whole, but not everything is well."

"I am sorry." He folded his hands with a swish of sleeves. "And you are here because you wish to help him? How can I help you to do that?"

There was nothing Luca could do, nor this priest. "I am a slave, my lord," he said, tasting acid. "I can do nothing but pray."

"That is not nothing."

Words into air felt like nothing, but a slave could not argue with a priest.

The priest smiled at his silence, but it was a wry smile, not belittling. "All our platitudes can smell like so much tripe, when one feels helpless."

Luca doubted this man had ever truly known helplessness.

"But every mill grinds with all its parts; a machine is not built with disused pieces. The smallest cog in a mechanism may be vital to the whole."

These were platitudes, and they did smell of tripe.

"And you can do more than you think," the priest said gently, almost whispering. "You prayed for your master because you wished to do so, not because he ordered it. Each of us serves more than a human master."

Master Shianan had not been there to order it. This priest talked nonsense. Luca looked down, avoiding the priest's kind eyes and childish words.

"Luca." That was Shianan's voice.

Almost relieved at the interruption, Luca turned and saw Shianan coming from the rear entrance. But something was wrong, Luca could see it in his gait and in the set of his shoulders. New trouble, or this morning's? He glanced at the priest—"my master"—and then moved to meet Shianan.

"Someone saw you come here," Shianan muttered distractedly. He glanced over Luca's shoulder at the priest who had followed. "Yes?"

"I'm pleased for your safe return," the priest offered, "and I thank you for your efforts in protecting our kingdom."

Shianan nodded curtly. "Glad for my part," he answered briskly. "Thank you. If you will excuse me, I need—"

"What shall I ask for you, my lord?"

"I beg your pardon?"

"I will pray for you, my lord, as I have since this young man came to petition for your safety in battle. If there—"

"Not me." Shianan wrapped his fingers around the sheath of his dagger without looking and ripped open the buckle with a sharp movement. He held the weapon out horizontally to the priest. "Pray for the prince. Pray for his recovery."

"I will." The priest nodded, making no move to take it. "You need not purchase my prayers."

A moment passed, and then Shianan let the hand with the dagger fall to his side. "Let's go, Luca."

They left the temple, Luca following an appropriate short distance behind. "What's wrong?" he asked quietly.

Shianan shook his head. He wouldn't speak until they had reached privacy.

They passed a square of soldiers marking where an herbal trade would open shortly. A Ryuven vendor would sell his wares within the fortress walls, allowing for easy regulation. The merchant would arrive with his stock in the defined, guarded space, sell for three hours or until his supply was depleted, and then his assistants would return home while he, escorted by soldiers and a captain to keep order, made his own purchases of human goods. Already there was a line of people forming to wait for the Ryuven and the dall sweetbud, gathered in little groups to gossip and speculate.

"My cousin lives west of the river, and he said the plague's not as bad there."

"Maybe it's abating all over."

"No, it's still strong in Far Point, I hear."

"It was rife in Harrowford until they got the dall sweetbud."

"So it does work?"

Luca wanted to walk more slowly, to listen and overhear, but Shianan did not hesitate.

"And it's Mage Callahan!"

"No, no, he said himself it was Hazelrig's daughter who found it. She identified it, she went for it and brought it back—he admitted she only gave it to him to confirm, as he's supposed to be some sort of fancy herbalist. She did it all."

"She did? She's just a girl, isn't she?"

"She's a Mage of the Circle, mind."

"She's still girl enough." A soldier laughed. "You should have seen her coming out of the sky, hair whipping around her and her robes flapping up her legs—and us down below! Heh."

Luca hurried after Shianan.

Shianan slipped his cloak off and tossed it as he entered, so that Luca leapt to catch it. Shianan strode across the office without pausing and began to pace, eyes on the floor. "Close the door."

Luca did.

"They think I tried to kill him." Shianan reversed direction. "They think I tried to kill the prince—or might have succeeded. I can't see him, I can't have word of him, and they may blame me if he dies." He clenched his fists. "I tried to save him, Luca! I carried him on my back for miles, trying to get him to healers, and they say I meant to kill him?"

Luca stared in horror. If the king truly thought Shianan guilty of trying to murder the prince...

"King's sweet oats." Shianan ran a hand through his hair.

Luca took a breath. "You can't stay here. Don't you remember the Court of the High Star?"

"Yes, Luca, I remember it well." Shianan's voice had gone flat. "Quite well. But if I run, then—"

"Then we would have a head start!"

Shianan sighed. "Thank you, but I'll be no safer at Fhure than here, should the king choose to seize me. But if you would rather go..."

Luca bristled. "You won't send me away again."

Shianan blinked. "I won't?"

Luca caught himself. "I—that is—well, no, Master Shianan." He straightened and looked evenly at his master. "You won't."

Shianan raised an eyebrow. "Dare I allow you to dictate to me?" He smiled slowly, almost tentatively. "I own you."

Luca felt the tension drain from the air. "You owe me."

Shianan's shoulders dropped. "Fair enough." He sighed and sank onto the edge of the desk. "All right, then, you stay. But I wish I knew how he was." He bit at his thumb, his eyes going distant again. "If he hasn't woken—but that's likely fever, then." He spat a piece of nail. "And I want to see him, regardless. If he's—I want to see him." He looked suddenly at Luca. "If you aren't willing to go to Fhure, are you willing to risk yourself with me?"

"Master Shianan?"

"Tonight. 'Soats, if they're going to arrest me anyway, they might as well have a reason."

CHAPTER 4

Ariana closed her eyes, willing the knocking at the door to end. She should have known it would be impossible to hide; even without her black robes, someone must have known her as she crossed the courtyard. She had only wanted to see Shianan. She had not believed the street news at first, of Prince Soren and the bastard. She could not help but go to him, even before going to her own home.

But she wished now she had never gone. It was almost better to think him dead, unable to see her, than to know she had lost a friend.

No, that was not so, of course; she was desperately glad to know he was safe. But she wished just as desperately that he was not bound and punished for the sin of his father. And he had sought to court her...

The knocking continued. "My lady mage! Are you there?"

Ariana pushed her face into her knees and pulled her arms more tightly about her, as if to hide from the voices. She had been through the worst days she could imagine—abducted, thinking Shianan dead and her father likely so, helpless before Oniwe'aru's implacable resolution, thrust abruptly into horrific battle, forced away by the man who had only just confessed his love——could they not leave her in peace?

Someone tried the latch, and hot anger flashed through her. But she had overlaid her magical lock on the physical one, and it resisted their rattling efforts.

She did not want to answer questions. She did not want to hear praise or criticism or anything at all.

Someone shouted outside, muted by the stone walls. All of the Wheel's walls were of stone, a sensible if expensive precaution in a place designed for magical experimentation. Ariana raised her head; was that her father's voice?

The latch rattled again. There was a snapping sound and a flash of yellow light, and the black door swung open. Her father looked across the room at her and closed the door behind him, magically resealing it without looking. "Ariana."

She leapt off her seat and ran to throw her arms about him. "You're safe," she breathed. "I heard you were—they said you had shielded—but to see you..."

He held her tightly, letting the words spill out of her without interruption.

"I'm sorry, but I couldn't—I couldn't stay there, not with the battle, I—I was just so... I didn't want to talk about it, I just wanted the fighting to stop..."

"I know, darling." He released her slowly. "You were obviously upset. And I wasn't near enough to reach you."

"I went home. You weren't there."

"I haven't been home yet. I've been in the Naziar or the Wheel since the battle. I slept in my workroom." He looked down and met her eyes. "Shianan Becknam is alive."

She nodded, her throat clenching. "I know." She swallowed. "I spoke to him this morning."

Her father knew her tone. "And?"

"And—and he has been ordered... the king... He can't even speak to me, he says. He won't be near me, because he's afraid of embarrassing me. As if I'd be ashamed of him!" She looked up. "He said—but he loves me! And what if it were known that he courted me?"

Her father pursed his lips. "How's your history?"

"What do you mean?"

"The Laguna line traditionally gelded their bastards."

Ariana blinked.

He pulled her close again. "Give it time. I know that's not what you want to hear—but we can't make any decisions now. We're all exhausted, and distracted with the Ryuven and the fighting and the herbs."

"Did he speak to you? Did you know?"

Her father chuckled wearily. "I've known for a long time, darling. I only wasn't sure if or when he would act." He squeezed her. "There will be time to think through this and find an answer. Wait for it."

She nodded against his shoulder. "But what about Shianan?"

"He'll wait. He isn't going to take up with another girl in the meantime. And then we'll find a way—if that's what you want." He looked at her. "Do you love him?"

26

"I—I'm not sure." Ariana swallowed. "That's a terrible thing to say, isn't it? But I can't even think anymore."

"No, darling, that's fine. You have more than a few concerns bidding for your attention, and it's not a decision to be made in haste." He took a breath. "You were safe with the Ryuven?"

She nodded. "I declared myself a diplomat and treated with Oniwe'aru as an ambassador. But..." She gave a small, wan smile. "Don't tell anyone, but it didn't go well."

"I suspected as much when we went to war." He chuckled gently and then sobered. "We gathered the truce was as much a surprise to the Ryuven as to us. Tamaryl was even fighting for them for a time." He paused. "He fought well; we avoided one another."

"I knew he was fighting." She withdrew and began to walk the room. "Oniwe'aru would not discuss peace until his warriors had raided fresh supplies. He told me we could talk further after the battle. I was furious, but there was nothing I could do. And then Tamaryl came from the battle, and you know the rest."

"What made him leave the fighting and help you bring about truce?"

She shook her head. "I don't know. We didn't take the time to discuss it."

"Have you spoken with him since then?"

"No. I wanted to be alone. After the Ryuven palace, I needed time... I haven't heard from him. I think maybe he wanted to be alone, too. The fighting and then the truce, and that he didn't want to be fighting at all, really..."

Her father didn't answer.

She stopped and leaned against the table. "I thought you were dead, too. Oniwe'aru said you'd raised a shield—but I worried." She crossed her arms defensively. "You and Shianan both, and I couldn't even think about it, because I didn't dare to miss my only chance at speaking with Oniwe'aru."

Her father held out his hand to her. "You are the most popular member of the Circle at the moment," he said. "You are the only mage to have survived abduction by the Ryuven—twice. You used the Ryuven's own magic, and in our own world. You brought the dall sweetbud we needed to stave off the plague and you bought our peace. You are the heroine of our day. I think we can justify slipping out and hiding you at the Kalen Baths for a time."

She nodded, thinking of deliciously hot water and locked doors. "I wish I had the energy even to anticipate that."

CHAPTER 5

The rattling bolt woke Tamaryl from his half sleep, and his shoulders twinged painfully as he lifted his head. His crossed hands, numb behind his neck, pulled the binding cord against his throat. Everywhere the fup-forged chains touched they burned faintly, destroying what power he might restore.

The che entered, his forked rod raised like a badge of office, and Tamaryl's heart sank. But Oniwe'aru came next, freezing his sinking heart in his chest. Behind Oniwe'aru followed a half dozen sho. This was a formal court event, then, and no private word between half brothers.

He should have expected as much. He could not hope for mercy twice.

It was difficult to move with his arms and wings fixed tightly, but he rolled his weight forward and onto his knees. Briefly he considered raising one knee so that he knelt in the courtier's position, but he was a bound prisoner and it was not wise to presume.

The sho fanned into a semicircle on either side of Oniwe'aru, staring down at Tamaryl. He felt their eyes burning into him, and his blood ran hot. Deliberately he drew one knee upward.

"Hm." Oniwe'aru made a faintly amused, disdainful sound. "Arrogant as ever."

Tamaryl stared at the floor before his feet. "I am still your loyal sho, Oniwe'aru. That is all."

"Loyal?" Oniwe'aru began to pace across the cell, making the others shift out of his path. "You left the field of battle, which would ordinarily make you a coward. But then you carried our prisoner to her own world again, which would make you a criminal. And you gave your authority to a truce that we had not discussed, that we did not want, in direct contradiction to your orders, and that makes you a traitor. Again."

Tamaryl swallowed against the biting cord, unsure of how to answer the charges. "She was no prisoner, Oniwe'aru, even in your eyes, for you met with her and treated with her as a diplomat." He could feel the aru's eyes, and he kept his head respectfully low. His shoulders and arms burned. "She was trying to return to her world when I found her; I only helped her to do it safely."

There was a stir among the sho until Oniwe'aru silenced them with a glare. "No human mage has ever crossed the between-worlds," he said firmly.

"No human mage has ever survived coming here, either." Tamaryl took a slow breath. This was not the crux of his accusation, and he could not afford to argue over this point. He should concede. "I was thinking only of our warriors. I did not consider that transporting—"

"By the Essence," one of the sho murmured. "If their mages have advanced to—"

"Athre'sho," interrupted Oniwe'aru sharply.

Tamaryl swallowed against the cord again. Oniwe'aru would hear no excuses, no protests today.

"So, Tamaryl," Oniwe'aru continued, and the omission of the honorific was loud in the crowded cell. "You protest that you are not a criminal who released and carried away a prisoner. But you have not denied that you are a coward and a traitor."

Heat boiled through Tamaryl, and chains pulled at his raw flesh as his wings flexed. "I am no coward, Oniwe'aru." Didn't Oniwe'aru realize the courage it took to defy orders? "And I am no traitor, despite appearances. I have acted by my conscience in service to you and our clan."

"Your conscience was under orders to crush the human army and sweep the countryside."

"My conscience was to spare as many Ryuven lives as I could. If I had to sacrifice our warriors to preserve the rest of our clan, that was my duty. But if I could spare our warriors and preserve our clan together, I could not but follow that action."

"You could follow your orders!"

"You could hear the alternative!" Tamaryl snapped, looking up. "If you had let us trade before opening fresh war, we might—"

The fork of the rod caught his exposed throat and shoved him backward. Without arms or wings to catch himself he fell, crushing one wing painfully. He tried to roll but the rod pinned him by the neck, holding him arched and choking over his crossed wrists.

"You will not rise before Oniwe'aru," sneered Vermi'che, smug in his exalted company.

Tamaryl twisted, but his wing remained trapped. He stopped himself and lay still, trying to control his breathing through the tight cord. He spoke past the che. "I meant no discourtesy, Oniwe'aru."

"Let him up, Vermi'che. He is no danger," Oniwe'aru said heavily. "He has less power than you at the moment."

The rod moved away from his throat, leaving only the biting pressure of the cord binding neck and wrists. Tamaryl rolled onto his side, swallowing against the squeeze of the cord, and sat awkwardly upright. Chain tore at his skin. He paused for a moment, trying to collect himself.

"You will not sit so before Oniwe'aru!" Vermi'che stepped into Tamaryl's shoulder, pushing him so that he fell again.

Tamaryl's elbow struck the stone floor with a shock of pain and he landed heavily on his side. He gritted his teeth and carefully closed his eyes, refusing to see the sho staring down at him. "Stop."

"What was that?" Oniwe'aru sounded remote.

"Stop this." Tamaryl rolled slowly onto his stomach, his head toward Oniwe'aru, his face against the stone. He could not spread his hands, bound behind his neck, in the appropriate position, nor could he flatten his wings against the floor, but his abasement was apparent enough. "Oniwe'aru, I have done no harm to the clan."

Please, Oniwe'aru. This is a matter of your pride. It is a matter between you and me alone. Send them away and let us talk. You'll never hear me while they listen.

He did not move, despising how he lay shamed before their eyes. But he was trapped here, and he knew nothing of the battle and the truce, and his pride had won him nothing.

Oniwe'aru sighed at last. "Leave us," he said. "I will speak with him privately."

The sho moved obediently from the cell. Vermi'che hesitated and then set his jaw, leaving with an air of injured betrayal.

Oniwe'aru waited a moment and then crouched on the floor. "Tamaryl," he said softly, "do you know that it is possible to believe passionately in a cause, and to be wrong?"

Tamaryl turned his face to one side. "Of course. But I am not wrong in this. Not for so many lives."

"Human lives, some of them."

"Yes, human lives. And Ryuven lives." Tamaryl licked his lips. "You would not listen. You did not even try to trade for what we needed."

"We could not afford failure."

"We could not afford not to try." Tamaryl drew his legs slowly beneath him, but he could not raise himself from the floor, with his arms and wings bound and weighting his torso. He slid onto his side again and regarded Oniwe'aru. "Will you help me?"

"Don't think that because we have no audience you are any less in disfavor."

"I know that." Tamaryl shifted his aching arms. "But I can hardly explain myself on my face."

"I think you have done enough explaining," Oniwe'aru said dryly, standing again. "But still you've never addressed the flouting of my authority."

Tamaryl rolled and pulled himself upright, and then he shuffled on his knees a respectful distance from Oniwe'aru. It was humiliating to look up at him with his arms bound painfully to his neck; it was difficult to speak forthrightly from chains. "Your authority? This is more than the appearance of obedience—this is the welfare of our people!"

"And what kind of welfare will that be if my authority is not respected? I have set guards on our warehouses and along our fields to protect our harvest workers. If my word meant nothing, how long do you think our stores would last?" Oniwe'aru shook his head. "You did not recognize the importance of this. Even if I thought trade feasible, I could not allow you to offer truce without my approval."

"You didn't support the truce?" Tamaryl wriggled against the wall and stared upward. "Essence and flames, Oniwe'aru, tell me you let them try—tell me it wasn't all for nothing!"

Oniwe'aru regarded him coolly. "That's what would upset you? That you had lost your status and rank for nothing?"

"Yes," Tamaryl answered. "That I had lost my position, lost your trust in me, lost my dear friends, and all without benefit for the Ai." He clenched his fists behind his head. "Did they even offer to trade for the herb?"

Oniwe'aru frowned. "They did." He shifted his weight. "They are eager to gain the herb, and their fighting men are guarding our merchants in their marketplaces. They will trade their grain for our samur." He scratched at his chin and looked at Tamaryl. "That is why you are still alive."

A chill ran through Tamaryl's gut. "Oniwe'aru..."

"You have defied me more than once, Tamaryl. No matter what blood runs in us both, I cannot allow that to pass without note. I have order to maintain." He crossed the cell and turned back. "But your willful disobedience has potentially benefited us, so you are here, awaiting the results of our venture with everyone else."

Tamaryl caught his breath. "Then we're trading?"

"Some. For a time. And then we will meet to discuss it." Oniwe'aru eyed Tamaryl. "You should pray it is as successful as you hoped."

"Where—where's Maru? He acted under my instruction, obeying his lord of obligation, so he—"

"What do you take me for? Maru is working for an herbal trader. There's a demand for unattached nim to carry samur, and he needed a place."

Tamaryl felt simultaneous relief and fresh worry. Why was Maru unattached—what had happened to Tamaryl's house?

He bowed his head again. "Let me help, Oniwe'aru," he pleaded quietly. "I will carry the samur and the risk."

"No, no. You will not leave this cell until I know whether your scheme was disobediently useful or merely anarchistic." He sighed. "By the Essence, Tamaryl, you could have been great. You were so... Why couldn't you do as you were told?"

Tamaryl didn't answer. He had already offered all the explanation he had. If Oniwe'aru could not understand, there was nothing else he could say.

Oniwe'aru turned toward the door. "In the next turn of the moon, I'll meet with their King Jerome. We will see then what your future holds."

"Oniwe'aru!" Tamaryl said quickly. "For that time—here—leave me unbound, at least! You took my power yourself, you know I am no threat—don't leave me like this." The intensity in his voice surprised him.

Oniwe'aru hesitated, looking back, and then he turned to the door again. "Any other twice-traitor would be dead already," he said shortly. He went out the door and the bolt slid home with a sound of grating metal.

CHAPTER 6

Shianan unbuckled his weapons and left them lying across the table. He did not want to harm a guard performing his duty, and he would not carry a blade into the presence of royalty—even were he not already suspected of seeking to murder a prince.

He glanced at Luca. "Are you ready?"

Luca nodded and held out Shianan's cloak.

They crossed the empty courtyard, two obscured figures in the dark. They entered via a servants' door and passed a few sleepy slaves kneading dough, who ignored them. Shianan let Luca lead, as the slave had been able to explore the servants' passages that afternoon. They climbed three narrow spiraling flights of stairs and passed through long, darkened corridors. They passed no one; there was no activity at this late hour, and it was early yet for the pre-dawn chores.

"Here." Luca paused near a single tall window at the end of a corridor. "This is the one."

Shianan looked out the window at the private garden below. Few eyes to see. A strip of linen fluttered at the latch. "You marked it?"

"So I could confirm it from outside, yes. You want the next one left." He hesitated. "If you want it at all."

"I do." Shianan unlatched the casement window and leaned out. There was a narrow ledge of stone directly below, just the span of his hand, and then smooth masonry across an arms-length of wall until the next window and its ledge. "King's oats."

"There's no other so near. And these are the largest windows."

"I know." Shianan considered. "But I see what you mean... Luca, I don't want to drag you into this."

"I'm already here."

"Then go and find a tray, with a pitcher and cup. Several of them."

As Luca returned to the kitchen, Shianan began casting about the area. There was no entry to the royal wing here, which was good; any guards would be a fair distance away. But he didn't know the layout of the wing beyond what he could guess from the windows. He was relying a good deal more than he would have liked on fortune.

He found what he sought around a corner, where old weapons supported a thick layer of dust in an antique display. He took down a short, heavy mace, wondering briefly whose it had been.

Luca returned with the dishes as Shianan knotted the mace into a corner of his cloak. "I have them," Luca explained unnecessarily, his voice muted. "What are you doing?"

"If anyone hears the window break," Shianan instructed, "tell them it was you dropping the tray. Glass doesn't sound anything like that, of course, but distance will be on our side. I'll try to be quiet."

"How will you return?"

"Out a window on the lower floor." He pushed the hinged window all the way back and sat on the little lip. He then fed his cloak though the open window until it hung below him, the mace swinging slowly. "Once you've locked this behind me, go home. Stay well out of trouble."

Luca nodded seriously. "You, too."

Shianan tested the heft of the weighted cloak and swung it experimentally. Then he shortened his grip, leaned out with one hand steadying himself against the wall, and swung the cloak so that the weighted end crashed through the window, snapping the thin strips of lead and glass.

Shianan released the cloak, leaving it hanging out the far window, and got to his feet in the open casement. 'Soats, but this was insane. It was only an arm's reach to the next window, but it seemed a league at least... He pressed his body to the glass and stone, edging as far as he could. Then he stretched out his arm, hugging the masonry to his face, and lunged.

His foot caught the far ledge and he grasped frantically for the broken window, shoving his hand inside and hooking his forearm about the horizontal saddle bar. It held his weight as he pulled himself securely onto the ledge, balancing at one end while he fumbled through the broken window for the latch. He had to stand on one foot for the casement to open, but it cleared him and he was able to slip inside the palace.

He stood inside the window, heart pounding, and looked around. He was in a disused chamber, and no one was shouting for guards to check on the sound of breaking glass.

He leaned out the window and saw that Luca had already closed the window he'd left; good man. He closed his own window—the break would be harder to notice from outside—and shook broken glass from his cloak, which he tied loosely out of his way. A pocketful of feathers mingled with the shards would provide an explanation for the broken window. He left the mace beneath an old chest as he crept from the room.

Somewhere beyond this empty stillness lay the royal family's bedchambers. He had to identify which was the one he wanted.

He came to a more commonly used section, evident from the cleaner hangings, the small lights left burning in the hall for late servants, the faint warmth of bodies and braziers. He had to be more cautious, now. Which room was Soren's?

He paused outside a door, listening. He was debating whether he dared to open it and peer within when he heard a faint sound. He flattened himself against the wall, wishing for more shadow from the dim betraying hall light, and saw someone with an armload of bedding nudging another door softly closed.

Servants didn't change linen in the middle of the night, unless for a sickbed. And, Shianan noted as the servant turned toward him, that was Ethan. Soren was alive, and he was behind that door.

Shianan exhaled and made his muscles loosen. Ethan, tired and unwary, was an easy target; he turned into a narrow servants' passage and Shianan slipped behind him. One hand clamped over the servant's mouth as the other jerked him backward by the throat.

Ethan dropped the bedding and struggled, trying to cry out, but Shianan leaned close to his ear. "Quiet, Ethan," he whispered. "It's Becknam."

Ethan ceased struggling, but Shianan did not release him.

"That was His Highness's room you left?"

Ethan nodded mutely.

"I'm going to see him." Ethan's eyes widened and he began to struggle again. Shianan tightened his hold, muffling the protesting noise. "Quiet!" But Ethan didn't stop, and Shianan changed his grip on the servant's throat, squeezing the two great arteries until Ethan went heavy in his arms.

Shianan hefted the unconscious man—'soats, why hadn't he done that for the injured prince back in the ravine?—and dragged him through a narrow door in the servants' corridor. It was a small storeroom, as he'd hoped, with spare blankets and ink and such as royal masters might request but didn't want cluttering their chambers. He tied Ethan, not uncomfortably, and gagged him with clean bedding. The dirty pile he kicked into the storeroom where it wouldn't draw notice. Ethan would be awake again in a moment, but he might have enough sympathy and trust in Shianan not to kick over too much furniture in an effort to be freed. Shianan hoped the servant would work to free himself, rather than waiting to be found or trying to attract attention. It would be to the advantage of both if Shianan's visit was unknown.

He checked for anyone else in the corridor and then moved silently to Soren's door. He eased it open—there might be a healer at the bedside—and entered.

The large bed was opposite the door, curtains tied back, and the room stretched darkly away to the right. Shianan closed the door behind him and stared at the bed. The single candle on the narrow table cast eerie shadows over the still form, but it was easy to see that Soren was not well.

He was very thin, Shianan saw as he moved closer. His body was consuming itself in an attempt to fight the sickness. His skin was brightly pale, even in the candlelight. Shianan reached to touch his shoulder, knowing what he would find, and the heat was palpable.

There was nothing Shianan could have done to prevent this contagion. Only prompt washing of the wound could have slowed the infection, and he could not have dared to draw out the spearhead in the ravine, even had he wine or antiseptic herbs to clean it. Still, if he'd been able to bring the prince out more quickly...

There were healers and mages working for Soren, certainly. He was receiving the best of care. Shianan could do nothing now. But he could not leave his prince, his lord, lying so quiet and still.

He moved his hand to Soren's arm, a low ridge beneath the blankets, and wrapped his fingers about the forearm as he crouched beside the bed. "My lord," he said softly. "If you can hear me, somehow—I'm sorry I couldn't do more. I tried, 'soats, I tried, but it wasn't enough... Stay here. You have work here, important work. And you wanted to come visit Fhure again."

It was not right, not fair, that he had finally been given those he could trust, lean upon, hold close—and that they were taken from him. Luca he had again, at least for a time, but Ariana and then Soren... *Holy One, I cannot do this on my own!*

"If there's a plan," he whispered, "if there is a plan to this... Keep him here. Your Highness—my lord—stay here."

He stood and leaned to feel Soren's hot, dry forehead. How could he be so hot? Why weren't the healers here with him now?

Some instinct made him glance up, and he caught a reflection of light from the far side of the room. He tensed and reached for the candle, holding it higher to throw its light. A large, stuffed chair sat across from him, a private place for the prince to read or relax. Curled tightly into the chair, enveloped in a blanket, huddled Prince Alasdair, his eyes wide in the flickering light.

They stared at one another for a long moment. Shianan's heart raced. A single cry from Alasdair would have guards rushing to the room, and he could never outrun them all in this unfamiliar wing. Any move to prevent such an outcry would prompt one and be interpreted as an attempt upon the second prince. *Please...*

Alasdair made a tiny choking sound. "Don't hurt him," he managed, his voice shaking.

Shianan felt something wrench within him.

"Please don't hurt him."

"King's sweet oats." Shianan exhaled. "You think I did this? I'm begging for his life, and everyone thinks I'm the one who killed him."

Alasdair blinked. "You didn't do it?"

"Your Highness, I have sworn my allegiance and service to Prince Soren. I tried my best to protect him and to bring him to help. I want very much for him to live." He took a slow breath, thinking of lingering weakness and permanent impairment. "To live and live well."

Alasdair shifted within his blanket. "Are you going to hurt me?"

"King's oats! I don't want to harm any of you. I wish you'd leave me alone, but I wouldn't kill for that." He looked again at Soren. "I wouldn't risk coming to kill a dying man."

"Why—why did you come?" Now Alasdair was looking at Soren, too. "What do you want with my brother?"

My brother. The words sliced through Shianan, but he did not look back at the younger prince. "Your brother is an excellent friend."

He couldn't stay here. If he were discovered with both princes... He swallowed and looked across the bed. "I must go, Your Highness. I—I know I have no right, but—would you let me go in peace? Without calling down the guards on me? I only came..." He stopped, hating to hear himself ask mercy from Alasdair and hating that it was necessary and hating that he'd tried, when it would do no good.

But Alasdair made a single, silent nod, his eyes wide and shining in the candlelight.

Shianan stared a moment, disbelieving, and then he gave a quick nod in return. He bent over Soren and whispered, "If you can hear me—if this is my last chance—thank you, Soren Laguna, for extending your arm." His throat closed, and tears seeped onto his cheeks. "Thank you for the tea in the rocks. Thank you for the flowers to Ariana." He hesitated and then—what would it matter if the younger prince saw?——he bent and touched his forehead to Soren's. "Thank you for everything."

Soren lay silent and still, his skin hot and paper dry. A tear fell onto his face, but he did not move. Shianan rose and, without looking at Alasdair, left the room.

He found the narrow servants' corridor and followed it, one hand on the wall to steady himself as the other rubbed savagely at his eyes. He could not afford to give in to grief, not yet. He had to get out of the palace and safely back to his own quarters. Even now he was not safe from Alasdair, who had only to mention his name—but what could he have done, once the young prince had seen him?

And Soren had never seen him. Soren lay too quiet and too hot, and there was nothing to be done for him now...

He stumbled down narrow stairs, barely remembering to check for others as he exited below. There was a casement window not far from the stairs. He let himself out, pushed the window behind him, and pulled his cloak close as he hurried back to his quarters. Far away a dog barked, too distant to be a threat.

Luca leapt from a chair as he entered. "Did you find him? Did anyone see you?"

Shianan made a single, weary gesture that silenced Luca. He unfastened his cloak and pushed it at its peg, but it fell to the floor. Luca moved quietly to retrieve it.

Shianan swallowed. "I saw him. He's—not well. There's infection in his gut, from the wound, and... He didn't know I was there." He rubbed again at his eyes, not caring if Luca saw. "And Prince Alasdair was there, in the room. I didn't see him at first. He saw me." He took a breath. "He let me walk out, but all he has to do is mention me."

Luca folded the cloak without looking at it. "Prince Alasdair."

Shianan shook his head. "It won't do a thing to worry over it. Either they come for me or they won't. And I'm getting tired of telling myself that."

Luca picked at a tiny shard of glass trapped in the cloak's weave. "I—I'm sorry. About your brother."

Shianan looked hard at him. "Watch your tongue, Luca. A slip like that could cost us both." He let his expression soften. "But thank you." He sighed. "I wish I could carve out this day and forget that it ever happened."

Luca nodded. "Is there anything else I can do?"

Shianan shook his head. "No, no. There's no help for this."

Luca hung the cloak on its peg. "Try to get some sleep before dawn, anyway. It will only look worse without any sleep."

"Worse? I'd hate to see that." Shianan started for the inner door. "Let's see what dreams wait to haunt me."

CHAPTER 7

Ariana tugged her cloak back from the wind to shield herself from its cold—not her black robes, because she could still pass largely unrecognized without them—and turned into the market street. The market traffic was thinning in the lateness of the day, and she made it into the bookbinding shop without incident. "Hello, Vaya," she called.

"Ariana! How good to see you. And come here and let me hug you." Vaya rounded a workbench and embraced Ariana. "We heard so many things, and we didn't know what was true, and we were worried."

"I'm sorry," Ariana answered, muffled against her. "Everything happened so suddenly. Thank you for worrying about me, but I am fine now." She pulled back and smiled. "Is Ranne here yet?"

"What?"

"We were supposed to meet tonight. We arranged by note."

"Oh." Vaya sobered. "She's not here. I don't think she's coming."

Ariana's heart drifted lower.

"She told me yesterday she was helping the baroness to plan a dinner, and I know she's been meeting some of the other families." Vaya tried to say it gently. "She's been very busy, marrying into a new household, and a noble one."

"Of course." Ariana could hardly protest, when she had gone abruptly to another world. There was time enough to catch up with Ranne, when they each had fewer obligations.

"I can tell her you came by," Vaya offered.

"Thank you," Ariana said, "and I'll send another note. I hate to drop in at the baron's house as I do here."

Vaya nodded. "She'll be sorry that she missed you. I'm sure it just slipped her mind."

Ariana nodded and went out into the twilight. Vaya was right; Ranne would not have meant to leave Ariana unmet, and she would be upset and apologetic when she realized her mistake. Ariana wasn't angry, not really. Only, despite all the claims on her attention, a bit lonely.

Overseer Alenn gave his team a breather at the head of the Farron bridge. The hills were hard going even without winter weather, and he had hopes of getting further than usual today, and that meant resting the slaves more often to work them longer. The time could chafe, but it wasn't truly lost time if they made it further by the end of the day.

There was a curious dull sound from upstream, but when he glanced toward the peaks, he saw nothing. The wide stream burbled a pleasant treble over the distant sound, shallow splashing around countless smooth stones long descended from the mountains' ice.

Alenn had been promised a fat personal bonus if the offered contracts in this transport made it to Ivat before a competitor's, and that was worth a little discomfort. He could exchange his team of four at the next village, and there was a good chance he'd make it out of the foothills by nightfall. After that it was a steady push to Ivat, and this load of letters, contracts, packages, and other correspondence could be someone else's worry.

But, for all that to happen, this breather could not turn into a nap. "All right, now, up!" he called. "Let's move."

The slaves shrugged harnesses into place and stretched their necks and legs. The sound from the mountains was louder, audible over the familiar noises of the wagon's start. Alenn walked alongside the wagon, watching the slaves lean into the traces to bump the wheels over the bridge's end. It was a hundred paces to the other side over the wide, silty stream.

What was that sound? It wasn't wind, though it had the same raw quality. It sounded almost like waves at a seashore, heard from a distance. But there was no seashore here in the lower mountains.

One of the front slaves slowed, turning his head to catch the sound. Alenn called for them to keep moving. But the slave looked upstream, and Alenn followed his eyes, and for just a moment he wondered why there were so many fewer rocks in the wide stream bed. Then he realized the water had risen, swallowing the river stones.

It didn't make any sense for the stream to rise, and certainly not in a wide crossing like Farron. That could only be—

"Run!" he shouted, rushing to the back of the wagon. "Run now!"

The slaves may or may not have understood the danger, but they leapt at the whipcrack of his voice, and the wagon lurched. Alenn pushed hard with them, and the wheels jolted against the bridge's planking. He watched the stream swell into a river.

And then the high water came around the bend, like a separate frothy beast riding atop the stream, all jagged with turbulence and dark with silt and mud. It hurtled toward them, less like a clear stream and more like furious porridge, and it rose in height as it came, a stooped monster straightening to enter combat.

"Run, curse you!"

The flood slammed into the bridge like an adze into wood. The bridge groaned and shook, and Alenn stumbled and grasped at the wagon, heavy with letters.

The end of the bridge could not be far. If they just kept going—

The foundation stones shook themselves apart, and the bridge stretched like pulled candy, bowing downstream. Then it broke.

The planking lurched and fell from beneath Alenn, and he was first thrown forcefully into the wagon and then scraped along it. His frantic grasp slid away. He was choking in the roiling water, spinning so that he could not guess which way was up, crushed beneath the unfathomable weight of an unleashed lake.

He would not receive his bonus upon delivery.

Ariana thumbed through a worn copy of *Hosthagel's Umbras*, blinking blearily at the half-familiar diagrams. The Wheel's library was a good place to avoid well-wishers and curious eyes, as generally only mages, their apprentices, and occasional servants came to this room. Tam had spent a great deal of time here, allegedly fetching for the White Mage but, she realized now, likely reading on human magic.

She closed the book and realized she was hungry. She hadn't had much appetite since returning from the battlefield, and she supposed hunger was a sign of recovery, in a way, though she wasn't entirely certain yet from what she was recovering. She stood and went to replace the book on its shelf.

The door opened and Ariana glanced back to greet whichever mage she might see. But the newcomer, a woman near her own age, was unfamiliar to her. She was no Mage of the Circle, and she was old to be starting an apprenticeship. Her clothes, however, were too fine for those of a servant. Ariana hesitated, watching suspiciously as the woman closed the door behind her and held it a moment, as if afraid of pursuit.

The newcomer glanced at the empty reading tables and seemed to relax. She started forward, looking about the room, and wandered to the pedestal where the Claire Ledger was chained. She opened the priceless book and flipped the pages.

"Could I help you find something?" Ariana's voice startled the stranger, who leapt and released the book. Ariana stepped away from the shelf, still holding the *Umbras*.

"I never saw you there," laughed the stranger, too brightly. She took a breath. "I just—the library is open, isn't it? Not private?"

"Guests are permitted," Ariana allowed, "though only members of the Circle may take books from this room. Were you looking for something?"

The woman shook her head. "No, I—only, could you whisper to me if any mages enter? Any of the Circle?"

Ariana regarded her dubiously. She was dressed in her own black robes. After her celebrity, her sudden obscurity was surprising and nearly galling. "Any more, you mean?"

The woman looked about again. "Are some working here?" She offered a slightly flustered smile. "I've been watching for colored robes."

Ariana kept her voice even. "In some chromatic theories, black is a color."

For a moment the woman stared, and then she gasped. "Oh! Oh, please forgive my ignorance. I truly didn't—I thought you were—I, as may be painfully obvious, am not of Alham and am unfamiliar with...everything."

"I am Ariana Hazelrig, the Black Mage."

"So I see, now. The most talked-of mage, even." She brushed uneasily at her dark, waving hair and smiled with embarrassment. "I mistook you for a librarian."

Ariana set down the Hosthagel, freeing her hands. "Why are you looking for mages?"

The woman flushed. "Raw childish curiosity. We don't have a Circle at home."

"Were you trying to sneak up on some?"

"What? I—oh, the door. Yes, I supposed I was sneaking—but away, not in. I wanted to come to the Circle's home, and I am not supposed to be here. Or anywhere."

46

Ariana relaxed and gave her a small smile in return. "Let me guess—you're really the Wakari princess, creeping away from your watchful attendants for a glimpse of the country you are to wed."

She laughed. "Almost, but not quite. No prince for me, I'm afraid." She folded her hands as if embarrassed by them. "My name is Calissa, and I did come with the Wakari contingent, and I am shamefully curious about the Circle and the Ryuven."

The Wakari Coast had only a few Ryuven raids each year, mostly near the mountains and the Chrenadan border. Mages speculated the between-worlds was more difficult to cross there, but no one knew for certain. Regardless of the cause, the result was that most eastern lands knew Ryuven raids as an exotic subject for storytellers and bards, something to be depicted in art but rarely experienced oneself.

Ariana had known all this, of course, but she had never actually imagined growing up without a knowledge of the Ryuven, without understanding that the greatest mages had a responsibility to the greater good.

The Wakari woman offered a smile. "I'm afraid I don't know the proper address for a mage of the Circle."

"'My lady mage' is the usual phrase." Ariana retrieved the book and turned away to shelve it. "And you are 'my lady,' I presume?"

"That will do very well, my lady mage."

"If you are new to Alham, you likely haven't yet tried the pies at this corner of the market. I was about to treat myself to one, but they're large enough to share."

"I should be delighted."

CHAPTER 8

Tamaryl dozed. It was difficult to really sleep, alternately propped uncomfortably to ease the pressure on his wrists and throat or trying to lie so the chain about his torso didn't grind into his ribs or tear at his wings. Still, sleep provided a brief escape from his thirst. No food or drink had been offered since his capture, and he had only licked at an intermittent rivulet on the wall. He would not have been able to take offered rations, anyway. With his arms bound, he could not lift a bowl nor cleanly relieve himself nor adjust the twisted link that scored his wing.

At the appearance of the lone che, he came fully awake.

Vermi'che braced the forked rod before him and advanced. "Get back against the wall," he ordered.

Tamaryl complied. There was no hope in refusal.

Vermi'che jabbed the fork at him, and Tamaryl twitched as he was pinned by the neck to the wall. He tensed as Vermi'che advanced up the stick. What did the che want? He had his legs free, he could kick the che away, but that would buy him only a moment...

Vermi'che reached into his belt pouch and brought out a small blade. His face was set in tight nervous lines. "Hold still."

The wall was very close at Tamaryl's back. He drew his legs under him; if he lunged sideways, the forked rod would probably dislodge. "Oniwe'aru has not given orders for my death," he said, trying to sound confident. If Tamaryl were to die, he would die as a traitor, a public warning.

Vermi'che gave a high-pitched laugh. "Scared I'll kill you?" His jaw muscles twitched. "Put your legs flat and sit down, or I'll leave you trussed like that for the next moon."

A quick rush of eager relief passed through him, and Tamaryl pressed himself against the wall. His heart pounded as the shaking knife came toward his neck, and he hoped Vermi'che could not hear it.

Vermi'che kept one hand on the rod, ready should Tamaryl move. The knife brushed Tamaryl's skin and began to saw at the outermost wrap of cord. The sound grated at Tamaryl, making him want to shudder, but he forced himself to hold still. He kept his eyes on Vermi'che's shoulders, watching for predictors of sudden movement.

The knife slipped and cut skin. Vermi'che caught his breath, but Tamaryl remained still, locked in place.

The cord parted, and there was a loosening about his neck. Vermi'che backed to the end of the rod, keeping it in place. "Now you stay there," he warned, and then he retreated to the door.

Tamaryl let his arms fall, and muscles and ligaments screamed. He had never realized how excruciating a lack of motion could be. Humans added more to their tortures; perhaps barbarism wasn't an unfair accusation, after all.

The bolt scraped home. He was still a prisoner, but he had the use of his arms, anyway. Or, he would. He sat still and let the blood seep agonizingly through them. It was a long time before he felt he could move.

He reached shakily for the chain about his chest and tried to run his thumb beneath it to smooth the links, but his arms were unreliable. No matter, his dexterity would return in time. As would his power, if he were ever freed of the fup-forged chain.

Still no food or water, but perhaps his jailer would bring that later. At any rate, he was pathetically grateful for his new freedom of movement. He touched the cut on his neck, still seeping blood. To be unable to heal something so simple...

He wondered how the fledgling trade was progressing. Were the farmers willing to sell to their longtime enemies? Would the proud Ryuven descend to purchasing what they had once taken? Would the exchanges remain peaceful? How had Ariana fared—was she named a traitor, too?

He reached over his shoulder to pull gingerly at the chain on his sore wing and then slumped with his shoulder against the wall. He could only wait and hope.

The winter sunlight came low and bright through the city streets, making Ariana shade her eyes. She wanted a walk before she went to her workrooms at the Wheel; perhaps the people often waiting for her would grow bored and leave.

She was uncomfortable when people thanked her for her efforts and the bringing of the dall sweetbud, and she was irritated when grey mages gathered without any particular goal. She had been a grey mage herself not so long ago, and she did not deserve or want their devotion.

There was a crowd gathering in the marketplace, and soldiers pushed their way through to form an orderly circle in the center, while others tried to urge those waiting into queues. Ryuven were coming with their herbs. Ariana moved through the crowd, anxious to see how the trade was progressing.

She sensed their coming before the soldiers or tradesfolk could. A moment later, several Ryuven appeared one by one in the ringed area, each with a large basket strapped on either side of the torso. One, better dressed, moved to the encircling crowd and began speaking and gesturing. The crowd murmured and stirred; for most, this was their first time to see a Ryuven. The throng shifted like water lapping at a shore, some wanting to shrink back while others wanted to be first to purchase the herb.

Ariana knew one of the basket-carrying Ryuven. "Maru!" she called, pushing through the crowd. She received more than a few dirty looks—some had gathered to buy the herb, and others only to see the Ryuven, but none wanted to lose place to her—and she made her way to the far side, opposite where the Ryuven merchant took coin and handed out paper packets of herbs.

Maru caught sight of her. "Ariana'rika!" He glanced at the Ryuven merchant and then came to meet her, shifting his baskets. "I'm glad to see you."

"And I you! How are you? How's Tamaryl?"

Maru's smile faded. "I'm well. I'm carrying samur, as you can see. I'd rather be in Ryl'sho's house, but..." His fingers tightened on the rim of a basket. "Ryl is imprisoned. As a traitor."

"What? But—how?"

"He helped you define a truce, when Oniwe'aru had ordered battle. He disobeyed and risked starvation for our clan. Should this trade fail, we will have nothing, and there have been more hunger riots at home." Maru looked ill. "I've not been able to get much word of him, except that I think Oniwe'aru is waiting to see how this progresses before judging him."

"He's a prisoner?" Ariana repeated dumbly.

Maru looked down at the half-dried leaves. The Ryuven were losing little time in preparing their new goods. "So I'm doing my best to see that the trade prospers, for Ryl's sake as well as the rest."

Ariana had done just the same as Tamaryl, had interrupted the battle with him—but she had not defied orders to do it. She had not guessed that Tamaryl had sacrificed himself for her desperate attempt to quell war with trade. She pushed down her futile worry and nodded. "At least you have a good crowd today. And the soldiers will keep it quiet."

Maru tapped the shoulder straps. "At the first sign of trouble, we'll leap, taking the samur with us. We're careful." He smiled gamely. "But it is not so worrisome, after all. Humans in markets carry fewer bows and axes."

Fewer, not none. Ariana could see a group of men standing to one side with weapons visible, watching the herb trade.

She fixed her eyes on Maru. "I hope you do well today."

"Oh, we'll sell all this." Maru sobered. "But I don't know how much will be needed to placate Oniwe'aru."

Ariana exhaled. "I wish I could do something. Will Oniwe'aru hear another voice?"

"Not yours, certainly." Maru hesitated. "I think he's waiting to see if your prince lives. If he dies, Oniwe'aru expects the humans will want blood."

Ariana nodded. It was a fair apprehension. "Perhaps you should make a gift of dall sweetbud—samur—for the prince."

"I know some has gone to the palace already," Maru confided. "We can only hope that it helps."

"It's got to be boiled for four and one half minutes exactly!" snapped a healer. "No wonder the prince isn't recovering, with idiots like you at work. By five minutes, all the good has been boiled out!"

"You sound like an old hedge-witch peddling herbs," retorted another. "A few seconds more or less? It's about the speed of the boil and the consistency of the heat, after all. And the purity of the source."

"Then you say the prince's fever hasn't broken because we're using impure medicines?"

Taev Callahan, watching from his corner of the table, rolled his eyes. "All fevers break sooner or later," he muttered to no one in particular. "The only question is whether they break alone or along with the invalid."

"You could demonstrate a bit of respect, my lord mage." The honorific was more a mockery in the mouth of the angry healer. "We haven't seen any improvement from your arcane assistance, either."

Callahan shook his head. "Not *my* arcane assistance, no. I have not so much as seen the prince. You should ask Mage Rumbt why his work hasn't shown any results."

"Don't try to make this my error," snapped the grey mage across the table. "We all know why the Circle's herbalist isn't working directly with the prince."

"Because I didn't want to argue with a pack of self-important blathering goats, all more concerned with personal aggrandizement than the prince's cure?" Taev swept the table with his gaze. "Do you think the queen would be half as glad for your help if she saw what squabbling took place down here?"

Pearst, the chief physicker, straightened in his seat. "Don't think to threaten us, my lord mage," he warned.

"That was no threat at all, only a question prompted by observation." He gestured. "And here's another: Why is no one adding chrysogenum juice to the prince's medicines?"

"Would you kill him?" demanded another physicker. "That's hardly known. We can't risk it."

"While if you continue as you are, there's no risk?" Callahan crossed his arms. "I haven't even seen the patient, but I've listened to you argue enough to know you're quietly delaying the inevitable. Am I right?"

There was a swell of indignant and furious silence. At last Pearst spoke again. "We are doing our best to support him in his fever. We hope it burns out the poison in the wound. We might have prevented this if we had received him immediately following his injury, but by the time anyone saw him, infection had already set in. Feeding energy to the injury to fuel his natural healing also sped the growth of infection, as the same metabolized—"

"I am familiar with the process," Callahan interrupted dryly. "But you have not answered my question. What risk does chrysogenum juice offer that is not already present?"

"One does not experiment on a prince-heir!" snapped a healer.

Callahan sat back in his chair. "Meaning, you are too afraid for your positions and reputations to try it. You know he will die, and you will not confess to a grieving kingdom that you tried an unconventional treatment—and you hope you will not be asked if there was anything more you might have done and did not."

"That is quite enough, my lord mage," Pearst said icily. "I think we have no more need of your botanical expertise for now. You are excused."

Callahan's eyes narrowed. "If you think it best." He rose, his indigo robes shifting about him. "I pray for the prince's sake you have somehow been wrong in your observations and that he will recover despite your timid orthodoxy."

The table erupted in angry protestations, but Callahan was already sweeping out the door.

CHAPTER 9

Mage Parma called a distracted permission to whoever knocked at her door as she sorted her newly purchased powders into their appropriate drawers. She was mildly surprised when she turned to see two Gehrn priests.

"Well, I suppose this was inevitable." She strode to her worktable and sat down, facing them. "What have you come to say?"

She did not offer chairs, but they took them anyway. Both wore blue garments, marking them as significant members of the Gehrn hierarchy, but neither wore the layered robes of the high priest. Flamen Ande still lived, prisoner though he was.

"I am Flamen Mennti, acting high priest of the Holy Order of the Gehrn. This is Flamen Gregorio."

"I see." As she was not pleased to meet them, she did not feel obligated to say so.

Flamen Mennti folded his hands. "I presume you are aware of our petitions regarding the trial of Flamen Ande."

"I am. The trial has been suspended once already, to allow mages to review the magic in the ritual—the ritual you did not provide us with the others, I might mention, the ritual that destroyed the shield protecting the kingdom. The unworking of the shield could not have been accomplished with the actions originally described to us. Flamen Ande must have done other than what he said, and he must have had Ryuven blood to use, which suggests forethought and intent. This has made your petition to release him, shall we say, unrealistic."

Flamen Mennti shook his head. "That is not true. Flamen Ande would have followed the rituals exactly, both the annual rites and the purification of a new site—"

Elysia turned up a palm, a gesture of self-evidence. "That is something you must discuss with Flamen Ande, not me."

"But we have come to talk with you," he pressed. "We have written our petitions for the release of Flamen Ande, both to the crown and to the Great Circle."

"It is the White Mage who would receive such a letter," she said. He had, she knew, and she had been grateful it had not been her responsibility.

"We have not had a satisfactory answer."

That meant Ewan had not promised them the release of their high priest.

"We have also sent several letters to you, the Silver Mage, but we have had no answer."

She had burned them. "The Great Circle does not have authority over legal affairs," she said, mostly patiently. "Ande is a prisoner of the crown and charged with treason."

"But the mages of the Circle are well-respected and have great influence." Mennti leaned forward. "You could speak for us."

Revulsion lanced through Elysia's gut like a bolt of battle magic. "I could, but I will not," she said flatly. "If that is what you have come to ask, then we are finished."

"We are not finished," Flamen Gregorio said, speaking for the first time. His penetrating eyes were fixed on her.

Mennti raised a hand. "Not yet. I believe Mage Parma may still wish to help us."

"Not likely," Elysia said.

"If reasonable talk will not persuade her, perhaps she can be persuaded in other ways."

Elysia did not like the tone this conversation was taking. "You have already heard that the Great Circle cannot interfere in a legal trial, and especially not one for treason. And you have been reminded that I do not wish to involve myself in this particular trial. Nor do I think that Mage Hazelrig, the elder, will be particularly anxious to help free the man whose actions nearly cost the life of his daughter, the younger Mage Hazelrig."

"That is why we have not approached him again," Flamen Gregorio said, biting off the words as if they offended him.

"And you think I will be a softer mark for your petition?" Elysia shook her head. "I'm sorry, I don't think I can accommodate you. Please close the door as you leave."

Gregorio shifted forward in his seat. "Mage Parma, are you familiar with the Gehrn order? Our history, our—"

"If you mean to ask if I am aware of what you are and what you do, then yes, I am," Elysia interrupted. "As it had never been previously important or interesting, I made time to look into it after your first message. I have read your history, both the alleged founding by Red Harper after he left Bloody-Neck Jacko and the truth that no such connection was ever claimed until two centuries after. I know how you prepare for an all-encompassing war, I even know how you practice the arts of war, to a degree." She crossed her legs. "But you might recall that I, too, practice war, and not in philosophy but in fact, and not against slaves and prisoners in ceremonial fittings but against winged and magical opponents with proper armor and weaponry. So if you mean to intimidate me, Flamen Gregorio, as your Third Tenet encourages in negotiations, you should be aware that what you attempt is both illegal and difficult."

"You cannot charge that we have come to intimidate you," Flamen Mennti said quickly. "We have only knocked at your office door and asked for your help."

"And I have told you I cannot give it." Elysia sat back in her chair and waved her hand in a half hearted dismissal. "The door, if you please."

After a moment, the two Gehrn priests rose. Gregorio glanced back over his shoulder once as they left, but Elysia was pretending interest in a scale left on her table and could avoid his gaze. They closed the door behind them, somewhat harder than necessary.

Elysia pursed her lips and exhaled in a long stream. With the trial restarted, and the damning evidence against Flamen Ande, the Gehrn would be growing more insistent and perhaps more desperate. She did not think they could mount a serious offense, whether physically against the jail that held the prisoner or politically against the trial and sentencing, but it would not hurt to be prepared.

CHAPTER 10

Marla curled her fingers about the cup of warm soup and retreated to a darker corner of the kitchen, less busy now that supper was finished and the day's work nearly done. She wanted warmth and privacy for her moment of melancholy. But one of the kitchen cats followed her, interrupting her musing with a rumbling insistence on a scratch.

She couldn't complain of her new life, of course—she had returned to her mother, to her home, to the place where any word of her lost husband might come first, and her master was not only not cruel, he was not even present. She helped with the routine tasks of the manor house, simple enough. She could hardly complain.

But she could not cease thinking of Luca, and poor Isen, and even Cole. There was nothing she could do for them, but restless worry kept her awake at night and plagued her through the day. Even if she only knew whether Luca lived—if he were dead, at least she could cease to worry for him. And if he were a slave, if she knew where he had gone, then she might beg her new master to find him. But she knew nothing.

If Shianan Becknam ever returned to Fhure—and they said he had visited only twice—then she would unhappily inform him of his friend's loss. To search for a single slave, who might not even live, across the whole of Chrenada or even through the Wakari Coast... It would be impossible.

Still, there was nothing else she could do for Luca.

She had promised to work tonight on Kraden's shoulder, as he'd fallen and pulled something out of place. She finished her soup, gave the cat a final ear rub, and rose to leave.

Shianan had never wished for the luxuries of the Kalen Baths. The soldiers' baths were good enough; he needed no colored, scented salts or silken bath sheets.

But tonight he thought he might have liked the privacy of the elite bathhouse. The military baths were full of soldiers calling to one another, milling on the edges as they complained about water temperature, occasionally splashing in good-natured combat. Shianan could have snapped at them to be more orderly, but he did not want to punish them for his strained mood.

He closed his eyes, water to his chin, and wondered if he should go home and try to sleep. It was early yet, but if he could sleep, it might be a respite from his worries.

The trade with the Ryuven was going well, by all reports. The only trouble was the high demand for the dall sweetbud, requiring careful management of crowds, and the rash of complaints regarding false herbs in the market. With the Ryuven selling only a few hours at a time, resale was common and lucrative. But few knew the extinct herb by sight, and often the miracle plant turned out to be trefoil, or young buttercup, or liverleaf, or even poison ivy.

Still, the presence of such schemes indicated the successful demand for Ryuven trade. If things continued as they were, the temporary peace could be made permanent.

But there was no good word from the palace regarding Prince Soren. Shianan understood the unwillingness to risk the fragile peace. The heir to the kingdom had been wounded in the battle with the Ryuven, and yet the ill-feeling against the Ryuven needed to be suppressed if peace were to be maintained. The king walked a fine line as he waited to see his son die.

And Soren would die. Shianan had seen the wound, and he knew the lethal grip of infection. Soren would have the best care in the kingdom, but healers and mages could do only so much. It was only a matter of time.

He cupped tepid water and pushed it over his face and hair. He missed Ariana—missed her already, though of course he had often gone much longer without seeing her. It was the finality of this parting that pained him. His gut ached with it.

And there was something bothering Luca—something he'd hardly had time to register in the frenzy since Luca's return, but it was there. He wanted to ask about it, but he recoiled from further ill news. He wanted no more hurt. He felt as he had when just a boy, too young for Torg's outpost, bruised and exhausted at the end of a day of training meant for men and knowing that, no matter how he wished, he would face the same the next day.

He'd thought briefly of escaping to Fhure again, but the army could spare few officers during this trial peace. And, if he was honest,

Soren's talk of visiting again was too fresh. Shianan did not want to sit and stare at a door the prince would not walk through.

This was no good. He rose from the bath and scraped water from his skin, ignoring the cool air that prickled. He would find work in his office to occupy him until he could fall asleep without reflection.

But Luca came from the other room when he heard the door. "I have your supper here, kept warm."

Shianan shook his head. "I had a pie at the kitchen."

"Yes, but I've brought more."

Curious, and happy for distraction, Shianan followed him to a covered tray. "What's this?"

Luca shrugged. "You haven't been eating well, and it's starting to show. I thought you could try something."

The tray was filled with more than the usual staples from the military kitchen. There were slices of tenderloin, roasted white, and apples drenched in maple syrup. There was sweet yellow corn in cream and eggs. There was even a handful of winter berries in a small bowl. "'Soats, I know this wasn't in the communal pot. Where did you get this?"

Luca grinned. "I hope they don't keep a strict count in the storerooms."

"You stole this?"

"I mean, it's there for the kitchens, right? And the kitchens are to feed the officers and soldiers, right? And you're a commander, even." He drew Shianan's chair. "Eat. You wouldn't want this to be wasted."

Shianan moved to the table. "King's oats, Luca." He looked at the food, his mouth watering. "You had to have cooked this yourself."

"Not entirely, but in part, and I apologize for that. I was trained in accounting rather than cookery. But I had enough help that I think it should be mostly edible."

"Why?"

"I told you, you haven't eaten. It's my place to note such things. Please, eat."

Shianan sat, shaking his head. "You shouldn't be here. You shouldn't be a slave."

Luca smiled faintly. "I'm not. I chose to come again."

"You chose nothing. You told them I'd pay for you, true, but you—"

"I could have begged them to ransom me to my brothers." Luca looked steadily at him. "It was my own will that brought me here, so I do not think of myself as a slave. I look at it rather like an oath of allegiance to my liege lord, only instead of risking my life on the battlefield and my honor among rabid courtiers, I fulfill my pledge in mundane, safe services such as laundering shirts." He made a little bow and poured from a small jar. "Wine, for your appetite."

Shianan stared at him. "King's sweet oats, Luca, I—"

"It's getting cold, Master Shianan."

Shianan hesitated and then picked up his spoon. "Thanks." He took a piece of the sweetened apples first. "Mm. Luca, you may rummage through the storerooms whenever you like."

"Try the pork," Luca suggested eagerly. "I hope it stayed tender."

"Try it yourself," Shianan returned. "It's not as if I'm the only one who could use an extra meal. You still show wear from that trek from Cascais." He nodded across the room. "Bring that chair."

Luca didn't move. "Master Shianan..."

"No, we are not going to argue about this. Bring the chair. I order you to sit with me. Does that make it simpler?" Shianan gestured. "Or don't you recall I said you weren't to keep your Gehrn's respectful distance while I ate?"

"When I said I was not a slave, master, I—"

"King's runny oats, Luca, if you speak to me like that I will beat you until you find a less courteous tongue. You know double-dyed well I would free you if I could—but I can't, and I'm too much a coward to send you across the border again right now. You're my slave by law, but you are also my dearest friend, and we'll not be bullied by custom. Now sit."

Luca did, his eyes bright over his sober expression. "Thank you."

"No, I thank you. As you are so fond of reminding me, I owe you." Shianan indicated the pork with his spoon. "Did you taste this? It's delicious."

Luca cut a piece of meat and lifted it on the tip of the knife. "It is good," he agreed.

Shianan took another bite. "I'm glad you're here," he said quietly. "I hate myself for it. What I said—I don't want you enslaved, but I am glad you're here."

Luca gave him a self-conscious smile. "I'm glad I'm here, too."

Shianan set his elbows on the desk. "There's something else... You left someone, and it wasn't your brother."

Luca looked away. "No."

"What happened? I don't even know anything of after you left Alham. We haven't had much chance to trade stories."

Luca stiffened. "I went home, and I was not welcomed with open arms. But... Jarrick tried, so hard, and Sara was so forgiving... And Thir. Flames, I never knew Thir even—but it was not what we hoped. I couldn't stay."

Shianan waited.

Luca swallowed and kept his eyes away from Shianan. "And then I was captured on the road and I came here."

Shianan hesitated. "Luca... If I can, I'll hear you. You know all my secrets, and—"

"Do I?" Luca looked back suddenly. "I guessed you stole the Shard, and I guessed you stole it to save Lady Ariana Hazelrig. But you were very careful not to speak of the Ryuven we saw when the shield failed."

"I didn't know you!" Shianan was stung. "We neither of us knew the other."

"But we trust one another now," Luca returned. "So, tell me about Tam. How does a young slave know more about the Ryuven than soldiers or mages?"

Shianan froze. "I—it's—that is not my secret." He exhaled slowly, dropping his spoon to the tray. "But... If you can bury the Shard of Elan, you can keep this."

Luca waited, motionless.

Shianan clenched a fist, ordering conflicting emotions and unreconciled thoughts. "The boy Tam... He isn't a boy. He's not even human. He's a Ryuven called Tamaryl, and he's Pairvyn ni'Ai." He swallowed. "When Pairvyn ni'Ai was missing, and we thought him dead—he was only hiding here in our world."

Luca stared.

"He got into some sort of trouble and had to hide here—as one of us. A human. And the White Mage knew it, and in exchange for his silence Tamaryl helped him to advance our defensive magic enough to produce the shield."

"Pairvyn ni'Ai?" Luca managed. "That boy was—Holy One protect us."

"He did, it seems." Shianan sighed. "Tamaryl wants Ariana, too. And 'soats, as a rival... At least I know she can no more openly claim him than me. The only suitor worse than the bastard is a Ryuven, and he's the most hated Ryuven, at that."

"And that's why he took her?"

"I don't know. I thought so, but it seems... She said she treated with Oniwe'aru as a diplomat." He sighed. "But that is Tam, and I couldn't tell anyone. At first, it would have been only the word of the bastard against the word of the White Mage. But then, I couldn't risk the Hazelrigs. And by the time you were guessing my secrets and saving my life, he was already gone."

Luca shifted. "I didn't so much save your life—"

"Yes, you did. More than once."

"Then it was only recompense."

"Enough. We are where we are, and there'll be no arguing over how we came here." Shianan lifted his wine. "Pick up the jar and take a swig in the name of good friends."

"In the name of good friends."

They drank, and then Shianan set down his cup. "And now that you know all my secrets and some that aren't mine, will you tell me what's been bothering you?"

Luca sobered and looked down. "I don't want to talk about that. Not now." He licked his lips. "This is the first moment of quiet either of us has had, and—and nothing will be solved tonight. Let's just eat and drink and not think of what else remains."

Shianan looked at him and nodded. "All right. But you know..."

Luca nodded. "I'll tell you. I have to, it's important. I'll want your help. But not tonight."

"Fair enough. Pour more wine."

CHAPTER 11

"Excuse me? My—hello?"

The Ryuven turned and saw a woman in what he'd surmised was common garb for human cities. "I'm sorry, but I can't take your coin here. If you'll step around to the queue—"

"No, it isn't the herbs. You'll be going to Alham, won't you? To sell there?"

The Ryuven nodded. "In two days. Why?"

"Could you take this?" She thrust a packet at him with both hands, obviously a little apprehensive. She probably viewed him much as he viewed the human soldiers standing nearby. But she was anxious to have her message delivered. "My cousin has a stall in the center of the prime market, right where you'll be. He has to get this—there'll never be time to carry it there by foot. Please, I'll pay you of course, but will you take it?"

She seemed earnest, and her money would spend well enough. More, this coin would be entirely his own, and not belonging to the sho, and he would bring home more meat and grain for his children and mate. "Yes, it's small enough. What's your cousin's name?"

"Commander!" General Septime raised a hand to catch Shianan's attention as the dismissed troops began to disperse. "A moment?"

Shianan spun his staff behind him and joined the general. "Yes, sir?"

"Pack a bag, commander, you're leaving."

"What?" Shianan blinked. "I mean, sir?"

Septime dropped his voice. "Get out of Alham. I don't know what's coming, but I know enough of what's going on. I don't believe you meant to kill the prince, of course. You'd have done a better job of it. But if he passes, I don't want you within easy sight."

Shianan felt as if he'd been struck in the gut. "But—sir, I can't leave, it will look—"

"It will look as if I've ordered you to our outpost in Dhubria. The men there need an experienced hand, as they're a bit twitchy about the Ryuven and the truce and all."

Shianan eyed him warily. "Sir, we don't have an outpost in Dhubria."

"Which is why you'll stop at your Fhure, or anywhere else you've a mind to visit. Only see that I can get word to you, in case of need." Septime shook his head. "It won't be the king who comes for you. If the prince dies, it's the streets where you'll be in danger. People are upset and nervous, with the battle and then this truce on its heels, and the Ryuven in our very markets... You're a good man in a fight, Becknam, but I don't see you sticking your blade into a shop boy without hesitating. And 'soats, I don't want to see you do it, either."

"But I didn't do it. Not the prince."

"I know that, man! That's why I want you well out of here."

Shianan looked away. "Will you send me word of him?"

"What? Oh, you'll hear if he dies, sure enough. And I can let you know what the air is like here."

"No, I mean—how he is. Whether he... How he goes."

If Septime understood, he gave no sign. But then, there was no reason for him to suspect. "I can, if you like. Every week or so, if it lasts that long. You'll be at Fhure, then?"

Shianan nodded as his stomach clenched. He had wanted to see Soren there. "Yes, sir."

"Good. Go and tell that slave of yours to pack. I want you gone in the morning."

"Yes, sir."

The Ryuven appeared in their market space one by one, with baskets of herbs slung about their torsos.

Medeth'che, whose company this was, arrived last, bearing a low-backed chair. Despite the gatherings of watchful folks who loitered near the sales, staves in their hands and cudgels and knives in their belts, just beyond the soldiers' influence and just in case, their fears or hopes of violence had not flared to life. He had found selling in the human markets less eventful than he'd feared, and after several hours the cobbled plazas grew wearying. He could sit occasionally and still supervise his sales.

A soldier confirmed that the samur leaves were fully dried, the new rule for herbal stock, and then gestured that sales were open. The waiting humans gathered about them, nodding and gesturing to one another as well as to the che and nim selling the herbs. Medeth'che had instructed them on the prices they were to accept. He had a large family and he wanted to stock his cellar before this tentative peace ended. He was not the only one to suspect that the rationing warehouses were near depletion.

Fortunately, the humans were willing to purchase the herb, if unenthusiastic about its origin. The sickness seemed to be vanishing as the samur became more available, but that did not stop goodwives wanting a supply on hand and herbalists and healers wanting a store for future use. The Ryuven could trade directly for grain, preserved produce, and cured meats or sell for coin and negotiate their own purchases separately—not bad returns for an herb they found less useful to themselves.

A few human merchants waved and called for his attention, anxious to advertise their own products. Medeth'che spoke with them at a cautious distance, and a butcher had reasonable prices. He asked the man to return later with smoked pork. They would carry it home in their emptied baskets.

He'd just finished when another human hailed him. "I like that seat," the man said, nodding toward the chair. "Good workmanship."

Medeth'che glanced at the chair. It did have fine carving, showing a group of young Ryuven at aerial play. Its low back was a luxury. "Yes, I think so," he agreed.

"What do you want for it?"

Medeth'che was caught by surprise. "For my chair?"

"For the chair. A hundred pias?"

Medeth'che did a rapid calculation in his head, counting how many bushels of grain were in one hundred pias. "Don't be insulting," he returned. "I'm sure even human craftsmanship is worth more."

The human grinned, caught in his stinginess. "Three hundred, then, and that's a fair offer."

Medeth'che wasn't convinced. "Three hundred seventy-five."

The negotiations would continue for a time, but one thing was certain—he would return home with more wheat and no chair. It was a trade he was comfortable making, and he was already planning to bring another chair on his next visit. He'd never considered this kind of market, but it could be profitable as well.

Ariana had barely opened the door when Calissa pushed inside. "Close the door, quick. I left an annoyance at the corner."

"Oh? Is everything all right?"

She shrugged off her cloak. "Oh, it's just a guardsman puppy-dogging about after me. Valetta was in a bit of a snit and she grumped about me going out."

Valetta was the Wakari princess and Soren's bride, should he live to marry. Ariana regarded Calissa with concern. "You're not going to get into trouble, are you?"

"No, no. I just had someone to keep an eye on me, but I didn't want him spoiling our fun here. He knows better than to report that I left him outside."

Ariana led the way to where hot drinks waited. "You refer to the princess so lightly. I suppose growing up with royalty lends a certain blitheness."

"At least I have the sense to do it when I'm with you. Not that anyone would notice even in court."

Ariana had not quite worked out Calissa's relation to Princess Valetta. The Wakari Coast had grown its royalty from its foremost merchant houses, and after centuries of intermarriage, the family trees resembled something of a hedge. The Wakari royals themselves were a large family, with a spreading canopy of royal siblings and cousins. It was likely Calissa was one of these. Calissa would explain if asked, but Ariana felt she had waited too long and now was embarrassed to admit she did not know her friend's position.

"I'm just so relieved when I can join you," Calissa continued. "All anyone thinks of is Prince Soren's condition, though we of course barely speak of it. And my lord Adoniram fusses continually because a bridge has gone—an ice dam gave way in the mountains, they say— and so there is no news from Ivat." She made a gesture as if to brush these annoyances away. "Will we have a clear night? You promised me a comet."

"Yes, a comet, and tonight should offer a clear view. But it will be tiny, you know, just another speck in the sky."

"But you'll tell me which is special? Which speck I can brag of seeing?"

Ariana laughed. "Indeed."

CHAPTER 12

Shianan rubbed at his nose and sniffed in the cold. Fhure House was not much further. It had been a long road, and he would be glad of a warm fire and hot soup. A bath would be nice, as well.

He glanced toward Luca, on his left. The slave had been in ardent agreement when Shianan related Septime's order—he was anxious to have Shianan out of Alham, too—but he'd seemed reluctant when Shianan had mentioned Fhure. Shianan was puzzled by that, as Luca had visited only once and briefly, but he had not asked.

But Fhure would be a good resting place. Enraged men might catch someone in the street or even storm an office, but few rioters would leave their homes and businesses to hunt someone after a day or two of travel. The king's guard could certainly find him there, if they chose, but if the king meant to find Shianan, there would be few places he could hide. He might as well be comfortable and frugal.

Fhure was also near enough, if he allowed himself to admit it, to rush back to Alham should Soren wake. And if he died, and if Septime thought it safe, Shianan could return for the prince's rituals and burial.

The oaken doors were shut against the cold, and Luca beat the knocker several times. After a moment someone opened and Shianan entered eagerly. "Sorry I sent no word ahead," he said, "but I'll be here for some time, I think. Please tell Kraden to see to everything."

"Yes, your lordship." The servant bobbed and hurried away.

Luca frowned. "It would have been a bit more correct to see to your comfort and then tell Kraden," he criticized. "Your majordomo could see to their instruction."

"I think they're all a bit rusty. I caught them unaware last time, as well." Shianan grinned. "Perhaps I'll set you on them, and you can scold them into proper service."

Luca smiled, self-conscious. "Sorry." He bowed. "As to that, your lordship, may I take your cloak and establish you before a fire?" He took the cloak Shianan handed him and shrugged off his own with the small pack he'd carried on the road. "Let's find that fire. Where is your room? Does it have a sitting area?"

"The west side." Shianan led Luca to the stairs and down the corridor to the master's room. It had a window, which was pleasant, a large bed to one side, and three chairs clustered across the room. Luca nodded toward the chairs as he set the pack and cloaks on a chest. "I'll find something for the fire, and I'll bring something for you to eat and drink."

"Don't forget yourself."

Luca didn't know the servants' ways, so he descended the main stairs again—there was no one to see—and went in search of someone he could ask about fuel. If all else failed, there would be wood in the kitchen.

He found the kitchen and glanced about for someone to ask. The other servants would be unhappy if he took wood they'd carried, and he didn't need to invite grudges from the beginning. Everyone in the room seemed occupied with a task, and Luca wasn't sure whom to interrupt.

A plump woman hummed as she sorted something at a nearby table: Marta. Luca's stomach clenched. Before he could decide what to do, she glanced up. "Hello, there. Who are—but have we met?"

He nodded, reluctant to speak to her.

"Oh, you came with the accounts once, right?"

He nodded again. "I'm the master's servant. I mean, I'm his attendant, if you like."

"Right. The diligent one."

Luca braced himself. Explaining he had found and lost her daughter would not be easy. "I met your daughter."

Marta looked mildly surprised. "Marla?"

Luca nodded yet again, feeling foolish and uncomfortable and anguished. He did not want to bear such news to a mother. "I met her... I'm sorry. We were coming here, but—I lost her. I don't know where she is now."

"Well, I dare say she'll find her way." Marta continued with her sorting. "Did you need something, lad?"

Luca was stunned at her callousness. Surely not—surely there was more. "It was bandits—I've written to ask about her, but..."

Marta glanced up, vaguely annoyed. "What? Speak up, lad, if you've got something to say. If not, then get what you need. I have work to do."

Luca stared at her.

Shianan entered the kitchen and crossed to a shelf of earthenware cups, Kraden trailing behind him. Shianan was saying something that Kraden seemed to hear with reluctance. The majordomo cast a glance toward Marta, and Luca bristled at the forbearance it seemed to imply.

If Shianan noted it, he gave no sign. He poured himself water from the pitcher on the shelf—Kraden should have done that—and continued speaking.

Luca took a deep breath. "Your daughter, Marla—she may have been taken by bandits on the road. Near Cascais. I don't know if she escaped, but if we ask Master—"

"Bandits?" Marta looked at him sharply. "Lad, that was—she's come home weeks since. She hasn't been back to Cascais and I pray she never goes." Her eyebrows moved. "You—you didn't know her then? Before she came home? Were you with her then?"

Heat scorched through Luca. "She came here? She came here?"

"'Soats, lad, didn't you know? She's here, all right, safe and sound. You weren't on the road with her, were you?"

But Luca's attention was caught by Marla herself, who entered the kitchen with a basket and started toward them, her eyes on her dried fruit. She glanced up and her eyes widened. "Luca?"

Luca's throat closed. "Marla..."

She shoved the basket at a table and ran. "Luca!"

She embraced him without hesitation, shocking him with her force. He rocked a few steps backward, surprised, and his arms closed about her as well, and he breathed deep the scent of her, all fire and almond oil and lavender.

"Sweet Holy One," Marla whispered, "I prayed you were safe. I prayed you'd lived, and that you would get free."

"Marla..." He couldn't begin to express the gladness he felt, the dizzying relief that weakened his knees.

Her mother was on her feet. "Him? It's him you've been worrying for all this time?"

Shianan's voice cut through the kitchen. "You two know one another?"

Luca, self-conscious before her mother and his master, stepped back. "I met Marla in Abbar," he offered. "On the Wakari Coast."

She nodded. "It was Luca who—but what happened?" Her hands slid down his arms to the new wristbands. "Luca, you're not..."

71

He nodded. "I was sold to merchants going toward Alham, and I convinced them to ransom me to my former master."

"But your freedom! Your inheritance!" she protested, her eyes wide.

He shook his head. "I am a slave again."

She squeezed her hands about his. "At least—at least we're here now, together now. Where's Cole?"

"I don't know," Luca confessed.

Shianan held up a hand. "What happened?" He glanced to Marla. "Is all this what I don't know?"

"It's all right," interjected Luca, surprising himself as much as anyone else. "I came to Alham anyway."

"But you're a slave!" she protested. "And you were a freeman!"

"Who is this?" demanded Shianan.

"I'm fine," Luca said to Marla firmly, not wanting to discuss it before so many strangers. He half turned toward Shianan, keeping his eyes on Marla. "Master, let her be…"

Her mother's eyebrows rose significantly. Shianan glanced away. "Who was this Cole?"

"My—my slave," Luca answered. "We were meant to come together to Fhure."

"But the bandits came," Marla picked up, "and he was taken. And now…"

"And now Luca is a slave again," Shianan said. His face was carefully expressionless, but his voice had taken its ring of command. "Luca—you should have told me of her."

There was something subtly wrong in Shianan's tone, something wrong in the way his eyes moved. Luca spoke carefully. "We hardly had time, master, with the Shard, and your injuries, and the battle…"

Shianan gave a curt nod. "Then go. Take the evening as you please. I'll want someone to bring me supper—I'll take it in my room—and, king's oats, I want my fire. Luca, your time is your own. Use it as you like." He turned and strode from the kitchen, his spine erect.

At her table, Marta shook her head, as if to clear it. "He's stiff, that one."

Luca ignored this. "Where can I find wood or charcoal? And can someone assemble a supper tray?"

"Luca." Marla looked as if she wanted to say more.

Marta said it. "Leave the master to us, Luca. It seems you've got some explaining for my daughter. We can scrounge a drudge to carry the wood, and I'll take the tray."

Luca shook his head. "No, I want to see to him myself." He looked at Marla. "I am overjoyed to find you. But I need to see to him. I'll come shortly, I promise."

She somehow understood, bless her. "I'll wait here for you."

Luca carried the wood first. He entered without knocking, finding Shianan pacing the length of the room. Shianan glanced up and then away. "I said you had the evening to yourself."

"Thank you, but I'll see you settled first." Luca began arranging the wood in the fireplace.

Shianan dropped into a chair and began toeing at his boot. "Settled." His foot slipped against the leather as the boot resisted removal.

Luca lifted the little fire pot carried from the kitchen and set an ember against the fresh fuel. "I'll bring your supper, too. Or I could have a bath drawn, if you want."

Shianan's foot slid uselessly against the boot again. With a grunt he bent and seized the boot, tearing it off and throwing it to the floor.

Luca froze.

Shianan hesitated, as if he'd recognized something in the sharp action. He set his face in his hands, his elbows on his knees. "King's oats. I'm sorry, Luca. It's not your fault."

Luca took a breath. This was Shianan, not Ande. He moved toward the chair and bent to take Shianan's other boot. "Take the arms of the chair."

Shianan obeyed, looking unhappy. Luca drew off the boot and set it beside the first.

"It makes sense now," Shianan said. "You lost her in Cascais, and you didn't know what had become of her. And, if I think on it, I know there is no cause for me to resent that you've found her again." He ran his fingers through his hair. "I'm glad you've found her."

Luca waited.

Shianan rubbed at his forehead. "Go and see her, Luca. Don't mind me. I'm being unreasonable and I know it."

"I'll just bring your supper, then."

"No, send someone else with it. I won't tear off any heads, I swear. Go to her."

Marta looked across the table at her agitated daughter. "That's the man you lost on the road? The one you worried over?"

Marla stared back in surprise. "What's wrong with him?"

"I've met him only the once before, but he was—he's a quick and obedient servant, I'll say that. The kind a strict lord likes, I'm sure. The master uses him hard, I think, and he bows under it. He was like to kill himself carrying accounts from Alham the once, and for no better reason than the master wanted us to look over the numbers—those we'd already sent him, and they were fine. There was no hurry at all, and your Luca came all the way at once, arrived in the middle of the night and gone before the bakers were up."

"That's no fault of Luca's."

"And he's not well-spoken, if I can say so. He's about as eloquent as a kicked dog."

Marla's jaw tightened. "Leave him be, Mama. I know him better, and he's a good man. Educated and clever. He was freeborn, but he's had a rough time of it. He was good to Cole, too, when it would have been easy to bully him to salve his own pride. You don't know him, Mama, and when you do, you'll like him."

Marta was taken aback. "He doesn't seem—"

"There are a lot of things that don't seem what they are, Mama. Luca fought a bandit for me." She folded her arms. "You'll like him when you know him better."

"And you mean to keep him here long enough for me to like him?"

Marla made a face at her. "Don't pick at him. He deserves better."

Marta sobered. "You really like him?"

Marla took a breath. "I am still hoping for Demario. But Luca is a good friend."

"All right." Marta nodded. "If he did save my daughter, then that is indeed enough reason for me to appreciate him. Though I can't see him fighting, I must say."

"That's what I mean about things being different than they seem."

Marta rose and began assembling a supper tray: a small brown loaf, a thick slab of butter, half of one of the chickens roasting over the fire, a generous pile of roasted root vegetables. "Well, I'll take your word for it. At any rate, we'll need to feed them."

CHAPTER 13

Queen Azalie leaned over her son's still body to rest her hand against his cheek. His skin was dry and hot against hers, as the fever still struggled wildly against the infection within him. He could not last like this.

She left her hand against his face, imagining she could draw some of the heat from him. The healers said the fever was a part of his healing from the infected wound, but it could also do harm itself. They were doing all they could now, treating him with herbs and poultices and collaborating with the mages in arcane healing, but Azalie knew it might not be enough.

As disheartening as it was to find him lying so still, it was far better when Soren was asleep. Her heart wrenched to see him in pain, groaning and clutching at the festering wound he couldn't even in his state bear to touch, sometimes needing Ethan to restrain him as he struggled without strength. Worse, even when awake, he was not awake—not really. He did not know them, he breathed broken phrases that meant nothing, he seemed to follow a stream of invisible attractions that moved about the room and the air. Weakly conscious and yet incoherent, he was terrifying when awake.

One day he had in a feeble, urgent whisper asked about the battle. Each time she had answered, he had looked across the room, watched something unseen for a moment, and then turned back to anxiously ask again how the battle had gone with no hint of memory. At last he had fallen asleep once more, mid-sentence. She had trembled for hours.

He had slept more and more of late, which was both relieving and frightening. She wanted her son back.

She felt a pressure and glanced down to see Alasdair resting his head against her. She wrapped her free arm about his shoulders. "He's trying, dear," she said softly.

"He's going to die, isn't he?" Alasdair's voice was thin and uneven.

Azalie closed her eyes. Not her Soren... Soren was to be the next king, and she had done her best to see that he would be a good one.

Soren was her firstborn, her hope through the series of lost babes that followed until Alasdair, her precious son—not her Soren...

Someone tapped at the door, and Ethan went to it. Good Ethan, who had been so solidly dependable through this, though she guessed he was nearly as upset as any of them. Two healers entered. "We've brought a new compound, Your Majesty," one volunteered.

They had tried so many, now—how would they ever know which did what for him? She nodded wearily. "Let's pray it helps."

It was growing late, and she was tired. She had been beside Soren nearly all of today. She waited until the healers had reported that there was nothing to report, and then she rose wearily. "I'm going to bed," she said aloud. Ethan made a small bow, but Alasdair didn't move. She looked at her younger son. "Will you watch him again?" she asked.

Alasdair nodded, unspeaking. She set a hand on the back of his neck, wishing there were something more she could do. She was their mother—Soren's and Alasdair's. She ought to be able to do *something* more. But she was helpless before Soren's terrible sickness.

"Wake me if there is any change," she instructed as always, and she hated the necessary ambiguity of the words. She bent to kiss Soren's forehead and then left the room, wishing she had tears left to release the ache in her chest.

Marla sat and tugged Luca down beside her. "Tell me everything," she said. "The last I saw was you turning back. What happened?"

The wide kitchen fireplace was empty of meats and kettles now, but for a single iron pot at one end. Several blankets padded a bench Marla had tipped to form a backrest before the hearth. Despite the difference in size, the cozy feel was almost like Isen's house on the mountain.

Luca told her, speaking flatly of Cole's reluctance to risk escape, of his bargain with the merchants, of Shianan's willing redemption. The narrative flowed easily into the Ryuven theft of the Shard and Ariana, Shianan's nearly fatal magical injury, the battle at Arakadamia, Shianan's return. Luca caught himself just as he began to speak of Shianan's worry over Prince Soren.

Marla tipped her head. "What? What about the prince?"

"You've heard he's injured," Luca ventured carefully. "Some would like to accuse Master Shianan of having done it. He didn't, of course." He did not want to keep anything from Marla, but Shianan's friendship with the prince was private and politically sensitive. "But rumors spread."

Marla looked indignant. "No matter if he is the bastard, that's no reason to kill the prince. It isn't as if he could inherit."

"No." Luca gnawed at his lip. "If the prince should die, and they say it was Master Shianan's doing..."

"Luca," Marla interrupted. "The master has his worries, and it does you credit that you worry for him—but there's nothing to gain by fretting at it."

"But if he is accused—"

"His troubles will resolve in time, one way or another, and there's nothing we can do about it, or about what will come of it. Leave Shianan Becknam for a little while and take your happiness where you can."

"They could kill him."

"And they won't let him live because you fret!" She looked at him unhappily. "Just for a little while, Luca. Be his servant, be his friend, but don't deny yourself all joy because he presently has none."

Luca waited a long moment. Finally he spoke. "I understand you, I do. But I can't just pretend that all is well for him and us. You and I—you can't know how glad I am to have found you again. But if our master is imprisoned, then—"

"Then we'll deal with it as it comes," Marla interrupted. "He owns us both, he owns our lives—leave him out of this moment, at least."

Luca went quiet and still.

Marla relented a little, easing the sting. "Holy One knows, worrying didn't keep me here when the proxy steward saw his end. Worrying won't help any of us. Besides, I think he's worrying enough for the both of you."

Luca acknowledged this with a grim smile. "That's true enough."

Marla sat back and sighed. "Mama said once it's the things we like most that most vex us." She rolled her eyes in mock irritation. "And I like that you think of others. Still, he's given you the evening for yourself, which means you're not to brood on his behalf, either."

Luca exhaled. "All right, I understand."

She looked at him. "I was so worried for you."

Luca's fingers and gut tightened. But he forced a smile. "While you couldn't do anything about it?"

She grinned and looked down. "I concede the point."

Luca's tight smile faded. "I wept and prayed for you."

"While you lost your inheritance and your freedom?"

Luca shifted. "It was only a bit of paper; it wasn't so hard to steal. It was gone before my head cleared after the fight." He shrugged sardonically. "It wasn't much of a fight, either."

"It was enough. I'll never forget that."

Luca hesitated. "I couldn't see them hurt you."

There was a moment of awkward quiet, and then she placed a warm hand on the back of his neck. "I thought as much." She began to rub at the tight cords of muscle. "Relax, Luca. It's all right. No one here will harm us."

He closed his eyes. "But—"

"Hush. Just sit for a time. When did you last do that—just sit, without fretting?" She moved and began to use both hands on his shoulders, shifting his heavy tunic so she could better reach the tense muscles through his shirt. "This is your evening of leisure. Take it."

Luca didn't answer, yielding slowly to her insistent hands. After a moment, she changed the direction of her pressure, pressing him toward the blanketed floor. "Lie still."

"How will this look if your mother comes—"

"Don't be silly. I'm an aelipto, this is what I do. No one will think anything of it." She pressed him toward the floor.

Luca made an incoherent sound of protest but submitted, and the resistance in the muscle began to fade. Marla worked for a moment, using the shirt to ease the friction in place of oil.

He looked better, without the lines of tension in his face. She pushed the long black hair aside and pressed between his shoulder blades. He lay still, his eyes closed.

"Sit up a moment," she said, "and let's slip off your shirt. It'll be warm enough by the fire."

Luca didn't move.

She leaned over him. "Luca?"

His soft, slow breathing betrayed his sleep.

Marla sat back, frowning to herself, both pleased and frustrated. Clearly he needed the rest. She sighed and laid a blanket over him.

What if his worries were justified? If Shianan Becknam was somehow blamed for the prince's injury, if he was arrested, what would become of all of them at Fhure? Such a transition was how she had been sold away the first time.

She shook away the thought—as she'd told Luca, nothing could be solved by fretting over it now—and wrapped a blanket about herself to stay warm as she went to her own bed.

CHAPTER 14

Shianan awoke upon an unfamiliar pillow. Normally such things were not worthy of notice—he had slept in far too many camps and barracks to be picky about his bedding—but this pillow was noticeably plumper with feathers than the one in his quarters in Alham, and his neck had registered the difference in angle. He sat up and stretched.

Luca was nowhere in the room. But there was no servant's bed in the room, so of course Luca had found a place elsewhere.

That—his stomach tightened uncomfortably—or Luca had spent the night entangled with the slave woman. They might still be wrapped about one another now, sleeping after a night of lovemaking in happy reunion...

Steady, he warned himself. *It's not good to be envying the slaves as soon as one wakes.*

He pulled his arms across his chest to feel the muscles reluctantly lengthen. 'Soats, but he was stiff. Maybe he would run today and see if he could sweat out the worry.

He might send someone for word of the prince's condition. It had been only two days, but already Shianan was chafing. If only it were finished, one way or another—*but not by dying, please, Holy One, let him live...*

Shianan sighed and began to dress. Someone knocked at the door, and he called them to enter.

It was the woman—Marla—who came in, carrying a tray with a steaming pot and a cup of tea leaves. "I've brought tea, master. And I thought I might give an account of myself, since there was hardly time last night."

Shianan sighed. "Who are you, then?"

"I was born here; Marta is my mother. I was sold away before Fhure came to you, but I'm glad to come here again. I am an aelipto. My previous master was also a soldier, and he found me invaluable."

She wanted him to want her here. "Massage. I see."

"My lord," she said, "an aelipto is a trained healer. We offer physic as well as relaxation. It is not what you might have experienced at public bathhouses."

"A healer." He exhaled. "You must not think much of my soldiering."

She opened her mouth, flustered and seeking words, and then he saw her notice the tiny crook of his mouth. She relaxed and smiled. "The best of soldiers can have a poor day."

He liked how she fell into gentle jest at his lead. "Then I suppose you might bring some use to Fhure after all. Thank you for the tea."

She smiled. "Of course, master. Thank you."

The quiet rattle of wooden rods and bowls nudged Luca from sleep. He blinked his eyes open, finding himself before the kitchen fire, a blanket tucked about him and his loose tunic. A cat lay atop his legs.

"King's oats, lad, just because you slept there once doesn't mean from now on," came Marta's voice. "We can find you a place. But in the meantime, move yourself. You're in the way."

Luca sat up, displacing the cat, and dragged the blanket away with him, sheepish. "Sorry," he said. "I didn't mean to fall asleep."

Marta gave him an indifferent smile as she set a kettle over the fire and then went on her way. Luca glanced about the kitchen, busy with morning chores. Neat rows of rising loaves and the delicious yeasty scent of finished bread indicated that Luca had slept through the early part of the work.

Long iron skewers for roasting lay on a center table, freshly scrubbed of old juices and ready for new meats. Someone was cutting sausages into a pan, preparing breakfast for the household. Loaves of finished bread for breakfast sat on another table beside a plate of thick, fresh butter, and a pot of cream awaited the finished porridge. Luca's stomach rumbled hungrily.

His master would be equally hungry after the journey, and Luca should see to him. He laced his tunic as he scanned the kitchen.

A shoulder slammed into Luca, checking him so that he half spun with the impact. He blinked, startled, and started a mumbled apology—had he been in the way?—but the broad man who passed him, carrying a wide platter, did not look back. The words faded as Luca hesitated, and then he turned back to the worktables.

There was a suitable serving tray sitting unused at the far left. He would take some of the fresh-baked bread, warm from the oven, and butter. Preserved fruit would go well with the warm bread, too, and some sausage. Maybe a delicious breakfast would help coax Shianan from his dark mood.

He had nearly filled an earthenware plate with porridge, cream, and thick preserves when the shoulder caught him again, sending him stumbling. Luca felt the plate slip, reached for it, caught his toe against something immobile and went down, catching himself on one arm as the plate shattered and spattered the floor.

He looked up and saw the broad man again, this time looking directly at Luca from his intimidating height. His mouth twisted in a pleased smirk. "Stay out of the way and you might not trip like that."

Luca was shocked by the tone that came from his mouth. "What was that for?"

The servant's smirk vanished, replaced by quick anger. "Watch your mouth, or I'll fill it with knuckles for you. And stay away from Marla."

"What?"

"She doesn't want a skinny lick-boot, not really, and you'll just end up looking stupid and missing teeth."

Luca blinked. "What are you talking about?"

All eyes were on them, it seemed, and the kitchen activity had slowed. Luca didn't dare look around for friendly faces. There would be few, anyway. Several spectators were chuckling, sharing in the broad man's power. Luca took a slow breath. "Marla is married and watching for her husband. And even if we were together—Marla can make her own decisions."

Apparently that wasn't the right thing to say. A hand caught Luca's shoulder as he started to rise, and he tensed with all the old terror as he was pulled off-balance toward the big servant—

"What's this?"

It was Shianan's voice, and relief rolled through Luca. Shianan wouldn't let him be beaten. He pulled free of the surprised servant's grasp and took a few steps backward.

"Someone answer me," Shianan said irritably, walking from the entry. "Luca, what's going on?"

Luca looked from his master to the man who'd threatened him, uncertain of how to explain. "Er..."

Shianan crossed his arms and glared over the worktables. "You, what's your name?"

The broad servant frowned but answered, "Gordow."

Shianan raised an eyebrow.

The servant shifted and added, "My lord."

"Gordow, what's between you and Luca?"

"We, uh, we were just talking about, uh, the kitchen. My lord."

Shianan's eyes slipped from Gordow to Luca, looking coolly at the spilled porridge and cream, the broken plate, the ringed observers. "Personal disagreement?"

Gordow seemed to weigh this. "Yes, my lord. Personal."

Shianan made a tiny shrug. "I see. Then finish it."

Luca and Gordow swung as one to stare at him, each remembering belatedly to take a short step back to guard from the other. "Master—" Luca began in disbelief.

Shianan's voice was dispassionate. "Go on, end whatever you've started. I'm a fighting man, if you recall. I dislike unfinished business." He turned his head to Gordow. "Luca has a wicked tongue. Choose your weapon."

Gordow hesitated, unclenched his fist, and then glanced at the long table beside him, where dark iron fireplace skewers lay. He glanced back at Shianan, and when the master made no sign of disapproval, he reached for the longest of them, a heavy rod of eight or ten feet. "I'll take this."

Luca's heart twisted in his chest, and he glanced at Shianan. But his master said nothing, only looked at him with a strange expression. Luca felt as if there were something he was meant to understand, but he couldn't grasp it.

"Ready, boot-lick?" Gordow raised the long roasting spit and rushed forward.

Luca snatched at the table and caught a skewer as he ducked. Gordow wielded the spit as a club, swinging it as he came. The tight rows of worktables meant he had to whip it horizontally, and Luca dropped beneath it.

Luca's own iron spit was so much shorter. He would never be able to reach Gordow.

Gordow's iron rod swung back and he heaved it overhead, ready to bring it down on Luca's crouched form. Luca felt the tables close on either side of him, trapping him beneath the descending spit. He rose and shrank to the side, brushing a bench with his knee as he struck the falling rod sideways with his own.

Gordow growled and pulled the heavy spit up again for another attack, and as Luca fled backward he suddenly saw his chance. Gordow used the spit only as an exceptionally long club. Its length was no asset in the narrow aisle or in his reliance upon raw strength. Luca's shorter skewer, though, could be as versatile and agile as any staff.

He checked his flight and waited as Gordow swung the spit. The rod plunged toward him, and he fell back as Shianan had taught him, bringing his own iron staff up as he did. It cracked against Gordow's elbow in a lucky blow, jarring the spit loose as the big man yelped. But then Gordow punched at Luca with his other arm, and the shorter skewer seemed to move of its own mind, reversing as he fell back again and striking upward into the outstretched punch. And then it reversed again, falling downward into the same arm, and as Luca's feet shifted it spun once more and whipped sideways into Gordow's skull.

The broad servant stumbled back and staggered to the ground. Luca seemed bound to the skewer, following as it pursued Gordow and rose over him, and then as Luca watched, numb with horrified realization, it plunged its sharp point toward Gordow's rolling chest—

"Stop!"

The iron staff obeyed Shianan's voice, and Luca froze. Gordow stared at Luca, wide-eyed, one hand to his temple. Luca wondered if he himself looked as frightened.

"That's enough. I think the point was made." Shianan leaned a hip against the table nearest him. "I want no killing in my kitchen, not before breakfast. Luca, bring my meal upstairs, as it seems a bit too lively here. Gordow, clean the mess on the floor and then find Kraden. Tell him I want a speedy messenger." He glanced about the room, as if daring anyone to protest, and turned to go.

Luca stepped back, hoping the trembling in his legs didn't show within his leggings. He dropped the iron spit and swallowed. Where had he left the tray?

He kept his eyes well away from everyone as he filled another plate, especially away from Gordow mopping up the floor while other servants edged away, pretending not to see his humiliation. Luca dipped a small pitcher of water, gathered the tray, and started for the door.

He nearly collided with Marla, entering breezily. "Oh, good morning," she offered. Then her smile faded. "Wait, what's wrong?"

Luca hesitated, unsure of how to answer. But a voice behind him piped, "He just beat the pasty snot out of Gordow!"

Luca winced—that was not how he would have put it—but Marla had already caught her breath. "What? Are you all right? Is he?"

"We're fine," Luca managed. His face was flushing hotly, and he started for the door. "I need to take this..." He fled.

Marla didn't follow him.

Shianan was sitting in his chair when Luca entered, frowning at the fire. Luca hooked a toe around a light table leg and dragged it nearer so he could set the tray upon it. "Breakfast, Master Shianan," he said. "Tea, sausage, porridge, cream, fresh bread, butter, and preserve. And what exactly did you mean to accomplish, there? We could have been killed, either of us!"

Shianan gave him a look of faint surprise. "What? Of course not. And you wouldn't have wanted me to save you, anyway. You can't survive here with just my shadow on you. They need to respect you, not eye you as a protected craven to be seized when my back is turned."

"But skewers? King's oats, he could have killed me. I nearly killed him!"

"Luca, give me more faith than that. I've managed bravado and posturing for years." Shianan shook his head, smearing butter across torn bread. "I knew he'd pound you to a jelly if we left it at fists, so I quietly encouraged him to choose a weapon you could match. I had every hope you'd manage a defense." He took a bite. "You did surprise me, though. I thought you'd quit once you'd knocked him down."

"I don't want to kill a man just for that!"

"I don't want you to, either," Shianan answered quietly. "And you didn't." He stabbed a thick piece of sausage with his knife. "And don't flatter yourself. If you'd placed those strikes better, if you'd used the tip and the full speed of it, you would have broken his arm, knocked him senseless, and opened his face from temple to nose—much better for a battlefield." He looked up at Luca. "But not for a kitchen brawl." He smiled tiredly. "What started that? New boy in the kitchen?"

Luca felt simultaneously embarrassed and guilty. "Yes. And, also—Marla. I think."

Shianan glanced down at his plate and nodded. "I see." He bit off a piece of sausage. "I hope last night was worth today's fisticuffs."

"I—oh, no, Master Shianan, it's not like that. We're not..." Luca faltered. It seemed awkward to explain. "She's married."

88

But Shianan merely nodded. "I see. Too bad." He took a drink of tea. "I'm sending to Alham, about the prince."

Luca nodded silently. There was little he could say to that.

CHAPTER 15

Queen Azalie returned to Soren's room, feeling her brief meal heavy and undigested within her. Her son had been asleep for two days now, which alarmed her, but she would not let herself think on that. She nodded to Ethan, who bowed silently but said nothing. There had been no change.

There had been no change for a very long time.

She took her seat beside the bed and leaned forward. "I'm still here, Soren," she said softly. She doubted he could hear her, but she had to say something when she came to him. Silence was even worse.

Was his breathing easier today? It was difficult to know. He was still hot and pale.

She found his arm and held it through the blanket. "Your father and brother are worried for you, too. All your friends at court—all the people, Soren. Everyone is worried for you. We have this sort of peace with the Ryuven now; we only need you." She took a breath, steadying her voice. "The Wakari contingent is being surprisingly patient. We've given them a wing and they're keeping largely to themselves. They have not suggested a change in contract, as they're waiting to see you. We need this match, after years of being bled by the Ryuven. But this new truce has made us stronger in the eyes of others... Stowmarries is squawking again about that money he wants. Your father will deal with him. Wallescourt is marrying a daughter of Bathurst, and some minor baron is seeking—"

Soren's lips moved. Azalie froze, staring at her son. Was he awake? Was he trying to speak?

She leaned over him. "Yes? What is it?"

"By," he breathed, the sound faint as dreaming.

Her heart leapt—but it was *not* "goodbye," it was *not*. "Soren..."

His eyes opened and focused—focused on her. His expression was urgent, and she felt him twitch weakly beneath the blankets.

"Bai—la—ha..." The last syllable faded in a long exhalation, and he was once more deeply, feverishly asleep.

She sat back, clenching his arm. He'd spoken, and that made her heart race—but what had he meant?

She'd heard the rumor that Bailaha had been responsible for the prince's condition, but she had firmly forbidden herself to even think of it. How the prince had come by his wound did not affect how it might be treated, and even in her dismay she saw the kingdom could not afford distraction. The peace was too tenuous, the situation too delicate, to hear rumors of a crime that could not be proven, and while the courtiers disdained him, Shianan Becknam was popular in much of the military.

Still, this could not be ignored. Was Soren accusing his murderer?

Azalie raised a hand, but Ethan had rushed forward during his master's brief effort, waiting breathlessly. He hardly needed summoning now. "Ethan," she ordered, "I want to see Bailaha immediately."

Taev Callahan looked mildly surprised when he answered Ariana's knock. "What brings you here?"

"May I come in?"

"Certainly." He held open the door. "Only I thought you would have more duties than would allow you the leisure to visit."

She gave him a confused glance and then turned away. "I don't want that. I didn't do anything so grand." She walked through the room, looking absently over his work. "I came to say... You were the one to identify the dall sweetbud, and yet everyone is coming to me. I'm sorry."

"I don't mind that they—leave that!"

"What?"

"Come away from there." He guided her firmly away from a bubbling pot.

"Why?"

"Because when an arcane botanist tells you to move away from something, it's generally a good idea to do so!" He sighed. "Because teardust root produces a particularly nasty vapor when it's boiled."

She glanced back at the pot. "Then why are you boiling it?"

"Because," he answered irritably, "there are other results that can be useful. And because I know better than to stand in the steam of it." He gave her a long-suffering look. "Look, I don't mind that they think it was your doing. They would be less comfortable lauding me for it, anyway. And I'm just as happy despising them as they are despising me, so this works out well for everyone."

"But what about you? Your standing? Your work?"

He rolled his eyes. "You are the Black Mage. I am the Indigo Mage. You won't advance unless I advance, and they will want to advance you after all this. Your fame benefits me, my little Black sister." He grinned unsettlingly. "And of course, I expect you won't forget your friends, should the opportunity arise to do some good."

Ariana regarded him warily. "What do you want?"

He shook his head. "I am only teasing you, of course."

She sighed. "I don't understand you, Taev Callahan, but thank you for your help. And I do want to see you receive some credit for your work."

He gave her an odd half smile. "No one will ever know much of my work, I'm afraid. Don't worry too much over it."

When she had gone, Taev carefully placed a lid over the boiling pot and removed it from the fire. It wasn't teardust root at all, and this particular variety of fungus had a unique odor. While he didn't think Ariana knew enough to identify it, it paid to be cautious.

Ariana Hazelrig was a nice girl, both talented and useful. Her strong ideals and sense of justice would obligate her to stand up for Taev in future business of the Circle, and with these successes behind her and the influence of her renowned father, it would require a phenomenal failure to put out Ariana's rising star. Even if the peace faltered, she would still be the only mage to have survived Ryuven abduction and to have used Ryuven magic. They would want to promote her through the Circle, and while it was technically possible to elevate one mage beyond another in order, it was rarely done.

He hummed a bit as he decanted from the pot, letting the contents separate by weight. He painstakingly measured an extract into a tiny vial. It was touchy work, slipping chrysogenum juice into the dall sweetbud supplied to the prince's healers, but worth the risk. The death of the prince-heir would upset too much, and there would be few opportunities for him in the resulting disorder. A private visit every evening to their medicinal stores was not too much to pay for national stability.

Luca opened the door, balancing folded laundry on one arm, and saw Marla on the bed straddling Shianan's bare form. He froze.

Marla placed her thumb precisely along the inner edge of Shianan's shoulder blade. "Quiet," she whispered. "I think he's sleeping."

Luca made himself close the door. Shianan was facedown, naked to the blankets over his hips, and unresponsive to the quiet voices. He was asleep, even with Marla over his legs.

"I dislike this bed," Marla commented quietly. "I can't get the leverage I need. Do you think he'd have a proper bench made?"

Luca had interrupted nothing more than a massage. He felt himself flush. "I don't know that he'll be here often enough to use it."

She shook her head, digging into Shianan's flesh. "He'll need something. His *teres* is so tight it's pulling his—"

Shianan shifted as she pressed, making a soft sound of pain or relief, and then subsided into sleep again.

Marla opened her hands, gently flattening his back. "Well, anyway, he needs more regular attention. And the scars, too. Why haven't you taken better care of your master?"

Luca answered the smiling demand with a smile of his own. "I haven't been with him long enough; he had those before I came. But since..." He stopped. Since then, he'd seen Shianan's ribs cracked by the king, Shianan beaten in the street by an angry mob and tortured, Shianan wearied by battle and worry... He shook his head. "His isn't an easy life."

"We'll have to look out for him, then."

Luca set down the laundry. "How long has he been asleep?"

"Since I convinced him to lie still. He seems worn pretty thin."

Luca nodded, knowing better than anyone that his master was at the edge. "Thanks for treating him."

"That is what I do." But she glanced again at Luca as she bent over Shianan, and he knew that she'd done it as much for him.

Before he could think much on this, though, Marla slid off the bed and gestured him close so she could drop her voice. "I'm sorry about Gordow. There's nothing there, but I might have guessed he could feel...proprietary. But flames, Luca, what did you think would happen? And we didn't even—you fell asleep!"

Luca protested indignantly, hot with embarrassment. "I didn't say anything! And I'm sorry, I didn't mean to sleep. I'd love to stay with you—I mean, that is..." He flushed hotter.

She laughed. "Then we were seen last night. Fair enough. Would you build up the fire, please? I don't want him to chill now that I'm finally loosening these muscles."

Luca did, leaving his hands in the warmth, and hoped they could stay at Fhure a while.

CHAPTER 16

Tamaryl shivered; the stone sucked all warmth from the air. The motion brought fresh twinges along the scabbed paths the chains had worn in his torso and wings. He twisted, trying yet again to find a way to flex the bound and cramped muscles, and again there was no relief.

Tears burned in his eyes at the pain, the frustration, the hopelessness of it. Never, even when he had first been exiled and confined in the body of a powerless human, had he been so utterly helpless. At least then he had been free to move, if not free to work his natural magic, and while he was nominally enslaved, his master was kind, respectful of his true nature, and a friend. Now he had only unceasing twilight within cold stone, and he was no more than a victim of his jailer's arrogance, without the power to heal even his minor wounds.

At intervals, the door would be unbolted and Vermi'che would leave food and water. The food was never enough. Tamaryl wondered whether that was a deliberate reminder that he had risked their welfare or a sign that their stores were failing. Or perhaps it was just another cruelty of Vermi'che, who seemed pleased with his role as the Pairvyn's keeper, often pushing Tamaryl to the wall with the forked rod as he collected the empty dishes. Tamaryl burned with humiliation, but there was little he could do. He was partially bound, sore, artificially weakened, and utterly helpless before whatever retribution Vermi'che might invent.

He longed for a bath. That seemed to him silly, in the face of all that plagued him, but he wanted to be free of the dust and sweat of the battlefield, the dried blood where the chains scraped him, the reek of a closed cell with only a tiny grate in one corner for waste. If Oniwe'aru came again, he would hardly recognize his Pairvyn.

If Oniwe'aru came again, Tamaryl would beg him for forgiveness, for release. He could not endure the cold isolation, the thousand tiny hurts of this. He would rather be a slave in the human world, carrying weighty loads, than bound here in the dark where his muscles screamed in the agony of immobility.

He wished he knew how the traders were faring in the human markets. He was still alive, and judging from what Oniwe'aru had said, that meant there had been no disaster. Still, that was hardly hope.

He wished he knew what had become of Ariana. Had she been deemed a traitor to her own people and imprisoned as he had been? Each of them had only wanted peace and prosperity for their own.

He wanted Ariana to be safe, and free, and happy. And he wanted her to look at him as he looked at her.

He rested his face in his hands. It was easy enough to explain that she had been the only female he'd known for years, but that was hardly an excuse. Ariana was young, idealistic, innocent, even naïve in some ways—but that compassionate optimism was balanced with intelligence and ability, and he had few friends now, and thoughts of her occupied entirely too much of his mind as he brooded, bound and solitary.

But she favored Shianan Becknam. At least, she seemed to favor him. At least, she had mourned his supposed death. But then, tender Ariana would mourn the death of any friend, of course—and Becknam seemed disinclined to press his suit, even alive. Tamaryl might yet sway her, despite the war, despite their separate species, despite everything...

But all this was foolish, and he knew it, even through the desperate circling of his thoughts seeking relief from his imprisonment. He loved Ariana, yes, but he loved her as the family he had known for years. In his giddy joy at becoming himself, his true self, once more, he had allowed himself to believe and act on wishes and whims, indulging an affection beyond its merit.

Likewise, in his terror at being exiled once more and his anger at discovering Ryuven prisoners, he had let himself betray his old friend and ally, thieving from him and using his daughter as hostage. He'd let his frustration and despair build until he had nearly committed the murder that would have destroyed any chance of ending the war he'd sacrificed all to end.

Tamaryl shifted in his biting chains. He wanted out of the dark silence that left him exposed to his most scathing thoughts.

But there was nothing to be done. Becknam was with Ariana in Alham, and Ewan knew Tamaryl had stolen their fragment of the Shard, and Tamaryl was chained in this cold, stinking cell.

Maru had endured this. He had been imprisoned in the human world, injured and afraid. Tamaryl could endure it, too, at least until he learned what was decided at the end of the trial peace.

He was cold. *A bath*, he thought. *A hot, steaming bath, with water that never cools.* He curled more tightly into himself and wondered how many days had passed, how many remained.

A runner arrived breathless at Fhure House, bearing a sealed message from General Septime. Shianan retreated with it to his room. He did not want to read of his prince's death before other eyes.

But there was a soft rap at the door just seconds after he closed it, before he had even broken the seal. "Yes?"

"It's Luca," came the low reply.

Shianan sighed. "Come." Luca had a right to know. He would be involved in whatever resulted.

Luca slipped inside, closing the door behind him. "I heard there was a message from Alham."

Shianan held up the folded paper. "From General Septime. I'm a bit afraid of it."

Luca didn't answer. But it was unfair to expect the slave to know how Shianan should navigate the labyrinth of court politics, public opinion, and his own bastard state.

He broke the seal. *Her Majesty has sent for you. Come immediately.*

After a moment, Luca leaned in and stared at the page. "That's it? That's all?"

"It's no less than I'd expect from a military order." But Luca's question prompted more unease. "I don't know what the queen knows or thinks. Maybe it was something he couldn't risk writing. 'Soats, that makes it worse."

"Or perhaps..." Luca's voice trailed away. Neither of them believed the summons could be anything good.

Shianan sighed. "It says immediately. I'd better go."

"I'll get some supplies for us."

"Us?"

Luca looked at him, surprised. "Don't you want me to come with you?"

"I thought you might want to stay." He paused. "With her."

Luca gave a rueful smile. "I told you, she's married to another." And then, more soberly, "And I don't want to wait for word, either."

Shianan nodded. "No one else saw the bill of sale I gave you before, right? For Mage Hazelrig? Then I could write out another, use the ruse again—for the two of you, you and your friend. I don't want you to suffer for this."

"It's no one's fault," Luca answered quickly. "And we don't know why the queen wants you."

Shianan made himself lift a corner of his mouth. "You're right. She might want to ask if I will take the place of the elder prince. Even a bastard is a better prince-heir than the little turd."

Luca smiled bravely. "Exactly so. I'm surprised they didn't send a horse for you."

"I'm sure they didn't want to give away the surprise when I entered the city in glorious honor." Shianan jerked his head. "You go and pack for us."

When Shianan started down the windy road half an hour later, Luca was with him, leaving behind a companion and relative safety, while at the end of the road some unknown force waited to seize his master. Only a fool would take such a road. Or a friend.

They spoke little as they walked, the wind giving them an excuse to stay quietly tucked into their cloaks. No one hailed them; there were few travelers, and Shianan's short sword discouraged any potential thieves. They overnighted at the small inn along the road and lingered over their breakfast before the fire, putting off the start. But at last Shianan pushed back his chair. "Come on, then."

They entered Alham at dusk, though it was not so late as the early nightfall made it seem. Luca dropped to a more appropriate position just behind Shianan, though the streets were not crowded, and followed him through the torchlit gates.

Luca did not know how he did it—how Shianan put one foot down and then another, moving inexorably toward the palace-fortress without slowing or deviating from his path. He knew what lay ahead of him better than Luca did, and Luca knew enough. Luca knew how Shianan had been accused of treason with manufactured evidence, how he had been beaten to injury by his royal father, how his life had been in danger for lesser causes than the death of a prince-heir.

The queen had been adamant in her feelings for her husband's bastard. If Shianan went to her now as the last person to see her firstborn alive, would he come back?

Shianan went directly to the nearest door of the Naziar, drawing his windblown hair back into a fresh tail at the base of his skull. "You have the bill of sale I gave you?"

Luca nodded, his throat suddenly closed.

Shianan unbuckled his sword and dagger, passing belt and weapons to Luca. "If you go to Mage Hazelrig," he said evenly, his eyes on the door before them, "tell Ariana that I love her."

Luca's heart raced. "Wait—at least in the morning—you've been traveling."

Shianan gave a short bark of bitter laughter. "Somehow I doubt what awaits will be steered by whether my boots have been freshly dusted. I will go now." He looked at Luca. "King's sweet oats, Luca, I don't want to do this to you. You've been the best friend I've ever known."

Luca tried and couldn't speak.

Shianan faced him and put a hand on his shoulder, looking over the gear in Luca's arms to hold his eyes. "Don't do anything foolish, Luca. Take care of yourself." His throat worked visibly. "Thank the White Mage for me, and don't forget to tell Ariana." His fingers tightened on Luca's shoulder, and then he turned toward the door, pulling it open and disappearing into the dark.

Luca stared at the closed door, barely visible in the torchlight, and clenched the weapons belt. He thought that he would always remember how, in those final moments, he had stood helpless, unable even to attempt to stop or spare his friend.

CHAPTER 17

Shianan went directly to the royal wing, where the guards tensed at his approach. "You'll need—" one began.

"I am here at the request of Her Majesty," Shianan answered stiffly. His fingers were numbing, and he hid them behind his back to flex them. "Please inform her I await her pleasure."

The guards frowned, but they exchanged glances and one of them passed through the doors. The other made no offer to speak as they waited. Shianan's stomach churned.

Someone moved at the distant end of the corridor, far past the guard, and Shianan turned too quickly to look. Alasdair looked back at him. For a moment they stared at one another, caught in mutual surprise, and then Alasdair turned away and hurried up the corridor.

After long minutes, the guard returned. "She will receive you now."

Shianan followed him to a small apartment—not far from Soren's room, though he wasn't supposed to know that.

The guard knocked and then stepped aside. A maid opened the door and gestured for Shianan to enter. He did, dropping to one knee and bowing his head as soon as he was through the door.

"Rise, Bailaha," came the queen's voice.

He obeyed, looking at her for the first time. She looked tired in her chair, pale but for the dark shading beneath her eyes. She raised an eyebrow. "I see you came directly from the road."

"My orders were to present myself immediately to you," Shianan answered. "Not knowing the cause, I obeyed as best I could."

"I see." The words gave him no indication of whether his choice had been correct. Queen Azalie accepted a warm drink from the servant. "Thank you, Eve. Now, if you would please leave us for a moment?"

The maid blinked and then nodded gracefully, withdrawing through a door in the far end of the small room. Shianan's stomach twisted—private meetings were never good meetings, though it was hard to imagine the refined Queen Azalie kicking or striking him as the king might.

She must have seen his reaction, though she misunderstood its cause. "I am not afraid to speak privately with you. I do not believe you are foolish enough to attempt to harm me in my own apartments, and even so this wing is filled with guards. At the slightest prompt they will enter."

Shianan swallowed. "As it was Your Majesty's summons that brought me here, I hope it is obvious I have not come with intent to harm."

She dismissed this with a wave of her hand. "To the point, then. You are not a stupid man, Bailaha. You are no doubt aware of a certain rumor regarding you."

Shianan's pulse quickened. How was he to answer? "I'm sorry, Your Majesty?"

"I have said you are not stupid; do not attempt to disprove it. I refer to the rumor that it was you who wounded the prince, my son."

Shianan's throat closed. "It—it is not true, Your Majesty. I hope that would be obvious. I have only ever served the throne and the royal family."

"So?" She straightened in her chair, moving with a brittle economy and staring at him with cold eyes. "Others say you only meant to carry the wounded prince to safety."

She shifted in her chair, as if she would rise, and Shianan's stomach twisted. His muscles braced, too tight for closing in battle. But she remained seated, her fingers tight on the carved wooden arms.

"Before asking for you, I questioned General Kannan, General Septime, Marshal Vanguilder. Each of them reports that you held your assigned position all through the battle and then were suddenly nowhere to be found."

He had pursued the prince's mad charge and dived over the ravine's edge within seconds of the prince's fall. The soldiers there had been under attack; they might not have seen what had happened— must not have seen what had happened.

"I am assured it is most unlike you to abandon your duty. So why then did you disappear?"

He had gone after the prince without hesitation. But if she had questioned his superiors, she did not believe his actions had been in good faith.

"Each of them also confirms both that the Ryuven do not favor spears, and that you are well-regarded for your prowess with a spear." She paused, steadied her voice, and continued. "My son has been insensible since the battle. It seems you were the last to see him as himself. All this time, I have watched by his bed or left trustworthy others in my place. Only once has he roused, showing any signs of returning."

Shianan caught his breath.

"He didn't wake, not fully, but he spoke and then fell unconscious again." She paused, breathed, spoke again. "I am watching my son die. In all that time he has spoken only one coherent word. If the rumor is untrue, Bailaha, then tell me why the only word he spoke was your name."

The room swam about Shianan. Soren had—what? Called for him? Tried to speak of him? He had thought of him, at least, that much was true. And yet he remained wholly out of reach...

Shianan ducked his head, suddenly afraid he would weep before the queen. But as he fought the tears, they began to edge over his cheeks. He squeezed his eyes tightly shut, holding his breath and trying to force iron control.

"Bailaha?"

His throat closed, and he could only shake his head for a moment. That was no way to answer a queen. "I'm sorry," he whispered. "Forgive me." He had to push away the tears.

He heard her soft intake of breath. "What is it, man?"

It only grew worse. "I—I'm sorry, Your Majesty, I don't mean..." He coughed and took a deep breath. "I'm sorry. I don't know why he..." He hesitated, swallowed. Blinking, he straightened to face the queen. "I do know something, Your Majesty, but it may not be easy to hear."

"Not easy to hear?" She pinned him with suspicious eyes. "I have heard you might have killed my son. We are waiting to learn if you were successful."

Shianan closed his eyes against fresh tears. "No," he answered softly. "Never."

He didn't want to stand here, exposed and vulnerable in this unfriendly apartment before a grieving mother and hostile queen. He didn't want to uncover his only treasures to a woman who had no reason to believe him and every reason to hate him.

But she was the queen, and he was the bastard.

She drew herself erect in her chair. "I have heard hard things before. Tell me."

Shianan swallowed against the thickness in his throat. It hurt. He took a knee, apologizing in advance for what he would say. "I met His Highness by chance when the young prince was lost," he began shakily. "We—talked. And after that, we spoke more, and—and we became friends. That is, His Highness was generous enough to extend himself to me..." He kept his eyes on the floor, unable to watch her learn her precious son had befriended the bastard she had so hated. "After the trial—the Court of the High Star—he was a good friend to me. And forgive me, Your Majesty, but I swore my allegiance to him, over what I had been ordered to swear to Prince Alasdair."

She sat immobile.

"At the battle, I saw him attacked on the field, and I could not reach him in time. I went over the edge after him, but he was already injured, impaled as he fell. There was no way to take him directly to the plateau, so I carried him up the ravine, looking for a path or a wall I could climb with him." Curse everything, he was crying now. "And all the time I feared that he would die, that I would not reach the healers in time, and then at last the searchers found us." He gulped. "And after that—I could not see him, no one had word of him, and he was my friend, my excellent friend! And they said I was the one to strike him, that I meant to kill him—but if I could somehow exchange myself for him now, I would do it. So believe me, Your Majesty, when I say I mean no harm to your son. I love him, he is my brother—"

He caught himself with a ragged gasp. How could he have spoken that?

Azalie twitched, her expression unmoving. "How casually you say it."

"I didn't mean—I would never have..." His voice failed. What could he say, after all, after saying so much?

She shook her head slowly. "I know." Her voice was strained. "And you meant to help Soren? Your friend?"

Shianan shivered and closed his eyes. "If there were any way I could have brought him out sooner, I would have done it. I tried to find a way up, I searched, but he could not climb, he could not even hold to my back, and I could not find a place where I could carry him up. We had no rope, I did not want to leave him unprotected for the Ryuven again—"

She was abruptly close, he realized, bending beside him. "It's all right. You were a friend to him, after all."

106

Shianan went rigid, his heart pounding certainly loud enough for her to hear so close beside him. Her presence burned like a coal.

"You are alike, after all," the queen breathed. "And you—ah." She retreated, standing again, and the relief of the empty space was a tangible pressure lifted. Shianan resumed a formal position on his knee, hiding his face.

The queen made a small sound, as if clearing her throat. "I suppose I deserve that," she said softly. "But you... I am sorry, Bailaha. It seems you did love your prince, and yet you were kept from him, even accused of attacking the man you sought to save. I am sorry."

Shianan did not answer; he did not trust his voice, and he had nothing to say. That the queen—that she might apologize to her husband's bastard— He could not comprehend it.

She cleared her throat again. "I saw that Soren liked you. I should have trusted more to that." There was a brief pause before she continued. "I called you here because I wanted to hear your own defense and your own explanation of why Soren breathed your name. But you have explained yourself." Her feet turned away from Shianan. "Would you like to see him now?"

Shianan's chest tightened anew. "I..."

"Come this way."

There was no argument to be made, and he wanted desperately to see Soren. He rose, keeping a respectful distance, and followed her out of the room.

She had spoken the truth about the guards; there were several outside the door. They glanced curiously at the queen and Shianan but stayed where they were. She passed through the corridor to Soren's room and tapped. "Ethan?"

Ethan opened the door, bowing to the queen and bugging his eyes at the sight of Shianan.

"I've brought him to see Soren," Queen Azalie explained shortly. She looked toward the bed. "How is he?"

"No change, Your Majesty," Ethan answered. His voice was worn rough, weary and disheartened.

Shianan privately disagreed. Soren looked thinner than even the last time he'd seen him, when he'd crept in during the night. The illness was taking him.

Shianan forgot all etiquette and moved toward Soren's bed, staring at the pale, motionless form. "My lord prince," he said softly.

The queen came to stand beside him. "I watch here every day. And only that once, only your name..."

He felt her unspoken question. *Why you? Why not his own mother, or his brother or father?* He licked his lips. "Perhaps he thought he was still in the ravine."

"If he even knew what he said." She took a carefully measured breath. "We'll never know."

The words struck Shianan like the spear that had taken the prince, driving up through his gut and all the way to his heart.

Queen Azalie opened her mouth, hesitated, gnawed her lip, spoke. "Speak to him."

"Your Majesty?"

"Speak to him. If—if he called to you, then answer him. Maybe he will hear you and—" She stopped. Some hopes were too fragile to be spoken aloud.

Shianan looked at the prince, hot and still, and he thought of the night he had whispered his hopes as Alasdair watched. He wondered what he could say before the queen, in their own nascent truce.

He leaned close and tried twice before he could make his voice heard. "Your Highness. I came."

Soren lay too still, too hot, his thin breath coming too fast. He did not react to Shianan's words.

Shianan felt something crumple within him. He did not look at the queen, unable to bear her disappointment.

Her breath was audible and uneven. She moved forward, and Shianan slid back out of her way. She bent and kissed the pale, dry forehead. "Goodnight, my son."

Shianan could think of no words, could not even formulate a prayer. Everything in him had gone numb.

Ethan made a small bow to the queen. "I need to attend to him," he said gently.

Azalie nodded; even an unconscious prince had his dignity. "We'll go, then. Thank you, Ethan." She turned to Shianan. "You may go, Bailaha. Thank you for coming, and—I'm sorry. I'm sorry for all of this."

She left Shianan standing alone in the corridor. He bowed as she departed, rigid and frail. His arms felt weak, like the prince's pale, loose hands.

He wanted Ariana. He wanted to tell her about Soren, about their blooming friendship and the prince's generosity, about his worry and his grief. But all that was impossible. King Jerome would have a strict temper with his elder son dying and the Ryuven war balancing on a knife's edge, and he would welcome a chance to vent his anger on the bastard's disobedience.

He thought of Soren, thin and still.

CHAPTER 18

The ever-twilight of the prison wore on Tamaryl like the pressure of the chains. Ryuven were creatures of air, as he had chastised Ewan Hazelrig, and they could not be kept underground as the humans had kept their prisoners. Buried their prisoners.

And yet, here he was buried.

There was a squeak and a bang from out of sight, echoing down the corridor to his lonely cell. Vermi'che was coming with a meal, such as it was. Tamaryl steeled himself for insults and small abuses.

But the figure that came into his cell was not the che.

Tamaryl struggled to straighten, but the chains and his long stiffness held him in place. "Edeiya'rika."

The Tsuraiya ni'Ai shuddered slightly as she looked about the room, and then immediately apologized. "I am sorry. I am not typically squeamish. It is more... If you will forgive me saying so, I did not ever expect to find you like this."

Tamaryl gave a grim smile. "Nor did I."

"May I sit?"

"If you dare."

The cell stank, and he stank, and he was humiliated by his bonds and his disgrace. He had not imagined what might be worse than Vermi'che's little cruelties and Oniwe'aru's rejection, but now he had discovered it was the warleader of the defensive force, his counterpart in the Ai warriors, visiting him in his shame.

She chose a spot of floor and sat cross-legged, propping her wings behind her. "I thought you should know what's happened."

There could hardly have been a more ominous opening. Tamaryl's heart iced in his chest. "What?"

"There was another riot at the storehouses. A larger one. Hundreds rushed to force entry and take the rations. There was fighting, of course. One guard was killed. One will never fly again, and another will never walk again. More were injured in lesser ways, and they are being treated."

Tamaryl closed his eyes against the imagery the words brought. "And the nim and che?"

"I am not certain yet of the numbers; many are hiding their injuries to avoid identification. I cannot blame them. They only wanted to feed their families."

"So these were families. Not bandits seeking to steal what we have put away for rations."

Edeiya looked down. "Many had brought their children, hoping to raise sympathy from the guards as they attempted to persuade and beg. It did not start as a riot."

"By the Essence of all," Tamaryl breathed. There had been children.

She lifted her head. "Oniwe'aru had to go himself to calm it, and he has been speaking strongly against those who would steal from the common pot. But he knows they are only doing as they think they must. The situation is growing desperate. He can open the storehouses and bring temporary peace, at the risk of total starvation later, or he can continue to ration and allow the unrest and anger to build."

"He is not taking grain from the humans then," Tamaryl said. Their best hope, all he had sacrificed for, ignored. He should have been outraged, but his stores of frustration and fury had been exhausted.

"It is not quite like that," Edeiya said. "There is trade, and it is bringing meat, produce, and grain. But it is not enough. There are only a few merchants going to the human world, and there are so many mouths to feed."

"Why aren't we trading openly and in quantity?"

"There have been a few incidents," she said levelly. "It seems we are not always welcome in their markets."

Tamaryl blew out his breath. That was only to be expected; they had warred for generations.

"And we have only a truce, and a fragile one. There cannot be an open market until there is a real peace."

"We have need on both sides, in every way. What more do we need to make a real peace?"

"A treaty."

Tamaryl sagged. "And our leaders are too wary and too proud to write one."

"Have some sympathy for Oniwe'aru. His people are suffering and rioting, and you ask him to bind himself to their enemy."

"They need not be our enemy," Tamaryl said tiredly. His fup-forged chains burned, his scabs pinched, and none could see the way out.

For a moment they sat in silence.

At last Tamaryl shifted. "I do appreciate knowing, even if it is not good news. But this is not your task. Why did you bring it to me?"

Edeiya sat back, leaning upon her wings. "A good question, Tamaryl'sho. I am not entirely certain of the answer myself." She tipped her head. "But I respect what you have done, even if I do not agree with it—or, at least, with all of it. And even if I would not have done it—or, at least, not all of it—myself."

This slight allowance of sympathy with his actions was more than Tamaryl had heard from any Ryuven but Maru, and even Maru had never hinted that he might have been tempted to do a fraction of the same. The faint praise struck Tamaryl like sweet perfume in the dank cell.

"When you had a dilemma that demanded sacrifice, you sacrificed your status instead of your people's welfare. That is the mark of a true leader, and not something we see often in politics."

Tamaryl huffed a derisive laugh. "And we see how that worked out. That sacrifice bought nothing."

"It seems it has bought a few exchanges of samur for food. It has opened the possibility of a treaty where none has existed before."

"But not the treaty itself."

She snorted. "Do you put so high a price upon yourself? You cannot buy everything, Tamaryl'sho, even with sacrifice. You can only do what you can do, and then leave the next stride for another to take."

"But—"

"But that is all anyone can ever do. You could bypass Oniwe'aru, I suppose, seize power for yourself and overturn the Four Houses and the Union. But do you think that would have no ill consequences for those you mean to help? Even if you executed the most peaceable coup imaginable, and somehow managed to prevent all the ill-willed from taking advantage of even momentary disruption, what would happen once you had established that power might be brutally and defensibly wielded in the name of conviction?"

He looked away. "I don't require a lecture."

"No, I suppose you don't. And this is a miserable schoolroom." She sighed. "But you elected this path when you returned from the human world. Twice."

You came home. You chose.

He nodded. "I chose, and it's a choice I must live with, no matter its wisdom or the outcome."

"That is all we can do." She straightened. "You have been brave to advance your ideals, Tamaryl'sho, and you have been noble, and you have been valiant." She looked at him. "When will you be wise?"

He had no answer. He had done only as he felt he must.

After a moment, she rose to her feet. "I am sorry I could not bring you better news." She looked discomfited at departing so awkwardly, but she left him alone to reflect on his failure.

Taev Callahan unbound the lock he had made for the royal herb storage—that had been a long while ago, and no one had thought to change it after he had been unceremoniously dismissed from those consulting on the wounded prince-heir—and slipped into the dark room. It smelled gloriously of mint, of rosemary, of mushrooms and moss, of a hundred different items that could be used to heal, if one had the knowledge.

Taev had the knowledge. Chrysogenum juice was nearly unknown and then distrusted, brewed as it was from unsightly and unhealthy mold. But Taev had been experimenting with it for three years—and what did they have to lose, trying it on a dead prince? The physickers were only prolonging his slow death, and all of them knew it, if none would say it aloud. There was too much death in the wound, which had gone deep and gone too long uncleaned. And then the camp healers, panicked with the terrible wounding of a prince-heir, had used the healing amulets immediately, without first purging the nascent infection, thus spurring the growth of poison as well as closing wounded tissue. Idiots.

If Prince Soren died, then the court physickers had all done the best they could, in their various ways. If he lived, then the kingdom would not suffer an heir's death and the devastation of the fragile peace Ariana Hazelrig had bought.

If he lived, then Taev would have saved a life.

Taev found the samur reserved for the royal invalid and decanted the chrysogenum juice into it, watching as it soaked slowly into the half-dried leaves. When it was gone, no drop remaining to betray him, he slipped out the door and locked it again behind him.

CHAPTER 19

Maru shivered in the cold morning. Even after their trade visits in towns and cities prompted them to adopt human styles of practical clothing, they were not prepared for the bitter cold of the open plain. Battles were fast and heated; this waiting in the dark of the morning was chilling.

But they had to wait, for they could see the royal procession climbing the hill. The king's coach, drawn by six big slaves, made its weaving way up the steep side. Inside sat the man who would help to determine Tamaryl's fate.

Maru glanced at Oniwe'aru, erect and wrapped in a feather cloak, watching the king's approach. Maru had not dared to ask directly about Tamaryl; he did not want to antagonize the aru further. But from what he could piece together after much questioning and eavesdropping, it seemed if this meeting went very well, Oniwe'aru might show mercy to his traitorous subject. If the meeting did not promise an abundance of trade and supplies for the Ai clan, however, Oniwe'aru would have no reason to withhold his demonstration of authority and discipline, and indeed might require such a demonstration to quell the growing unrest. The aru who would execute his half brother and Pairvyn was to be obeyed indeed.

But he had given Tamaryl this chance, at least—he had waited to see how the unwanted truce profited the clan. Maru clung to that narrow hope.

Did King Jerome know he held the fate of the hated Pairvyn ni'Ai? Would he sacrifice peace to avenge himself on the warrior who had wrought so much damage to his kingdom?

The royal coach arrived at the top of the hill, the slaves panting with exertion. A ridiculous custom, Maru thought, to display strength by relying upon others' effort. The attending human soldiers spread themselves into a line facing the Ryuven, two silent rows awaiting treaty or resumption of war. Maru shivered and prayed for peace.

King Jerome looked ill, leaving his coach. For a moment Maru wondered if this was really the king who had withstood them for so long, but then he remembered that the elder prince lay near death.

Jerome was no doubt suffering from the double burden of his son's and his kingdom's precarious welfare.

Oniwe'aru inclined his head, the greeting of an aru. "Good morning, Your Majesty."

King Jerome returned an exactly equal nod. "Good morning, Oniwe'aru."

The aru straightened for the traditional expression of good faith. "I am Oniwe, aru of the Ai. My people have guarded our raids upon yours jealously and prohibited other clans from encroaching; our peace and our trade would be guarded in the same way. Thus I pledge my worthiness to enter into negotiations and to uphold whatever agreement we conclude."

King Jerome nodded. "I am Jerome Laguna, king of Chrenada and father of its prince-heir. My rule is absolute and I bear no small influence upon our neighboring lands. I pledge my worthiness to enter negotiations and enforce our agreements."

Oniwe'aru made a graceful gesture toward a tent erected against the wind. "Then let us sit and talk."

Ariana wished she could pace. She wished she could be in the privacy of her own workroom, shattering glassware in her impatience and anxiety as she waited for news. But she stood outside the Ryuven tent, her black robes billowing on the windy hilltop, and tried to look patient, dignified, confident.

She wanted to scream.

King Jerome's procession had left the palace before dawn, passing through Alham's gates just as the sun became visible over the eastern road, and yet already the streets had been lined with quiet, hopeful citizens, waving and clasping their hands before flooding to the temples to petition. Ewan Hazelrig was with him, the White Mage of the Circle of course being one of those who would attend the negotiations. Ariana Hazelrig would not have been included—only the foremost were accompanying the king, as the complete Circle might have been seen as a show of force—but for her part in working the temporary truce. She waited outside the Ryuven tent, ready should her opinion be wanted.

It would not be, of course. She was only the Black Mage, she had enacted the truce only with Tamaryl's help and fortunate timing. She was not of sufficient rank or knowledge to actually influence decisions; she had only bought time to consider their reasoning and the possibility of more.

And so she waited and worried.

From what Maru had told her so briefly in the street, the outcome of these talks would color Oniwe'aru's judgment of Tamaryl. There was no reason that should worry her more than the fate of a kingdom, but it seemed to hang equally large in her mind's eye. He had helped her for the good of both their peoples; he deserved better than a traitor's death.

Peace would spare the lives of human soldiers and Ryuven warriors. Peace would keep Shianan Becknam from further battle. Peace would bring mercy for Tamaryl. Sweet Holy One, how could they even consider returning to war?

What was being said within the tent?

She spotted Maru among the opposite Ryuven, and her stomach tightened. Was he here as a warrior? A servant? Did he know anything more of Tamaryl? He must have seen her arrive; she was obvious enough in her mage's robes. She might catch his eye when he looked back.

What were they saying inside? Surely they would agree to make the peaceful trade permanent? She should have asked her father to keep one of the harmonized crystals in his robes, so she could secretly listen. But such a spell would be unwieldy to maintain during negotiations...

A percussive sound interrupted her anxious thoughts, and she turned with the others to look over the road that had brought them. A horse was galloping at speed, its hoof beats audible even at this distance on the paved army road. A rider balanced over its neck, motionless in the saddle; it was someone skilled and in great hurry. Ariana's chest clenched.

No one spoke until the horse and rider began to climb the hill, making it impossible to deny that an urgent message was coming. Someone murmured at the entrance to the tent, and a moment later the rulers and advisers exited, their faces tight with strained politeness, residual fear and dislike, and fresh worry.

The horse labored up the trail and the soldiers split before it. Reaching the level top of the hill, the horse stretched out again under the rider's urging and finally slid to a halt within the silent group. The rider threw himself from the saddle, wristbands showing between sleeves and gloves, and dropped breathlessly to his knee.

"Philip." The king's voice was carefully controlled. "What news do you bring me?"

"Your Majesty," panted Philip. "Your son."

CHAPTER 20

Shianan was instructing soldiers in their morning practice—the pretense of routine helped them all to keep their minds off irritable and fruitless wondering about the state of negotiations beyond the city walls—when the palace guardsman arrived. Shianan noted him but said nothing, as guardsmen were not a part of his command. This one, though, scanned the assembly and then started deliberately for Shianan.

Shianan's pulse quickened. "Carry on," he ordered. He turned aside and waited for the guard. "Yes?"

"Her Majesty calls you to the prince's quarters, your lordship."

For a moment Shianan could not breathe. Finally he managed, "Thank you. I'll come directly." He turned back to the soldiers, engaged in their drills. "Finish this set and then you are dismissed. No, there is no news from outside. Continue."

He headed for the Naziar palace at a steady jog. Soren... Had he woken for one final moment of coherency? Had he quietly slipped away in his sleep? Or had he, somehow, miraculously, unbelievably awakened as his fever faded?

Shianan ran for the royal wing.

Soren was cold, so cold. The ravine blocked most of the wind, but it was still bitterly cold. Becknam had made a fire, but it hardly helped. Even when he spread the fire over Soren and tucked it about his shoulders, Soren still shivered.

The piercing spearhead throbbed in his side. He did not want to move for the pain of it. He was afraid of being cold, afraid he would shiver and the agony would shock through him.

Sometimes he heard voices, carried down the ravine by the wind. He could never quite make out the words, though he listened. He thought he might hear news of the battle, but the sound was never clear.

He was so tired, and so cold, and it hurt so much... Occasionally Becknam would lift him or treat his wound. It was excruciating sometimes, and yet Soren could not tell him to stop. Other times, though, it was hardly perceptible, the movement as slight as if Soren bobbed in a boat upon a gentle river.

His cloak was heavy over him, but the rocks on which he lay were soft and even. He wondered if Shianan had found a way out yet. He wanted to ask, but it was so hard to speak, so hard to do anything. He worried that the Ryuven might return. They had come, he knew, twice for him. What if they came again, while Shianan was looking for a way out?

Bailaha is my champion, he thought. That was what he would tell the Ryuven; that was what he would tell Pairvyn ni'Ai when he returned. *Bailaha is my champion.* Then they would let him be.

He could hear more voices and footsteps now. Where was Shianan? Was he near? Soren knew he could not move, could not flee or defend himself. He was helpless, waiting. He wanted desperately to be able to see through the dark night.

There was no recourse; he had to see them coming. He summoned his fading strength and opened his eyes.

His vision was hazy and indistinct; it frightened him. The ravine had changed, transforming strangely into something like his own familiar room. That frightened him, too. He was seeing visions. "Becknam," he tried, but his voice failed.

'Soats, he was weak.

"Becknam," he mouthed again, feeling his lips crack. "Help."

A form appeared over him, but it wasn't the commander-count. Soren tried to focus, but it was the voice that came clearest: "Master?!"

Ethan. *Ethan.* "Ethan?"

"Master!" The servant seemed to glow with sudden joy. "You're awake!"

It wasn't a vision—he was in his own room, in the palace, with Ethan. Panic seized him. "The battle? Where's Becknam? How did it end?" His limited vision swirled black and he caught at his breath.

"Hush, steady," urged Ethan. "Let me send word, and then I'll help you. Lie still, master, you're very weak."

He closed his eyes as Ethan rushed away and fell asleep before he returned.

Voices woke him again, and this time he recognized another face. "Mother..."

She was crying. "Oh, Soren, my Soren!" She clutched his hand and squeezed tightly. "Thank the Holy One."

Was she weeping for him or the kingdom? "The battle..."

"We know, you were injured, but we've brought you—"

She didn't understand. "The Ryuven—how is it?"

Ethan leaned close from the other side. "The battle ended in truce, my lord. Negotiations for peace are in progress now."

Alasdair pushed into Soren's field of vision. "You—you're here!"

Where else would I be? Twit. But that irritation was his own denial. It was terrifyingly clear that Alasdair had worried he would die. His mother and Ethan, too. They were all crying for him.

Where was Becknam?

"We've called the healers, Soren, so just lie still and rest. They will—"

"Becknam?" he managed. King's oats, if anything had happened to him...

His mother wiped her cheek. "He's fine, if that's what you want to know."

It would do. The battle had ended in truce, and Becknam was alive... Alasdair and his mother and Ethan were all right. There was so much more that he wanted, but he was so tired...

Shianan fought the powerful urge to seize the guardsman by the throat. "No," he said curtly, "I am called by Her Majesty, who sent word to me by one of your turnip-headed own. I am called to the prince's rooms. You must let me through."

The two guards exchanged nervous glances. "We don't have any word of you," one began again.

"Then get it!" snapped Shianan. "But hurry!"

The guard's jaw set. "I will have to speak with my captain," he answered deliberately, making it clear that Shianan's military authority meant nothing to the palace guard. "And then we will go and see if there are any orders indeed sent for you." He looked significantly at Shianan's swordbelt. "You do not come as if for a royal visit."

Heat burned through Shianan as he jerked the buckle open, swinging the swordbelt free. "I came directly from training my men," he replied shortly. "I was in a hurry. And I am still in a hurry."

"Then we will see what can be done," the guard answered.

CHAPTER 21

Ariana could almost feel the shifting behind her as the soldiers exchanged anxious speculations over the horseman's arrival. The king and messenger had gone together a few paces away, speaking closely, and she could not guess from their posture what news he had brought.

She prayed Prince Soren was not dead. She did not want that—not for Shianan, not for the kingdom and today's negotiations, not for Soren himself. *Please...*

Her father stepped close to her, blocking a bit of the wind. He placed an arm about her shoulders. "Holding up, my girl?"

"I wish I knew what they were saying," she answered. "But it has to be bad, racing like that to interrupt the talks—"

"Prince Soren is not dead," he interrupted softly.

She looked at him, startled. "How do you know?"

"The king would never be given such news in view of others, especially of an enemy. There would be a polite request to return for today, and then he would be told in appropriate privacy."

"Then this is..."

"In all likelihood, the fever has broken." He squeezed her closer. "This will be very good news indeed."

They could just see the king and slave around the edge of the wind-whipped tent. Ariana felt guilty watching them, but she could not tear her eyes away. The king was staring intently at the slave, bound to his words. The slave nodded, and Ariana saw the king turn away to shield his face.

The prince—?

But a moment later, the king turned back, his reddened eyes and tense mouth betraying him but his features mostly composed. He nodded to the slave and came around the tent as Ariana tried desperately to find a place to rest her eyes where it did not seem she was staring.

But all eyes were on King Jerome as he faced Oniwe'aru. "I have had word from my queen," he said hoarsely. "My son's fever has broken, and he has awakened briefly."

The quiet words were repeated through the line of waiting soldiers and mages, gaining intensity as they went. A cheer half rose and died quickly, elation bowing before sober duty and anxiety for what would come next.

Jerome did not look at the spectators, keeping the eyes of the Ryuven. Ariana saw Oniwe'aru's shoulders relax slightly; had he worried, too, that the prince might have died and thus ended their negotiations with a fresh blood-feud?

"With your understanding," Jerome continued, "I would like to go to him."

"Of course," Oniwe'aru replied, and Ariana thought she could detect faint relief in his voice. "But—if we could take but a few minutes more, I think we could resolve what we've discussed thus far, and you would be able to take good word to your son as well."

Ariana's heart leaped. Were they so near?

The king hesitated and then nodded once. "Yes, yes, I see. Let us do so." He turned and beckoned. "Mage Hazelrig—both of you."

Ariana entered the Ryuven tent, surprised at how effectively the fabric dulled the wind and its noise. The floor was laid with rugs. There were two backless Ryuven chairs in the center, and the king and aru gave each other precise nods before settling into them. Ariana noted how King Jerome shifted awkwardly, unused to the seat. Advisers and officers ringed them, their eyes flicking over the circle watchfully.

King Jerome spoke first. "Then our proposed terms are acceptable, my lord?"

"I believe so, Jerome'aru."

The exchange of honorifics made Ariana smile.

Oniwe'aru gestured. "Our trade has been very limited, but most reports have been of success. Regarding the incident in the market in..."

"Forgestone," supplied a tall Ryuven.

"Forgestone, as you say, but our trader and his assistants were able to escape without injury."

King Jerome nodded. "Forgestone is very near to Caftford, my lord aru, and we might have anticipated that there would be local resentment. We might send a military escort to ensure fewer disruptions."

Oniwe'aru nodded. "Our traders will likely avoid rural areas in the immediate future. Your cities have proved receptive enough. And our trade has expanded beyond the herbs and foodstuffs, as well. We have seen profit from carrying messages, trading furnishings and fabrics—minor in themselves, but a complement to our primary exchanges."

"Indeed, the craftsmanship of this very setting is magnificent," King Jerome commented. "You have provided a most comfortable surround for our discussion."

"It is my pleasure to present it to you," Oniwe'aru said graciously. "The tent and furnishings are yours."

"I thank you most sincerely," King Jerome replied. "And I have brought gifts for you and your people, as well." He signaled, and someone went out the door. "But let us swear our agreements, if we may?"

Oniwe'aru stood, and the surrounding Ryuven took a step backward. The humans mimicked them, uncertain of these strange protocols. Oniwe'aru pressed his palms together against his chest and rolled his lower lip into his teeth. Power hummed silently through the air, and then he lifted a hand and pulled his lip free with a little sound of tearing skin.

Ariana flinched.

Oniwe'aru raised his hand and drew a bloody streak across his forehead, left to right. "The Ai will raise no offensive action against Chrenada while we are welcome in your lands, permitted to trade freely and openly. We will suffer no other clan to raise offensive action against Chrenada. We will shepherd our own, keeping our traders safe in strange lands and guarding the honor of our oath. This I swear, the oath of Oniwe, Altayr ni'Ai cin Celæno, Alcyon ni Pairvyn, Majja to Pleione."

King Jerome seemed as startled by the physical sign of the Ryuven oath, but he stood erect and faced Oniwe'aru squarely, raising his right hand. "Your clan will be welcome traders in our kingdom, free to..."

Ariana hardly heard the king's oath, critical as it was. A strange prickling was running over her, and she tried to follow it, to find its form and origin. Why had the Ryuven used magic? Was there danger? Couldn't anyone else feel it?

Her father touched her arm. "Steady," he breathed, too softly to disturb the central exchange. "It's only the binding."

Ariana didn't understand him, but if he thought there was no danger... She swallowed and straightened, flexing her knees slightly within her robes.

And then there was cheering as King Jerome and Oniwe'aru nodded to one another, and someone must have signaled to the waiting humans and Ryuven outside, for a greater roar rose there. Two men entered, carrying a chest and bowing before Oniwe'aru. They opened the chest to display jeweled articles. "Chrenada's gift to you, my lord aru," explained King Jerome.

Ewan Hazelrig leaned close to Ariana. "I knew power might be associated with the oath," he explained. "They use a metamorphosis to sharpen their teeth, and magic with the oath itself. It is the same formal oath Tamaryl swore to me years ago, when we first met."

She could hear the sadness in his voice. "I'm going to ask about him."

"Now?"

"When will I have another chance? And whom better to ask?"

He nodded. "You'll be careful, though, yes?" He smiled. "You won't endanger him, or yourself, or the kingdom?"

He was not really joking. "I'll be careful," she promised.

"Mage Hazelrig!" They turned together to the two rulers. King Jerome beckoned. "My lady mage," he clarified. "Please come. Our esteemed guest would like a word with you."

Her chest tightened. What did Oniwe'aru want? Perhaps he himself wanted to speak of Tamaryl? She curtsied low. "Yes, my lords?"

Oniwe'aru gave her an intent look. "I want to thank you for your persistence in the face of my initial skepticism. It seems you knew the mind of your countrymen better than I—a fact that should have been evident, one might suppose. You should be honored as a mother of this peace, an architect of our new trade."

Ariana curtsied again, warm with flushing. "I—thank you." She straightened. "But it was not I alone who—"

"Of course not," Oniwe'aru interrupted. "There are so many parts of this whole. But yours was significant." He turned to King Jerome. "And now, Jerome'aru, let us dispense with ceremony. You must go to your son. I am truly pleased that he recovers; go to him and share our new peace."

"Thank you, my lord aru. I will tell him most gladly."

There were shouts as the king exited, and then the royal coach began its hasty journey. The rest of the company would stay, packing up the gifts and then making its more conventional way home.

Ariana had not moved from her place, and Oniwe'aru turned to her again. "I do thank you for your dedication to this peace. Do not disparage that."

"I do not, Oniwe'aru," she answered. "But I did not act alone. There was—"

"You found the key product of trade. You were the only ambassador, the only diplomat, the only one who did not disobey direct and specific orders," Oniwe'aru replied significantly. "You were not sent by your king, but you never flouted his command or overturned his authority. You pledged your strength to convince him, but—"

"That's not so," cut in Ariana sharply. "I disobeyed no direct orders, but my interrupting a battle of defense might be considered a form of treason. If we had failed, it certainly would have been." She took a steadying breath. "I have not had word from Tamaryl'sho."

"Did you expect a message from him?"

Now they played word games, and it angered her. "I have heard he is imprisoned."

Oniwe'aru's expression did not change. "He has done disobedience."

Ariana held his gaze, ignoring the bustle about them. "We have peace now. He was right; he did what he thought best and it has profited us all. Won't you release him now?"

Oniwe'aru narrowed his eyes. "The governing of the Ai is none of your concern, Ariana'rika," he said shortly. "Nor is the fate of Tamaryl."

He made a gesture over his shoulder to the other Ryuven, and then with a clap of disturbed air he was gone.

Ariana stood a moment, shocked.

"He called him Tamaryl."

She turned and saw Maru behind her, worried and wind-tousled. Ariana faced him. "Shouldn't he?"

Maru shook his head unhappily. "Not Tamaryl'sho, but Tamaryl. As if he were nim." He swallowed. "He's lost all rank, all position. He is nothing."

She stared at him. "What does that mean?"

"I don't know."

"Maru!" called a voice. "Your work is here!"

Ariana reached for his arm quickly. "Send me word. Whatever you can."

He nodded and then turned to obey the summons.

Ariana looked after him, a heavy weight settling over her. They had a new peace between Chrenada and the Ryuven, and that was good. But both Shianan and Tamaryl were trapped in this new peace, unable to celebrate what they had sacrificed to gain. The people cheering the happy news did not even know. Only she could act.

But what could she do?

CHAPTER 22

Soren became hazily aware of someone clutching his hand. He fought to listen; there was a voice near him. He was so tired...

"My lord," came the voice, broken and hoarse. "My lord..."

Recognition raced through Soren. He tightened his fingers as he opened his eyes. "Shianan Becknam."

Shianan was crouching at the side of his bed, watching anxiously. "My lord? Highness?"

Soren tried to smile, but it was difficult to know if he'd succeeded. "I knew you would bring us out."

"I didn't, Your Highness. A search party found us, looking for you. I couldn't reach—"

"You did enough." It hurt to speak, and he hardly had the strength.

A soft gasp came from the door, where his mother had just entered. She rushed to the bed, taking the hand Shianan had held. He ceded it and bowed his head as he moved to one side. The queen did not look at him, but threw her words toward Ethan as she bent toward Soren. "I wanted to be here."

Ethan gave a bob of his head but said nothing.

She squeezed Soren's hand. "I'm sorry to ask you this, but what happened when you fell?"

He was tired, and he didn't want to tell stories yet. There was too much else to ask. "Becknam can tell."

"I want to hear it from you, Soren."

It took him a moment. King's oats, she distrusted Shianan. "He saved my life," he said, dismayed at the effort it required.

"How?"

Soren did not understand the strained urgency in her single word. Shianan could explain it for them both. He was so tired...

Shianan cleared his throat. "Some say I tried to kill you, my lord," he explained quietly.

For a moment the words made no sense, and then came strengthening outrage. "What? That's—ridiculous. I fell... Ryuven pushed me over the edge and I fell onto a spear. Becknam came after me." He paused, breathing hard with the effort of protesting. "He fought—"

"That's enough, Soren; don't strain—"

"Hear me! Pairvyn ni'Ai came—Shianan defended me. Then he carried me. Ryuven came again; I don't remember much but clearly he protected us both. For hours he carried me, and I owe him my life." He gasped for more air. "King's runny oats, why would he kill me?"

Shianan looked away. Soren wanted to meet his eyes, but he could not move. Why was he so weak? Why did it require so much air even to speak?

A hand settled on his shoulder; Ethan stood opposite the queen. "Quiet, my lord," he urged softly. "We understand."

Soren lay still, grateful. Shianan meant to kill him? What idiocy was that?

"Rest a while, Soren," his mother said. "We've sent word to your lord father. The healers were here while you slept, and they are bringing fresh medicines, but they say you will need sleep. Try to get some now."

He was not a child to be tucked into bed so, but he didn't have the strength to argue. His mother bent and kissed his forehead. "Welcome back, son," she said softly, and she turned away.

Shianan shifted beside the bed, and then he took Soren's unresisting hand and pressed its back briefly to his forehead. Before Soren could think to speak, Shianan rose and followed the queen.

"I'll bring more pillows later," Ethan offered, already guessing his mind, "for speaking. But you should rest again now."

"Thanks," managed Soren, and then he slipped into soft sleep once more.

Queen Azalie went to the far end of Soren's room and turned back, facing Shianan as he followed. He bowed his head and waited for her to speak.

"I'm sorry," she said at last. "I thought—I thought if I could see him when he first saw you..."

She thought she would learn the truth of Shianan's defense. Shianan said nothing.

"You spoke the truth, but not all of it. You did not say you had defended him from Ryuven in the ravine."

"To what purpose?" Shianan's fingers twitched. "If it were alleged that I meant to kill him instead of to save him, talking of Pairvyn ni'Ai would hardly have made my story more credible."

She sighed. "I am sorry I doubted you. I—I did believe you, when you told me before... But I had to hear it from him. I had to—" She stopped, lifted her chin, tried again. "It is a great thing, to trust someone with the life of a son. If there was a chance that you did mean him harm, then I had to know."

Shianan looked at the floor between them. "Your Majesty, I have sworn my life to my prince. I would have died for him if necessary."

She nodded. "I see that now."

Ethan opened the door to a group of healers, and she glanced over his shoulder. "Let me speak with them," she said. "Excuse me."

Shianan turned and saw Ethan move out of the way while the healers prodded at Soren, already newly asleep even beneath their examination. Alasdair stood against the wall, watching the healers and mages clustered about Soren's bed. The younger prince hugged himself, one heel resting on the wall, looking lost in the large room.

Shianan had no purpose here now; he should go. It was inexcusable to leave without royal dismissal, but the queen would hardly miss him in her anxiety for her son.

He went to the door and let himself quietly out.

Word of the newly sworn pact spread outward from the path of the king's coach as it raced through the city to the Naziar palace. It reached the military barracks as the king raced up stairs, pushing through doors even before servants could open them. By the time Jerome bent over his son's bed, his eyes damp with relieved joy, there was already music and dancing in the streets of Alham.

In the Wheel, Ewan Hazelrig drank toasts with the other mages. Elysia Parma hugged Ademar Carrock and then kissed Ewan's cheek as Alan Odderman held forth on the glorious history of the Circle, gold robes sweeping with his grand gestures. Ariana watched them all, smiled with them, but thought privately of Shianan, Tamaryl, Maru, and all that was given or lost.

CHAPTER 23

The bolt drew back and Tamaryl raised his head. He didn't bother to move; his back was already against the wall, and Vermi'che could not push him further.

But Vermi'che looked nervous as he entered, glancing from Tamaryl to the door, and then the cause was revealed as Oniwe'aru came behind him. Tamaryl blinked and then shifted weakly to his knee, bowing over it as his pulse quickened. Had Oniwe'aru met with the human king? Would there be peace or fighting? Had Oniwe'aru come to condemn him finally?

Vermi'che fingered the forked rod. "Do you want me to stay and hold him?"

Oniwe'aru gave him an impatient look. "I think I'm capable of defending myself from a single bound and weakened prisoner. And what I have to say is not for you. Go."

Vermi'che retreated. Tamaryl felt a slight relief at his departure but a greater worry for what Oniwe'aru had to say. A pardon would be public news.

Oniwe'aru took a step forward, so that Tamaryl kneeling could see his feet. "Tamaryl."

The lack of suffix was painfully obvious. Tamaryl shifted so that he rested on two knees and spread his hands on the floor so that the forefingers touched. "Oniwe'aru."

"You present yourself as a supplicant?" Oniwe'aru observed in cold amusement. "You think your petition might yet move me?"

Tamaryl's breath caught. "I have made my defense, Oniwe'aru," he answered, his voice hoarse with disuse. "I do not ask you to hear it again."

"What do you ask, then?"

His throat closed with sudden emotion. "Mercy, Oniwe'aru—I ask mercy." He gulped. "Do not leave me here, bound and weak and hungry. No matter what I've done, I have the dignity of my past and of our blood; honor that, at least." Shame filled him as he heard himself beg, but there was nothing left to preserve. "Please, Oniwe'aru, mercy."

"By the Essence, you can be broken," Oniwe'aru observed quietly. "And by such simple means."

Tamaryl squeezed his eyes shut, humiliated. He rotated his hands so that the long middle fingers touched and lowered himself fully to the cold stone, abasing himself utterly. He could not flatten his bound wings, but the position was clear enough; this was no ceremonial petition but abject groveling.

Oniwe'aru placed his foot across the back of Tamaryl's neck. "My proud Pairvyn now crawls before me. You spurned my word, Tamaryl, my law, and see what you've become."

Tamaryl wanted to weep. It was difficult to breathe.

"But I perceive that you once again had reason for your actions. You disobeyed, but in good faith, as it were."

He could hardly hear Oniwe'aru as the blood pounded in his ears. He gasped for air and choked as Oniwe'aru's foot pressed more firmly into his neck, bending it against the stone.

"Hear me and answer me, Tamaryl," said Oniwe'aru evenly. "You are in prison, you are neither Pairvyn nor sho, and you are bloody with injuries from che. You were a prince doniphan of the land, and you have fallen, Tamaryl, until you are less than nim." He lifted his foot, letting a rush of blood sweep through Tamaryl's brain so that the room swam about him. "Tell me, Tamaryl—did you do the right thing? Do you still think we have a chance of trading with those who hate and fear us? Would you see us treat with the humans?"

Tamaryl panted, his face pressed against the stone. Was this his chance—his sole opportunity for mercy, for escape from this cell?

But he had done only what he'd thought right. He had never meant to betray Oniwe'aru and the Ai clan; he had only sought to help them, despite themselves.

He pressed himself against the floor, breathing deep. "I would see us at peace," he whispered. "I would see us trade our goods rather than our lives."

There was a long pause, and Tamaryl wished he dared raise his eyes. Would Oniwe'aru forgive him? Kill him where he cringed? Curl his lip in disdain at his weakness and leave him to molder forever beneath Vermi'che's humiliations?

Oniwe'aru took a slow breath. "You are not broken, after all," he said softly. "You are just as you were."

He turned and passed through the door, closing it behind him. Tamaryl remained on the floor and wept.

Ariana turned the crystal over in her hands. "But she only touched it. Just touched it and spoke."

Her father nodded, intent on his work. "That's right." His workroom at home was too small to share easily, but Ariana had been his apprentice in this space and they were used to moving around each other.

"She said the difficulty wasn't in the technique, but in the execution." Ariana set the crystal in her flat palm and held it level at her eyes. "But every technique I can think of requires more than mere physical contact."

"Give yourself some time. She did tell you it wasn't a common technique."

"She said only a scant handful could do it."

"Mm-hmm." He measured out a blue-grey powder.

Ariana set the crystal down on the table and frowned at it. Across from her, a matching crystal did nothing. "She touched it, and she spoke, and you could hear her voice from the other crystal."

"Something like her voice, yes."

"And you're not going to help me with this, are you?"

"Didn't she tell you that you should be able to work it out for yourself?"

Ariana growled in her throat.

She flicked the crystal in front of her and its consonant mate whined and buzzed like a honeybee. That was simple enough. But how to do what Mage Parma had done in sending her voice?

"When she said a scant handful could do it...did she mean only you and she can?"

Her father coughed to hide his chuckle. "That's not quite true."

"Mage Odderman? Can he do it?"

"Tamaryl could."

Ariana flung the crystal down in mostly mock frustration. "No wonder I can't work this out."

"Be patient." He siphoned the powder into a vial and set it over his athanor. "It took us some time to polish it into working order."

There was a knock at the front door, and Ariana thought momentarily of ignoring it, but then she left the crystals behind.

135

She opened the door and was swept backward by the combined enthusiastic embraces of Calissa and Ranne. "Ariana, Ariana, you did it!" Ranne cheered. "The war is ended! Truly!"

"It wasn't—"

"I know, I know, it wasn't only your doing," Calissa interrupted her with good humor. "We'll let that pass for now and focus on celebrating. You won't mind if we toast you, will you?" She sailed into the sitting room like a Wakari three-master, pulling seats together.

Ariana conceded. Her friends meant no harm, and their good cheer was warming her brooding. "You may toast me only if we have something worthwhile, and I haven't been to the market—"

"You didn't think we'd have you supply your own toast, did you?" Calissa drew a bottle from a covered basket as Ranne arranged cushions on the gathered seats. "I do hope you'll provide the glasses, however."

"I hope someone brings a glass to me as well," came Ariana's father's voice from the workroom. Ranne laughed and called back a promise.

A few minutes later, Ariana was surprised at how glad she was of their presence. The wine was excellent and she drank it rather more quickly than she was accustomed. They relaxed into their cushions, settling into comfortable companionship with legs drawn beneath them, and Ariana reflected that she should have brought them together sooner.

"Now that we've toasted Ariana, and the prince-heir, and Chrenada, and the Wakari Coast, and a good percentage of the populace," Calissa said laconically, "let's turn to another theme, shall we?"

Ariana gestured lazily. "What's that?"

Calissa glanced in the direction of the workroom and then turned back with a dramatically lowered voice. "Tell us about your secret lover."

Ariana jerked in her seat, her blithe mood instantly dissipated. "What?"

Calissa exchanged glances with Ranne. "That itself was worth the price of the bottle. Did you ever see such a leap? If we had doubted..."

Ariana couldn't answer. "I..." She glanced at Ranne helplessly.

Ranne only bared her teeth in a bloodthirsty grin. "There's no denying it now, Ariana. And there's no point in delay, either. Connor is away on a business trip to Nalarbor, and I can stay to work at you all the night if necessary."

Calissa laughed and turned back to Ariana. "You've already confirmed we're right. Now, who is it, and why is he such a secret? Or is that answer one and the same?"

Ariana tensed. "Sweet all, no."

Ranne laughed. "No, you can't tell us? Or no, that isn't the same answer?"

Calissa took up the jest. "Or are there really two? Let's guess. Who would have to be kept a secret?"

"He's a commoner," ventured Ranne, "unworthy of the Circle's finest."

"No, that wouldn't be scandalous enough. He's aristocracy—but he's married."

"He's a Ryuven!" They shrieked with laughter, missing Ariana's quick catch of breath.

"No, no," panted Ranne, "that's too much. Who else?"

"It's the prince-heir," suggested Calissa, "and they have been suffering beneath the threat of this promised Wakari match."

Ranne laughed. "That's good! Or, even worse—it's the bastard." She looked at Ariana, ready to share laughter, and saw something that gave her pause. "It's—oh, sweet sunrise. Ariana? Is it...?"

Ariana flushed hotly, wishing a plausible lie would spring to mind, but she could think of nothing but fear for Shianan. "I—he—oh, please, please don't tell anyone."

"The bastard?" Calissa's mouth worked in uncharacteristic dismay. "I thought—that is—everything we've heard..."

"Court rumors are tools to curry the king's favor," said Ariana firmly, "and the king hates him. But Shianan Becknam is a good man, really—brave and considerate and nothing at all like one would think. I—I'm not ashamed of him, I'm not, but if it were known that he courted anyone..."

"Oh, it's not for you, it's for him," Calissa breathed. "It's for his safety, is it?" She sobered. "This is a better tale than I'd guessed, and I'm sorry." She hesitated. "It cannot be easy. He really is both above and below you, isn't he?"

Ariana gave a bitter little laugh. "Indeed. Do you know what I did once? I was going on about trying to accomplish something for myself, wanting to achieve something notable. You know, Ranne, you've heard me wax fantastic over it often enough. And I complained—can you believe—I complained to him I was tired of being known only by association with my celebrated father." She rubbed at her face, warm with embarrassment. "I still writhe when I think of that."

Calissa looked sympathetic but said nothing. Ranne reached forward to touch Ariana's arm. "What will you do? Have you made any plans?"

Ariana took a slow breath. "You know that if either of you mentions even this much, he'll suffer for it. I don't mean mere reprimand. If he's known to be courting..."

Calissa's eyes widened. Ranne nodded seriously. "I know how to keep a secret. You know I'd never betray you."

Ariana nodded. "We haven't made any plans. And how could we? There has been so much..." She stopped and forced herself to take a slow breath. "When I was carried to the Ryuven world, with the Shard, he tried to stop them. I thought I saw him killed alongside my father."

"Oh, Ariana!"

She shook her head and tried to smile. "No, it's all right—they both survived. I'm fine now. It's fine."

By their expressions, her friends knew better.

"But after that, when I returned—he won't see me, now. He's afraid."

"He won't even see you?" Ranne's voice carried surprise and sympathy and indignation. "The coward—"

"No," interrupted Calissa gently, "he may have cause. He might be protecting you, too, Ariana."

She nodded miserably. "I know. And I think that might be worse. If I had the courage to face whatever might come, then he wouldn't be..."

Calissa moved and pulled Ariana into her arms. "Royals are complicated beasts," she whispered. "They do silly things for the sake of their own names. Half royals are no better. He's trying to protect you, and it doesn't matter if you can face it, he thinks he's doing the right thing."

Ariana nodded, pressed tightly between her friends, warm with their love and concern. Ranne had kept her own courtship secret until after their marriage, and she would hold Ariana's secret secure.

They had known Calissa for less time, but the Wakari would not have included an untrustworthy tongue in their delegation.

Ariana had friends. She had support, no matter what came, while Shianan did not. She could not expect him to act where he had no footing. She would work out her own solution for them.

CHAPTER 24

Shianan received another royal summons the next morning. "I suppose I should be getting used to this, but it makes my stomach clench every time."

Luca nodded. "Is it the queen again?"

Shianan nodded. "Find me something presentable to wear. I won't go in travel dust or training clothes this time."

The queen received Shianan in a small audience room, not far from where he often went before the king. Shianan's rigid posture betrayed his anxiety as he knelt to greet her. "Your Majesty."

"You may rise, Bailaha," she said. "Thank you for coming."

"It is always my pleasure to obey."

A corner of her mouth turned downward. "They do teach you the most ridiculous things to say."

Shianan did not know how to respond to that.

"Bailaha, I asked you to come...for..." Queen Azalie bit at her lip and turned away. "What is the price of a prince?" she asked after a moment. She turned toward a window, though she did not seem to see through it. "I don't know, but it must be at least that of thirty slaves. Or a horse. Then, what is the price of a thousand horses against a son?"

She turned back toward Shianan, who floundered for a response. "I... I wouldn't know—I wouldn't dare to guess, Your Majesty."

"Speaking of horses, you know of my herd at Kalifi."

"No, I don't, I'm afraid, Your Majesty."

"What? My herd—some of the finest horses on the continent. I breed horses, of course. Whatever did you think I was doing there?"

"I..." Shianan was unable to regain his equilibrium. He had never thought on what the queen did when avoiding Alham and the bastard.

"I have learned a few things in that pursuit," the queen continued, "and not only about the combining of bloodlines, selecting for the fastest or strongest or longest-lived and above all, pursuing those elusive successful breedings. I've also learned about their management and about the feasibility of keeping the creatures. Horses are frightfully expensive—and with good reason—but while I may sell a young half-trained horse for twenty or thirty thousand pias, I cannot give one away even if I wish. They are dismayingly valuable and thus such a burden to the recipient, who must now lavish a fortune on their care and protection. There is the fodder, and bedding, and the armed men for the stable guard, and—well, you can see that it is a considerable undertaking.

"In fact, the gift of a horse from the royal stables is a useful way to break a man. He may not sell a royal gift, of course. Nor may he fail to keep it in good condition. This gift of apparent generosity might bankrupt a man of mild fortune. You may recall the Baron of Shuile, that pompous self-important toad who claimed he single-handedly drove off a whole company of Ryuven no one else ever sighted and hinted loudly that he deserved royal gratitude? He was given a horse, an extravagant gift that inspired much talk and jealousy in the court. He retired to his country estate three years later, leaving a large debt in the city."

Shianan nodded once, choosing to wait and see where the queen meant to lead him before commenting.

She began to pace, still dignified. "Horses are beautiful creatures, elegant, strong. However, they are difficult to exercise properly in the city. Alexander—he's Philip's son, of course, my stable-steward at Kalifi—Alexander tells me they are wandering grazing animals in their own homeland, and he believes pasturing helps them to thrive. That is our practice at Kalifi. But in a city like Alham, one cannot pasture a horse. You see the difficulty."

Shianan nodded again, watching the queen in concealed puzzlement. Surely she had not called him to lecture him on the husbandry of horses.

"So, Bailaha, I am afraid I must ask this favor, as you have already proved so useful and dedicated to our royal household." She faced him. "Would you exercise my young stud here in Alham? Kuolema is his name. He is well-started, still excitable at times, but he needs exercise and experience. He needs riding, in the streets and outside the city."

A thrill like magic ran through Shianan. "Your Majesty..."

"I'd expect Philip to assist you of course, but the bulk of the duty would fall to you. You may set your own schedule. As owner I would bear the responsibility of his care, but yours would be the chief exercise." She faced Shianan. "So? Could you agree to this?"

Shianan sank to his knee. For a moment he couldn't form words. "Your Majesty, I—I am... Me?"

She chuckled. "You." Then the smile faded, and she turned partly away. "You saved our son's life, Bailaha. You saved his life and you received not praise but censure. Allow me this chance to honor you as I may."

"I never did it for reward, Your Majesty."

"I know. That is precisely why you shall have one."

Shianan gulped. "Thank you, Your Majesty. I am very grateful. Very pleased."

She smiled, a bit self-satisfied. "Philip will be waiting for you this afternoon, if you would like to go to the stables then. And, Bailaha—see that you travel all the primary market streets. For the education of Kuolema, of course."

Shianan entered the stable gingerly, almost guiltily, expecting to be challenged at any moment. Horses were living treasure; those without business in the stables were not suffered to remain long.

Even the slaves here knew the sanctity of the ground. One emerged from a stall bearing a basket of grooming tools and paused at the sight of Shianan and Luca. "How may I be of service to you, my lord?" he asked suspiciously, his tone implying that he knew my lord was not a regular visitor and he would be happy to show my lord the way out.

Shianan straightened; he had come by royal direction. "I've come to speak with Philip. I'm Shianan Becknam, and—"

"Oh, right, my lord," answered the groom immediately, his demeanor altering to willing accommodation. "One moment, and I'll tell the stable-steward you're here."

"She told them before she told you," murmured Luca. He had spotted Shianan's suppressed amazement as he left the queen, and they had ducked into an empty corridor so that Shianan could break the news. Luca had been nearly as pleased as Shianan himself.

Philip hurried down the aisle toward them, bowing respectfully toward Shianan as if he were one of the council or a general rather than a mere commander-count. "My lord, I have been awaiting you. Come, and I will show you Kuolema."

Kuolema's stall was the size of Shianan's office. The horse put his head over the door to greet them, his ears pricked sociably. He was a dark bay, Philip said; Shianan thought the red and black shading on his head was simply beautiful. "He's...amazing."

Philip nodded proudly. "He goes well, too. Alexander started him. He'll be a bit anxious about the city, but he's honest, and he'll settle soon enough. He's young, mind; my lord will need a patient hand with him."

"I'll need your guidance," Shianan said quickly. "I won't pretend to know more than I do, and I would hate to harm such a magnificent animal."

Something brightened within Philip, lighting his eyes, and Shianan realized he had just made an ally of the horse-steward. "I would be glad to assist you, your lordship. He is a wonderful horse, and he deserves careful treatment." He nodded appraisingly. "Has your lordship much experience?"

Shianan shook his head. "I know only the rudest theory of it, and I place myself wholly in your tutelage."

Philip beamed. "Let me bring him out, my lord, and I'll show you the handling of him." He glanced at Luca and then back at Shianan. "You'll do well, I'm sure."

Shianan did not ride Kuolema that day, content to learn the basics of grooming and moving about the horse on the ground. He would not be responsible for the horse's care, of course, but it seemed a good way to accustom himself to the young stallion and to learn the basics of handling horses. Philip was plainly delighted that Shianan did not arrogantly assume expertise, and he was eager to teach him.

Shianan could not stay the day; he had other duties that demanded his time. He left with a fine layer of dust over his hands, a comfortable warm scent of horse in his nose, and a calm satisfaction. "That was gratifying. Even—fun," he said to Luca. "I'd wanted to ride a horse, yes, publicly, but even the grooming... I enjoyed that."

And the generals would see him ride. Ariana would see him ride.

"When will you ride him?" Luca seemed as pleased for Shianan as he would have been for himself; this represented an enormous trust and honor, besides its inherent excitement.

"Soon," Shianan answered quickly. "Privately, in the training ring. And then in the street." His heart swelled warm in his chest. "Oh, but this is going to be fine."

Tamaryl was sleeping when the door opened, and Vermi'che rapped his shoulder with the forked rod. "Up! Get up!"

"What?"

"You're wanted. Now. Move!"

The hurry surprised him. The chains rubbed as he stood and moved unsteadily toward the door. Flames, but he was weak. Where would he go? What did Oniwe'aru want with him now?

Hands seized him as he exited the narrow cell and pushed him against the opposite wall, pinning his arms to the stone. He looked over his shoulder. "Wait!"

But it was water that struck him, cool thick sponges from the distant bay, not the scourge the humans used on their prisoners. Tamaryl shivered with relief and cold. The water reached the gouges left by the crossed chains, and he drew in a quick breath as it stung him.

They wouldn't clean him for execution, surely. He would go before Oniwe'aru—he would appear in the Palace of Red Sands, or they wouldn't scrub him of his filth. He would be heard once more.

CHAPTER 25

Shianan tapped softly at the door, still not quite accustomed to expecting admittance. But Ethan's welcome was genuine. "Come in, my lord. He's awake and will be glad of your company."

"Indeed," came Soren's weaker voice, "any change is welcome, but especially you. Please come and sit."

Soren had several pillows behind him, and he seemed less pale and a bit less wasted. Shianan took the chair beside the bed. "You look improved. How are you feeling?"

Soren made a face. "I am sick to death of this room, there's still a goodly dent in my ribs, and I'm told—I can't even try to bend and look—that the burning pain on my backside is an oozing wound from nothing more than sitting on that same backside too long. Can you imagine anything less dignified?"

Shianan tipped his head. "You'd think a pampered royal backside would be used to it."

Soren laughed and then winced. "Oh, 'soats, man, don't make me laugh."

"Then I'm afraid I can hardly do much to cheer you, my lord. Shall I recite drill patterns for you instead?"

"You can tell me tales of the outside world, if you would. I've heard the primary news about the Ryuven, of course, but I want to hear about anything that isn't this room."

Shianan shrugged. "Merchant news? The state of the crops?"

"King's oats, the only good part of this has been relief from dry reports on the number of bushels of wheat expected per acre in a particular district. Can't you speak of something human? Your mage, for example—how is she?"

"I—I haven't spoken with her."

Soren looked contrite. "I'm sorry. Not her, then. Your Luca? I saw him in Alham again, but how did that come about? Did his family sell him back again?"

Shianan shook his head. "No, he was a freeman there, but bandits took him."

When he'd finished explaining, Soren shook his head emphatically. "A freeman enslaved without reason is no slave. Bandits cannot make a man a slave."

"It is done frequently, my lord. How can a slave, once stripped and chained, prove he was a freeman?"

"Then it needs reform," Soren said stubbornly. "A registered paper, perhaps—it would slow transfer and somewhat raise the cost of slaves, true, but we can't lose our subjects to false slavery, either. And it's a better project for my staring at the ceiling than counting projected bushels of wheat."

"There is one piece of news," Shianan said, and he hated how his stomach tightened. Soren would be glad for him, of course, but...

"What's that?"

"The queen has assigned me the task of exercising a horse."

"A horse?"

Shianan's stomach clenched further.

But Soren needed only a moment to work out the politics. "Oh, she's clever. Given you the status without the burden, and under the guise of an assignment. Oh, she's brilliant. What's that face to mean?"

Shianan hadn't realized his expression had betrayed him. "What? No, it's an honor, of course." It only felt wrong to be telling the prince-heir he would ride a horse, and a royal horse. As if Shianan were over-reaching his place.

"What horse? Not that I really know her horses. But tell me about yours."

"Not mine," Shianan said quickly. "The horse belongs to Her Majesty, and I am only to exercise him."

"Only to exercise him?" repeated Soren expectantly.

The grin broke out of Shianan. "Publicly, she specified."

Soren nodded in approval.

"He's a bay colt—which means he's dark reddish-brown and black, and a young stallion, though I'm sure you know more about it all than I did this morning. His name is Kuolema. He's quite a handsome fellow. And so personable! Did you know horses were so affectionate? He's more like a dog than a—a—what I thought horses were."

Soren laughed.

"If I could ride him at the Founding Festival next year, I—" Shianan stopped abruptly.

"What?"

148

But the words did not want to be spoken, to be given breath and thus brought to life. Shianan looked down, away, down again. "If I am at the Founding Festival next year."

Soren, still slow with his illness, did not understand at first. In fairness, much had intervened to distract him. But Shianan could see the moment in which he remembered. "He can't. Shianan, he can't."

"He can." Shianan forced himself to speak, to blunt the pain and prepare for the blow yet to come. "He said he would take the title, and he as good as said he would take the commandery. The council did not have the opportunity to confirm it because the shield fell and we had the battle. But now there's a treaty, they'll have time for less urgent matters."

"Shianan, you fought at Arakadamia. You saved my life. You're a hero."

Shianan returned his gaze levelly. "After my return from Arakadamia, the queen thought me your would-be murderer until you confirmed my telling. How much less does the king hold me?" The words grated across his soul.

Soren deflected with another argument. "Even if he wanted to, he cannot punish a hero. My mother was suspicious, yes, but now she has put you on a horse. My father—our father—"

Shianan shook his head at the awkward stumble. It was kind of Soren to try, but it made it worse.

"He will not embarrass the kingdom, and especially when he has no cause to argue other than his own temper. To strip title and command, he would need an accusation of treason."

Shianan stared at him incredulously. "Do you think that is so hard to come by? Have you not heard of the Court of the High Star? Do you not understand that treason, stretching from my natural place, is the doom I have lived under my entire life?"

Soren had no ready answer.

"You argue as if the rules you know are the only rules. But I have lived within different rules from my birth." Shianan looked away, hot and embarrassed. "I'm sorry. None of that should have been said."

Soren looked down. "I'm sorry. But... It's hard for me to believe it. Not because you are untruthful; you are not. But if it is true, then I have been complicit in it. And if I cannot change it, I am helpless, and I am not accustomed to being helpless."

"It's not helpless," Shianan said quietly. "It's knowing what can and cannot be helped."

Ariana would say it could all be helped. But Ariana was not here, and wouldn't be.

They were saved from their talk by Ethan entering. "Excuse me, my lords, but I've brought the meal."

Ethan brought a tray to the bed, and Soren curled his lip. "Broth, bread, and bland," he observed. "What I'd give for a piece of real meat."

"Not long now, my lord," Ethan answered mildly, a faint smile curving his mouth. He arranged the tray at Soren's side. "Would you like help?"

Soren made a show of cringing. "Please, Ethan, Becknam has already seen me at my worst. I'm going to make a show of feeding myself while he's here to watch."

Shianan laughed. The prince was certainly improving, and all would be well.

CHAPTER 26

Tamaryl was cold. His grimy clothing was damp; they had scrubbed the worst of the crusted filth from him but had given him nothing fresh to wear. His hair was wet, too, and the breeze coming off the hills and through the airy passages of the palace carried the warmth from him.

He told himself this was why he shivered.

The Ryuven on either side of him, wearing the leather bandoliers of Oniwe's guard, seemed ill at ease. Tamaryl could not guess whether it was a reluctance to handle the former Pairvyn ni'Ai as a treacherous prisoner or whether they knew the mind of Oniwe'aru and wished to distance themselves from what would come. He thought he was sweating now as well as shivering.

He was tired already from standing, hungry and cold, oddly weak without his natural power. The chains still about his torso bit at his chafed skin.

There was a raised voice from within, cut off suddenly. One of the guards sniffed. A moment later, a Ryuven stalked away from Oniwe's audience chamber, wings raised and quivering, fists clenched. He had long orange hair bound into a knot high on his skull, and he turned his face from the group even as he passed at a distance.

The guard sniffed again. "Never should have come back," she muttered. "Kala'rika, five down that he'll try once more?"

"Surely no one is so shameless," Kala'rika replied. "Not again."

"Five, then?"

Kala'rika considered. "Say instead a drink at Lana House. I don't feel so confident in him."

Tamaryl did not think he recognized the rejected courtier, but it was not the time to question Oniwe's guards.

At last someone came into the passage and made a sign to the guards. "Let's go," muttered Kala'rika.

They entered the audience chamber—a small one, not grand, but better than he'd expected—and Tamaryl sank to the floor before the seated Oniwe'aru. He bent low, long middle fingers touching and face to the floor, dropping his shoulders as if he would spread and flatten his wings if he could. He was a beggar here; he knew that.

"Leave us," ordered Oniwe'aru, and Tamaryl heard the guards retreat. What did that mean? Why did Oniwe'aru want to speak with him privately? Was that a good sign? His pulse raced.

"Tamaryl," Oniwe'aru began. "What do you think of me this moment?"

Tamaryl's mind reeled. What kind of question was that? What did Oniwe'aru want to hear?

What did Tamaryl want to tell him?

"Oniwe'aru, I don't understand."

"It's a simple enough question," Oniwe'aru responded. "What is your opinion of me now? What do you think of my actions, my decisions?"

Tamaryl swallowed. "You have always been most concerned with the welfare of your people," he began slowly, "and you have always sought the best for them in your own way. Though the time came when we preferred different methods, I never thought you meant anything but the good of the Ai."

"And my treatment of you?"

Tamaryl closed his eyes against the floor. "You have done what you thought best, Oniwe'aru. You see me as a traitor to your dedication to the Ai, and you've tried to safeguard your way of serving the clan. You have done what you think is right, and I flatter myself that it was not easy for you to do." He took a slow breath. "You are no madman, Oniwe'aru. I regret our present situation, for my own sake of course, and also for that of the Ai—but I know you do only what you think is right, even if I believe you are mistaken. I wish we were in agreement, but...but I understand why you think you must do this, even if I do not understand why you cannot see the way to peace."

Oniwe'aru sighed heavily. "We are in nearer agreement than you may think, Tamaryl."

There was a long moment of silence, and Tamaryl fought the urge to shift on the floor. He could not fidget, not before Oniwe'aru. Flames, what was Oniwe'aru thinking?

At last Oniwe'aru spoke again. "The humans are barbarians. You should know this better than anyone; you spent years among them. As a slave, no less."

Tamaryl gulped. "Look at me, Oniwe'aru. I am lower now than ever in the human world."

It was a foolish thing to say, and he knew it. He squeezed his eyes shut and waited for the response.

"Your enslavement was hardly typical," snapped Oniwe'aru sharply. "I have seen your master, a man who notably protested the institution and argued for benevolent treatment of slaves."

"Then you contradict yourself," answered Tamaryl, "for such a man is decidedly no barbarian."

"Tamaryl," Oniwe'aru said firmly, in a voice that somehow emphasized the lack of honorific suffix, "you have no leave to speak in that posture."

Tamaryl bit hard on the inside of his lip, wanting to weep and argue and shout and beg, all at once.

But how had Oniwe'aru seen Ewan Hazelrig? How had he known of the White Mage's position on slavery?

Oniwe'aru made a small sound of grim amusement. "Your imprisonment has sapped you; once you would have caught that clue instantly. Yes, I have met your Mage Hazelrig, in the human world—when I went to treat for peaceable trade."

Tamaryl jerked upright, forgetting all strictures of his low position. "You—when?"

"A few days past. Just before I last came to see you." Oniwe'aru looked unhappy. "I did not know what to do with you."

"Then we have agreed to trade? To try it, to honor it and to find exchanges?"

"We have."

Mingled relief and joy flooded through Tamaryl. "I am glad. I am so glad."

"Not everyone shares your sentiment. Many think we have given the humans our greatest weakness, so that they may starve us out at their pleasure."

"Those who think so are wrong and short-sighted, speaking in fear instead of acting on opportunity."

Oniwe'aru shifted in his chair, looking as if he wanted to chastise him. "Tamaryl..."

Tamaryl bowed his head, remaining on both knees but above the floor. "For the sake of my past service and our shared blood," he said hoarsely, "if you mean to slay me, say it plainly and let me die with some grace. If you mean to grant me mercy, then please don't torment me longer. I am too proud, Oniwe'aru, but it honors neither of us if I continue to grovel."

Oniwe'aru laughed aloud. "By the Essence, I was right," he mused as Tamaryl stared at the floor. "You are not broken, not yet."

153

"Oniwe'aru, I mean no impudence—"

"Nonsense. There is nothing more impudent than a scabbed weakling in chains refusing to abase himself before the one who could end his life with a word. And you still maintain that you're right—and yet you do not blame me for our differences. I could not be more satisfied."

Tamaryl could not help himself; he lifted his head and stared. "Oniwe'aru?"

"I must send a liaison to the human court. I need someone who will be courteous of their ways, but who will not bend beneath their pressure. It also need be someone they will respect, of high enough rank to honor them as my emissary." He raised one corner of his mouth in a smirk. "And there are very few among my sho and princes who wish to be sent to the human world."

Tamaryl's heart quickened. "And you are thinking of sending me?"

"You know the human world better than any other. It would be an elegant solution to my dilemma; my court would see you exiled again to an unenviable duty in an inhospitable court, a fit recompense for a headstrong prince, while the humans would be pleased to see someone of such high rank sent to them." He paused. "And I would be pleased to have a reason to spare you."

Tamaryl bowed his head. "Thank you, Oniwe'aru."

Oniwe'aru seemed to soften. "For all that you grieve me..." He sighed. "Tamaryl'sho, please kneel as befits your rank."

Tamaryl, stunned, needed a moment to assess his limbs and then shift onto one knee. "Oniwe'aru, I thank you. I will serve you to the best of my ability in this new charge."

"I swore a binding oath to their king. I will see this peace go well, now that I have committed to it. I must have someone equally committed in that place—and you have demonstrated your foolhardy determination." He smiled. "But just now, you look utterly shameful as you are. I think you will find a bath a welcome relief. I, at least, will find it a welcome relief when you no longer stink as you do. Go and make yourself presentable, and then we will talk further." He stopped and stepped forward, gesturing for Tamaryl to stand, and then he reached for him. "Tamaryl, my—" He stopped, his embrace interrupted by the wings trapped securely against Tamaryl's back. "Oh, these are unnecessary now," he muttered, and with a jolt of power he severed a link. Chain rang noisily to the tiled floor, and

Oniwe'aru rested his arms above and below the wings as friends and brothers did.

Tamaryl gasped as his wings shifted, the first motion in a very long time. Oniwe'aru released him with an apologetic look. "Go slowly, Tamaryl'sho. Your power will come, now that the chain is off, and we can have a healer speed your recovery as well."

The pain in his wings was excruciating, but Tamaryl nodded gamely. "I just need some time." He moved his arms carefully and returned his half brother's embrace. "Thank you for— understanding."

"I would not lose you, Tamaryl'sho." Oniwe'aru stepped back and gave him a steady look. "You are my Pairvyn ni'Ai and the son of my mother. You know that, were you not who you are, you could not have survived this experiment in defying the aru's vision for our survival."

Tamaryl smiled without humor. "If I were not who I am, I could not have tried it."

"Boldly spoken, but not inaccurate," acknowledged Oniwe'aru. "Now go and bathe, before my rooms reek of your stench as well."

CHAPTER 27

Soren was dozing, but he awoke at the sound of heavy tread crossing the room. "Father," he greeted, hearing the sleep in his voice.

The king bent over the bed and took Soren's shoulder gently, kissing him lightly on the forehead. This, his father's renewed demonstrativeness, was the greatest sign to Soren of how narrowly he'd missed death.

King Jerome sat in the chair beside the bed and smiled. "How are you feeling today, my son?"

"Better," Soren answered sleepily. He shifted, knowing he should try to sit up and greet his father properly, but muffling weariness seemed to slow his thoughts and movements. His talk with Shianan that afternoon had been enjoyable but exhausting; he still had trouble comprehending how weak he was. Ethan came to the bed, opposite the king, and quietly eased another couple of pillows behind Soren so that he was not quite supine.

King Jerome set his hands on his knees, bending forward a bit in the chair. "We've been busy. One would think it would be simple enough to end a war, once the haggling of terms is done, but that's not so, it seems. Soldiers are meant to fight and kill, not to hold hands and discourage brawling... And the generals are fussing, of course, because they're trained to see all that can go wrong, that's their duty. And we haven't even touched on the Devinne agreement, or the warlords and bandits, or the complaints of trade in false herbs, or anything else that came along with this. We need you on your feet, son." He beamed. "They'll listen to the hero of Arakadamia."

"I'm no hero," Soren protested weakly. "I should have been dead."

"A dead man can be a hero," answered his father amiably, "and you aren't dead, after all."

There was a rapid knock at the door; that would be Alasdair. The younger prince entered before Ethan could open, impatient. "Is he—you're awake! And, oh, my lord father." Alasdair straightened, checked somewhat. "Good evening. Soren, how do you feel?"

It seemed Soren would have no more rest, after all. Soren made himself smile for his younger brother. It was not Alasdair's fault Soren was tired. "I'm all right."

"Mother's coming, too," Alasdair announced.

"Alasdair, come and sit beside your heroic brother," the king said. "We'll need another chair for your lady mother."

Soren shifted his eyes to Ethan, who nodded and moved to fetch a chair. Good man.

Alasdair moved as if to sit on the bed, but he glanced at Soren's sudden apprehension and aborted his movement. Soren exhaled, relieved, and watched as Alasdair turned and pulled a chair closer. Perhaps the little turd was learning to be considerate. Soren felt a slight guilt; his mother said Alasdair had passed many nights in Soren's own room, watching his unconscious elder brother. Perhaps the little turd was not wholly one, after all.

Alasdair was staring at Soren, looking as if he wanted to speak but saying nothing. Ethan brought the chair.

Queen Azalie entered without knocking. "Hello, dearest." She bent to give Soren a kiss on the cheek, and in return he caught her hand and pressed it briefly to his lips. "How are you feeling?"

"Better and better," he answered. "I still need too much sleep, but I was so sick of my own dreams that I sacrificed a nap for conversation."

"I'm sorry I left you to scavenge for conversation," she answered with a smile. "Who came to see you? My lord Hastings was asking after you."

"No, it was Becknam." Belatedly Soren glanced at his father. He had not yet heard the king acknowledge Shianan's part in Soren's rescue, and he didn't know where opinion stood.

Azalie turned to assess Jerome's response as well, her mouth set in a warning that frightened Soren, trapped on his back and unable to escape.

Jerome was not looking at either of them, however. "I don't like him coming here," he muttered. "He did you good service, and we are appreciative, but I have warned you before, Soren, beware of that man's ambition."

"Ambition?" Soren hadn't the strength to protest properly. "I've told you, Father, that Shianan is—"

"He is a mistake," snapped Queen Azalie. "A glaring error in judgment."

Soren and his father looked at her in surprise. Soren felt as if he'd been slapped. "Mother, you..."

"No, I don't mean the spawning of him; only one of us had anything to do with that." Soren saw his father actually flush. "But we all have used him shamefully since."

Alasdair withdrew into his chair.

"Becknam is a talented man, as I hear. You've praised him enough, Jerome, when you thought you could." She gave him a narrow look. "I admit I resented that and therefore resented him. And that was wrong. As was treating him as a trespass to be punished."

Jerome retreated slightly before her steely glare. "He has been given opportunities to earn advancement."

"You brought him here and ennobled him, certainly, but you haven't truly included him in your court, have you? You've made him a scapegoat and laughingstock." She whirled on Alasdair, who shrank in the chair. "And you—sweet heaven, he is a nobleman and a member of the court, and he rescued you. By what madness did you think it your place to arrange his humiliation or murder in the festival military displays?"

Alasdair gaped. "You—you know?"

"I am your mother and the queen. How could I not know?"

Alasdair writhed. "I... I thought... He was supposed to be such a fighter... And my lord father said..." He glanced quickly at King Jerome and then as quickly away, suddenly aware he would find no help there. "He's supposed to be a fighter!"

"And so you took it upon yourself to use the seal—a hanging offense in anyone else, you realize that?—to forge the king's name? To kill royal blood?"

Alasdair seized desperately on this. "He's not really royal blood."

"No? If he does not carry the blood of his royal parent, why has Chrenada taken such pains in the past to ensure a bastard cannot form his own line?" She fixed icy eyes on Alasdair. "Bastards have claimed the thrones of honest sons—as you'd know if you gave a better showing in your history lessons—and supported their claims, too. Tarik reigned thirty-seven years while his legitimate half brother lived in exile. No one argued Tarik's blood."

Alasdair shrank in the chair and stared fixedly at his feet.

"You contradict yourself," protested Jerome. "Yes, bastards have seized the thrones of legitimate heirs, and that is exactly why I have kept Becknam in his place all these years. He is not suffered to have any illusions of power or possibility; he is a useful tool and nothing more. That is what was needed—that was what you wanted!"

"Half right," returned Azalie sharply. "I wanted him, not useful, but gone. I wanted it to be as if he had never existed. That was impossible, a foolish wish. Instead, you more than kept Becknam from presuming to power, you abused and abased him in the most shameful manner." She hesitated, took a breath. "I was wrong. But you, my lord husband, you were more wrong."

Jerome stiffened, his face reddening. "I have managed him as—"

"No." Azalie's voice had changed, chilling the room and stilling the king's protest. "No, I say. Of all of us, I had the most cause to hate him, to resent him, to despise him. He was an affront to me most of all. And I did hate him, as you well know. But now—now I have met the man, I have seen him for myself, seen what he has become and what he has been made, and now I owe him the life of my own son. And I can see clearly I was wrong to hate a boy who had no part in his birth." Her eyes blazed. "You also owe him the life of your son. Both sons. And you, his sire, owe him a respectable existence. If I, who have the greatest grievance against him, can recognize this, surely you must know it."

Jerome swallowed. "I have made him a courtier."

"You have made him an animal." She turned her awful glare upon Alasdair. "Do you understand me, Alasdair?"

The young prince nodded tightly.

She faced Soren. "You recognized his merit first of all. You should have argued for him before now."

Soren was pinned by that gaze, trapped in the bed. "I did not think anyone would hear me," he answered weakly.

"I suppose that is true." She nodded. "And it is good that you befriended him," she observed, her face softening. "I don't know that anyone would have done as much for a man who reviled him and shamed him before the court." She looked toward the king. "Or privately. If you speak of him so callously to us, what do you say to him yourself?"

Alasdair's eyes widened and he looked suddenly at his lap. Soren's pulse quickened; the boy knew something. The obnoxious little turd had espied out what Soren had only wondered at.

Jerome swelled angrily. "What I say to him privately is our private matter. But I praise his accomplishments and scold his failings as with any other."

Alasdair curled into the chair, hugging his knees to his chest, and stared at the floor.

"I hope that is so, for a king must be consistent in all things." Azalie nodded meaningfully. "It won't be long before Alasdair will enter the military himself to learn to support his brother. He will expect the same even-handed treatment from you, I'm sure. And I hope that Shianan Becknam will be eager to serve his princes." She glanced to the side. "Alasdair, sit up properly."

Alasdair slid from his huddle and sat dolefully upright.

"And now that we understand one another," Azalie said, "explain to me how you intend to honor this man by stripping his title and property."

Jerome stiffened. Soren's chest tightened. Too many had heard the king's intent, and Azalie did a cruel kindness by forcing the question here, privately, instead of letting rumor and speculation build.

Jerome looked, to Soren's eye, embarrassed. Despite Shianan's worry that the blow was yet to fall, the king had hoped it would be forgotten. "I...had not thought on it."

"I could have guessed as much," Azalie said. "To set a precedent of taking land and title for spite? Not for something properly treasonous, but just to quell a noble who served too well? That's a dangerous path to walk, and your court will not be pleased."

"It was not for spite," Jerome protested. "It was for treason, or something near enough. He wanted to marry."

Soren clenched his jaw with the feeble energy he could summon and looked at his mother. She did not disappoint him.

"To marry?" she repeated, and her voice was low and steady. "Treason needs a heavier charge than a desire to marry."

"You have only just said yourself that bastards cannot be permitted to form their own lines."

"You cannot demote and humiliate the commander who just saved your prince-heir's life."

"And so I should let him position himself to inherit instead?"

"He's not inheriting!" Soren interjected with a little stab of pain in his side. "He doesn't want that." Why couldn't his father see that? What did he imagine in Shianan?

King Jerome scowled at the blankets over Soren's knees. "You don't know that, Soren. It isn't—the line of inheritance doesn't always go as planned." He set his jaw. "You can't dig out a trench and expect water won't run down it."

"So don't name him an heir." But even as he spoke, Soren finally realized what his father had never said aloud and never could. *The line of inheritance doesn't always go as planned.* Jerome had not been a prince-heir, either. Had he desired more than his brother's bride? Had he coveted the throne which then came to him, leaving him with a lifetime of self-reproach?

But his expression now was only firm dismissal. "Letting him marry would be setting him above his established place, setting him to imagine himself as more than he is, a potential heir—or, just as dangerous, to let others imagine him so, a pawn for others' ambitions."

Soren shook his head, struggling for words. "That's not what he wants."

"For now," Jerome said. "But give him gold and he'll begin to think of money. I don't care what he wants, or might want, my duty is to protect this kingdom and the succession."

Azalie answered, "Then let's think on how we might do that without punishing one of its greatest servants." Her tirade ended, she turned to Soren. "I'm sorry for shouting, dear. Take some rest now; you look weary."

He was. "I..." He wanted to protest, but he was indeed tired and a little daunted.

She shook her head. "Get some rest; we'll leave you to it. Come, let's let him sleep. No, Alasdair, if you have questions they'll wait a moment. My lord husband?"

They left Soren to worry and then slide helplessly into sleep.

CHAPTER 28

Elysia Parma poured herself additional wine and looked across the table at Ariana. "I don't mean to pry, young Mage Hazelrig, but all evening you've looked as if you had a boulder strapped across your shoulders and a death warrant to sign in the morning. Would it help to talk about it?"

Ariana stirred, looking at her father and Mage Parma, and then back at the supper laid between them all, which she'd been ignoring in her daze. "Oh," she said lamely. "I hadn't realized I was being such poor company."

"You're always lovely company, but just now you're not yourself." Mage Parma tore another piece of bread. "And I certainly don't believe that just because some things have gone very well, such as your triumphant second return from the Ryuven world, something else may not undermine your joy. I am not so foolish as to think success is a panacea for all of life's conditions." She dipped her bread in the juices on her plate. "I do know your father and I would do anything to help you, if we can."

"I don't know..." Ariana trailed off. "I know you would—both of you—but I don't know..."

Her father smiled. "Well, we certainly cannot help what we don't know." He sobered and leaned over the table. "You've had a turbulent time, even in the best of it. It may be that you're only struggling to keep up with being thrust so prominently into the public eye, and with so much pressure for this trial peace to work."

"That also," Ariana admitted. "If it fails, I failed, and all Chrenada suffers for it." As they started to answer, she shook her head and held up a hand. "Maybe not, but that's what it feels like. But I don't want to talk about that. That's not what I've been thinking about."

Her father folded his hands. Elysia Parma spread fruit butter across the remaining bread and waited expectantly.

Ariana took a breath. "I'm trying to decide if I am in love. If I want to marry. Don't laugh, please."

Neither of them laughed. Her father's mouth crooked upward slightly, but not in a mocking way. Elysia only looked very interested. "Who is it?"

There was no one else in the house to hear, and she trusted them both. Ariana rubbed her clammy hands on her thighs. "Shianan Becknam."

Elysia's eyebrows rose. "Shianan Becknam?" She did not add, *the bastard*, for which Ariana was grateful, but her tone was surprised. "I confess, I had no idea. But Ewan, you look very pleased with yourself. I suppose this is no surprise to you."

He grinned. "They have been stepping out occasionally. I had my suspicions."

"And you were—are—comfortable with this?"

"I know the man better than you might suppose, and I believe in his integrity and his dedication. He's no social prize, I'll grant, but I believe he would be a good husband, if he married." He looked to Ariana. "And that's the question, isn't it."

She nodded. "As a king's bastard, he's not permitted to marry. I think—he went to the king to ask permission, and he was denied. So..."

"So there's no way but to defy the king," Elysia finished. "A bold and dangerous choice. And what you're wondering is, if you have done enough at Arakadamia to rely on your reputation and fame to save you."

Ariana's muscles tightened all at once. "I had not put it in those words, exactly, but yes, that's the general sum of it."

They sat silent for a moment.

"Let me go back and ask another question," Elysia said. "You started by saying you were trying to decide if you were in love. Tell me about that."

Ariana's pulse quickened in a moment of panic. "I—sweet all—I don't know. How does one know? There are stories, so many stories, but I don't trust stories, not for something like this. I love Shianan, I know, but I love Father and you and—Tam, and I don't know how to know if love is *that* kind of love, or if—or if it's enough. Because I'm not a complete fool, I know if we try it will be hard, harder than if I loved a merchant or a noble, and I'm ashamed to admit it but I'm afraid. What if I love him, but it's not enough? What if I make everything worse for him by trying to act on my love?"

Elysia nodded. "These are wise questions."

Ariana swallowed. "You've never married?"

Elysia's eyes darted to the table, as if caught by some movement there, and then she returned to looking at Ariana. "That does not mean I have never loved, or never wrestled with these questions."

Ariana bit her lip, chastened. She had not thought the question might be unkind. Perhaps Elysia had wrestled with these same questions and found the answers Ariana was most afraid of. "I'm sorry."

Elysia waved the words away and looked at Ewan. "You've been watching them. What do you think?"

Ewan propped his chin on his laced fingers, elbows on the table. "I cannot say if someone is in love. What I can tell you is this: being in love is delightful, but it is not enough."

Ariana caught her breath.

"Hear me out," he said patiently. "Being in love is an emotion, a glorious giddy rush of fire and wind, reveling in your own flames and burning with excitement. It's wonderful—but it is a gorgeous bright flash, a burst of sparkling color and sound, and it will inevitably fade. And you are too clever to make such a crucial, life-altering decision on an emotion, no matter how glorious or intoxicating."

Ariana nodded despite herself, not knowing if she understood, not knowing if she wanted to hear this.

"But being in love is not the only kind of love, though it claims most of the attention in stories and songs. True love burns steady and strong beneath layers of ash even when the bright flame dancing above may flicker or falter—love that does not offer so much color, but steady warmth and useful heat. It may be set by a bright spark, and that is how it often begins and that is beautiful, but that is not its true nature, which is far more powerful. It requires tending, but properly tended, it will not go out."

Ariana's throat was too tight for her to speak even if she had wanted to.

"So you are absolutely right to question being in love. The question is, are you considering a bright firework or an ever-burning hearth fire?"

Ariana gulped air and tried to clear her throat. "That's a good question, Father. But you have not made me less afraid."

Ewan looked at Elysia, who planted her elbows on the table and matched his posture. She observed to Ariana, "What I heard earlier, in your fears, were concerns for *his* welfare."

Ariana nodded. "I am the Black Mage. I have a place in the Circle. My father is the White Mage. Shianan is the bastard, and—and it's worse than I'd thought. If something goes wrong, I will not be the first to suffer." She pressed the next words out, hating them but needing to acknowledge them. "And it doesn't matter what I want, if I ruin him to have him."

Elysia nodded. "It seems to me, this sounds like the right kind of love."

Ariana tried to breathe through her tight throat, her pulse heavy in her hands and ears. "So you think...?"

Elysia shook her head. "I can't tell you what your answer should be or how things will go. But to me, your hesitation speaks better for your chances than a giddy determination to act. I think you should consider your options and see if a route might be open to you." She smiled. "You have always been a bright and optimistic thinker. I can't say I've thought much on when you might fall in love, but I've certainly never pictured you with an ordinary farmer or merchant— nothing against merchants, of course, but you were raised a mage, and the extraordinary is your ordinary. I suppose it shouldn't surprise me that you were attracted to someone who should have been outside your reach."

Ariana looked from her to her father. "And what do you think?"

Ewan looked embarrassed. "I think I've known the decision you now face for longer than you have," he said, flushing a little and looking down at his mostly empty plate, "and I did not know which path I wanted you to choose."

Sweet Holy One, he was talking about both Tamaryl and Shianan. He did not even know what had happened this last time in the Ryuven world, but he had *known*.

Attracted to someone who should have been out of her reach, indeed.

Twice.

But even when she had thought Shianan dead, she had resisted Tamaryl. He was a friend, a dear friend, someone she had known or half known most of her life and her only help when she needed it most. She did love him. But she loved him as a friend and a brother, not as she loved Shianan.

"But if you have chosen," her father was continuing, "then I will support your choice. You are the Black Mage and you have done a great service to the kingdom. There may be a way to leverage that into permission to marry the man of your choice."

Emotion crushed Ariana and she wanted to cry, despite feeling no sorrow whatsoever. "Do you think so?" she half whispered. "Do you think we could, without harming him? But—oh, sweet all, I'm still afraid."

"That's good," Elysia said, pouring more wine into all their glasses. "Fear exists to prevent the doing of something stupid. Fear makes you think before acting. But it shouldn't prevent you from acting when appropriate." She set down the ewer and lifted her glass. "A toast for Ariana and her Shianan Becknam—to the difficult task ahead of them and the rich reward behind it."

Ariana, watching them raise their glasses and look at her, felt a swell of confidence and joy. If they loved her and supported her, it would be all right. She would find a way. It could be done.

She lifted her glass to the task ahead of her.

CHAPTER 29

Tamaryl straightened, reveling still in the movement of his body and the luxury of extending to his full height. His power was returning, steadily if gradually, but he still felt the effects of the forcible draining and the fup-forged chains. It would be days yet before he had his full strength. But he was fully clean, after a long scrub and a proper soaking bath, dressed in his own clean clothing in his own home—it was good to be out of prison, home, in command of his own name and actions. He stretched overhead, possibly just to prove that he could.

So often he had sacrificed his natural self to his principles.

He rolled his shoulders. Nori'bel the healer had given him something to drink several times a day, which she said would ease the discomfort somewhat. It was difficult to treat magical malady with physical means; she had helped Maru to recover from the Subduing, but the human technique was a little different than the Ryuven method. It was easier to treat a human Subduing, she said, once the Ryuven was returned to his native atmosphere. Still, Tamaryl would be whole again, and it was more than he had expected, so he could hardly complain.

Someone clapped outside the door, and Maru entered without waiting for permission. "Tamaryl," he said, and his tone carried so many more words, words of relief and gratitude and joy and affection.

Tamaryl faced him. "Maru. I owe you everything."

"What?"

"So much. You stopped me from killing the human prince-heir. You talked me back to myself and helped Ariana and me to stop the battle."

"I only did what I had to," Maru protested. "What you would have done, if you were thinking as yourself."

"But I wasn't thinking as myself, that's the point. You had to do it for me." Tamaryl took a breath. "You're the hero of this success, Maru. And I owe you everything."

Maru shook his head. "Not quite everything. I wasn't the one who convinced Oniwe'aru to give you another chance."

"Another chance, after the second chance I did not expect." Tamaryl gave a wry smile. "But I thought there might have been another hand beside Oniwe's own. He is shrewd, and generous when it suits him, but I would not have thought this reprieve suited him. It will make trouble for him in the court."

Maru nodded. "There's been talk that he was pressed into it."

"Pressed?" Tamaryl raised his eyebrows. "By whom?"

Maru gave him a steady look. "Edeiya'rika."

Understanding struck Tamaryl like the cleansing waters of his bath. Edeiya'rika had influenced Oniwe'aru as only she could; Oniwe had already said that she would be Edeiya'silth soon, likely the next leader of the Ai clan. If she had urged Oniwe to a particular course, she had the wisdom and prestige to be convincing.

And she had lobbied for his release.

"I must find a way to thank her," he said. "But not so overtly it mars her coming rule." And that would be a subject to occupy his mind for many nights. "Speaking of court affairs... There was a sho in Oniwe'aru's court, one I did not know. From the guards' talk, he has been making a nuisance of himself. He had a striking color of hair—"

"That is Ronal'sho." Maru knew him immediately. "He is of one of the outer branches of the North Family. He thought to be Pairvyn, after Gann'sho died, and was slow to give up hope. After you were imprisoned, he must have thought the opportunity renewed."

Tamaryl thought back to what Edeiya had told him. "But Oniwe'aru did not want to give the position to another family, not while there was unrest." So Ronal'sho might think himself cheated of the title. He must have resented Tamaryl's return after long years to reclaim the rank he had simply abandoned. "Should he have been?"

"Of course not."

Tamaryl laughed. "I appreciate your loyalty, but my question is sincere. Would Oniwe'aru have been wise to choose him?"

Maru screwed up his face in concentration. "He is a good fighter, there is no question of that. He has a name as a dueler. I do not know if he would be as good at strategy. He would be a better Pairvyn than an aru, I am certain of that, but I do not know that I would have wanted to fight under his leadership."

Tamaryl nodded. Then he smiled. "Which of us would win?"

"What?"

"In a duel. Which of us would win?"

Maru shook his head. "Twenty years ago, you, I am sure. But now—now he has been trying to prove himself, and you have been trying to make peace. He bears a grudge you do not, while you have been softening to practice diplomacy. And you are still not recovered from your imprisonment, so—"

"Thank you, Maru, that is more honesty than I may have wanted." But Tamaryl gave him a reassuring smile.

The darkening grey clouds overhead were an apt mirror for Ariana's mood. Her knocks at Shianan's door had gone unanswered, though she could not say whether he had barricaded the door against her or was out training soldiers or on other work. His servant Luca had not answered, either, but again, she could not be certain if he had been there to refuse. She had left a note the day before and had heard nothing, which was more suggestive of avoidance, but it had been necessarily oblique, and Shianan might have let it pass in his belief that there was no hope for their future and it was better to sever all ties.

But he had asked to court her. Dared she rely on what he had done then?

Despite the clouds, she turned her steps toward the market. Ryuven merchants were bringing more dall sweetbud today, and she thought the sight of successful trade would cheer her. By all accounts, the sales had been going well, and trade had even broadened beyond just the medicinal herb and foodstuffs. If nothing else, she could be proud of this.

The Ryuven were already in place, selling on three fronts as soldiers ringed the group. But Ariana, approaching, wasn't sure if they were there to guard the market from the visiting Ryuven or the Ryuven from the men gathered in the market. A dozen and a half men scowled, their arms crossed or cradling a staff or cudgel, standing in a loose group to one side or patrolling back and forth along the south side of the plaza.

Ariana had seen men like them before when the Ryuven had come to sell, but their numbers seemed to be growing. There had been few clashes with the Ryuven traders, and soldiers were already in place; why did these men come, and keep coming, and keep bringing more like themselves?

The breeze strengthened, heavy with the coming rain. Ariana turned away from the rushed sales and started back toward the Wheel.

She kept her head down as she walked, ducking the wind and the eyes of those around her. Were the men arming in the market defending against the Ryuven, or looking for an opportunity to attack them? Did they believe those to be the same?

How could she reach Shianan, and did he still care for her as he had? He had asked the king for permission to court her before he had spoken to her—possibly to avoid the embarrassment of having to reverse his suit if he was denied. Should she likewise act before speaking to him, relying on his former commitment?

"Ariana! I was just coming to look for you!"

Ariana turned and saw Ranne hurrying toward the Wheel. She had a bag hanging on one shoulder, which she held close to keep it from bouncing as she jogged. Ariana moved to meet her and gave her a quick hug. "Ranne! What brings you up here?"

"I have something for you."

"Come to my office, then, before the rain."

Ariana and Ranne ducked inside as the first fat drops began to splatter the paving stones and then followed the curved outer corridor of the Wheel. Ariana tapped her black-painted door to release its magical lock. "Have a seat."

But Ranne stood at the table, struggling with her bag. "This was such a tight squeeze... Here! I thought it was most fitting that you should have the first copy."

Ariana set the athanor to heat water—it worked just as well for tea as for more arcane purposes—and turned to see a large book on her worktable. "Oh, it's gorgeous."

Ranne had bound it in a deep green leather of a gentle texture, with external stitching in a wine red. More wine-red stitching wrapped from the spine across the cover, forming the raised shape of a Ryuven in flight. Silver leaf formed the mace in his hand, matching the bright edges of the pages. All the space between the embroidered Ryuven and the cover's edge was filled with delicate silver leafing in intricate patterns, occasionally opening around a radiant silver star.

"But wait." Ranne lifted the book and flexed it to spread the pages slightly, and a hidden scene opened on the ends of the pages, a cavalcade of officers on galloping horses, banners and spears high in the air.

"Oh, Ranne, this is amazing work," Ariana breathed. "What is it?"

"One of Connor's father's friends purchased a book from a Ryuven merchant, and he's had it copied and bound," Ranne explained. "He's giving some to friends and we're selling the others."

"So this is his?"

"No, silly, I said this was yours. Don't worry, he's paid enough for the lot that this one is covered as well. But can you imagine? I'm binding a Ryuven book!"

"It's fantastic." Ariana stroked the cover, her fingers tracing a brilliant star. "What's the book?"

"Oh, that's the best part. You'll love this." Ranne opened it to show the title page.

The Stars of the Firmament and Their Tales: An Accurate Reproduction of an Authentic Ryuven Text on the Astronomy of the Ryuven World.

Ariana caught her breath. "Oh, that's wonderful."

Ranne grinned. "I thought you'd be pleased. And since you brought the Ryuven merchants, and since I'm making a tidy sum, I am also pleased." She gave Ariana a quick hug, too enthused to linger in one place. "So I know it's a large beast of a book, but find somewhere large to put it."

"I'll treasure it," Ariana assured her. "Thank you."

As Ranne left, a servant in royal livery was coming down the hall. Ariana hesitated at the door, and he hurried to her. "For my lady mage." He presented a heavy document, folded and sealed, and bowed. She took it and he departed.

She closed the door, looking over the missive. Something official, anyway. She broke the wax seal.

The letter begged to invite her to a grand ball held by the House of Laguna, to commemorate jointly the new peace with the Ryuven and the prince-heir's recovery. She would be a guest of honor.

It was dizzying—she was only the Black Mage, and that less than a year. It was stunning that she should be a guest of honor at a royal ball. And yet...

...And yet at the last ball she had danced with Shianan, and she wanted that again.

Shianan entered Soren's room to find the prince seated in a chair. "My lord, you're out of bed!"

"More, I walked over here myself," bragged Soren with a grin, "all six paces of it. Well, Ethan was at my shoulder the entire way, but I managed my own feet."

Shianan laughed. "I'm glad to see you moving."

"I'm glad you're glad, because I have a boon to ask of you." He gestured to another chair, and Shianan moved it so the prince could face him without twisting. "The healers tell me I'll be recovered enough to stagger from place to place during the coming ball. I hope they're right, because I cannot fail to be there. It's our grand celebration of a new peace, the apparent defeat of the plague, and even my own recovery. Of course I'm quite pleased to be breathing." He smiled. "But if my present state is any indication, my lurching about the ball isn't going to be graceful and may not be terribly reliable. I'll want someone to keep me steady and prevent my embarrassing the kingdom by pitching down the stairs face-first. Will you stand with me and be my human crutch?"

Shianan looked at him in surprise and then shook his head. "Surely my lord has many friends of more suitable rank—"

"I am not concerned with rank," answered Soren sharply, suddenly serious. "I want someone I can trust to look after me, not someone who will be stealing glances at the court women while letting me flail for help. I want someone demonstrably trustworthy."

Demonstrably trustworthy. Shianan's fingers flexed into the upholstery. King's sweet oats, this was for him as much as for Soren. "My lord, I hardly—"

"Shianan," Soren interrupted, "I have many friends in the court, but few I believe would be as good if I were not the prince-heir. You, on the other hand, I believe would be an even better friend were I not the prince-heir, because you wouldn't hesitate for these questions of courtly protocol." He paused. "Do this for me: let me do this for you."

Shianan answered slowly, "If you ask it of me, my lord, I will do anything."

"Thank you." Soren looked somewhat relieved. "And 'soats, I hope I'm well enough to hold myself upright, at least. I can't imagine much more humiliation than—no, Ethan, don't turn away! That look—you know something. What's planned?"

Ethan's face smoothed into concerned sobriety. "I believe my lords Their Majesties intend to tell you themselves."

"And they will, certainly, but you'll tell me first. That expression frightened me. What do you know?"

Ethan looked sympathetic. "My lord, Her Highness will be present at the ball. For the formal introduction."

Soren stared at him. "She—of course, that only makes—oh, king's sweet double-dyed oats."

Shianan looked between them. "What is it?"

"You might as well drop me back into the nearest ravine, because I'll be as much good there as here. What possessed anyone to think that I could—"

"Who?" interrupted Shianan, surprising himself.

"Princess Valetta," answered Soren unhappily. He gestured at the well-appointed sitting room as if it offered an explanation. "Of the Wakari Coast. My betrothed in all but official acknowledgment. Whom I've not yet met, and whom I'd rather not meet while I have to be propped up like a top-heavy drunkard."

Shianan was helpless to aid him. "She'll be in awe of a prince-heir no matter what, and the betrothal secured."

"Would that were true. The Wakari merchants are a match for our army—no offense, my lord commander. We need this marriage, after so many years of being bled by the Ryuven. Thank the Holy One we have a reprieve from that."

"Maybe you'll be much improved by then. It's days away, after all."

"Mere days, you mean," Soren replied gloomily. "I've seen her miniature, and she probably has mine. It more than likely didn't show me a cripple."

"Surely she will understand an injury." Shianan shrugged. "And at least you can think of all the fun you'll have watching Lady Bethia Farlyle meet the princess."

"'Soats, yes. I hope someone has taken her aside and corrected her mistaken impression." But one corner of Soren's mouth twitched. "That ought to be suitably embarrassing for everyone, I think."

"It might take some of the attention from your imperfect form. I mean, imagine my lady sweeping down the stairs, nodding imperiously to courtiers on either side, giving a contemptuous glance to the woman at the far side of the room, and then—"

"Curse you, Becknam, I told you not to make me laugh."

"Sorry, my lord." But they both grinned.

Chapter 30

Shianan stroked Kuolema's muscular neck, admiring how the red coat gleamed as the colt arched and turned his head to lip at Shianan's hair tail. Shianan laughed and pushed him gently away.

Philip cleared his throat from across the aisle, and Shianan jumped as if guilty, and then he grinned at the horsemaster. "It's only a little."

"He shouldn't be nibbling on you at all."

"There's no teeth to it. He's just returning the favor as I scratch him."

Philip nodded with a growing smile. "Ah, well spotted."

Theirs was a curious relationship. Philip was a slave, and Shianan a commander. Yet Philip was the horsemaster, and Shianan an untrained ignorant permitted to approach the precious animals. It would be a foolish man indeed who meant to throw his rank about Philip's stable.

"He's a good fellow," Shianan said, scratching the horse's neck near the dark mane. "And he's comfortable with my handling his feet." He had lifted and cleaned out the young horse's hooves.

"I saw," Philip said. Of course he had. Philip saw everything, even from the far end of the stable. But then, he would not allow any possibility of harm to his charges.

There was a slight cough at the door, and Philip turned. "Yes?" Even the palace messengers deferred to his authority here.

"Commander Becknam is called for, at the palace."

Shianan's stomach flipped and roiled. These days, a royal summons could predict honor and friendship or shame and humiliation. The not-knowing was somehow even worse. "Who calls me?"

"His Majesty King Jerome."

His stomach settled into a dark pit. "Thank you," he answered dully. "I'll go immediately."

The messenger left. Shianan avoided Philip's eyes; it was bad enough when Luca knew, and he would not betray himself before another slave. Nor any other, he hoped.

Philip came and pulled Kuolema's halter rope free. "I'll put him away. Best not to keep the king waiting."

It was what he might have said to any of the king's courtiers. It should not have sounded like a bell's knell of doom.

At his quarters, Shianan changed his clothing dusted with horse hair for fresher garb, and then he turned his reluctant steps to the royal wing. He was admitted into King Jerome's office—not in the old wing, which gave him hope—and noted immediately that they were alone. Hope fled.

He knelt and waited.

"Rise, Becknam."

Shianan did, raising his eyes only to the king's torso. He would not look the man in the eye, and not merely for decorum. Words hung between them, words and blood and years of unspoken emotion like a mist in the air, obscuring vision and muffling words.

The king had summoned him. The king must speak, if Shianan waited.

Time weighed on King Jerome, and he cleared his throat. "I have been made aware of what service you did the prince-heir on the field of Arakadamia," he began, as if something had lodged in his throat. "How, though Prince Soren came very near to death, he should have certainly died, and much sooner, if you had not acted so promptly."

Shianan did not respond.

"My—advisers," continued King Jerome, "have suggested it would be ill-seen for the council to consider taking titles from a courtier who so lately has saved the prince-heir's life."

Shianan waited and kept his face strictly impassive, a soldier's resolute face, though a flicker of hope sparked low in his chest.

"And," King Jerome continued, as if the words warred in his mouth and had to be forced over the precipice of his teeth, "I am glad of what you did, and I would not see you punished for it. There was foul rumor about you, and I'm sorry for that. I won't add to it now."

It was the nearest he would receive to either apology or gratitude, and he recognized it for the rarity it was. It should have been precious to him. Once it would have been gold, clutched to his heart for a week of sustenance.

Now he saw through the words, saw the conflicted effort behind them, saw they would never swell into more no matter what service or love he brought. Now he held them against honest joy, the prince's affection, the queen's kindness, and he wondered that he could ever have been so swayed by so little.

But still—he would remain the Count of Bailaha. He would remain an acceptable friend to both Soren and Ariana. It was a good gift, though stolen for the gifting.

Now he had to speak, and he gave back the mealy lukewarm words he had received. "Thank you, Your Majesty. I am glad to have been able to serve the prince-heir."

The king turned and went to his desk, sitting in the fine chair. "I have been at a loss," he said, toying with a pen. "The Ryuven are sending a liaison to our court as part of our agreement and treaty. To honor us and to show their dedication to this treaty, they are sending a courtier of some stature, a noble of high rank. I'm afraid you will know him by the reputation he once had years ago, before he retired from the battlefield. The guest to our court will be Pairvyn ni'Ai."

Shianan's muscles convulsed, making him jerk as he stood. He fought down the visceral betrayal and swallowed against the hot lump forming in his throat. "Pairvyn ni'Ai?"

King Jerome kept his eyes on his pen. "Yes, it seemed in poor taste to me also, at least in the beginning. But now I understand how it is meant, to send the one who was once our greatest enemy to now shepherd the fledgling trade and guard the peace. It is a strong statement to make, and we should be worthy of it."

Shianan made himself nod. "It will be fitting for such a proud warrior to now be responsible for safe trade." And at least Tamaryl would be caught up in merchant affairs and council politics, keeping him well out of Shianan's military circuit.

"Exactly. But, as I said, I have been at a loss, as I must assign a fitting liaison to the Ryuven, guarding and escorting him on his inspections and giving him an appropriate status in our court. I had not known at first who should be assigned to this task, at once critical in its importance of the Ryuven noble's safety and critical in visibility to our court and theirs."

Shianan's heart sank. "No, Your Majesty," he started, before the king could say it aloud. "No, I—"

"You are the ideal choice, Becknam. *Bailaha.*" King Jerome straightened and looked at him. "You are a titled noble and a member of my court, so you have the proper status to honor him. You are an excellent soldier, renowned for your ability, so you have the capacity

179

to protect him. And it will be a prestigious assignment for a soldier who has served well."

"The Pairvyn ni'Ai does not need my protection," Shianan snapped. "He is a butcher."

King Jerome held up a hand. "That may have been true in the past, but things are different now. And no matter his ability, past or present, we cannot have the Ryuven emissary killing citizens, not even in self-defense if an angry mob should start an assault. That would shatter any hope of peace."

That was true, no matter how Shianan might resent it.

"You are the logical choice," King Jerome continued with a hint of pride, as if it should have been a compliment. "And even if there were another similarly qualified in both rank and ability, you would still confer additional honor upon our guest, being someone so close to the royal family."

Sweet all, even his own bastardy, denied all his life and at long last now dangled as a gilding on the welcome to the Ryuven champion. Shianan's pulse pounded heat through him, and he clenched his teeth on his frustration.

"And so, Commander Becknam, Count of Bailaha, I am pleased to entrust this assignment to you. You will welcome this—" King Jerome checked a paper on his desk "—this Tamaryl Pairvyn ni'Ai to our court, you will accompany him on his duties, and you will ensure his safety and comfort while he is here."

Shianan could not trust himself to answer. If he opened his mouth, his fury might escape, and he could not risk that again. So he only jerked his head in a nod.

King Jerome smiled, pleased. "Perhaps you are embarrassed by this show of good faith so soon after such ugly rumor. But this will help to assuage that, I am sure."

Shianan swallowed. "Is that all, Your Majesty?"

"What?"

"Thank you, Your Majesty, but is there anything else you require of me?"

"Of course you must have much to do after such a battle and a new peace. Yes, go, and you need not keep your new assignment to yourself. He will be arriving soon."

"Thank you." He bit out the words, bowed, and fled.

He walked at a furious pace, passing all with his eyes forward and fiercely alone, until he reached his own quarters. Then he slammed the door, as if it might block out the onerous duty pursuing him, and swore loudly enough to bring Luca from the next room.

The slave stared at him. "What is it?"

Shianan fumbled for words through the swirl of hot emotion. "They want me to take him around, hold his hand, play nursemaid to him! To that winged—to that lying, pretending, murdering—to that overgrown chicken!"

Luca tried to pick out his meaning. "You are—escorting a Ryuven?"

"Escort and aide to Tamaryl! The Pairvyn ni'Ai! Spy on him, keep him from trouble, play the sycophant to him. The king claims I'm the logical choice, as a military officer who is also a member of the court... Bah. This is nothing more than yoking the bastard with a task no one else wants, tricked up as a shallow honor." He curled his lip. "The only joy in this is that I just might be an insult to Tamaryl as well. He can't be happy to have me."

Luca looked puzzled. "But why would they assign a military officer to our greatest military opponent? Wouldn't that strike sparks and endanger the peace?"

"No, no, it demonstrates our willingness to extend friendship, as we put aside our past. Unless, of course, the Pairvyn and I exchange words and cross swords, which would require immediate punishment in demonstration of our commitment to peace, ridding the kingdom of both the bastard and the enemy's champion at once." He sighed. "King's oats. He meant to kill the prince and me both."

"He came very near to killing you," Luca reminded him quietly. "But you can't fight with him—for your sake and for the peace."

Shianan clenched his jaw. "I know that. I know that."

CHAPTER 31

There was a clap at the doorway, and the silver-haired servant waited for Tamaryl's attention to turn to him. "Tamaryl'sho, you have a guest."

"Who?"

"It is Edeiya'rika. She is waiting in the courtyard, beside the fountain."

Tamaryl's stomach tightened, to his surprise. Edeiya, competent and cool, had come to collect for the service she had done him in Oniwe's court.

Aloud, he said, "I will come directly." Better not to make her wait even a short while. Tamaryl rolled his shoulder, cramped as if the prison bonds still constrained him.

Edeiya sat on the edge of the courtyard fountain, looking into the water as if there were still fish there to amuse her. Her black hair gleamed emerald green in the sunlight, the high-set tail slipping behind her as she straightened to look at him.

"Edeiya'rika," he said, and he wondered if he had pitched his tone too enthusiastically. "Welcome. Your visit is an honor."

She smiled. "Thank you, Tamaryl'sho." She stood. "I hope you are well."

It was a subtle question, a mere polite inquiry but also more. "I am well enough. I am glad to be in the sunlight, and glad to have full reach of my limbs." He hesitated. "I suppose you must have heard what I have become."

She raised an eyebrow. "You have become many things, Tamaryl'sho. You are a traitor, a rebel, a hero, a visionary." She crooked a wry smile. "I think it depends on whom one asks."

He felt warm with her words. "I think some of those may apply more than others."

Her eyes laughed, if her mouth did not, and she turned away to stroll across the courtyard. He remained where he was.

He had always admired Edeiya'rika. She had been a strong figure from the beginning, predicted to be a powerful player in politics as she matured. Her parents had been significant, of course, but she had more than an inherited bloodline to commend her.

Her next words seemed to argue with his remembered impressions. "I prefer action to words," she said, turning back to him.

"You are not above diplomacy when it will serve your purpose."

She nodded. "Of course. There are times when diplomacy is more efficient. And less messy."

He should have chuckled, but knowledge or suspicion weighed on him. "Was it diplomacy you used on my behalf?"

She raised an eyebrow. "Has someone been carrying tales?"

"I have heard only rumor, and only from nim, so not undiluted from the court itself. I would prefer to hear the truth from you."

She snorted. "Do not pretend to me that you do not value the word of a nim. You listen to everyone, Tamaryl'sho. And also to no one, when it suits you."

He inclined his head to acknowledge her point. "Still."

She faced him squarely. "Yes, since you ask me plainly, I did speak to Oniwe'aru about you. I suggested you were a valuable tool, not to be discarded for its misuse, and a convenient scapegoat. He does like you, even if you vex him and embarrass him, and he was more glad than he cared to admit to be talked into preserving you."

Tamaryl drew a steadying breath. "I owe you my life."

"Very possibly." She was not one to hedge about the truth, not when they both knew it. "But it was a good investment on my part. The Ai need strong warriors, Tamaryl'sho, even headstrong ones. And if we are to pursue this peace with the humans of Chrenada, we should have to advise us someone who knows them well and understands them. We would be foolish to throw away the one best able to help us achieve peace because he pursued it too closely."

"You say it better than I might have said it myself. I can see why Oniwe listened to you."

She shrugged. "As I said, he was glad to be convinced. He did not want to execute his own blood, even one who was a well-meaning traitor."

"If only there might be some way for me to repay such a favor."

She smiled. "I do not know if Oniwe'aru will see it as a favor. Having you to send to the human world in place of anyone less inclined has saved him a great deal of political angst."

"I did not mean him." Tamaryl straightened. "You are a rika of position. You do not waste your efforts. What do you want of me?"

She gave him a faintly disappointed look. "How baldly you put it, as if my interests were mercenary rather than for the benefit of all."

"They were certainly to my benefit, and I will not complain of them. But I ask nonetheless."

She pursed her lips. "What I said was indeed for the benefit of all, Tamaryl'sho, as I truly believe that you can serve the Ai better alive than dead, and that you have significant service yet to offer." She looked past him, inhaled, looked back, but at his forehead rather than his eyes. "And I am one of the all."

Tamaryl hung in a gap of turbulence, not yet falling but unsupported and seeking air beneath his wings.

Edeiya straightened, looking slightly down on him; she was not tall for a female. "It is postulated that, after Oniwe'aru steps down, I will become Edeiya'silth. I am thinking ahead to the situations I will face and the decisions I must make in that role. I would much prefer to have someone with intimate knowledge of human character and culture to assist in some of those decisions."

"You preserved me for political aid."

"Yes," she said. "But you are a political liability, too, Tamaryl'sho. You have a history of acting independently, even against orders, of abusing your privilege as Pairvyn."

He nodded, stung but understanding. "I will not look like the best courtier."

"And I," she continued, her bright eyes fixed on him, "as silth, cannot have a poor political alliance."

An alliance—what did she hint at?

"Do not leap to conclusions," she warned. "I am thinking still of the benefit of all, as well as my own. If I wish to keep a knowledgeable adviser at my side, that adviser must be acceptable and must not put off my other political allies. I need you to check your impulses and trust in what you've started, at least for now. You will be of greater use to the Ai if I can keep you in my court."

Her words chafed. He had waited fifteen years in the human world, he did not act on impulse—but he had nearly killed Prince Soren in his frustration, and he had reversed his position to join Ariana's interruption in a moment of conviction. Even if Edeiya'rika did not know how near he had come to ruining what he had worked to bring about, she could argue her point, and she was right about staying in a place where he could do greater good.

More, she was all but promising him that place, if he could keep from being a liability to her.

He nodded. "I understand that."

She relaxed a little. "Good. I am—thank you." She flattened her lips and glanced to the side, weighing her words. "As a warrior and as a courtier, I have always held a great regard for you, even when you acted out of line with our ruler's orders, because you acted on your principles for common goals. Today I will not see your skills lost when we need them, because I still respect those skills. And principles." She moved, her green-black hair tail sliding over one shoulder, and met his eyes again. "I would be glad to see you comport yourself in such a way that my urging to Oniwe'aru will not look foolish, and that will benefit the Ai and its rulers, present and future, now and in years to come."

Tamaryl understood the immediate meaning of her words. He wanted to think on them, to consider if there was another meaning behind the first, but he could not think fast enough to be certain.

She had stopped speaking, and now it was his turn, and he was mired in trying to divine her meaning. "Before," he said, "with Daranai—you influenced Oniwe'aru then, too. You suggested to him—it was subtly done, but I caught it. It was brilliant."

She laughed aloud, a bright sound. "That was simple. Daranai fled; who could respect a rika who could not stand to defend even her own home? We are the protectors of homes and homeland, and she could not have disgraced herself more."

"No one was thinking of it in that way, not yet," Tamaryl said. "They were thinking only of the human mage. You framed her flight for them."

She gave a little shrug. "Daranai was a coward and a bully—though I repeat myself. As Tsuraiya ni'Ai, it matters to me that inferior warriors are neither given to me nor entrusted with our safety."

Tamaryl laughed aloud. "That is well-said, Edeiya'rika. But I thank you for it. It was a kindness to Ariana and to Maru."

She smiled then, and it was a different smile than before, more private and almost shy. "I did not do it for your notice, but I am glad of your thanks."

"You have it again, for speaking to Oniwe'aru. I know my debt; you did me a great service."

"And that means nothing, so far as obligation. Kindness is not compulsive."

A tiny tingle of relief ran through Tamaryl, a release of tension he'd only barely registered. He swept an arm to indicate the courtyard and the rooms beyond. "I have come but lately to my neglected house and my larder is poor, but would you care to stay to what supper I can offer? If I am to redeem my reputation in time to serve in your court, I should start by associating myself with the right names."

She laughed. "I would be delighted, thank you."

"I just thought you should see it for yourself, sir," Captain Torg explained in a low voice. "You'll see it differently than if you just read a report."

"I trust my reports," Shianan answered, "but I also trust your word. Should we come in from the side? What about our uniforms?"

Torg shook his head. "No, I think you should see how they view us."

The rain had given way today to soggy snow, in small dirty piles in the streets. They entered the market and made their way through the crowds. Those waiting to buy dall sweetbud were irritated at the intrusion but gave way when they saw the military uniforms; the commander and captain were organizing, not jumping line.

"Dead across from us," Torg muttered as they reached the ring of soldiers.

Shianan half turned and casually looked across the Ryuven wearing baskets of dried leaves. Beyond them, he saw the men Torg had described, waiting outside the ring but not to buy, weapons in their belts or their arms, their quiet menace forcing those waiting to buy to split around them with wary glances.

"Try to make eye contact, if you can," Torg suggested.

Shianan abandoned his casual observation and turned to look at a man standing a little in front of the others, leaning upon a cudgel the length of his leg. He noted Shianan's gaze and raised one corner of his mouth in a knowing smile, nodding slowly, an intimation of brotherhood across the noisy trading ground.

Shianan turned away and swore.

"That's a look that doesn't come through so clearly on a report," Torg said. "But you see it now."

"What are they thinking?"

"They're thinking they're their own army. Part of ours, but doesn't stand to our orders. Ready to go around us if they decide."

"Do they talk about it?"

"I expect an eager recruit could get more."

Shianan nodded. "I don't have much to do with agents or informants, but I'll see what we can find."

Shianan entered his quarters to find Luca counting over coins. "What's that, do I owe for something?"

"Not yet," Luca answered distractedly. He set a pile of silver to one side. "But there's not enough here..."

"For what?"

"Your new clothes." Luca looked at him. "I will go to order for you, you needn't be bothered, but I'll need more."

Shianan looked back blankly. "My new clothes?"

"For the ball."

Shianan shrugged. "I have a set, the black with gold and silver."

"You told me you wore that to the last one."

"What of it?"

Luca stared at him. "You should have something new!"

Shianan stared back. "Why?"

Luca all but rolled his eyes. "If you appear in the same clothes, it advertises to one and all that you are not of enough consideration to be invited frequently—"

"But that's the truth," Shianan interrupted. "I'm no one of consequence. I am very near to not being a courtier at all. Why spend coin to pretend otherwise?"

Luca tilted his head and frowned at him. "Because others will assess you as you present yourself, and if you are a count, you should appear as one. Even more so if there has been a question of who you might be, count or not."

"Luca—"

"And you are not no one of consequence, you are the demon commander, the count of Bailaha, and the rescuer of the prince-heir, who counts you a close friend."

Shianan gave him a long-suffering look. "And few know, and fewer care, if I am the prince's friend. I certainly don't intend to parade it."

"Parade, no—but will you shame the prince by appearing beside him in old clothes?"

Shianan crossed his arms. "That's hardly fair. And they're not old; I've worn them but once."

"They're years from fashion, they've been seen recently, and you should be in better."

Shianan scowled at him. "Prancing merchant's son."

"Mud-flecked soldier."

"It's no use, Luca. Even if I agree—"

A knock at the door interrupted them. Luca left the sorted money and opened it. "Yes?"

"From Prince Soren." A liveried servant proffered a wrapped package. "For his lordship."

Luca thanked him, closed the door, and turned back, weighing the package in his grasp. His eyes were bright. "Here, open it!"

Shianan knew already, judging by Luca's grin, what he would find. He undid the wrapping and uncovered a fine new set of clothing, deep green with trim of gold. He held up the doublet obligingly.

Luca beamed. "And you cannot refuse the prince's gift," he said with the air of closing an argument.

"No," Shianan conceded. The green and gold were tasteful and handsome. He sighed. "And you may gloat. But it won't spoil my mood." He grinned. "Philip thinks Kuolema is steady enough to try in the market this evening. It won't be so busy, so it will be a good introduction for him."

More, Philip had complimented Shianan's improvement in handling the horse and this, Shianan suspected, was as much the cause for today's venture into the market. It pleased Shianan hugely that the stable-steward was beginning to think him competent to handle the priceless young stallion. Of course, it helped that Kuolema's temperament was sweet and generous and decidedly stable.

Perhaps tonight he might sight Ariana in the street, and she might see him on the horse's high back.

Luca grinned, pleased for his master's success. "I'll put these up, then. Do you know when you'll want supper?"

"I'll find something in the market after we've finished with Kuolema."

"All right. I'll just finish filing the new rosters and then fix that buckle—"

"Luca, no," Shianan said. "Take the night to yourself."

Luca hesitated. When he spoke, his voice was quiet, with just an edge of uncertainty. "To do what?"

"Anything. Go out, eat, drink, see friends."

Luca's mouth turned down. "As you do?"

Shianan did not answer. He did not go out either, rarely had. He had always told himself it was because officers did not fraternize, but that was not strictly true.

"Point awarded," he answered gruffly. "I'll find something to do. But first, I'll go and parade the queen's horse through the public market."

CHAPTER 32

Tamaryl rolled his shoulders, savoring the movement even as they twinged. His lingering disability from the prolonged fup-forged chains would not matter so much in a court assignment; he did not go to fight. He would join their human court as a sign of Oniwe'aru's good faith and to represent their Ryuven interests. There would be time enough to recover fully there.

He did not relish the idea of going in his Ryuven shape without his Ryuven abilities. That was somehow worse than being limited in a human body.

Maru appeared at the door. "How are you feeling?"

"I've been better, but I've been much worse. I'll be fine."

Maru extended a small package. "Here. It's hard to find, after the battle, but I managed to get some."

Tamaryl recognized the exotic aroma of chocolate. "Oh, Maru, thank you," he said in heartfelt gratitude. "I'll want this." Briefly he wondered what the nim had needed to barter for such a luxury good.

"Eat some now," Maru urged, "before you cross." His eyebrows drew close. "And you're sure you won't need someone there?"

Tamaryl broke off a piece of chocolate and shook his head reluctantly. "Not in the beginning. They will be uncomfortable enough with the Pairvyn in their midst; they won't know how to accept more Ryuven. And they will be happy to give me a servant for my needs. More eyes to spy if I am trustworthy." He smiled. "You may come later, I think, but not just yet."

Maru nodded. "Then I'll help Fasi'bel. Your household will be fully reestablished when you return."

Tamaryl chuckled grimly. "I'm afraid no one will know what to think of me by then—exiled and restored, jailed and restored, my household dissolved and reestablished once and again... No one will trust credit to me." He forced a smile.

Maru didn't laugh with him. "Be careful there, Ryl. They know who you are now."

"And they know we have what they need, and that they have what we need. No one wants fighting. It will come only when they do not see how to go otherwise. And I am there to speak for the otherwise."

"Still, be careful." Maru hesitated. "And, be cautious of her. And the commander. You didn't make much of a friend of him."

Tamaryl's smile was bitter. "No, I suppose I didn't. I'll be careful of him."

Luca accepted the sealed packet, closed the door, and turned to deliver it to Shianan's desk. "What does the prince send you?"

"You're quite inquisitive for a man in your position," Shianan said in mock complaint.

"My position is to keep your correspondence in better condition than if you were left to yourself," Luca answered.

That wasn't quite true; Shianan managed the eternal paperwork of his rank well enough. But Luca's aid was appreciated, and his efforts in other areas made the burden of the paperwork easier to bear.

"With any luck, this will be a report from a research agent," Shianan said, slicing open the packet.

"Your informant is the prince-heir?"

Shianan made a face. "Don't play ignorant at me. No, but the informant is one of the prince's. The military doesn't keep a network on the citizens of Alham, but the prince-heir had set someone to gather soldiers' gossip about me, so I asked to pass on a question to such an informant." He raised an eyebrow. "I don't even know who received the task. It could be you."

Luca shrugged. "You know I wouldn't be able to say if it were true."

Shianan sobered as he drew out folded notes. "Quite a bit here. I hope that's good."

He settled back to read. The informant had been thorough, posing as a retired soldier and detailing the public rooms in which he'd joined the armed men from the marketplace, their origins and reasons for joining the affiliation, and even reproducing large passages of conversation.

"A Luenda veteran? That was hard fighting, I hear."

"It was. And you're in now? That's good to hear. We need strong minds these days. What unit?"

192

"*Well, I'm not in the regular forces, not exactly. But I'm two weeks into my recruiting and I'll be taking my initiation in four days.*"

That sounded more organized than a loose gang of bullies looking for trouble. Shianan turned to another conversation.

"*We have to be prepared to step up and do what's necessary. Look at what's happening, with the soldiers and mages not only letting the runny Ryuven into our world, but bringing them right into our cities and towns, bringing them right in. These are our cities, our towns, and we haven't kept them safe for generations to allow our own runny soldiers to bring Ryuven right into them.*"

"*And they say it's in the name of peace—but no one asked if we wanted peace, did they?*"

"*Right again. When Mennti talks about war being the more natural state of things, that's what makes sense. A man's got to be strong, got to protect his own. Peace leads a kingdom into decline; the fires of war forge its pieces into unity.*"

These were ideas crafted to stoke resentment and resistance. Shianan tried to remember if he had truly heard the name Mennti before, or if he only grasped at straws in his eagerness to make sense of the problem.

"*The initiation is no easy thing, I'll say. We're not to talk about it with those who haven't done it yet, but it tests resolve, and concentration, and willingness to endure for the righteous cause.*"

"*And if I come in, it won't just be the three of us?*"

"*Oh, no, we have quite the band. More recruits all the time, now that people are seeing we can't trust the soldiers to—I mean, no offense, obviously you're in the right, being here. And we mean no disrespect to our fighting men. But it's no secret that some of the leadership is falling for this blather about a treaty and ending the war, and we all know how that must fail.*"

"*I understand, no worry. So just recruits, then.*"

"*Oh, no, we have others, and a few full-ranked, too. We're to be recognized as our own chapter. And Flamen Mennti says more will come as—*"

Shianan crushed the pages against his lap and swore.

Luca called from the next room. "Do you need something?"

"Nothing," Shianan called back.

But Luca came anyway. "I'll bring a warm drink. What's in the report?"

Shianan shook his head. He did not want to tell Luca that the Gehrn were recruiting in Alham. "That's informant business, not for outside eyes."

Luca did not look stung by Shianan's sharp refusal, and that meek acceptance hurt Shianan worse than if he had. "I'll bring something warm, as I said. It's cool in here."

Shianan nodded distractedly, and Luca went out the door.

Shianan drew a fresh sheet of paper and began penning a letter to General Septime, Mage Ewan Hazelrig, and the King's Council, all of whom would need to understand this new foothold.

CHAPTER 33

Tamaryl crossed the void of the between-worlds, and the polished walls of the Naziar palace appeared about him. There was a ring of people waiting, marking his arrival as a court event. So be it.

But he was cold and weak with the effort of crossing, so that he felt himself waver as his feet reached the floor. Bless Maru and his chocolate to shore him up beforehand. He swallowed and sucked air, trying to steady himself while hiding his fatigue.

Three men stepped forward from the ring and made bows of varying depth. Tamaryl bowed in return, hoping he was judging the degree correctly. Bows were a human gesture, and he had not learned their use beyond his limited slavery.

"Welcome, my lord Tamaryl," offered the first man in formal court dress. "I am Edmond Washe, Chancellor of the Chain, and I welcome you to Alham."

"I am honored to be here," Tamaryl answered, bowing to him individually.

Chancellor Washe gestured to his right. "You may recall Ewan Hazelrig, White Mage of the Great Circle."

Tamaryl bowed again, slightly lower. He owed this man so much. "My lord mage, it is an honor."

Hazelrig, perceptive as always, heard the additional meaning. "My dear Tamaryl'sho, you are most welcome here."

"And in recognition of your status and your commendable mission, in which we have the greatest faith and hope, we have made available to you an aide, who will give you safe conduct through the capital and attend to any needs you might have," continued Washe. "This is Commander Shianan Becknam, his lordship, the Count of Bailaha."

Tamaryl hesitated a heartbeat too long. Becknam noted it, recognized it, and resented it, just as he must surely resent his present duty. By the Essence, how had Becknam received this charge?

But Tamaryl had bowed to each of the previous introductions, and so he did so once more, a quick movement that he hoped looked sufficient to the human spectators. And indeed, he had no reason to discount Becknam's honor. The man was diligent in his duty and loyalty, and Tamaryl could hardly fault him that.

Becknam bowed in return, a tight, tense motion. Mage Hazelrig glanced at him, concern in his eyes.

"Thank you," Tamaryl heard himself say. "I am glad of your thoughtfulness."

Chancellor Washe smiled. "We have prepared a place for you in the palace, and Bailaha will lead you there. If you have need of anything, please inform Bailaha or the servant assigned to you. The king will be pleased to welcome you formally this evening."

Tamaryl nodded. "Thank you very much."

Long practice in bowing under humiliation allowed Shianan to incline his head and gesture for Tamaryl to accompany him, and to walk through the corridors without clenching his fists or otherwise betraying his emotion. At last he stopped and knocked sharply at a door. "This is yours, my lord," he said, biting off the honorific. "I will come for you in two hours' time, to conduct you to the throne room for your formal reception."

Tamaryl raised an eyebrow. "Am I to remain here until then?" he asked significantly. The door opened, and the chamber slave stepped back and bowed.

Shianan took a breath. "Of course you are no prisoner, my lord. You may move through the palace at your leisure. I am here merely to guide you and to serve you."

The words burned. The last time he had seen Tamaryl, he had stood between the Pairvyn and his intent to kill Soren. The time before that, Tamaryl had nearly succeeded in killing Shianan.

"Hm." Tamaryl looked into the room. "Very nice. And a sitting area, too, though I think I will not have many guests, at least at first." He looked back at Shianan. "Will you come, my lord commander? Be my first guest?"

Shianan's jaw tightened. He did not know what the Ryuven planned, but he could not refuse so soon. "Thank you, my lord."

"Tamaryl'sho," he corrected softly.

They went inside and started toward the cushioned chairs. The slave followed, looking nervous. He was probably no more pleased with his assignment than Shianan. Tamaryl paused and gave him a frank look. "What's your name?"

"Fulke, my lord."

"Well, Fulke, I'm glad of your attention. Would you please go and fetch some wine and something to eat? Sliced pork, if you can find some, with cheese. If not, whatever you bring will be fine."

Fulke blinked and then bowed. "As you wish, my lord." He fled the room.

Tamaryl made a sound of amusement. "He probably thinks I'm likely to eat him."

"You would know a slave's thoughts." Shianan was surprised by his caustic challenge—what was he doing? He could not taunt the emissary Pairvyn!

Tamaryl gave him a cold look. "I suspect that, compared to some, I have somewhat less experience in leaping to do others' bidding," he returned evenly. "Tell me, my lord commander, how you came to be my aide. Did you volunteer to attend me?"

The barb struck flesh, and Shianan fought to control his expression. "As I have both military rank and noble peerage, it was felt I was the best choice to look after you."

"I see." Tamaryl's tone was flat and meaningful. Shianan hoped he would not flush with shame.

The Ryuven went to a chair and eased himself into it, looking faintly pained. Shianan was intrigued. "Are you well, my lord?"

"Well enough," Tamaryl answered with a grimace, his voice pitched too casually.

He had not wanted his discomfort known. Shianan felt a strategic thrill; he had spied a weakness. And did Tamaryl look even more unnaturally lean than his Ryuven form should?

"It is only an ache; it will be gone shortly." Tamaryl gestured. "Please, my lord commander, be seated."

A muscle jumped in Shianan's face. He had wanted only to escort his charge and escape. Aloud he said, "Thank you, my lord."

Tamaryl sighed. "I would speak candidly with you, Shianan Becknam."

Good; at least the Ryuven was uncomfortable as well. And Shianan did not want to play courtiers' games of fine words, dancing along the edge of his escort assignment. "We are fighting men," he answered. "Plain speech is better suited for us."

"Honestly, and without offense."

"Honestly, and without intent to offend."

"Good enough." Tamaryl sighed and looked at Shianan. "Come, commander, we dislike one another, and not without reason. But I am here, and for some time, and you are here with me. For the sake of our peoples, we must find some common ground."

"We have much common ground," Shianan answered more bitterly than he'd meant. "We have each lost countless soldiers to the other. We have each seen our fighters die before the other's army."

"More reason to find ground we can share," answered Tamaryl sharply. "We have each tried to kill the other, as well, but that will not carry us into what must become a new age for our peoples. This is larger than us, commander. Our preferences, however justified, must not come between this treaty and success."

He was right, however much Shianan disliked it. Shianan did not want to lose more soldiers to fighting the Ryuven, and he did not want to see the fragile new peace crumble into another Luenda, another Arakadamia. He could not afford to argue too fiercely with the Ryuven emissary.

He took a slow breath and ventured the most dangerous tie. "We both admire Ariana Hazelrig," he said warily.

Tamaryl looked away. "That may be more contention than binding."

Shianan considered. "We both wish for Ariana's happiness, then."

"Hm. Better." Tamaryl propped his chin in his hand. "And each of us believes she would be better off with the other."

"No," Shianan said sharply. "I don't think she would be happy as the bride of a Ryuven, exiled from her world."

"You think you can make her happy with you?"

"No." Now Shianan looked away. "The only way we could make a life together is to flee to another country and live quiet, hidden lives, poor and unknown. She would need to give up her father, her home, her friends, her position, her magic, her whole life."

Tamaryl looked at him. "Would she do it?"

"I don't intend ever to know." Shianan looked at him sharply.

Tamaryl looked almost sad. "I see."

Fulke returned, sloshing wine in a pitcher and bearing a tray with thinly sliced pork and cheese over pieces of fresh bread. "Refreshment, my lords."

"That was quick." Tamaryl reached and took one of the pork and cheese assemblies. "Thank you, Fulke." He looked again to

Shianan, as the slave proffered the tray. "Will you drink to our common ground, my lord Bailaha?"

A salute to Ariana, concealed as political goodwill for the benefit of the watching servant. Shianan took the wine Fulke offered. "Gladly and always to our common ground, my lord Tamaryl—Tamaryl'sho. And may this temporary peace prevail."

CHAPTER 34

Tamaryl was not expecting guests—who would visit the Pairvyn in his Naziar rooms?—and so the knock surprised him. Before Fulke could emerge from wherever he hid when Tamaryl was not directly addressing him, Tamaryl rose and called, "Come in."

The White Mage came inside. "Thank you," he said as Fulke appeared at the edge of the room, "but I think we'll be all right by ourselves. You may go."

Fulke should have conferred with Tamaryl first, but he only glanced back and then bolted for the door, no doubt overwhelmed with the thought of the White Mage and the Pairvyn ni'Ai facing one another.

For a moment, neither spoke, as the treaty and the tentative peace and the Shard and Ariana hung invisible in the air about them.

Ewan's mouth turned down. "I dug through a midden."

For a moment, Tamaryl couldn't make sense of the words. And then he remembered—he had gone to the fishing village to find the broken fragment of the Shard of Elan before Ewan and the Circle arrived to search. The fragment had been lost by Ryuven raiders, who had received it from Tamaryl himself, who had stolen it from Ewan Hazelrig.

Tamaryl felt ill. "I... I'm sorry."

"You didn't even speak to me about it."

Tamaryl remembered those days as a dark smear, all frustration and rising dread. What he had done seemed necessary at the time, though now he could not meet his friend's eyes. "I panicked," he admitted. "I was afraid that—I needed a safeguard, a way to be sure my people would not starve if what we meant to happen did not."

Ewan heaved a sigh. "I know despair," he said quietly. "I know how it can blind one, when it seems there are no good choices left."

Tamaryl looked at the mage's chest, unable to raise his gaze. "I thought if there could be only one raiding party at a time... I had not realized how the famine had worsened. When I went back and saw... I could not cut off Chrenada entirely."

"We need trade, not war."

"I agree. I'm glad we're coming to that."

Ewan nodded. "But I am still angry about the midden." His mouth relaxed at last, nearly a smile. "I comfort myself with the thought that you must have searched through it as well."

Tamaryl felt his expression soften. "It was never in the midden."

"No?"

"No. I found it in a barn, where the raiders had tried to steal barrels of fish."

Ewan scowled, but this time with less sting. "And you never had to dig through that ditch?"

"It was in a rat burrow, if that helps."

"It does not." But the edge was gone from his voice, and Tamaryl knew that Ewan understood, somehow, and Tamaryl was forgiven.

Ewan had kept guilty secrets as well, even from Tamaryl. He was not a man to forget his own failings when considering another's.

"May I sit down?" Ewan asked.

"Please." Tamaryl gestured to a chair.

The side streets were nearly empty by the time Elysia Parma left the Wheel. Twilight filtered between the roofs enough that she could avoid the worst of the street debris. Silver robes, while impressive and prestigious, were a nuisance to keep presentable.

The growl of a street dog matched the tingle of alert sensation that ran over her. A tall figure stepped around a corner ahead, filling the end of the narrow walkway, and she came to a deliberate halt, her eyes on him. She did not speak. Let him reveal himself or move on, if that was his business.

He faced her; his business was here. "Mage Parma. I am Flamen Gregorio."

A wave of irritation washed through her. "I've already said I want nothing to do with you." She kept her voice even, neutral.

"And yet I suggested we might meet, and here you are."

"This is my way home, and you aren't worth altering my habit." She crossed her arms. "Stand aside and you'll save us both time, at the least."

The flamen started toward her. "I don't think you grasp the full significance of this final warning. We have requested your help, and we will have it, given readily or taken."

202

Elysia's pulse quickened. "That's enough of this conversation."

"If you continue in your stubborn refusal, I am prepared to persuade you to be more cooperative."

"I said we're done talking."

"I have evidence prepared of your treachery, to present after you are no longer able to mount your defense. Your reputation will be ruined, our cause secured, but that will be the least of your concern." He was close now, barely two arm-lengths away. "An assignment I will enjoy."

Elysia scooped energy from the air and brought her arms sharply together, and two invisible hemispheres crashed curve-first into the flamen from either side. She heard his ribs crack as the air grunted out of him. "Leave me," she ordered. "Go now with your life, and do not ever contact me again."

He bared his teeth at her in a defiant snarl. "No, it will be you who comes to me, after we inform the king how you have betrayed—"

She opened and spiraled her arms, sliding the hemispheres around one another so that he was nearly enclosed in an invisible sphere. He pushed against them, his hands spreading. One set of fingers found the gap, and he shifted to try to wrench it wider. With a sustaining burst of power to the shields, Elysia withdrew her hands and formed a ball of magic.

It glowed visible in the dark twilight, and if the flamen had known enough to recognize what that meant, he might have screamed for mercy in his final breath. But he did not, and Elysia thrust it sharply into the narrow gap in the sphere.

The Gehrn did not practice true magic, and so simple energy could not kill him so easily as it would a mage. But all men die to raw fire. The reflected heat from the shields she powered afresh made it burn even hotter than it would have alone, and the flamen charred to unrecognizability within moments.

She let the shields fade, and she regarded the twisted, blackened body with a sick feeling. The remnants of the Gehrn robes were still perhaps identifiable. She hit the body again, scorching the fiber dark with a blast that left the corpse smoking.

She looked away, trying not to inhale the scent of roasted fats.

Home. She had to get home. Had anyone seen this? She could explain—but killing a Gehrn on the streets could only lead to trouble, even if the high priest was not about to be sentenced for treason. Why had the vermin pressed her? Why had they come for her in an alley, forcing her hand?

She went home, keenly aware of all movement in the streets around her, and went through her rooms one by one with magic couched in her hand. It was perhaps over-cautious, but better to err on the side of too much than not enough.

With the house safely clear, she sat down and thought of what to do. The remains would be discovered—might have been already. Much of the flamen now was ash, separating in the alley, but she had left enough to raise concern. She had to alert someone before an alarm was raised, panicking the city.

And the killing of a Gehrn would certainly invite retribution, especially as they sought to apply leverage to free their high priest. If Flamen Gregorio had simply disappeared, unreturned from his mission to intimidate and coerce a woman, that would be more confusing and less immediately rallying.

She was too accustomed to war and its unencumbered solutions.

She would inform Ewan, and together they would ask the city guard to quietly clean it away. Surely the Circle could request them to refrain from inquiry, under the rationale of state business and the assurance that it was a threat the Circle had already dealt with and would deal with—for there was no doubt now that the Gehrn were prepared to escalate to have what they wanted.

She should have gone directly to Ewan, so together as the Circle they could inform the guard before someone else did.

She could go now.

She looked at the dark pressing against her window. She did not relish the idea of going out into waiting Gehrn; there were many ways to kill a mage, especially from a distance and in a city. But she could renew a shield about her as she walked.

She pulled a cloak against the chill and went out into the dark street. She met no one in the night.

Ariana answered the door, looking surprised. "I didn't expect anyone so late! Come in. What's wrong?"

"I need to speak to your father."

Ewan joined her in the sitting room. "Oh, Elysia—what's happened?"

"You know I've been approached by the Gehrn," she began, keeping her voice level. "I was approached again today, but on my way home, in an alley."

He went still. "Are you all right?"

"I'm fine. I'm here." She was keenly aware that Ariana was still in the room. "Their agent is not."

Ewan sat in a chair and blew out his breath. "Oh, Elysia." He gave a small shake of his head. "Not again."

Elysia could feel Ariana's shock like a palpable breeze from where she stood. Well, she would have learned at some point how a farm girl had earned her entry to the Circle. "We need to alert the guard that it was a Circle affair regarding a threat to the city, before they alarm the people with asking after a burned corpse."

"And you want me to explain they shouldn't be concerned with a charred cultist in the street."

"In an alley, less noticeable. And there's not enough to identify him as a cultist. Anyway, the bureaucracy is your work, and they'll take it better from you."

Ewan gave her a flat look, and then he rose. "I'll bring paper and we can write up a formal letter."

"And you'll stay tonight?" Ariana asked. "There's an extra bed. You don't have to go home." She made a confused gesture. "Not that you couldn't, of course, but—in case you didn't want to. And it will be late when you've finished."

Her concern touched Elysia. "Thank you. I suppose I will."

CHAPTER 35

Shianan nodded to the guards as he passed and knocked at Soren's door. Ethan admitted him with a polite nod of greeting. Inside, Soren stood uncertainly before a mirror. "Hello, Becknam. Come in and tell me if I dare go down in this."

The prince was dressed in a rich red, a striking color. He looked worried, and as he turned, the handsome color seemed to emphasize the pallor of his face. Soren frowned. "He had to take it in by four inches about the waist—and that's accommodating the protective wrap I have in case of someone brushing me in a crowd. 'Soats, Shianan, can I show myself?"

This was about the Wakari princess, Shianan realized. The prince was concerned about representing himself well to his people, but not to this degree, and the court would be understanding of his brush with death. But he did not want to appear an invalid before his betrothed. "The color is certainly noteworthy. Grabs the eye. And the cut isn't too thin; if anything it makes you appear taller."

Soren frowned and turned back to the mirror. "Taller?"

"And on that thought," Shianan followed quickly, "I should thank you for what I'm wearing tonight."

Soren smiled. "Well, I could hardly risk you coming in something near to this, could I? And the best way to be certain was to dress you." He grinned at the excuse and ran a hand over his forehead. "I'm glad it fits you. I told them about my size—my former size—but an inch or two shorter and with more muscle." He hesitated. "Just keep me from falling down the stairs. Please."

Ethan came beside them, offering watered wine. "My lords?"

They sat to wait. In the hall below guests were arriving, moving among the beginning music and exchanging greetings and gossip. Soren would make his entrance later, with fanfare appropriate for a surviving hero who had gone bravely to help an entrapped squadron. But he did not seem inclined to wait patiently.

Ethan came and went, occasionally refilling their drinks or straightening a piece of trim on Soren's boot. Shianan shifted subtly. Today's ride through the city's outskirts had gone well, but Kuolema had been nervous, and he'd tired himself sitting deeply on the dancing horse. Philip had been pleased, though, not only with his seat but with how he had calmly steadied the horse.

At last Ethan prompted, "It's time, my lords."

Soren nodded. "Let's make it through this." He braced himself against the arms of the chair and got to his feet, able to support himself but still cautious of quick movements. Shianan waited watchfully as he moved toward the door.

They paused at the long corridor above the great hall, hearing the music and conversation and able to peek out for glimpses of the colorful gathering without being seen themselves. "What a lot of them," Soren commented.

"It's a notable celebration," Shianan offered. "The Ryuven war ended, the plague ended, the prince-heir saved...and betrothed."

"Quiet. I don't need reminding of that, I'm nervous enough already. She didn't come all this distance to see a scarecrow manipulated down the stairs and introduced to her like a sorry puppet."

"You're no puppet, my lord," Shianan protested.

Soren gave a half frown. "I hope she thinks as much. This match isn't confirmed, you know, and the contracts are not signed. If she feels herself insulted—"

"You're worrying for nothing," interrupted a calm, feminine voice. Soren and Shianan separated and bowed to Queen Azalie behind them. "Thank you; be at ease. In all seriousness, Soren, you're thinking of this in entirely the wrong way."

He looked at her skeptically. "Oh?"

"Consider—a handsome young prince is injured in battle, nigh unto death, and then survives beyond all expectation. Important, heroic, dashing, and requiring just a bit of care and fussing over." She gave him a significant look. "You'll need Bailaha to prod the women away from you with a staff."

Soren considered, still skeptical. "You think so?"

"Of the three of us, my son, I suspect I have the best insight into the feminine mind. There is the matter of your response, of course. You can ruin the effect by being coldly independent, protesting too much that you need none of her concern. We like to be needed, Soren, in some fashion at least. Likewise, if you require her ministrations, delighting overmuch in careful attentions, you will seem a cad posing for benefit. She is well-bred enough to continue the charade in public, of course, but you will have lost her respect."

Soren stared at her. "So this is to my advantage, if I only play the game correctly."

"Of course. Only to play the game correctly is to play it honestly, not as a game." She smiled. "Good luck, my son. Good evening, Bailaha." She turned and went down the corridor to the primary stairs.

Soren turned back to the happy crowd below. "So not too much, and not too little."

"Right, my lord. Play the middle balance."

"Right." Soren bit his lip. "King's sweet double-dyed oats."

Ariana reached a hand up to touch the comb in her hair, making sure it was still secure. The black pearls were cool against her fingertips. She glanced around at the crowded room, watching brightly dressed guests mingle and talk.

She had not seen Shianan. Surely he had been invited? There had been the nasty rumors of his involvement in the prince's injury, and there had not been an official response. Surely that had not been enough to exclude him. He was a military hero, after all, and no one who knew him could believe he would harm the prince.

Still... She suppressed the disturbing image of the king kicking his bastard son as he knelt.

But that would change. For good or for ill, whether she deserved it or no, she was celebrated now, too, and she would use that to improve their situations.

"My lady mage."

She turned and saw Linner bow to her. She managed to suppress a scowl; she had dismissed the baron as politely as possible at the last ball, but he knew in such a public venue she could not reject him outright. "Yes, my lord? Did you want something?"

A flash of annoyance crossed his features. "I had hoped you would honor me with a dance, my lady mage."

She resisted rolling her eyes. "I am flattered, my lord, but I—"

"You have promised this dance to another?" He made a show of glancing about them. "But no one has come. I will keep you company, then, until your appointed one arrives, and then I shall surrender my claim." He smiled, knowing full well that she had no such previous commitment and could not wriggle free.

A sudden rush of frustration at everything took her, but he had not trespassed beyond entitled smugness. "Very well," she conceded reluctantly.

He took her arm and drew her toward the center of the room—the arrogant man meant to display her!—and turned to face her. He laced his fingers through hers. "Now, my lady mage—"

"I beg your pardon," came a voice beside them. "I may be mistaken, but—were you promised this dance, my lord?"

They turned as one to see Tamaryl, his face set in polite inquiry. Linner hesitated. "I—I thought to—"

Ariana felt her chest tighten. *Tam!*

"I'd thought it mine."

Linner blinked and wet his lips. "Of course, I meant no affront. I only—it is hardly good manners, my lord, to keep a lady waiting."

"Then I shall certainly ask my lady's forgiveness," Tamaryl answered simply. He extended an arm. "My lady mage?"

Linner had no choice but to retreat. Ariana turned to Tamaryl and they set off in the dance. "You may have to direct me," he whispered. "I've been watching, but I don't think I understand the nature of your human reeling about."

She was less concerned with the state of their dancing. "Tamaryl! How are you? I've been—I wanted so to be there when you arrived—I wept when I heard you were coming because that meant you were alive, and—"

"Ariana," he interrupted softly, and she saw his pained expression.

She took a deep breath as they turned. "Tell me everything."

"Everything, my lady mage? I think not. But I will give you an overview." They parted, took two steps backward, came together again. "After the battle, Oniwe'aru came himself for me. It was high treason, you know, what we did. I was imprisoned, and I worried that the same might have befallen you."

A wave of guilt crashed over her. "They called me a heroine."

"I'm glad. In the end, Oniwe'aru conceded I had acted in the interest of the Ai, and he appointed me his ambassador here as a form of useful exile. That pleased Oniwe'aru, the sho and princes, the humans, and myself."

She looked at him unhappily. "You were imprisoned—and Maru thought that—"

"Maru was worried," he interrupted. "Yes, I was imprisoned, but I'm free now and restored to my princely state. Stop that! It is the utmost rudeness to scry out someone's power, do you know that? Yes, there are some...residual effects of my confinement, but I'll be fine within a few days." He changed the subject firmly. "I've only just arrived, and I hardly have a network of friends in this court, and even I have already heard rumors. What's this about the prince and the bastard?"

"Don't call him that," Ariana responded sharply. "And I don't know where it started. I know it's ridiculous. Shianan would never harm the prince. He's devoted to the royal family, even though—well, someone else might resent... I don't understand why the king hasn't responded, though; surely ignoring it makes it worse."

"Questions could be asked of several decisions." Tamaryl gave a tiny smile. "I don't think the commander's assignment as my aide could have been planned more inappropriately, had anyone known."

Ariana gasped. "Really? How—awkward."

"Indeed. Didn't he say anything about it?"

Ariana didn't know how to explain. "We—haven't spoken."

Tamaryl gave her a curious look, but mercifully he did not ask. "I thought we had made a sort of temporary truce, but he sent word that he would not be attending me tonight, as he had been previously ordered to attend the prince-heir. So I am left to myself, to drift about the floor watching for mages making faces at small nobility."

Ariana suppressed a chuckle. "I am glad you were available. That Linner is slow to catch a hint, or rather thinks himself above them. But you and Shianan—to be assigned together..."

"We have duties above our personal antipathies. We have common ground."

The music ended with a flourish and was followed by a small fanfare. Ariana and Tamaryl turned automatically toward the grand staircase.

Prince Soren descended the stairs, easing himself one painstaking step at a time, his right hand upon the stone balustrade. A step behind him walked Shianan Becknam, his eyes wholly on the prince's progress. A nearly imperceptible ripple passed through the room. It was the bastard who accompanied the prince into the ball, ready at his side? Surely that honor should have gone to one of the dukes, or another distinguished courtier, or...

The entrance took a great deal longer than it might normally have, the musicians improvising, and by the time the prince reached the central landing, he was pale and visibly perspiring. He paused and leaned slightly upon the balustrade. Someone in the watching crowd helpfully began applause, and the cheering spread and filled the room while he regained his breath.

After a moment, Soren raised his hand, and the applause faded. "Thank you all," he began, grimacing with the effort of speaking loudly. His arm twitched involuntarily toward his ribs but was arrested sharply. "Thank you all for coming this evening to celebrate. We have so much for which to be grateful. We should especially note our commendable soldiers, ready for defense but welcoming peace, and our dedicated council who have devoted themselves to this new accord." He paused, took several steadying breaths. "There are others, of course, but my lord father will speak to you of that. And I myself wish especially to thank Shianan Becknam, Count of Bailaha, without whom I would not be here."

There was a soft murmur from the crowd. So it was true! The bastard had saved the life of the prince!

Soren glanced over his shoulder at the commander, as if expecting him to step forward. "Bailaha defended me from certain assassination and then bore me on his back to find help. I could not ask for a better friend." He hesitated, and then he turned back to the crowd. "I am very pleased to be here tonight, and I am most glad all of you are here as well. Please enjoy yourselves and this celebration." He gestured, and the music began anew. He waited a moment and then began inching down the rest of the stairs.

Tamaryl sniffed quietly. "Certain assassination... He owes more to Maru than to Shianan Becknam for that."

Ariana turned wide eyes to him. "What? You were there?"

One corner of his mouth quirked. "Between ourselves, my lady mage, I was very much there. And I can tell you that had I determined in the end to kill the prince, no mere commander would have stopped me."

Shock ran like jagged ice through Ariana. "But—but—you—"

"Maru talked me out of it. I'm glad some good came of it, at least. Still, a less generous nature might feel slighted, mentioned in such a way at such an occasion."

Her fingers tightened on his arm. "But if you were—"

212

"Oh, no worries. They can't afford to say it was I—how would that look, inviting the prince-heir's would-be murderer into the court? So Becknam receives some long-overdue credit, I have my place in the human court, my lord Soren continues living, and all is well."

She frowned. "If you say... And it's His Highness. Not my lord Soren."

"You have the most convoluted forms of address." Tamaryl made a face. "Well, shall we dance? Apparently we still have some time before either of us receives any attention."

She faced him and began to move with the music. "You sound almost resentful."

"I'm merely trying to cultivate my haughty demeanor. I am the Pairvyn ni'Ai, after all, and your court will want something of a show." He hesitated. "I do not resent the prince, in truth, nor even the commander, not much, and certainly not you, my lady mage. And I am most glad to be here."

She said nothing. So there had been something to his imprisonment, after all. Perhaps Maru had been right, despite Tamaryl's hasty dismissal.

It took time for Soren to reach the main floor and make his way to the dais, where the king and queen had taken seats to observe the gathering. Once he seemed to weave and Shianan caught him swiftly beneath the arm, but the prince steadied and moved forward without further assistance. At the dais, the queen watching anxiously, he sank wearily into a well-padded chair, and Shianan took a position behind him.

The dance ended, and as Tamaryl released Ariana she noticed several women watching them intently. It was only natural that Tamaryl drew attention, she supposed, though they might have been more subtle in their observation. Most looked rather severe, as if withholding judgment but reasonably certain they would dislike him, but one—Calissa!—seemed more curious than reserved. That must be the Wakari contingent, then.

Calissa's dark hair was braided elaborately; some maid must have spent a great deal of time working the coils. Ariana wished uncharitably that someone had taken as much time to remind the party that it was rude to stare at Tamaryl. Why weren't they dancing? Were they waiting still for their formal introduction?

Tamaryl must have felt their gaze. "If my lady mage will permit," he said quietly, "I will excuse myself. I believe you are wanted."

Indeed, Calissa had detached herself from the group and was beckoning Ariana to join her. "My lady mage," she greeted. "You do look lovely tonight."

"Thank you. I was admiring your hair."

"Thanks. Ariana, I have a confession to make, and I want to explain before you learn another way." Calissa gave her a worried, apologetic smile. "The day we met, you asked if I was the Wakari princess. I evaded. But the truth is, while I am not the Wakari princess you meant, I *am* a Wakari princess. Just not an important one."

Ariana wasn't sure how to respond. She remembered the trailing guards, the jests about royalty. "I—Your Highness..."

"I'm sorry I deceived you by omission. I only—I was under such orders not to speak out of turn, and at first I was worried I might have offended you, and—it just...happened."

"I'd guessed you were someone of rank, as you were important enough to have a bodyguard. I hadn't supposed princess, though." She was warm with embarrassment. "I did not know how to ask who you really were, not after we had spent so much time together. It seemed rude to say I did not know you, when we were friends."

"Well, and you know the Wakari royals, princesses everywhere but only a few who matter. Can you forgive me, please? I didn't want you to think I'd meant to trick you."

Ariana laughed. "Will you still come for tea?"

"Gladly, if you'll have me! Thank you, thank you so much, and now I have to get back to our group. Lord Adoniram is worse than a goose girl when it comes to keeping us together for occasions. We're to be introduced after the king speaks. And I think," she said as she glanced at the dais, "the king is preparing to speak now."

Ariana glanced where she indicated and saw the king gesture. The dance finished, and the musicians fell silent again.

King Jerome rose and addressed the gathering. "I should like to welcome you all again, as my son has done, and to recognize our special guests of honor tonight." He held out a hand. "First, we must welcome a guest to our court, a prince doniphan of his land who has come to inaugurate this peace between our peoples, Tamaryl, Pairvyn ni'Ai."

Tamaryl stepped forward and bowed precisely, as if he had practiced. He probably had. "I am pleased and honored to be here,

Your Majesty, and I look forward to long friendship between our peoples."

Soren pushed himself upright from the chair and took a step forward. "I am told," he said as loudly as his damaged torso permitted, "it was you who informed the search party where to find Bailaha and myself. I thank you for your service in that."

Only Ariana saw the embarrassed half smile pass between the men, the reason Tamaryl had known where the incapacitated prince was to be found. "It was my pleasure," Tamaryl answered politely. "And I am most pleased to see that you recover."

Soren gave him a smiling nod—an acceptable substitute for a bow, under the circumstances—and retreated to his padded chair.

"I urge you all to make my lord Tamaryl most welcome in our court and in our city," King Jerome continued. "We rely upon him to convey our good faith to the Ai."

Tamaryl backed away and moved beside the dais, seemingly unaffected by the stares of the hall.

"And we must certainly also recognize this night a prime architect of this current peace, our Black Mage of the Great Circle, Lady Ariana Hazelrig. Together with my lord Tamaryl, young Mage Hazelrig took great personal risk to bring about sudden peace in the midst of bloody chaos." He gestured. "Please come forward, my lady mage, and receive our thanks."

Ariana moved stiffly, uncomfortable with the enormous pressure of so many eyes upon her. It had not been only her doing—so many had helped to create this new accord... But they had chosen to recognize her, and this was her chance to make things different. She reached the dais, coming closer than was usual, and curtsied low. "Thank you, Your Majesty."

"You are a mage of great talent and great innovation as well as of great devotion to your kingdom," King Jerome said. "We should like to commend you and present you with—"

"Thank you, Your Majesty, I do have a boon to ask." She spoke quickly, her eyes still on the exquisitely tiled dais.

The king paused, disconcerted by this break from protocol. "Do you? Then you must come to us tomorrow, and we shall hear your—"

"I wish to marry," Ariana said in a rush, her heart pounding to drown the sounds of the watching ball behind her. "I ask for permission to marry."

The king's face relaxed infinitesimally. "That is an easy boon, my lady mage, and we can—"

Ariana dropped her voice so that it carried only to the dais. "I want Shianan Becknam."

CHAPTER 36

There was a moment of absolute stillness. The king did not move. Then, slowly, the onlookers began to nudge at one another, asking if anyone had heard what was said.

Ariana swallowed and pressed on. "I have heard it rumored his lordship may be transferred," she continued quietly. "It is my request that he remain in Alham, with Your Majesty's will."

She raised her head. The king was staring open-mouthed at her, struggling to maintain his composure. The queen had one hand hovering uncertainly about her heart. Soren was watching wide-eyed, while behind him Shianan wore an expression of undisguised horror.

Ariana licked her lips. "Your Majesty, if I may expl—"

"My lady mage," King Jerome interrupted, with enough recovered graciousness for the watching crowd, "tonight is a night of celebration. We would be happy to hear you privately tomorrow and to render unto you any suitable compensation." His eyes narrowed for just a heartbeat, and then he smiled. "Tonight, we shall dance and feast and celebrate. My good people, may this night be a night of joy! Make yourselves merry!"

There was a great round of applause, and then the crowd turned to their own pursuits, foremost the hurried queries as to what had been said. Ariana curtsied again and backed away from the dais, only to feel fingers close on her arm. She turned and was pulled close to Tamaryl, who drew her immediately into the dance. "That was interesting," he commented coolly. "Whatever prompted that?"

Ariana's throat closed. Having to explain it felt somehow worse than making the demand itself. And she did not want to explain to Tamaryl, of all people, whom she did not want to hurt, to whom she owed so much. "They won't permit Shianan to marry," she said unhappily. "Because of who he is. Nor even friendship; he was ordered—"

"It is not friendship you seek," Tamaryl snapped. "So you mean to demand him for yourself, then?" He shook his head. "And I suppose—that is your decision, obviously. I'm glad I was here to note it."

Her chest felt dangerously tight. "Tamaryl... I'm sorry. I do—"

"Let's not speak of it," he said shortly, executing a turn. "I hope his lordship is glad of this. As I understand, the sole advantage to his position was that he would not be married off as a political favor like the princes, but now you have made him a bartered commodity just as a radish or slave."

Ariana had not thought of it in that way.

"And I think you must not have mentioned this plan to him beforehand."

She looked up worriedly. "Why?"

He turned with the music so that she could see the dais. The king glared across the platform toward Shianan, controlled rage evident in the set of his features. Shianan was staring hard at the back of Soren's chair, flushed scarlet and immobile. Before him, Soren bit his lip and stared at his hands in his lap.

Ariana's heart sank. "You don't think... But if we have both rendered services to the kingdom—"

"Even that cannot change the succession," Tamaryl answered sharply, "which is what permitting Shianan Becknam to marry would be tantamount to doing. Treating him as anything other than an unacknowledged bastard places him ahead of young Alasdair and sets him as a potential rival to the prince-heir Soren. You've placed the king in a most awkward position, my lady mage, in choosing whether to overturn centuries of successive surety or to award a boon to a celebrated and popular figure. And you did it publicly."

"But it's wrong to prohibit Shianan—"

"Is it? I've read your histories, my lady, and your two bloodiest and most destructive civil wars came about because of half heirs." He sighed. "Besides, your Shianan Becknam was resigned to life without a bride. He's told me as much himself. Now you have angered the king on his behalf."

Ariana felt ill. "But certainly the king has to consider—they honored both of us tonight, so they cannot refuse outright—"

"A ruler can do—must do—whatever he considers necessary for the good of his kingdom," Tamaryl said curtly. "Regardless of what others may think, regardless of what he prefers, regardless of what might be the best action in fact, he does what he perceives is best. King Jerome believes Shianan Becknam must be handled carefully to prevent disaster. You have demanded he do otherwise, and not for the good of the kingdom, but for nothing more than his consideration for you."

Ariana stumbled, no longer keeping time with the music. She swallowed, tasting bile. This evening had not turned out as she had imagined. "What have I done?"

Tamaryl sighed. "We shall see, my lady mage."

CHAPTER 37

Shianan could not move. He stared at the prince's chair, his mind blank with horror. She had—before all—she had demanded...

He hadn't spoken with her. He'd told her they couldn't even speak. He'd tried his best to put her from him. But the king would never believe that now.

Soren moved slightly in his chair, and Shianan knew the prince was trying to turn to look back to him, hampered by his injury. He was glad that he couldn't; he did not want to meet the prince's eyes now. He did not know how, standing immobile on a dais before all the glittering nobility and court, he would actually face anyone at this moment.

She had meant well, he was certain of it. She did not know— she could not have known what it would mean. She had meant well.

The music played on, a jangle of indistinguishable sound. Guests danced and talked and laughed, and he noted none of it. He could not move.

And then a voice cut through his miserable stupor. "Come with me, Bailaha."

He lifted his head and saw the king glaring at him, very close. Shianan gulped. "Your Majesty."

Soren caught his breath. "If I—"

"Stay, Soren," ordered Jerome. "I want to speak with Bailaha."

Shianan nodded, unable even to form words of agreement. There would be no help in resistance or delay.

But he had not moved quickly enough, and the king's hand fell on his shoulder heavily. "Go. Now." The fingers squeezed, though his controlled face betrayed nothing to the self-absorbed guests.

Shianan fled the dais and retreated before the king, backing down the little corridor that ran behind the rear hanging. "Your Majesty, I had no idea—"

"Shut up." King Jerome shoved open a door and stepped inside, turning to watch Shianan follow. As Shianan entered, the king clouted him across the ear. "What mutiny is this?"

Shianan reeled and turned to face the king. "It was not my doing—"

The king pursued him. "Did you think your celebrity would save you?" He struck Shianan again, though the blow only glanced off his skull as he ducked. "Did you think I would fear your renown? I can still have you imprisoned, flogged, stripped of what honor you have—did I not already tell you that you would not marry?!"

Shianan backed away, ducking, not even pretending to face the king properly. Jerome followed him furiously, swinging his fists. "How dare you?! You arrogant, incorrigible—"

Shianan shielded his head as the king struck him. He brushed against a wall and found himself in a corner. There was no escape. He hunched his shoulders and waited for the king's fury to spend itself.

"Unreasonable demand—"

"Stop!"

"Impudent—"

"Father, stop!" Soren grasped at the king's arm.

Jerome wheeled on Soren and struck. The prince fell back against the wall with a jolt.

Soren froze against the paneled wall, his arms at his damaged ribs, not even breathing as he choked with the impact. Jerome stared and then started toward the prince. "Soren—!"

With two quick steps Shianan slid between the king and prince. He did not breathe as the king hesitated. Soren's hand rested on his shoulder, but he did not move. The enormity of his own defiance frightened him in a way the blows had not.

"Get out of my way," Jerome bit out angrily.

"Not him." Shianan's voice shook, and he did not know if it was for fear or fury.

The king's eyes flashed. "I want to see to Soren!"

"I agree with Becknam," snapped an icy voice from the door. Queen Azalie's eyes glowed with rage, her face white with pure wrath. "Get away from my son."

The king turned to face her. "I never meant to strike him! It was only that he got in the way—"

"Not so." Her words cut through the room like frigid steel. She left the doorway and started toward them.

Jerome bristled. "He pushed in—of course I was angry, how could I help but—he should know—"

"For being king," Azalie interrupted in acid tone, "it seems you have remarkably little power. The cause of your action always lies in someone else, never in yourself. Even striking your injured prince is his

222

doing, not yours. Or is this all for the words of a young woman you meant to honor?"

"I act in the interest of our sons!"

"So I see." Her voice dripped contempt.

Soren straightened against the wall, his hand shifting on Shianan's shoulder. The fingers flexed, possibly trying to communicate something, but Shianan could not guess what.

Jerome jabbed an accusatory finger at Shianan, who flinched. "Don't you see the bid for legitimacy, clear as daylight? And Soren—you said he had no ambition! Do you see now why I told you he was dangerous? Don't you see his design?"

"I see a madman," Soren answered hoarsely.

Jerome blinked in astonishment. "I—but—Soren, you don't—"

"Not now, Father." Soren shook his head. "We are neither of us in a mind to speak reasonably."

Jerome moved toward him. "But—"

"Leave him be." Azalie's tone was imminently dangerous. The king hesitated and glanced at her, but she had not moved. "Not now, Jerome. Soren is right; you can talk it over in the morning, when your minds are clear. For now, you and I should go back to the hall, lest our guests wonder why Alasdair is alone there while we are supposed to be introducing our Wakari guests."

"Alasdair isn't in the hall," Soren observed.

Azalie turned toward the door. "No."

The cracked door opened, and the younger prince fidgeted under the weight of their eyes. "I..."

"Go back with your father," she instructed crisply. "I'll be along in a moment."

Jerome's jaw clenched. "I won't be ordered about—"

"Do you have a better suggestion to save face? Or do you want all the world to know we're in the back corridors arguing over your bastard?"

Jerome straightened. "You know well I would not sacrifice our dignity," he snapped. He glanced at Soren and Shianan. "Tomorrow morning, then. And I hope, Soren, that he has not already poisoned your mind against my wisdom."

Soren said nothing. Shianan bowed, acknowledging his sovereign's departure and hiding his own expression.

The king moved past Queen Azalie without meeting her eyes. When he had gone, and Alasdair had followed, she crossed the room.

Shianan stepped away from Soren and bowed again, his thoughts a whirl, wishing to be anywhere else, wishing none of this had happened.

A hand touched his shoulder. "I'm sorry about that last part," she said gently. "I hope you know the sting was meant for him and not for you."

Shianan's throat closed. "Your Majesty said nothing that was not truth," he answered unsteadily.

"Nonetheless." She tugged him gently upright and regarded them both, one hand resting on Shianan's shoulder, one on Soren's. "Are you badly hurt? Either of you?"

They shook their heads silently.

She sighed and moved to kiss Soren's forehead, drawing him slightly downward so that she could reach him. Then, amazingly, she turned and drew Shianan to her as well, brushing her lips across his forehead before he could react. "I'm sorry," she said. "He is—I'm sorry. I should not have stayed so long in Kalifi. Go on, there will be no dealing with him tonight. We'll meet in the morning."

"Thank you, Mother," Soren said flatly. Then his expression turned to sudden dismay. "Oh—Princess Valetta! King's sweet oats."

Azalie took in his pale, pained face. "You're in no shape to make a good impression. I'll make your excuses, and no one will be surprised if you retire early tonight. I will see the ball carries on, and we'll make the Wakari guests welcome even without you. Don't worry, I'll work it all out." She turned and went out into the corridor, toward the hall.

Soren looked toward Shianan. Hot shame crashed over Shianan like a wave, and he glanced away. "I'm sorry."

Soren swore vehemently and made a frustrated gesture. "You're the only man I know who can be beaten unjustly and then apologize for it! King's oats, man, you did nothing." He took a slow, careful breath. "Ouch. Don't make me shout at you again."

"I had no idea she meant to ask for—that."

"I know you didn't. But even if you had, he had no—it was not—there was no cause for that. She was open and straightforward, that was all. And only a paranoid fool would suspect it's your bid to seize the throne through an alliance with the Circle."

Shianan gulped at this frank assessment. "My lord..."

Soren shook his head. "No, I know I'm not being fair, either. But I—'soats, I want to sit for a moment."

Shianan glanced around, but the room was a mere antechamber for ambassadorial parties, barely and uncomfortably furnished. "If you can walk a bit, my lord, we'll find someplace better for you."

Soren nodded. "I can walk, yes. Let's go back to my rooms. At least we know we'll not be bothered there."

They went out into the corridor, Shianan watching the prince closely, and turned away from the hall. Music followed them for a time, fading as they moved further into the palace.

"At least there's no question of whether she cares," Soren ventured. "If she's willing to risk the both of you to have you."

Shianan did not have anything to say. He had put Ariana off, as he'd thought he must; he had not dreamed that she would defy his own word for him.

Soren nodded tightly toward a door. "Rear stairs."

Shianan pulled open the door and looked at the steep, narrow flight. It rose sharply, turned over itself, and continued on.

Soren gave them a despairing look. "Stairs."

"You've only to make the first few, my lord," Shianan urged. "That will take you high enough to reach my back."

Soren looked at him. "But—"

"Your healers will be furious if I let you try those," Shianan protested reasonably. "Come on. The sooner we reach the top, the sooner we may each have a chair."

Soren ascended the first four steps and turned to face Shianan, who backed to the stairs and bent forward. Soren eased himself onto Shianan's back. "I hadn't meant to make a habit of this."

"Let's make this the last time, if Your Highness does not mind." Shianan turned and began to climb.

"Oh, but I have grown to enjoy these little trips."

"If you grow much more, my lord, you may render these little trips impossible."

"With your sly flattery, it's a wonder you aren't at the front of the council."

Shianan climbed, losing count of the steps, passing door after door. "Which of these is it?"

"I'm trying to recall. I haven't used these since I was Alasdair's age."

"Shall I turn back if we reach the tower? Or shall I just collapse on a convenient landing?" In fact, Shianan had not started battle-wearied, as in the ravine, and the prince had wasted lean during his illness. It would not do to say so, however.

And then a door opened just above them, showing Ethan's concerned face. "How can I help, my lords?"

"Hold the door wide," Shianan instructed. "Thanks." He eased himself and the prince through and found himself in a rear corridor in the royal suites. "Which way?"

"Here." Ethan hurried ahead and held another door for them.

"Set me down, Becknam, I can walk well enough here," Soren protested. "Ethan, how did you know to find us?"

"My lord left the dais with the king," Ethan answered, "and did not return with the others. I assumed you were retiring, and it seemed logical you would use the rear stairs if you meant to avoid the crowds." He opened a door to Soren's rooms. "I hadn't thought you would ascend so unconventionally, however. Should I order you a litter in the Wakari style, master?"

Soren waved the joke aside. "Thank you, but no. I plan to be steady on my own feet soon enough. Ethan, do you think—neither of us had opportunity to sample the feast downstairs. Would you bring us something to eat?"

Ethan nodded. "Certainly, my lord. About how long would you like me to be about it?"

Soren shook his head. "I couldn't fool you if my life depended on it. Give us half an hour."

"Yes, my lord." Ethan poured out two drinks, left the wine pitcher within easy reach of Soren's chair, and closed the door behind him.

Shianan watched the slave go. Now, free of distractions like the queen's concern and the obstacle of the stairs, now it would come, and there was nothing he could do to stop it. Soren knew. Soren, who had liked and respected him at last, had *seen*. It was his worst humiliation realized.

He braced himself.

CHAPTER 38

Soren looked across at Shianan and gestured. "Sit down already. There's no need for ceremony here." He was glad Ethan had gone. He trusted Ethan implicitly, but he didn't think Shianan would want another face. "Sweet oats, man, are you all right?"

Shianan, still standing, nodded irritably. He turned partly away and inspected his wine. "Yes, yes. I bore you well enough, didn't I? Frankly, my lord, his fists are not enough to concern me."

"But that was..."

"Forget this!" snapped Shianan over his shoulder. "It's been far worse."

"Worse?" Soren repeated. "But he hit you—"

"Which was nothing; he would have spent himself in a moment. He kicked me before Alasdair." Shianan stopped abruptly, as his protestations undermined his protest. He clenched his fist and kept his face away.

Soren gaped and finally made his tongue work. "Kicked you? With Alasdair?" He shifted uncomfortably in the chair, partly from the residual pain of injury and partly because he felt nauseated with what he had seen, with Shianan's confession. "Where?"

"In the chest, mostly." Shianan began to pace. "Or, in an older audience chamber, if that's what you ask. When I was hesitant to swear myself to the younger prince." He was pacing furiously now, sloshing his forgotten wine onto the floor. "He's done me damage that way. Broke ribs once, but that was when we lost the shield." He spoke too fast, his words spilling free. "And I never meant for anyone to know, no one, because the only thing worse than the bastard is the bastard beaten, and if I thought I knew shame before...!"

"Shianan, I'm sorry." Bits of memories slid together, formed meaning. Soren licked his lips, faltered, and finally ventured, "Luca knew, didn't he?"

"'Soats, Luca, yes." Shianan reversed direction again. "I brought Luca back the night the shield collapsed. The next day, he saw me crawl home with my ribs kicked in and my tail between my legs. Not the way to impress a new slave, eh? He guessed the rest quickly enough." He came to a halt, his shoulders slumping. "But now? Luca,

Alasdair, you, the queen herself... He might as well make me the entertainment for the guests."

Soren fought mingled outrage and disbelief. "He—no, I can't—I've never seen..."

"Well, you saw it plainly enough tonight." Shianan turned back toward him. "I'm sorry, my lord. I've never said... I'm sorry."

Soren shook his head. "No, no, I believe you. I have to believe you. But I can't... I'm sorry. On his behalf, and on my own. 'Soats, I should have seen it, somehow."

"We were neither of us anxious that you should see it." Shianan looked away. "I suppose I should have noted that, never in the sight of others. I should have known then."

"Known what?"

Shianan hesitated. "That it was wrong."

The admission was a fresh blow, taking Soren's breath and leaving him stunned, not yet capable of anger. "How long?" he asked numbly.

Shianan moved uncomfortably, as if to shake off the memories. "From the beginning, when I first came to Alham. I thought—I had never seen him before. The king! The grand secret of my existence, the crowned head, the object of all our military service! I was in awe, of course, and it didn't occur to me that my punishment was anything other than just. It was small at first, maybe just a slap, and after all, he praised me as well, if I made a particularly fine effort." He glanced at the mostly emptied wine glass and swore softly.

Soren waved in dismissal of the spilled wine. "It isn't you. You're the living reminder of his mistakes, and that's what galls him. I tell you, he cannot praise you enough when he requires more of me, and only the Holy One knows what Alasdair hears. But whatever drives him, there is no excuse for him to—to strike you." He swallowed. "I'll see it stopped, somehow."

Shianan gave him a sad half smile. "I thank you, my lord, but—"

"I don't know how, but I will. 'Soats, I already told you I would be a lord who protects those who serve him. I can hardly swear that and then fail in this."

Shianan finally took the chair. "Again, thank you, but... I am more grateful for what else you have already given me. I would take a thousand kicks from His Majesty before I would surrender your friendship."

Soren scowled at him. "Flattering indeed, but no one has asked that trade. There is no reason I cannot claim you as my friend and keep you from unreasonable abuse. Indeed, it seems quite logical that I should do both."

Someone knocked at the door. "Ethan was a bit quick," Soren observed. "Come!"

But it wasn't Ethan. Alasdair entered hesitantly, closing the door behind him. Shianan stood and bowed, his face carefully blank.

"I don't think anyone saw me come," Alasdair began, his eyes darting everywhere about the room except for them. "I went to dance, and then I went to the privy, and then I slipped up the rear stairs when no one was looking. Could I talk to you for a minute? My lords?"

Soren glanced briefly at Shianan, whose face offered nothing, and then back at his younger brother. He didn't want to interrupt this rare and raw moment with Shianan, but he had never seen this look in Alasdair's eyes before. And Shianan might be glad of a change. "Certainly," he offered, beckoning. "Come and join us."

Alasdair curled into a chair, knees to chest, facing Soren. "I—I was—I didn't think..." He gulped and then let the words loose all in a rush. "I was here with you when he came, one night. The guards didn't see him, though they found a broken window later and I never said I knew why, and they thought it was a bird. But when he came, I thought—everyone said the bastard had tried to kill you! And we always knew he wanted our positions! And I was scared, because he was going to kill you, and he would kill me too, and—but he hadn't come for that, he just came to see you." He gulped. "And then it turned out that he hadn't tried to kill you at all, and...and I didn't know what to do."

Soren didn't understand everything, but it would not help to interrupt whatever confession Alasdair was attempting, so he nodded encouragingly. "Go on."

"I mean, when I received..." Alasdair's voice faded. He took a breath and began again, his eyes fixed firmly on Soren, as if determined not to see Shianan at all. "He hadn't wanted to swear to me, and Father had—had made him do it. So I knew that it was true that he resented us and that he wasn't really—if Father could..." He trailed off again.

"But that's not so," supplied Soren quietly.

"Right!" Alasdair nodded. "He saved you, and—he didn't do anything tonight!" He looked at Shianan for the first time. "You didn't tell her to say that, did you? And if he can—just for—I don't want that!"

"None of us do," answered Soren.

"Your Highness," Shianan said stiffly, "I did not mean any offense to you when I was reluctant to swear to you. My concern was—"

"You didn't want to swear to me instead of my brother," interjected Alasdair. "I know now." He gulped and stood, and then he bent in a formal bow. "Thank you for saving him," he intoned solemnly.

Shianan blinked. "My lord, it was—I never considered otherwise."

Alasdair straightened. "Thank you," he repeated. He licked his lips and seemed to fumble for the next words. "And—when I enter military training, I—will that be—if I am wrong, will he..."

Soren grasped what he asked. "Ah, you want to know if what goes around might come around." He shook his head. "No, it's not for Shianan being a soldier."

"But Father said—"

"Father's word is not to be trusted in this, I'm afraid." Soren nodded toward Shianan. "I don't know whom they've picked for you as a mentor, though. If you're fortunate, you'll have an opportunity to learn from the demon commander himself."

Alasdair paled and glanced involuntarily at Shianan. "You..."

Shianan half smiled. "It could be."

Alasdair made a brave face. "I'll be ready. I've been studying my history, and I have my weapons lessons, too, and—"

"If your swordsmanship is anything like your brother's, my lord, I wouldn't count too heavily on it," Shianan warned with faint humor. "But I daresay we could improve you, as I intend to improve him."

Soren lifted an eyebrow. "Oh?"

Shianan turned on him. "You don't think I'll let you go out so unprepared again, do you? And you agreed to train with me, that night in the ravine, don't you recall?"

"I remember very little of that night, thank the Holy One."

Shianan turned back to Alasdair and took a more serious tone. "My lord, I thank you for your frank speech. It could not have been easy for you to trust me that night, and certainly not for you to speak here tonight. But I thank you for it."

Alasdair nodded with as much dignity as a boy his age could manage.

Soren hesitated. "Could you do something for me?" Alasdair glanced at him, and he shifted uncomfortably. "When you go back, could you—just look, mind you—but see if you can guess what Princess Valetta is about? Don't ask her, 'soats, don't say anything! But just see if she's... Oh, you know."

Alasdair grinned. "I can."

Soren flushed and grinned. "Thanks."

Alasdair nodded respectfully to each of them, surprising Shianan again, and then left. Shianan dropped into his chair. "I had not expected that."

Soren nodded thoughtfully. "I think the little turd may be growing up."

Shianan did not ask what that would make him.

Another knock came at the door. "My lords?"

"Ethan, come!"

Ethan entered, carrying full trays of splendid tidbits from the feast below. Shianan looked at the array of food. "This is luxurious," he said, "and I have no appetite for it." He ran a hand through his hair. "Maybe I should go."

"No," Soren protested. "Don't go. Please, I feel responsible, somehow. Stay for a while. Stay all night, if you want."

Shianan laughed grimly. "Afraid I'll disappear in the night, my lord?"

"I hadn't thought that, no. But king's oats, Shianan, I'd never seen him like that. I can't..."

Shianan sighed. "I'll stay, my lord," he said quietly. "I'll stay, on the condition that we find something else to talk about."

"Agreed," Soren answered readily. "You can tell me all about the skills I'm lacking with a sword, and then we'll talk about Princess Valetta and whether she'll ever so much as speak to me after our marriage, and—king's sweet oats, the princess. We were to be formally presented after Father's speech."

Ethan bowed silently and retreated, leaving Shianan and the prince staring glumly across the room.

CHAPTER 39

The outer door rattled and then someone pounded on it. "Luca! Open the door!"

Luca unlocked the door and opened it, leaving Shianan with his fist hanging midair. "Oh, good," Shianan said. "I thought you might not hear, if you were still sleeping." He stepped into his office and shivered out of his cloak.

Luca only nodded. He had not waited up for Shianan after the ball, but he had worried when he woke and found his master had not returned in the night.

Shianan continued, "I thought I'd better come and change before the audience."

"Audience? Who sets an audience for early morning after a royal ball?"

Shianan opened his mouth to speak and hesitated.

Luca read enough in the lines of his face. "The king. Something happened with the king."

"I have an audience with the king," Shianan said heavily, "and possibly the queen and others, to reinforce my illegitimacy and deny my lady Ariana's request to marry me."

Luca blinked. "Master Shianan..."

"I'll be all right, Luca. Sticks and stones, and all that. Get me ready."

Luca was not convinced. There was nothing to do, though, but wait. Wait and hope. Shianan had weathered political menace before now. When Shianan had washed and changed, Luca followed him out the door.

Shianan was aware of Luca trailing dutifully behind him, and he knew his friend wanted to say something encouraging. The trouble was, there was nothing encouraging to be said. The king might reprimand Shianan with scathing reproof, or he might kick in Shianan's ribs in his anger. He might order Shianan to the furthest outpost to rot in forgotten exile or die at the hands of ambitious warlords. The only thing he assuredly would not do would be to grant

Shianan's request to court Ariana Hazelrig or her request to marry the bastard.

Shianan wanted to send Luca back. There was no purpose to the slave's presence, after all. But he couldn't bring himself to say the words. There was a narrow comfort in knowing that Luca, at least, wished him well and stood by him.

Soren would do the same. And whatever King Jerome decreed, Soren would do his best to mitigate it, that was sure. There was some comfort there, as well.

There was no one else in the antechamber, and Shianan allowed himself to pace. Luca already knew his nerves, anyway. At last the doors opened and a servant breathlessly asked Shianan to enter, his voice carefully flat and his eyes well away from the commander-count's.

Shianan kept his gaze from Luca's, took a final breath to still his heaving stomach, and entered.

King Jerome sat at the head of the long empty table, as if presiding over an invisible council meeting. Shianan dropped to one knee, mere steps inside the door. "Your Majesty." Deference first of all. And, if the king meant to beat him, so be it, but he would keep his distance until ordered to present himself a target.

"Bailaha." The voice was not welcoming. "I have been considering you."

There could hardly be a less mincing introduction. "Yes, my lord." He had to make the attempt, at least. "Sire, I had no idea my lady mage would—"

"You have not been invited to speak."

Shianan clenched his jaw.

"Slave! What do you think you're doing? Get out! This is not for the ears of your betters, much less yours. Out!"

There was a scuff of movement behind Shianan and the doors closed again. He had not realized that Luca had followed him into the council room itself. Bold, brave, loyal, stupid Luca.

The king left him kneeling. His voice was terse. "Bailaha, we should not be careful of words, now that things have come to this. You are aware of the constraints of your position?"

It was hardly a question. Shianan swallowed. "Of course, Your Majesty."

"You know that you have already been favored beyond your birthright?"

"Your Majesty has been generous."

"You know if you had been dealt with properly, you would not have the position and fame to attract a woman, nor the means to court her, nor the means to enjoy her."

"Yes, Your Majesty," he forced.

It was not my fame that drew her. It was your own doing, my lord. It was your distrust that forced me to keep her secrets and so made us friends.

"And yet you persist in abusing our generosity?" Jerome demanded. "You even seek countenance to marry—and into the Circle itself! Presumptuous! Do you think you can take a place alongside the princes? Pretend you are no bastard?"

Shianan's answer rasped in his tight throat. "Never, Your Majesty."

"Then why do you persist in this?" The king blew out his breath sharply.

Shianan's breath burned in him.

The door opened. "Why are the—" The queen's voice cut off abruptly. "Jerome!"

"Father, you told us to come on the hour!"

Shianan clenched his jaw. The king had meant to isolate him from his few allies.

"I wanted to speak with him myself first! Bailaha, come here."

Shianan rose, his pulse pounding, his movement stiff. He started toward the king.

"Come with me. I want to speak with you privately."

Soren started forward. "Surely—"

"Jerome," warned the queen.

The king gestured irritably at them. "I only want to speak with him! Sweet holy—come here, Bailaha."

There was a small room attached for closeted conversation. Shianan followed mutely, looking at neither king nor prince nor queen. He closed the door and waited, his eyes across the room as when Captain Torg would verbally eviscerate a too-young soldier.

He hoped it would be as simple as that.

"Shianan Becknam," the king began, and Shianan twitched at the sound of his name. The king didn't use it often. "You are a considerable problem."

Shianan said nothing.

"You are more than your birth. You are, by all accounts, a talented military hero, beloved of his men and respected by his officers. You are handsome enough, and clever. You are capable of much, and your lineage is evident in your face and ability. But that is exactly the problem—those men who love you might support you against the rightful prince, or—"

"I honor my prince," Shianan interjected, his voice thick. "I have no desire to oppose him, nor to compete for anything at all."

"So you say. But your actions imply ambition. You seek to marry, and to marry a Mage of the Circle, no less! And when you are expressly forbidden, still the matter is raised again. What are we to think but that you intend to rise above a bastard's place, set yourself at the top of the court and wait for opportunity? I was glad to offer you gracious treatment, to place you into the military early to protect you, to keep you intact and whole, to bring you to Alham and ennoble you—"

"Protect me?" repeated Shianan, frustrated and confused and afraid and angry. "Protect me from whom?"

"Raised at court as a bastard? Would you have preferred that? Castrated as a child? Would you prefer a late and nominal appointment with little real authority, a useless attachment needing a function? Is that what you would want?"

Shianan held his tongue and fought down his roiling thoughts. He should not have protested in the first place; arguing over the past helped nothing. He wanted only to last this day.

"No, you risked none of that. You were trained and ennobled and advanced as your skills merited. And now what is to be done with you?"

Shianan swallowed. "I have sworn my oath to the prince."

"Alasdair is not—"

"No, my lord." Shianan's voice quavered. "To Prince Soren. I have sworn myself to his service."

The king blinked. "To Soren?"

Shianan gulped again and met the king's eyes. "I have pledged my whole service to him. I leapt over a cliff when I saw him fall, I carried him on my back in search of help for his wound. My lord, Your Majesty, how then could I seek to displace him?"

King Jerome looked hard at him, flustered. "You are sworn to Soren? When? No—no wonder you did not wish to bow before Alasdair... But why? What hold has he over you that—"

"My lord, I gave it myself," Shianan answered abruptly. "Of my own will, unasked."

The king watched him for a long moment. "Yes," he said at last, "I think I believe you."

Shianan inhaled, dizzy with the sudden air. The room seemed close about them.

The king turned away. "I had prepared a proposal for you," he said slowly. "We need a new ambassador to the Soek court. It would be good to send someone with high standing, even royal lineage. If you will go, I will see you acknowledged."

Shianan's heart leapt. Acknowledged? It was a dream he had not dared since he was a child, imagining the king riding frantically into the cold outpost, declaring a terrible mistake and sweeping a tired, bruised Shianan through the air onto his great horse, turning to gallop back to the fabulous distant Alham and the royal palace...

And then his stomach twisted, dragging his heart with it. An acknowledged bastard was still a bastard, far from legitimacy. He would be a son, but the gulf separating him from the royal family and court would be as vast as ever. Even in this great offer, he was still held at arm's length, a muddied bit of refuse to be kept at a safe distance. *I will see you acknowledged*, the king had offered. Not, *I will acknowledge you.* It was a subtle distinction, but telling.

A year before, he would not have noted such a subtlety. A year ago he would have leapt for even a shred of recognition, rushed to see the king claim him. Now he had ceased bounding after scraps.

"Soek, Your Majesty?" he repeated, obligated to speak. "Why me?"

"Because you are Bailaha, the commander-count, famed soldier and noble of our court. Soek would be glad to receive you." The king hesitated for just a heartbeat, tipping his head as if considering. "And if legitimate, you could speak for our kingdom, a trusted ambassador. Soek is a rich court, and there would be much to amuse you."

The room seemed to spin about Shianan. Legitimate! Yes, if the king adopted him, it was possible. To be legitimate—no longer the bastard, no longer the ill-regarded politic tool, a threat to friend and foe alike... He could make a new name for himself in a court that had not known him first as the despised half son. He would move among Soek's lauded nobility and wealth. There was no dishonor in rising through adoption.

King Jerome crossed his arms. "Well?"

Luca would go with him. But Shianan would leave behind Soren—and Torg, and Kuolema, and even Alasdair, whom he despised but who might be changing, and the queen, who seemed to have a new regard for him. And he would leave Ariana, who would of course remain in Alham in the Circle. He would see her rarely, or perhaps never, if he went to Soek.

And then the bargain became clear in his mind. He was not offered legitimacy through any personal attachment, nor because of his superhuman efforts to win approval, for his deeds in fighting the Ryuven, for carrying the prince, any of it. No, this was merely a sop to distract him from Ariana, a baited lure to draw him away—because the bastard could be denied expressly and flatly, but an honored mage of the Great Circle could not be refused so bluntly, and it would be simpler to tell her that Shianan had chosen a post in another land.

It was a conciliatory bribe, nothing more. And Shianan would bear his hollow new status not in his own kingdom, but safely, distantly in another land.

King Jerome cleared his throat irritably. "Holy One, what's taking you so long? What's to think over? Sweet Holy One, Bailaha, I'm offering you an ambassadorship—will you take it or no?"

Shianan's arms trembled, and he thought he might be quivering with fury. "I thank you for your generosity, my lord," he said, suppressing the dangerous angry disdain he felt, "but I am surely more suited to military duty than to courtly diplomacy, and I have my oaths to the princes to fulfill."

The king stared at him in surprise. Of course, he would never have expected Shianan even to hesitate. He believed Shianan would crawl eagerly, groveling in gratitude for this scrap of commendation. "No?"

"I prefer to remain here, my lord."

"You would be my son in Soek!"

Shianan's heart spasmed. It was the first instance the word had been used, and it came with such a heavy condition. "But I would not be your son here," he answered quietly. Dry bitterness marked his voice, covering the soft, raw frustration. He sucked air through his teeth. "I would not be your son here."

Jerome's eyes widened. "You would not—!" He stepped close, and Shianan fought to avoid flinching back. "And if I order you to Soek? If it is not your preference, but my command, what then?"

Shianan's heart clenched, but he made his voice even, an obedient soldier's quiet response. "I have obeyed your every order, my lord. You know I am yours to command."

Don't do this. Please don't do this.

"And you would not refuse?"

A direct command refused by the bastard would mean court martial. Shianan would be imprisoned at the least; Ariana and Soren would be shamed before the court. Luca would be seized and sold. Shianan swallowed. "No, Your Majesty. You know I would obey."

Jerome fixed his gaze on Shianan. "I did not order you to refuse her," he said. "I could have told you to refuse the mage, deny her yourself—she will not press for you if you will not have her. But I did not."

Hot rage burst within Shianan, radiating outward, and his arm actually twitched with the desire to strike at something, someone. He stared at the king openly, mouth slightly agape, hurt and angry. Refuse Ariana himself? After he had risked all to petition for her? After she had petitioned for him? After he had told her there was no hope for them and they could not see one another?

"Do you understand?" The king looked at him, breath suspended, waiting for something.

Shianan understood; he waited for some sign that Shianan had understood the brutal choice. It was to be Soek, privileged and honored as the king's distant but legitimate son, or the unhappy task of lying to Ariana that he did not want her.

"Well?"

Shianan straightened and drew a ragged breath. "My lady mage's request is between Your Majesty and herself," he said, his voice mostly steady. "I cannot intervene. I will accept what resolution is reached between you."

The king stared at him for one eternal instant and then looked away. "I would have made you a prince in Soek. You have rejected this." He turned, staring at the opposite wall. "You have chosen against being my son."

Shianan's gut wrenched. "That's not so, my lord," he answered, fighting to keep his voice level. "I will continue to be what I ever have been." He swallowed forcibly through his closed throat. "It is your choice whether you will be my father."

King Jerome's jaw fell, and his mouth moved with speechless rage.

Shianan's heart sank. This was it, then—he had doomed himself, and his friends with him.

Jerome turned away, his shoulders twitching as if he fought some great argument. But that was ridiculous, as he had already vanquished his bastard and there was no one else to fight.

Then he wheeled on Shianan, who flinched, to his shame. "You miserable ungrateful whelp," he snarled. "Do you hate me so much?"

Shianan had no answer, and the king did not wait to see if he had. He turned and left the small room like a catoblepas shouldering out of its den. Shianan took a shuddering breath, relieved and furious and despairing, and then followed.

CHAPTER 40

The queen and prince-heir were waiting at the spacious table, and three courtiers had also arrived, standing to one side. Queen Azalie and Soren rose as the king entered, but their faces showed more impatience than respect. "Will you tell us now what you have planned?" asked the queen, her tone civil but edged with frustration.

King Jerome jerked savagely at a tasseled cord, and a servant appeared with near magical efficiency. "Guards," the king snapped, and the servant rushed out.

"Guards?" repeated Azalie. "For what?"

"Bailaha has refused orders," the king growled.

"What orders?" demanded Soren. "He's the most loyal man in the army. What reasonable order could he have refused?"

A half dozen royal guards poured into the room and, at King Jerome's gesture, flanked Shianan. He did not resist. What was the point? Fighting would only add to the difficulty of his situation. And there was nothing to fight for.

"I wanted to promote him and send him on a special assignment," King Jerome muttered, looking away from them. "It would be good for him as well as good for the kingdom, but he refused."

Shianan had not refused, but there was no point to arguing, either. He had offended the king, and that was sufficient; the king's telling would stand above Shianan's.

The door opened and a servant announced, "My lady mage Ariana Hazelrig, the Black Mage."

Shianan's eyes leapt to her. She had been summoned with the others, then. She looked less confident than the night before.

Ariana curtsied beside the table and then, as she straightened, she caught sight of Shianan, flanked by guards. Though they had only a hand on each arm, the meaning was clear enough. She gasped and then tried gamely to address the situation. "Your Majesty, I came as asked..." She faltered.

Shianan's chest tightened. *Ariana...*

"So we are all here," King Jerome observed, trying to regain an air of control. He straightened and inhaled, swelling his shoulders.

The queen looked irritated. "Now we're all here, will you now tell us what you intend?"

Jerome shifted from foot to foot and looked uncomfortable. "I had thought we would have something to say to Lady Ariana," he muttered.

Ariana's eyes widened, and Shianan thought she caught her breath as she glanced again at him. His stomach twisted. Her expression held surprise and excitement and alarm and hope. Shianan looked away, seeking a place in the room where he would meet no one's eyes, not Ariana's nor the king's nor Soren's nor anyone's.

Ariana glanced back at the king, wetting her lips. "Your Majesty—"

"No, I don't mean the granting of your boon." King Jerome straightened and scowled. "That is impossible. You knew it was impossible when you asked, just as it was impossible when Bailaha asked before."

"Oh sweet runny oats!" The queen rose from her chair and advanced on the group. "This is not the way to discuss this, or to dispense judgments when they are ready."

"Quiet!" roared the king. "I will have order in my own court."

The door was pushed open. "Your Majesty!" began a dark-haired man in fine brown clothing. "I must ask you—" He paused, blinking at the array of personages and guards.

"Lord Adoniram." Queen Azalie inclined her chin in a way that conveyed simultaneously gracious greeting and rebuke for his abrupt entry. "What may we do for you?"

"Your Majesty," the foreign courtier began, addressing her now. "I have come a great distance to help orchestrate a match between our kingdoms. Last night my princess was to have been presented to your prince-heir and yet she was left without any attentions, as my lord the prince was incapable of remaining, it was said." He gestured to encompass the table, the waiting courtiers, the king and Shianan. "And yet this morning—" He again swept an indignant hand across the room and nearly spat, "You look after a misbegotten by-blow while my princess sits solitary in her rooms!"

"Lord Adoniram," Queen Azalie answered evenly before the king could speak, "your insight into our private affairs is wonderful." Her voice sweetened. "As you may see, this is a delicate matter for us, and we would like to treat Her Highness with the greatest possible care. We did not wish her visit to be disrupted by these private concerns. We wish to conclude and set them aside first, to give her the fullest consideration."

Lord Adoniram looked dubiously mollified. "But to settle the bastard's marriage before that of—"

"The bastard will have no marriage," King Jerome pronounced firmly.

"Your Majesty?" Ariana's voice was hurt and confused.

"My princess cannot be left to wait upon the affairs of a bastard! She has not even been officially presented to your court, much less to your prince."

Azalie rose and started toward the Wakari courtier. "For the present, my lord, allow us to dismiss these distractions so that we may bend our efforts wholly upon the proposed alliance..." The queen led Adoniram toward the door, saying something conciliatory as she ushered him out. Shianan ignored them as the king turned back to Ariana, taking the chance of the queen's distraction.

"My lady mage," King Jerome said, "I must first emphasize how we are deeply grateful for your service to this kingdom. We are glad to recognize your devotion with a suitable acknowledgment. Regrettably, we feel an attachment to Bailaha is not the best reward for our esteemed and honored servant."

The king's words faded into noise as Shianan watched in mute hopelessness. It was crumbling away, all of it, dreams to despair.

"If you wish to marry, I will pledge to find you a suitable husband," King Jerome said. "You are a valuable servant of the kingdom, and we must consider your match for the good of the state, the good of the Great Circle, and for your own good, my lady mage."

Ariana stared at the king, surprised and disbelieving. "You have betrayed my service," she whispered.

King Jerome did not hear her. He gestured to the Chrenadan courtiers still standing silent and awkward at the side of the room. "I have asked Lords Devinne, Stowmarries, and Everingham here to consider—"

"Thank you, but I decline." Ariana's voice was clearer now. "You have betrayed us, Your Majesty. I am, as my father has ever been—as Shianan Becknam has ever been—I am your servant. I swore, like the rest of the Circle, to serve the crown diligently. In exchange for commission to experiment and research, I dedicated my gift to the kingdom and its defense. But in turn, my lord the king has obligations and responsibilities as well. While I owe obedience and service, you owe respect and the effective use of your willing servants."

Soren regarded her with something too faint to be a smile. Shianan stared in mingled admiration and horror.

"You have failed to hold your sworn vassals in good regard, Your Majesty."

King Jerome was incredulous. "This is insupportable!"

"To the contrary, I think my case is well-supported." Ariana's voice flattened as she answered. "Thank you again, for your offer to find me an alternative husband, but I must decline an offer that is no gift, Your Majesty."

Queen Azalie returned, her eyes bright as she scanned the room for signs of what had occurred while she was with the Wakari ambassador. She came to stand beside Soren's seat.

Ariana did not seem to notice the queen's entrance, caught up in her rejection of the king's solution. "You disregard and abuse your most loyal servants, Your Majesty, and you have cheated me of my boon."

"So you both are against me?" The king's face had reddened dangerously. "Traitorous bitch."

"Am I a traitor for expecting of my lord what my lord expects of me?" Ariana stood straight and stared upward at the king, politely defiant. "I have learned today how foolish I have been. I will never again ask anything of my lord king, nor seek to win royal favor. I was naïve to think service would win royal regard—to think royal regard would mean anything at all."

Shianan wanted to scream, to shout and warn her—Ariana was destroying herself. She was losing her position, her career, her freedom, and all for what he had done, foolishly daring to aspire to her and more foolishly revealing his desire. He should never have spoken of his desire—or he should have married her immediately, never asking for permission. A marriage would be binding, even through the king's wrath. Shianan would have suffered for marrying without leave, but now they would suffer regardless.

No one spoke into the shocked silence, not even the queen or Soren. Shianan's throat closed. He had tried to tread carefully to preserve his friends and himself, and now they would be destroyed despite everything. He should have seized a brief happiness when he could.

Ariana looked from the king to Shianan, and he saw a twisted, pained longing in her eyes, flaring brightly before its inevitable death. Desperate conviction flooded him and he lunged forward, catching the guards off-balance. "Ariana!"

The guards stayed with him and grasped him more tightly, pulling him back. Ariana looked at him with wide, hopeful eyes, and suddenly her eyes lit with understanding.

Even slaves could wed.

"Ariana, marry me! Marry me here, now!"

She gasped.

Shianan lifted his leg and dropped his weight into the guard on his left, throwing him off-balance as he stomped hard into his knee. The guard's hold loosened and Shianan wheeled on the other one.

"Stop him!" Jerome snapped. "And seize her! Don't you dare—"

Shianan spun and struck another guard rushing from behind. "Ariana Hazelrig, I take you as my lawfully wedded wife!"

There was a rush of livery toward Ariana. "Don't!" ordered the king.

Everingham, Stowmarries, and Devinne fled to the rear of the room. Ariana gestured and the guards reeled from her. A ripple of power brushed over Shianan, shifting his hair as he whirled and punched another guard. Ariana turned toward Shianan, her eyes meeting his across the room. "Shianan—"

"Stop! Don't finish that!" The king himself lunged at her.

Ariana's eyes widened, and for a moment she didn't move. She could not strike the king—that was not what she had intended, she did not want to injure him...

Shianan threw aside a guard and leapt forward.

Soren reached across the long table, unable to intervene. Ariana stepped backward and raised her hands, an involuntary defense as the king plunged toward her—

There was a dull thud of flesh striking something immobile. The king fell against the invisible barrier, catching himself on his outstretched hands, and then stumbled as the barrier vanished.

Ariana gulped, staring at the straightening king. She took a quick breath. "Shianan Becknam, I claim you as my lawfully wedded husband."

King Jerome's face reddened. Behind Ariana, Soren did not move, leaning on the table as if he meant to vault it but couldn't. Queen Azalie stared in mute surprise.

A guard swung at Shianan, who sank back easily from the blow and then rocked in to strike wrist and throat, leaving the guard gasping as he stumbled back. Shianan reached for Ariana.

"Don't let them fast hands!" someone called from behind Shianan. Arms seized him about the torso. Someone else seized Ariana as she started toward him.

Shianan dove forward and stretched out his arm—*Ariana, I'm sorry, I never wanted it to be this way, but I will have been your husband, and I love you*—and he grasped for her, seeking the clasp that would legally, irrefutably wed them—

His fingers struck against something cold and immovable, a solid barrier where there had been air. Ariana's hand slapped hard against invisibility, an inch of glassy air between them, and she stared with shocked surprise. Then she curled her fingertips, as if she could claw through it, and Shianan beat his fist against the invisible wall in anguished fury.

And then more strong arms wrapped about him and hauled him backward. He struggled but they were many and had him securely this time, and he could not break free. Guards wrenched him to his knees and forced his head low, holding him immobile.

Two more clutched at Ariana. She thrashed. "Let me go! Take your hands off me!" There was an audible crack of power and the guards jerked away from Ariana, shaking their hands as if they'd been singed.

"Enough! Stop!" King Jerome's thunderous voice froze all movement. He stalked toward them, livid in his fury. "What did you think to accomplish? You are both subject to my will, and I will not allow a bastard to—what are you doing here?"

Shianan followed the king's startled gaze and saw Tamaryl standing a few paces inside the door. His gut twisted. Worse even than brutal punishment or forced exile was either witnessed by Pairvyn ni'Ai.

Ariana fairly blazed with wrath. "That shield was yours!"

Tamaryl bowed. "I beg your pardon, Your Majesty. I came to beg audience and could not but hear the tumult, and I entered to see if there was trouble and if I could be of assistance. If you will allow, I believe I have been. And I am delighted that I may be able to further serve you in this, if you will hear."

King, queen, prince, mage, courtiers, and bastard stared at the Ryuven. "What do you mean, my lord Tamaryl?" asked Jerome stiffly.

Tamaryl spread his hands as if describing the self-evident. "My lord cannot allow my lady mage and the commander to remain in Alham, given the commander's, er, position in the court. If they marry, it could only be an embarrassment, as none would believe it permitted or blessed by the king; as I understand, my lord has not often recognized a soldier's service with a gracious display of generosity, and so such a boon would be questioned by many. I, however, can offer to—"

The king's eyebrows rose. "I have often rewarded those who serve me well!"

Tamaryl dipped his head in apology. "Forgive me, Your Majesty; I am new to this court, and of course there is much that has not been recorded in your reign's history. Regardless, I might provide another option. They could be removed to my own land, relieving Your Majesty of the potential dilemma their unsanctioned marriage could bring."

Shianan's contorted stomach wrenched further. King Jerome's eyes shifted to him. "Exile in the Ryuven world?"

"Yes, Your Majesty. It would conceal any marriage effectively while allowing my lord to honor the kingdom's law. It would also be fit punishment for their audacity, exiled forever from their own world." He smiled benignly.

King Jerome nodded, considering. "Yes, I see."

Soren stared wide-eyed, shaking his head, while Queen Azalie's jaw had dropped in open surprise. Shianan wanted to shout protest, but his voice had frozen. With the Ryuven—forever! Even with Ariana, what torture would that be? Peace or no, for the Ryuven to find an old enemy trapped among them, powerless to defend himself or to escape... What would they do to Ariana and Shianan?

"More, your choice would be seen as an act of great civility and friendship," Tamaryl continued. "To share a celebrated military officer and a mage of the Great Circle with your once-enemy, and so soon—you will be lauded as a ruler of great faith and pacifism. A few will protest, of course, but they will be soon silenced when they see how gratefully the Ryuven accept your gifts. We seek to further trade between our peoples, and what better way than the exchange of information? There is much we could learn from—"

"My lord Tamaryl," King Jerome interrupted, his voice edged with strain, "I appreciate your concern and your—innovative solution. But we should not be too hasty to respond to this...unexpected event."

Shianan, unaccustomed to court intrigue, needed another moment to recognize the cause of the king's abrupt reluctance: in Shianan and Ariana, the Ryuven would have access to all the military and magical techniques of Chrenada.

Tamaryl raised an eyebrow. "My lord?"

King Jerome looked unhappy. Though capable of diplomatic negotiation, he was not of a mind presently to fence verbally with the Ryuven emissary. "My lord Tamaryl, surely you can appreciate that we must keep our Black Mage here in Alham. She has only just begun her career, and it would be a tragedy to curtail it."

"His lordship, then." Tamaryl's eyes seemed to flash. "We would be very glad to welcome the commander—the count, I mean, Bailaha—very glad." His voice took on an edge, almost eager.

Shianan caught his breath. They would force every military tactic from him, they would use him to train their young warriors, learning at leisure how to defeat human fighting styles, and then they would take their slow revenge. A veteran commander and instructor would be invaluable to the Ryuven. And Shianan had come nearer Ariana than Tamaryl ever had; jealousy might require bitter retribution. He could hear it all in Tamaryl's voice, see it in the gleam of his widening eyes.

But King Jerome had heard it too. He did not know all, but he guessed enough. And no matter his anger toward Shianan, he could not surrender military knowledge to the Ryuven. He took a slow breath, buying time to formulate an answer. "My lord Tamaryl," he began, "your offer of assistance is noted and indeed appreciated. It is most generous of you to extend your hand in these private, internal matters." He stepped nearer Shianan. "However, you misunderstand our situation. I have no desire to exile Bailaha, who has done us much good service, after all. I would not send him so far."

Shianan released an exhausted breath. He was relieved, though he didn't know why. He was not yet out of danger.

Tamaryl inclined his head. "Forgive me if I have suggested an inappropriate solution. I am still learning the ways of this kingdom. I apologize if I have offended. I will read over the annals of your reign again and look for how Your Majesty has traditionally rewarded honored servants of the realm, and perhaps it will help me to be of greater service." He bowed. "Excuse me, Your Majesties." The Ryuven left the room, wings high.

Ariana looked at the king, her face tense with strain.

King Jerome cleared his throat. "Bailaha," he said gruffly, "I will speak with you again."

Shianan hastily disguised his shudder as a shake to free himself of the guards. "Yes, Your Majesty."

Soren and Azalie were on their feet, but the king shut the door firmly before they could protest. Once again in the adjoining room, he turned to face Shianan. "He would have taken you to the Ryuven world."

Shianan suppressed another shudder. "Yes, my lord."

The king looked at him a moment. "Well? Aren't you glad?"

Shianan looked at him in surprise. "Glad?"

"I kept you from him! I risked offense to the Ryuven emissary by refusing!"

Shianan's anger flared. "I am to be grateful I wasn't delivered to the Ryuven? My lord, we both know it was your military you protected, not me." He sniffed. Blood ran from his nose and down his throat, though he hardly remembered being hit. "You did not want them to study our tactics." He had nothing to lose anymore; he would speak his mind.

King Jerome stared, and for just a moment Shianan thought he saw surprise. *Did he think I would not know?!*

But then the king looked away. "No," he said, and his voice had changed. "No, it was the thought of exiling our celebrated hero. It would not look right to the kingdom, or to other lands." He turned and crossed the room.

Shianan clenched his fists and remained where he was.

The king turned back. "Go to your quarters. Remain there. Speak to no one."

"My lord, I have duties—"

"Leave them! Go. Go now."

Shianan bowed stiffly and left the room. He glanced at the guards still standing about the council room, nursing broken noses or blackening eyes or bruised throats, daring them to challenge him. They didn't. The courtiers were against the wall, looking as if they would rather be anywhere else.

Ariana was leaning upon the table. He started toward her, and she turned anxiously to him.

Soren straightened. "Shianan—"

Shianan reached for Ariana, clutching her close, and kissed her, desperately, trying to memorize the feel and taste of her. She reeled at first in surprise and then kissed him hastily in return, holding him with the urgency of her frustration and the fighting. Shianan ended it long before he was ready, knowing he was at the very edge of his fraying control. He stepped back, swallowing hard, and bowed.

She looked at him, her eyes frightened. Shianan started down the room, toward the doors.

Soren tried again. "Shianan."

Shianan gave a short twitch of his head and kept moving, knowing he could not simply walk away from the prince-heir but trusting, needing Soren to understand he could not stop. He escaped the room and went directly down the corridor without hesitating.

He had to reach his quarters. He was confined there by the king's orders; he could not remain in the palace or anywhere else. He would be safe there, he would have the privacy to sob and beat his fists and shed the hot furious tears that half blinded him now—

A shape joined him as he left the palace. Shianan recognized the movement, though he could not distinguish the features. His throat had closed too much to allow him to speak safely, but Luca spoke first. "Master Shianan?"

Again Shianan shook his head tightly. He would risk nothing until they had reached the relative shelter of his quarters.

Luca fell behind him, trotting to follow Shianan's brisk pace, until he ran ahead to open the door for his master.

Shianan could hardly draw a steady breath. His voiced sounded choked to his ears. "Leave me."

"What happened?" Luca asked.

"Get out!" snapped Shianan. "King's runny oats, I want to be alone. Out."

Luca hesitated. "Shianan..."

Shianan shook his head, not daring his voice further. Luca looked unhappy but went to the door, closing it behind him.

Shianan slid the bolt, barring entrance to all. Then he leaned forward upon the door, allowing his brittle façade to crumble.

Whirling, he seized the inkwell from the desk and flung it hard, spraying a dark stain across the wall. The glass cylinder bounced across the floor, spattering inky gobbets, but it did not break. Shianan kicked it, infuriated—it should shatter!—and cursed aloud. He kicked the desk, but it did not yield. He whirled and began furiously to pace, clenching and unclenching his fists as tears burnt their way down his cheeks.

CHAPTER 41

Ariana stood alone in the middle of the council room, surrounded by staring eyes. Shianan had gone, silent and rigid and ignoring both prince and queen, but the king had not yet emerged.

Tamaryl's words of betrayal still echoed in Ariana's ears.

She had to escape. Ariana curtsied. "Your Majesty, Your Highness, with your permission, I will retire."

"One moment." The queen detained her with a raised hand. "You have acted boldly and decisively today," she observed, "just as you did on the field of Arakadamia."

Ariana nodded anxiously. She wanted out—out to have time and space to decipher what had happened here, out to follow Shianan. If they could only speak, could plan together some desperate course—

"I am glad you acted thus at Arakadamia," Queen Azalie continued, speaking too slowly for Ariana's preference. "I hope you do not have cause to regret your decision here this morning."

Ariana's fingers twitched in her skirt. "Your Majesty," she answered, her voice faltering, "no consequences could change my reasons for acting as I have done. We serve in good faith, both his lordship and myself."

"So you do," the prince agreed softly, looking unhappy.

The queen held Ariana's eyes. "You have stated that the king has violated your oaths and you no longer seek to earn royal favor. Is it your wish to disassociate yourself from the Great Circle and the court and all corresponding duties? Or would you—"

Ariana's throat spasmed and she spoke immediately, before she lost the ability, cutting off the queen in unthinkable hurry. "I have dreamed of the Circle my whole life, Your Majesty, and I love this kingdom and its people. I would gladly keep my position if—" She choked. "I am the Black Mage."

The queen sighed. "You may go," she granted reluctantly.

Ariana curtsied briefly and bolted from the council room. She was shaking, sick with excited anxiety and dizzy with what they had done. She had defied the king, she had tried to marry Shianan— Tamaryl had stopped them, blocked their marriage—Shianan was in danger, something was happening—

Shianan was nowhere to be seen. Why hadn't he waited for her? Where had he gone—or been taken? She started toward the Wheel and then checked herself abruptly. Perhaps she was no longer a Mage of the Great Circle. King's sweet oats, what had she done? What would come of those few moments?

She pulled her black robes close about her, tucking her head against the wind and the eyes of passersby.

Soren stared at the door through which Lady Ariana had gone, his side throbbing, his mouth agape but without words. What had happened? What had been done here?

His mother glanced at the courtiers, huddled like alarmed sheep against the wall. "You may take your leave," she said curtly, and Soren was relieved to see them bow and flee.

His father emerged from the side room, head hanging and face uncharacteristically defeated. For a moment Soren nearly felt sympathy for him, trying to do what he thought—but no, there was no justification for what he did.

Soren settled into his chair and crossed his arms over his torso, hiding his pain behind anger. "What did you say to him? What weren't we to hear?"

Jerome stiffened. "Ungrateful grasping whoreson."

"That's not how I heard of her," muttered Soren.

Azalie cast him a warning look. That was not for Soren to speak of, not ever.

Soren avoided her eyes. "He saved my life, Father. Who would be the ingrate if we denied his only request?"

Jerome huffed. "Come, see reason and practical caution. He seeks to marry not merely above his station, but a Mage of the Circle! What better position to seek further advancement? With the Circle and the military to support him, he could threaten even your own seat on the throne."

Soren shook his head. "Shianan hasn't an ambitious—"

"Shianan?" The king shook his head reprovingly. "You cannot afford such intimate friendship with—"

"With the man who swore his fealty to me unasked and risked his life to save mine?" Soren gestured in vague frustration. "What is it that turns you so against him, Father?" Against all caution, he pressed. "He's never acted on his birth. What is it you hold against him now?"

Soren played with fire, but Shianan's welfare depended upon it.

"He takes too much for granted!" snapped Jerome. "He takes it as his due that he is intact, that he is respected in the army, that he is a count and a member of the court. He did not even appreciate how I risked angering our Ryuven emissary for his sake by refusing his suggestion so frankly. He took that as his due. How can I see him as anything but ungrateful?"

Insight came to Soren. "You didn't want him to go to the Ryuven because you didn't want to see him harmed."

"Of course not! Shianan Becknam is an honored soldier and a hero of our army. Our treaty with the Ryuven is fresh and untried; I would not give him into their vengeful hands."

And while he might strike or kick his bastard in anger, he would not see him in the keeping of his longtime enemies. But his father would not admit aloud to concern for Shianan Becknam.

Soren glanced at his mother and nodded. "He is well regarded among the army; it would be unwise to exile him ignobly. They would find that poor reward for his service." And their own.

The king frowned. "I—I reward well those who serve me, don't you think?"

Ah, so the Ryuven's words had struck a tender point there.

Queen Azalie made a show of considering. "I haven't had cause to think of it. But I'm sure you had meant to reward these two, didn't you?"

"Of course," answered King Jerome quickly. "In another, more appropriate manner."

"And what manner was that?" Soren let bitterness color his tone. "While I meant to publicly favor Becknam at the ball, your choice was to drag him away for a beating."

King Jerome straightened abruptly, his expression darkening. "Soren..."

"You discredit yourself, Father, by striking a man who has dedicated his life to serving you—and you discredit me, by beating like a slave the man I meant to honor." He set his jaw, pretending indignation to cover the horror, revulsion, shock, humiliation that still rocked him. "It's *shameful*, Father."

The king huffed. "It's only that he angers me so. He is a capable man, talented in many ways, and it angers me to see him fail reasonable expectations."

Soren fought a brief, familiar defensive jealousy and seized on the disputed point. "He would never disappoint you if he could help it, Father. He and I are too alike."

If King Jerome caught the layered meaning of Soren's words, he gave no indication. He stared at the table without responding. He turned from Soren and glanced at the queen.

Soren looked at his mother, certain she would speak first.

He was wrong. The king sank into a chair, looking terribly weary. "Well? Get on with it."

Queen Azalie stood still. "What is there for me to say? It all seems terribly obvious as it is."

"You should not have argued with me before the courtiers. You made me look a fool."

"You should not have asked them to come and watch you make a fool of yourself."

"I should have never allowed that mage to speak."

"What did she say that was wrong?" Soren interrupted. "All that she said, all that of oaths and exchanges, what of that was untrue?"

His father looked at him. "You did not tell me Bailaha had sworn himself to you."

Soren was caught unprepared. "I—I did not want it to seem that I was acting before your will."

King Jerome rubbed at his forehead. "Why won't..." He sighed.

No one spoke for a long moment. At last, Queen Azalie turned to Soren. "Let us speak alone for a time."

A leaden feeling settling in his gut, Soren bowed.

"Soren." The king's voice was quiet. "About last night... I'm sorry. I'm sorry for—for carrying too far. I didn't—I owe you an apology."

Soren took a hasty breath. "If you owe me anything, Father, give me my half brother and my friend."

"Enough," snapped the queen. "Soren, go and make sweet love to the Wakari princess. Salvage what you can of that before the Wakari leave as Lord Adoniram threatened. But leave us."

Soren bowed again and fled.

Azalie regarded her royal husband, slumped in his chair. Jerome appeared just as he had when waiting for Soren's condition to change—undecided whether to grasp for slim hope or to steel himself for the worst.

He kept his eyes down, unwilling to face her. It never felt right to chastise him when he was like this. But his hurt turned quickly to self-pity, and leaving him to his own choices in this state had proved disastrous in the past.

He took a breath. "I didn't mean for it to be like this."

She held up a hand to forestall him. "You are an impressive king, as your nobles acknowledge you. But their admiration fails you, in that you are not often challenged. I will say to you plainly, my lord, what your scraping courtiers will not—sometimes the greater error is not in the error itself, but in failing to admit that error. Your best course lies not in pressing further, but in finding the least ignominious way of withdrawing your hand."

King Jerome glared at her. "Do you take her side as a woman?"

"I take no one's side, and I speak not as a woman but a queen. You undermine yourself with this madness. Your nobles and your mages must be able to trust you. I speak to your own good; what you have done threatens your rule."

"To the contrary, if I allow her to defy me, I am undermined. I am the king, and my word cannot be—"

"Your word cannot be ridiculous! And that is exactly what you demanded, the ridiculous. She asked to marry a man—a man it seems you knew wanted her as well—and you offered her a stranger. It was an absurd and fearful reaction, and the harder you press this, the more absurd and fearful you appear." She stopped and took a breath, softening. "Jerome—you have done many wonderful acts as king. Truly, though I might not agree with all, there is much you have done well. But no one thinks of those good decisions as they watch you treat this young woman irrationally and wonder what irrational thing you might demand next of them."

He broke his eyes from hers. "And what would you have me do? Let the bastard usurp the place of our sons?"

"Stop crediting him with the sins of his father."

The words had never been spoken, his self-accusation never aired. Jerome's wandering eye had changed the succession and cost the life of his brother, and then he had done it again. Azalie was beginning to believe it drove him more than she had guessed. He had not betrayed only her.

Jerome's throat worked visibly and he looked away. He said nothing.

She sighed. "Do you truly believe Shianan Becknam is trying to insinuate himself as a rival to the princes? I cannot see it. I can hardly have a conversation with him; it's like talking with a half-drowned kitten. What do you see to fear?"

"I held him apart because you hated him. I protected our sons, your sons, and—"

"Do not pretend this is my doing," snapped Azalie. "I will not deny I hated the very name of Shianan Becknam, but you never acted on that. You praised him to me, you brought him to Alham though it drove me to Kalifi, you gave him title and land against my desire. All you have done with him has been by your decision alone." She pointed toward the door. "Your own prince-heir's marriage contract was set aside while you dealt with Shianan Becknam—not because his case was urgent, but because it mattered to you. If you had attended to the Wakari delegation instead of the bastard, we would have a betrothal now."

He stared at her. "Do you think I am pleased by the bastard's—"

"I never said it pleased you, my lord. I said it mattered to you." She steadied her voice, but it had lost no fervor.

Jerome turned away. "You needn't worry. He said he would not—" He stopped, tried again. "I offered to acknowledge him, but he would not be my son."

"Sweet all, can you blame him? After what he has been these years? After what was done today?"

Then she realized the magnitude of that sentence, the confession it hid. Jerome had offered the acknowledgment he had kept back for years, had defied her own anger to offer it, and he had been rejected, and it had pierced deep.

But she had no comfort to offer when he reaped what he had so dedicatedly sowed. What could she say to change the years?

Azalie came around the table, close behind him, and placed a hand on his shoulder. Jerome reached one hand to cover hers, and they sat a long time without moving or speaking.

At last, he sighed. "What would you have me do?"

"Assure the Black Mage of your appreciation for her service and her place in the Great Circle. She is a heroine and a valuable ally, politically and practically. Apologize to her for suggesting another

258

marriage; she has those near who will instruct her how to accept it gracefully."

He waited a long moment and then nodded. "And—and the other?"

"Well, it's a bit late to drown him at birth." She withdrew her hand and moved to his side to face him. "I cannot tell you how to deal with him. You know your own mind. But you cannot continue as you have, alternately pushing him away and granting him honors. It's untenable for both of you. You must decide—it must be all, or nothing. Bring him in, or cut him away entirely."

Jerome looked at her, startled. "What do you mean?"

"Acknowledge him, without condition, if you mean to bring him to you. Or, if not, prune him cleanly. Look at him now—he hardly acknowledges the title you awarded him, much less uses it to advantage. By all reports he lives beneath his military rank as well. If you break away utterly, making him a simple soldier, it will affect little of his present life. He might even be glad to be relieved of some of your attentions."

Jerome looked ill. "I—I can't do that."

"No?"

He stared ahead, lips slightly parted but silent.

"Then I will do what you cannot. Leave him to me." Azalie moved to catch Jerome's eyes. "But you must reach out to Ariana Hazelrig."

There was a stiff pause, and then the king nodded heavily.

CHAPTER 42

Luca left the office as ordered and jumped as he saw the guards on either side of the door. Shianan was under house arrest, then. What had happened? The guards eyed Luca but made no motion toward him, and he bolted into the relative safety of the courtyard.

But only a few minutes of walking later, he huddled into a corner of a foot traffic alley between buildings, his cloak pulled about him. There were few other places to go; slaves were not welcome in most public houses, he had no coin, and he did not want to risk recognition as Shianan's servant in any case. Soldiers, merchants, slaves, and others passed occasionally, but no one spared time to wonder about the figure tucked out of the wind.

A dull lump of fear moldered in Luca's gut. If Shianan were arrested... Luca would be forfeit, the property of the crown. Marla and the others at Fhure would be lost as well, sold away or turned over to a new favorite.

Luca could swallow his scrap of pride and write again to his brothers. They had not answered after he had explained he'd lost his inheritance, a third of their house gone to some bloody-handed bandit, and that he was a slave again, sold again into Alham...but he wanted to believe they had been sincere in their protestations. And if they had ignored his letter, if they had cut him off again, he had nothing to lose in writing a second time. He had already been sold a slave in his own house; he had little pride to protect.

But they could never receive the letter quickly enough. Even if they answered, by the time anyone arrived from Ivat, he'd be long sold or sent away into other work.

Still... There was money in the office, enough to send a letter to Ivat. At least he could tell them to watch for him.

He sat still, hardly noting the people ignoring him, testing phrases in his head. *Our caravan was attacked and we fell into the hands of slavers. I bartered with my new Chrenadan masters to reach Alham...*

Would he be able to enter the office? He would have to pass the guards to get coin for a letter, or the spare certificate of sale to Mage Hazelrig. There was no freedom in Chrenada but by the master's death-will—if Shianan's will was even heeded after he died a traitor's death. With good luck, he could go to Mage Ewan Hazelrig, and to that end a sale receipt would be more reliable than a traitor's will. Luca did not want to risk the auction block again. He wondered briefly if it would be possible to bribe a soldier if the office were guarded.

One does not bribe the One who created all things...

"Holy One," Luca breathed.

"You say something?" grumbled a passerby.

Luca instinctively ducked, all his old terrors reawakened with Shianan's arrest. "No, my lord."

The man moved on, leaving Luca with a quick flash of relieved embarrassment. He had never thought himself particularly adherent to the faith; his father's betrayal and his horrific spiral through slavery had cemented that. Only desperation had driven him to petition for Shianan's safe return from battle. And Shianan had returned. But was that because of prayer, or would he have come home anyway? Luca dug his knuckles against his eyes.

But it would be warmer in the temple, and what could it hurt? He rose and, keeping well out of soldiers' way, made his way there. He chose an out-of-the-way prayer alcove and sank to the floor.

Words did not come easily. "I don't know if any lord should listen to a supplicant who comes only in time of need." He clenched his fingers. "Or, will any lord heed a slave, especially in Alham? How many slaves cry daily for mercy? Their masters and their masters' master ignore them altogether." He took an unsteady breath. "But—but if you will hear a slave's supplication..."

The words failed and died, and he shivered silently within his cloak.

No one came to the alcove, and so no one saw the huddled figure leaning sideways against the wall, knees to chest, his back to the alcove's opening and his eyes gazing into the blank end where prayers went. He stayed for two hours, making prayers for desires he could not speak, fearing that what he could not articulate could not be granted.

Soren stood in the corridor three full minutes, steeling himself. Every passing moment made the offense worse, and an apology by even a councilor or a duke could not carry the weight of a royal apology. Best to do this directly, and himself.

At last he rounded the corner and knocked at the door to Princess Valetta's guest wing. A voice called within, and a moment later a young manservant opened. "Look, I already told you—oh!" He gulped and closed the door.

Soren stared at the closed door, bewildered. As the prince-heir, he was not accustomed to having doors shut in his face. Nor was a princess of Wakari, he considered, accustomed to her hosts departing before she could be formally presented, or a prince putting her off to discuss the affairs of a bastard.

The Wakari Coast was a land of integrity and honor, and they would be treated with the same. This was bone-gratingly shameful to his family, and there was no way to beg forgiveness without making his father look like a fool, making it still more difficult to close negotiations to bring the princess into his family—but he had to try. If he could get in. Had Princess Valetta been so offended that she'd ordered her servants to refuse him admittance? But even then, they would deny him in a more politic manner, surely?

As these thoughts ran wildly through his mind, there was a sharp exchange of voices within and then the door opened again. "My lord," a woman began, bending low, "I humbly apologize for the unspeakable rudeness shown you. Please come inside, of course."

Soren nodded briefly and entered a sitting room, where two servants guided him to a comfortable chair, anxiously offering wine, fruit, pastries. He declined all. He saw one of them make a furious gesture, and the youth who'd answered the door slunk out of sight.

"Her Highness will join you in a moment," assured the woman. "Are you sure there's nothing I can offer you, my lord?"

"No, thank you."

They retreated into the background like good servants. A moment later, a door opened and the princess entered.

Soren started to his feet, newly unsettled. She gave him a smile, but it seemed brittle. "Good day, my lord. We are honored by your visit. I can send for my lord Adoniram, if you like?"

Oh, 'soats, she was insulted. Of course she was insulted. "Oh, no, my lady, Your Highness, please—may we sit? I wanted to speak..."

One corner of her mouth quirked. "I should hope that is what you wanted, my lord." She gestured to his chair as she took a seat.

Soren hesitated. Had she made a jest? If so, what did it mean—that she was teasing him in their arranged courtship? That he should never hope for more?

The corner of her mouth moved again. "Please, my lord, be seated."

Soren did, feeling foolish.

He would have known her from her miniature, inexact though it was. The court painter had known his duty, giving her more cheekbone and greater color. In life, Valetta was not classically beautiful, but she had striking features and thick, black hair. The hair was mostly loose now, pinned back from her forehead and then falling in heavy waves about her shoulders. "I'm told you were greeted most inappropriately at our door," she said. "I apologize sincerely for that. It's hardly an excuse, but I expect no one thought the prince-heir would come alone and without announcement."

Another misstep. He had hoped it would be seen as a more personal gesture, but... "Yes, well, I'm sorry for coming so abruptly. I wanted to speak with you. We didn't have—opportunity... I came to apologize. Not diplomatically or officially, but—for myself. This has not been an easy time for our court, but I regret that you should have felt the effects of that."

She raised an eyebrow. "Are you asking us to stay?"

He smiled sadly. "I am not so naïve as to think a private apology can sway politics between nations, my lady. But it was important to me that you yourself know there was no offense meant."

"I myself? I—oh, no, I should think not." She smiled nervously, tipped her head, and looked at him. "I don't see you intending to offend, at least not by that manner."

Soren's gut twisted. "I had meant to welcome you, of course, and I even meant to try to dance, after a fashion... Something came up, something of immediate concern, and I wish I could—"

Valetta gave him a forbearing smile. "That is no secret." She gestured. "We've had our fill of whispering. Bailaha is equally known as a military hero and a royal bastard, though neither acknowledged nor accepted. The court admires and disdains him."

Soren glanced at her, interested. "Admires and disdains?"

"You know, certainly—they speak well of his accomplishments but are quick to add they have no particular attachment to the man himself. Wary politics."

Soren nodded. "I had hoped to change that somewhat last night, introducing him as the man who saved me. He did, of course. I owe him my life and more."

"He is by all accounts a man devoted to his duty."

Soren looked across the room. "He is more than he appears, and certainly more than is said of him. But that is beside the point. I should never have left you waiting."

"We were not left to our own amusements; most of the court was very welcoming."

"Most?"

She smiled uncomfortably. "I'm sorry. No one was rude, of course, nor anything but friendly."

Was she subtly chastising him for his departure? "Again, I'm sorry. When I left, it was not in the belief that I wouldn't return."

"Oh, no, Your Highness, I wasn't speaking of you. I'm sorry. It was—just between ourselves, there was a duke whose welcome seemed, perhaps, a bit strained."

Soren felt his mouth shift into a bitter smile. "Devinne."

"Yes, I think that was the name. His wife and daughter smiled and offered their hands, but they seemed somewhat cool." She sighed. "I would not have thought much on it, except it was so distinctly a family trait. I wondered if they had some connection to the Wakari Coast that had served them ill, or if I had somehow distantly offended them."

"Not in any fashion you could have avoided." Soren shook his head. "It was their assumption that the daughter, Lady Bethia Farlyle, would be my bride."

"Oh, my." Valetta drew her eyebrows together. "I'm afraid there's not much to be done to soothe that, is there?"

"I'm afraid not. But once more between ourselves, I am not disappointed."

"No?" Her expression darkened. "I am gratified to hear Wakari is not a disappointment."

Soren inwardly kicked himself. "That is not what I meant. Please... It has been a trying morning upon a trying night. Please forgive my poor manner of expression."

The door from the corridor opened and a woman with dark chestnut hair entered distractedly, with a maid trailing. "Calissa, time is short and—who's this?" She caught her breath. "Your Highness! I—I—Calissa!"

Soren struggled to his feet and turned back to the first dark-haired girl, who looked from him to the newly arrived princess.

She flushed. "What should I have done, turn him away?" She turned to Soren. "I am Calissa, of course. This is my sister, Her Highness Princess Valetta."

Soren felt ill. "But—I'd thought..." His side ached with the sudden movement and the fresh twisting of his stomach.

Calissa nodded regretfully. "I'm so sorry—I hadn't meant to deceive you, but at first I didn't realize you thought I was my sister. By then, I thought it simpler not to embarrass either of us, especially as we'll be leaving shortly. I—I meant the best."

Soren gave a single nod, not quite sure of his reaction.

She hesitated and took a breath. "Though, if I politely accept your apology, it might mean we could stay a bit longer, and I'd like that."

Princess Valetta was staring. "Calissa, what have you done?"

"I'm sorry! I didn't mean any harm. But, Your Highness, I like Alham. I like the city, I have made friends here, and I would like to know more of—Alham."

Valetta looked back to Soren. "Your Highness, I do apologize for my sister's—"

"No, no, the mistake was mine," Soren said hurriedly. "We had not been introduced, after all, and I had only a miniature..."

"It is a simple mistake," Calissa offered. "Valetta and I are rather alike, while I knew you immediately. It wasn't fair."

Valetta chewed at her lip. "It may be late to ask, my lord, but why have you come?"

"I..." Soren wasn't sure how to admit he had apologized to the wrong princess.

"He had a very pretty speech," Calissa put in, "and I wish you'd been here to hear it."

Valetta looked distressed. "I'm afraid I cannot stay to hear pretty speeches at the moment. We are packing for departure, and—I no longer have official leave to discourse with you, my lord. I am sorry. I thank you for your visit, Your Highness, but my sister and I must prepare—"

"I'll keep my lord company," Calissa said lightly. "We may not be in negotiations, but neither would we be inhospitable."

Valetta hesitated, caught between etiquette and political directive, and then nodded at her sister. "Please do," she said awkwardly. "And, my lord..."

Soren was sympathetic to her position. "We are bound by greater forces," he said quickly. "It was good to meet you even so briefly, Your Highness. I am sorry it was not in better circumstance." He gave her the best bow he could manage, she curtsied, and then with a final glance at Calissa, she retreated.

Princess Calissa gave him a concerned look. "Please, my lord, be seated. I can see your injury troubles you."

"It is not so bad as that," Soren lied, bracing himself against the chair's arm and lowering himself again.

She smiled at him, and for the first time he saw the warmth within it. "I hope so." She turned her head. "And I hope your next visit will be met in a more gracious manner. I haven't heard Abele's explanation—that's the boy at the door—but Ginevra reported he was intolerably rude. That's why I rushed out so."

Soren nodded. "He did gawk and then close the door in my face." He considered. "He must have thought I was someone else. He seemed to expect to continue an argument when he first opened."

Calissa shook her head. "Unacceptable, and worse to a prince-heir with whom we are in, if I may be blunt, dubious negotiations. His careless discourtesy might have cost a great deal." She looked at Soren. "I must offer reparation. How would you have him chastised?"

Soren's chest tightened. Was this a test? A Wakari custom? How should he respond? "I?"

"Yes, my lord. What would you have done with him?"

"He is young, your servant," he mused aloud, giving himself time. "Very young, it seemed. But if he would be an older servant, he must mind his ways."

Shianan Becknam had observed favorably how Soren dealt with his servants. But a prince had a certain position and could not surrender his dignity so readily to a young foreign slave. Was this a test of his nature? Would Calissa see a benevolent prince, or a weakling who could not defend his standing? Too much rode on this nonsensical and non-political exchange. How would his response affect the Wakari ambassadors' opinions, when they heard of it?

How would he react if Ethan made such an error? But he could not imagine Ethan ever making so gross a mistake.

Calissa was watching him, waiting. He took a slow breath. "I do not think he will answer the door in haste again," he ventured. "At the least, he'll be sure of the next guest before speaking. There was no harm done but to my own pride, and that's suffered enough of late so that one more prick can hardly matter. Scold him if you think it necessary, but please no more on my account."

Calissa raised an eyebrow. "I had heard Chrenada was more strict, what with the rebellions and such."

"In some ways, yes. But he will not make the mistake again, whether he's punished or no. Retribution is hardly instruction."

"So my lord needs no sop for his wounded pride?"

Soren looked at her worriedly, but Calissa was smiling. He gave her an embarrassed shrug. "My lady, after the entire court saw how I could barely stagger down steps, this is hardly worth noting."

"There are many in whom the greater embarrassment would have prompted a susceptibility to retaliation for the lesser." Calissa gave him an approving look.

'Soats, it had been a sort of test, and it seemed he had passed. Soren took a relieved breath. "I can't speak for another," he answered. He rubbed his slick palms over his legs.

There was a knock at an inner door, and a page stepped inside. "Your Highness, my lord Adoniram calls for you."

Calissa cast an apologetic look at Soren, who rubbed his palms against his legs once more and spoke. "I will take my leave, Your Highness, if I may. I have fallen somewhat behind in my duties of late and have much ground to recover." He gave her a wan smile. "I'm sorry I won't be able to see you again."

She nodded. "The wheels of state will grind."

He rose, bowed awkwardly, hoped his wince was not visible, and made his way uncertainly to the door. A servant appeared from nowhere to hold it for him, and he escaped into the carpeted corridor.

Princess Calissa... She was the third-born daughter, if he recalled correctly. Maybe the fourth. He'd known Valetta traveled with a sister among her entourage, but he had little reason to think more on it; his proposed bride had been ample to occupy him.

He made his slow way to his own rooms, taking his time now. Ethan would have something to dull the pain. King's oats, he wished this would heal more quickly.

But that was poor gratitude from a man who should have been dead, and he checked his complaint.

It was a pity Princess Calissa was so late born, and so less likely to make a primary political alliance. She would not be content to sit aside while the council argued politics and taxes. She would be demanding answers to her own political queries, Soren predicted, and defending her own suggestions. She would be a worthy opponent, or a valuable ally.

It would be good to form a friendship with her before she married into influence. She was only a third-born daughter, or fourth, but wherever she landed might become a seat of power after all.

He reached his room and sank gratefully into a supportive chair. He closed his eyes and wondered if the faint taste of bile from his throat came from his surprised lurch at the sight of the real Princess Valetta or from the disaster of last night and this morning. He wondered what his father had said to Shianan that had driven him to rush out without acknowledging Soren or the queen. He wondered if there was anything he could do to blunt his father's wrath when it turned to Shianan.

"My lord?"

"Oh, Ethan, thank the Holy One. Can you bring me something to make all this go away?"

Ethan returned a guarded look. "I'll bring you medicine and something to soothe the pain, my lord."

It would have to do. Anything to make him forget now would only make the situation worse later.

Princess Calissa was less beautiful than her sister, truth be told. But her dark hair was quite memorable...

Soren swallowed and pushed the thought away before it could grow. There was no alliance between their nations, and nothing at all between Soren and Calissa herself—nor likely to be, given the debacle of the past two days.

He would like to introduce Princess Calissa and Shianan, he realized. Once past their initial polite reserve, they would together offer good counsel and considered opinions, and they might even become good friends in the end. It would be advantageous to bring them together.

He wished he could have that chance.

CHAPTER 43

Shianan sighed and looked at the wall across from him. He had exhausted his fury, and now he had nothing. He could not summon the strength to even straighten in the chair he'd flung himself lopsided into.

It was the late night, he told himself. He had not slept much after the disastrous meeting, and the morning had taken what strength he had.

The time for the day's drills and lessons was approaching. But he was not to leave his quarters, and so the soldiers would not have him for sparring today, and if he were shortly to be exiled or otherwise removed, there was little reason to force his distracted mind to his reports. He faced a long day to himself, and nothing to fill it.

He wished he hadn't sent Luca away, with no way to recall him. He had wanted to be alone, but now he feared the silent hours looming before him.

What would the king do with them? Would Ariana be forced to surrender her position in the Circle? Would Shianan be dispatched to Soek, or Heege—or the Ryuven world?

He wanted to speak with Luca. Or Ariana. Or Soren. Even though the prince could not help him—even the prince-heir could not overturn the king's decision—it would be good to talk with someone. Shianan had gone too many years keeping his own counsel, and it surprised him to discover how he longed for the company of others now.

If he were to be exiled, he mused, he would rather go to Soek. He would be known as the bastard in Soek, of course, but there would be some who would respect his military reputation, while the Ryuven world would be pure nightmare. In Heege he would find battle to distract him, but he was disturbed to realize that he worried faintly for his safety. He wanted to return to Alham, to Ariana.

And the king had offered to acknowledge him, if he went to Soek. That was before, of course, but... Shianan clenched his fists. After a lifetime of disdain, he was offered at once a father and a proper name, and yet only in exchange for surrendering the sole other desire he'd ever permitted himself.

And he wanted Ariana. King's sweet oats, he wanted Ariana, right now, just to speak with her, even. If only she were here in his office, able just to put her hand on his arm and tell him that, somehow, it would be all right... If he could have just this day with her, just one day to be husband to her—to make desperate love to her in the short time left to him...

He could not sit here and brood, not for the hours awaiting him. He rose and went into his sleeping quarters, and he began to shove furniture against the walls, clearing a wider space in the center of the room. He would not lead the troops in their drills this afternoon, but he would train himself. It would occupy him for a time, at least.

A murmur of voices sounded at the front door of the house, and Ariana's heart leapt into her throat. She tensed and rose to answer it, but it was her father and Mage Parma who entered.

"Oh, thank the Holy One," she breathed. "Father."

He held out his arms and met her halfway, embracing her to him. "Oh, my girl. You've had a busy morning."

She clung to him, squeezing her eyes closed. "Oh, Father, it was awful. I'm so sorry."

"Easy, easy." He eased away from her. "That was a bold move."

"So the queen said. But—the king was unreasonable, he said he would marry me to a stranger he would choose for the benefit of the Circle, to breed more mages I suppose, and then Shianan called to me and I just—I just acted."

Mage Parma came and gave Ariana another fierce hug. "And the two of you disabled most of a squad of royal guards as you swore your oaths. At the least, it will be a splendid story."

"At least," Ariana agreed, trying to smile.

"And you know he loves you enough to risk himself and try once more," Mage Parma added. "If you wondered."

"We knew that," her father said gently.

The Silver Mage squeezed her shoulder. "You've broken a lot of rules and noses, but it's not finished yet. You have forced the king's hand with this attempted marriage, though, and I cannot say how this will end. He will want to spare you, I believe, due to your position— but it will be hard for Bailaha."

"Isn't there anything? Will he listen to you, maybe? Can I do something more?"

Her father shook his head. "The king will not hear me on this matter. I am the White Mage, not a councilor, and your father beside. He will want other voices than mine."

The kitchen door opened, and the boy Tam entered with a tray of cups and a teapot. Ariana went rigid. "Get out," she snarled.

Tam froze. "My lady..."

"Get out!" Ariana's vision blurred as she carved power from the air. "Get—"

"Ariana!" Elysia Parma snatched the waxing energy from her hand with a technique Ariana had never seen. "Control yourself! He's a boy, and no part of this." She waved sharply at Tam. "Leave the tea and go."

Ariana clenched her fists and glared at Tam. She was trembling again, as she had when she'd first hidden herself away at home, and she hated it—she was angry, so angry, and sick with fear at what might come and—

"Come this way," her father said firmly, guiding her to a stuffed chair. "Sit with us, and let's think of what may be done." He nodded to Tam, hesitating and silent near the door. "The kitchen is built for fire, separated by stone walls. You'll be safe enough there. Go on."

Tam did not smile as he placed the tray on a table and retreated to the kitchen. Ariana let herself be directed by her father, hampered while Mage Parma was present. There were still secrets to protect, and she knew she was dangerously near blind reactions. It could do no harm to sit and reason for a while, let her emotions cool, purge the ferocity that had come upon her in the council room.

She trusted them. If there were a way to recover, to come through this, then her father and Elysia Parma would find it.

Tam sat in the White Mage's kitchen, clenching and unclenching his boyish fingers. What had he done?

But Ariana had made her choice. She had chosen the commander, and he could not pretend otherwise. He even agreed. He knew his infatuation with her had been a product of his exile—but that made it no easier to see her turn to the bastard who hated his people.

Ariana...

The kitchen door opened, and he started to his feet, conditioned in this shape by long years of posing as a slave. Ariana entered—less furious than he had last seen her, but still with a dangerous set to her mouth. He remained standing. "My lady."

"Don't you dare *my lady* me," she snarled, leveling a finger at him. "And don't take an innocent child's face, either. Not after what you did."

His heart twisted in his chest. "I only did—"

"That was your shield this morning. We would be wed if not for you."

"Or dead!" he returned. "Do you think King Jerome would let you defy him so in his own court?" He took the offensive. "What were you thinking, trying to fast hands with the bastard in the king's own council room? Were you trying to throw away all you've worked for?"

Ariana was momentarily checked. "I hadn't planned—"

"And so you blindly followed Becknam, without thinking whether it was the right action?"

She was flustered now. "It was impulsive, but that wasn't..."

"You acted in desperation." He made his voice a sneer. "You'd have married anyone in that moment, I suppose, caught up in your defiance?" *Would you have come to me?*

Her face hardened again. "I wanted Shianan Becknam."

The words cut him, and he turned away, ashamed and embarrassed. Despite his bold words, he was not certain he had thrown that barrier to save them from the king's retribution. It had been purely instinctive, and he had not thought whether it was to protect Ariana from a politically foolish action or to keep Bailaha from her. But he could never admit that, and certainly never to Ariana.

And that, he realized suddenly, was why they would not be together in the way he wanted.

He slipped off the cuffs he and Ewan had made together—it was too difficult to hold such a different form for a long while—and released the shape of Tam to metamorphose into his natural body. Perhaps he would betray himself less in his own body, and perhaps he would feel less ashamed if he did not have to look up to meet her eyes. Perhaps he needed to be the Pairvyn again, a warrior Ryuven instead of the boy she had fondly regarded as family.

He took a breath as he turned back to her. "I tried to help you."

She crossed her arms, all disdain and skepticism. "Is that why you suggested exile? For both of us?"

He seized on this. "That was to your advantage! Did you not see it?"

She gestured angrily. "You wanted to keep me in your world forever! And you would have given Shianan over to—"

"And was it done? Stop and think!" Now he was in earnest. "Yes, I made it seem as if we wanted you ourselves. But you saw the king refuse. There was no better way to check his rage than to let him see another threat."

She regarded him dubiously, but she was no longer shouting. "Even Shianan?"

His wings clapped in frustration. "By the Essence—even if King Jerome hates him thoroughly, he wouldn't send him to the Ryuven. The man is a military hero as well as the prince's savior and friend, and he can't be disposed of during such a tentative time. How would the people, still skeptical of the Ryuven appearing in their markets, like to hear that their champion has been given over as a punishment to the very monsters they're told to welcome and trade with? And Shianan has all the knowledge of the Chrenadan military, which must be protected. The king cannot send him into the hands of his enemies."

Ariana gave him a narrow look. "Oniwe'aru did as much with you."

"That was hardly the same," he retorted, but his eyes fell from hers. He took a breath. "Believe me, everything I said regarding exile was to keep you safe. Both of you."

She crossed her arms again, but now it appeared defensive. "He wanted... I couldn't believe it was happening. I never imagined..."

Tamaryl didn't respond.

She rubbed at her arms as if cold. "I'm sorry," she blurted. "If you were only trying to help us—I should have known you wouldn't do anything so..." She tried to catch his eyes. "I'm sorry."

He did not answer. After a long moment, Ariana turned and left the kitchen without speaking.

Tamaryl watched until she disappeared down the short corridor, and then he wrenched the heavy door shut. Savagely he punched the stone wall, and again. Skin split and his light Ryuven bones cracked and fragmented, and he gave a cry of pain and frustration.

He threw himself onto a chair, catching a wing, and cradled his injured hand. That had been foolish and childish, he thought regretfully. Now he would need a day or two to heal, as he was still recovering his power.

It should be enough, he told himself. The fighting had ended, the nascent trade was spreading, and Ariana was safe. It should be enough.

CHAPTER 44

Shianan spun and struck through the air, his fist knocking back an imaginary Ryuven. It was easier to visualize his opponents these days, as most of them resembled Tamaryl, Pairvyn ni'Ai.

Tamaryl had danced with Ariana at the ball, while Shianan had been forced to watch from the dais. Shianan would not have been able to claim Ariana for long, even had he moved freely on the floor, but that did not make it easier to watch the Ryuven hold her, move with her, whisper to her. Shianan remembered too clearly Ariana shielding that same Ryuven, risking her position and life to shelter him just as Shianan had risked himself for her.

And Tamaryl had suggested to the king that Shianan and Ariana be exiled. Common ground, indeed! Shianan punched empty space. That was all but an open declaration of hostility. Once in the Ryuven world, Tamaryl would have Ariana and the Ryuven warriors would have Shianan. The idea had caught the king's fancy, for a moment at least.

Shianan paused, breathing hard after his exertion. If the Ryuven hadn't betrayed his eagerness to have a military commander, King Jerome might have let him go. *An act of great civility and friendship, indeed...* It was wholly a way for King Jerome to dispose of the inconvenient bastard while throwing a bone to their tentative allies. Tamaryl's mistake had been to Shianan's favor, turning the king from initial approval of the exile to wary protectiveness of his soldier.

But...oh.

A leaden feeling eased into Shianan's stomach. It was unlike Tamaryl to make such a slip. Shianan was an honest man, saying what he meant, but Tamaryl was a noble and a Ryuven who had lived for years as a human slave, successfully concealing his true identity; a glaring mistake would not slide out so carelessly. More, he had been a high noble in the Ryuven court before he became a human boy, and like any courtier he would have learned the art of guarding his motives and pitching his recommendation in the best possible light. It was hard to believe he would have entered unbidden into the king's private audience and accidentally betrayed his eagerness to have Shianan

Becknam given into his keeping. He had, in fact, manipulated the king into keeping Shianan close.

Why?

Shianan's head ached. He could not make sense of anything now. He was exhausted from trying again and again to consider their situation and falling into hopeless misery each time. There was nothing to do but wait, and waiting grated and tore at him. It had been the same after stealing the Shard, when he'd almost longed for the end to come quickly, sparing him the heinous waiting.

The bolts of the outer door moved, startling him. Someone had a key. Shianan felt ugly swollen anger and was unexpectedly glad of a target. If he was under house arrest, he should at least have the luxury of privacy during his imprisonment. He turned, prepared to snap at whoever entered.

The door opened and admitted King Jerome.

Shianan's anger dissipated abruptly, leaving him weak and alarmed. The king? Why here? He had no reason to come to Shianan's humble office. Even as a prisoner, Shianan was at the king's command, to answer when called. Why had he come?

King Jerome passed through the office and looked about the sleeping room, impassively curious. "These are your quarters?"

With a sense of panic, Shianan reviewed his disordered quarters—chest and chair pushed aside to make room for his exercise, his bed rumpled, a few items scattered loosely about... He fought an irrational urge to rush about snatching up objects in a mad attempt to straighten the room.

The king looked back at Shianan. "I suppose you did not expect to see me here." He glanced around the room again. "That chair...?"

Shianan jumped and drew the chair from the wall, facing it toward the king. "I'm sorry, but I did not expect Your Majesty, you see." His voice was hoarse in his ears.

"I can see." King Jerome lowered himself into the wooden chair and frowned. "I want to speak with you. I have asked the guards to ensure we will not be disturbed."

Shianan had not known there were guards at the door, but he was not surprised. He wondered if Luca had tried to return and been rebuffed. He wondered again why the king had come privately.

The king was looking at him. So much hinged on what might happen here, and Shianan had no idea what was happening. He bent his head. "I am your obedient servant."

King Jerome sighed. "I know." He flexed his fingers on the chair's arm. "Most of my courtiers say similar things, but with you I know it is true. If I ordered you to throw yourself upon a Heegeish sword or leap off a cliff, you'd do it, wouldn't you?" He sighed, not expecting an answer. "I have very few who offer that kind of obedience."

Shianan realized he was holding his breath. He tried to swallow. "Your Majesty, I—"

"Quiet, Bailaha. I have something to say to you."

But instead of continuing, the king hesitated. His fingers drummed on the arm of the chair.

Shianan waited.

"I had wanted..." The king's voice was quiet, softer than Shianan had ever heard it. He held his breath again, afraid he would miss a word. The king shifted. "I'd wanted..."

Shianan watched anxiously, but the king only looked across the room. He saw the king's throat work as he swallowed. The room seemed to lack air.

Jerome sighed. "I'm sorry it could not have been different," he said finally, heavily.

Shianan felt suspended, as if he had missed his footing. "Your Majesty..."

"I've wanted to make it...different. I've wanted... That doesn't matter now. You don't need a marriage to gain status—Becknam." He seemed to trip over Shianan's name. "I should have done more, I should not have... But that is done." He sighed. "I thought too much of—I saw only what..." Jerome hesitated. "A king does not apologize often."

To the contrary, the prince must be the first to apologize. He is held to a higher standard. Soren's words flashed through Shianan's mind. But he could not say that to the king, and he did not know what he could say, so he said only, "My lord."

"Kneel, Bailaha. Becknam."

Shianan did, his stomach clenching.

Jerome rose and stood before Shianan. Shianan stared at the golden buckles on the king's shoes, wondering inanely if they were solid gold or merely plated. How could his mind wander at such a time?

A moment passed. King Jerome had not yet spoken, and Shianan gathered his courage. "Your Majesty, I ask one thing of you."

The king was visibly startled. It was not Shianan's place to speak from such a position, and the bastard had not often dared requests. "You?"

Shianan wanted so much, but one thing was more urgent than all. "My lord, please forgive the Lady Ariana Hazelrig."

"Forgive her? That is what you ask? That is all you ask?"

"She did not mean to defy you. She did not know what had passed between Your Majesty and myself." Shianan stumbled, fighting fear for himself and terrible desperate fear for Ariana. "My lord, I beg you—"

"Don't speak!" snapped the king, turning suddenly away. "Don't tell me what you—I don't wish to hear it!"

Shianan's tentative effort collapsed beneath this incongruous order, and he fell silent. He might have pressed, but he was not sure whether the bastard's pleading for Ariana would benefit or harm her. He bit at his lip, tasting blood, and waited.

"She said she would do what I cannot."

The words were almost too quiet to hear, and Shianan could not guess their meaning. What had Ariana said to the king?

King Jerome growled. "I need you out of Alham. Soon, before the queen—soon." He turned and paced narrowly. "You shall escort the Princess Valetta safely home. Her leaving is your doing; her councilors could not be mollified, once you had disrupted this alliance—an alliance we sorely needed. See her safely home, and be sure you lick every toe of every boot in her party. I am half tempted to chain you to their wagons myself."

The betrothal, lost... Shianan's stomach fell. It wasn't his fault, not really, but they had counted on an alliance with the Wakari Coast. All eyes would be on his misdeed.

But...the Wakari Coast? Once there, would he find himself ordered to remain, in exile? At least, he thought bleakly, it would be possible to free Luca there.

After a moment the king turned back, and Shianan heard him sigh. Then King Jerome's hand fell on his shoulder, and he twitched. But the king's words were soft. "I am sorry. Serve me well, as you have done." He tapped Shianan's shoulder—the stiff, awkward touch of a man unaccustomed to demonstrating affection.

Shianan's vision blurred. He pressed a fist against his forehead, grinding knuckles against his skull. "My lord," he began hoarsely, but he did not know what he wanted to say beyond that.

The king froze. "What?"

"My lord, I..." Shianan swallowed thickly. There was so much, and so little that could be said. "Your Majesty, I am glad to serve without recognition. I only ask that..."

The king sighed. "The mage, again?"

No, breathed Shianan, *not this time*. But King Jerome could not have heard him.

The king sighed again, more deeply. "Mage Hazelrig will not be removed from the Circle by my doing," he pronounced heavily. "If she wishes to keep her place, she will."

Relief drained Shianan. This was, he knew, the very best he could hope after today's debacle—restoration for Ariana and potential exile for himself. At least Ariana would be safe, in her person and in her position. "Thank you, my lord. Thank you. And I will go to the Wakari Coast, where I will be no burden to—"

"Shut up," Jerome snapped.

Shianan did, biting hard at the inner corner of his lip.

Jerome seemed to hesitate, as if wanting to speak further, and then turned abruptly away. "Be careful," he said gruffly. "Stay out of the queen's way." He stood a moment, somehow less fearsome, and then he went to the door.

A cold blast of air blew through the rooms as the king exited. Shianan slid slowly to one side, catching himself on an arm as he sprawled. He rested an elbow on his upright knee and blinked against swollen pain in his throat.

Stay out of the queen's way. He had thought the queen warming to him, looking improbably favorably upon him since the prince's recovery. But the king's final statement had been a warning. Was Queen Azalie regretting her gracious overture? Had Shianan's actions that morning infuriated her anew? Was it the loss of the Wakari alliance for her son?

There was a frantic scrabble at the outer door and then Luca pushed into the office. "Shianan!" he called, his voice tight with anxiety. He swung into the room, eyes wide. "Are you all right?"

He was afraid. "I'm fine," Shianan said quickly. He brushed his hand across his eyes.

"Who was that?"

"Couldn't you tell?"

"He was hooded," Luca answered curtly. "There were guards—when I first left and when he was here. I thought he might have been—that you had—why are you on the floor? Are you all right?"

"I'm all right, Luca," Shianan answered gently. "I'm sorry to have worried you." He got to his feet. "They wouldn't execute me in my own room, you know. There would be a quiet trial and a clean beheading."

Luca's expression was stern. "What's happened?"

"That was the king. He came himself to see me."

Luca gulped. "And are you..."

Shianan shook his head. "I'm fine, Luca, really. He wasn't... It wasn't like that." He took a deep breath, feeling oddly detached. "This morning he offered to legitimize me. Adopt me."

Luca's eyes widened. "By what condition?"

How telling that it was Luca's first question. "By no condition, except effective banishment to Soek. But I... I declined." Shianan sighed. "I don't know what I was thinking, except that I didn't want to be a son in Soek when I could be nothing here. I am not willing to trade what I do have for legitimacy in a foreign court."

Luca nodded slowly. "I understand."

That crumb of validation, from a slave rejected by his own father, was surprisingly welcome.

"But," Shianan continued with a determined tone of presenting good news, "we are going away for a time." He took a breath. "It's the Wakari Coast, so you'll feel at home."

"What?"

"I'm to escort the Princess Valetta home. There I'll write your manumission, and at least some good will come of all this." He tried to smile at Luca's conflicted expression. "Go ahead and be glad of it. I'd rather one of us were happy today." Shianan took a breath. "Do you know where Lady Ariana is?"

"No."

"Then I..." Shianan trailed off uncertainly. The king had indicated Ariana might recover from this morning's debacle, but if Shianan were in disfavor, the best he could do for her was to give Ariana space to regain her position. "I will not trouble her for a time."

Not until after dark, when he would go quietly to the Hazelrig home and beg entrance, if the White Mage would admit him after his reckless actions. He would beg forgiveness of them both and just cling to Ariana how he could, as long as he could.

"He told me to stay out of the queen's way," Shianan said. "I don't understand that; I thought she had forgiven me, or near enough. Was it the attempt to marry? Was that enough of a threat to her sons' succession? 'Soats, I don't know how to do more."

Luca gave him a steady look. "Do you want to know more?"

Shianan tried to smile. "What, will you use your secret servants' intelligence network, passing notes and whispers?"

"Don't be ridiculous," Luca answered, forcing a smile in return. "You know we slaves can't read." He sobered. "But if you want to know, I will ask Ethan."

"If anyone knows something, it's probably Ethan," Shianan agreed. "But can you be subtle?"

Luca gave him a disappointedly patient look.

"I'm sorry, you're right," Shianan said. "I doubt Ethan is capable of being unsubtle."

CHAPTER 45

At the mid-afternoon knock, Luca jerked his head to check the closed door and then looked at his master.

Shianan sighed, propped an elbow on his desk, and pushed his fingers through his unwashed hair. "King's sweet oats, what now?"

Luca went to the door. Whatever waited, nothing could be gained by denial or delay. He steeled himself with a quick breath and a wordless prayer, and then he opened the door.

It was a slave who waited without, dressed in royal livery. It was not Ethan, but still Luca felt a small relief; the king would have sent guards, not a single slave. Almost grateful, Luca gestured for him to enter. "Yes?"

The slave acknowledged Shianan with a quick dip of his head. "Good morning, my lord. I've come to fetch the slave Luca." He looked at Luca. "Would that be you?"

Luca was taken aback. "I—yes."

The slave nodded and turned back to Shianan. "With your permission, my lord, he and I will go."

"Wait." Shianan stood and came around the desk, eying the badge on the slave's sleeve. "What does the queen want with him?"

Luca looked at the badge, subtly different than that of the prince's slave who had summoned them after the Court of the High Star. His slight relief vanished utterly, replaced by fresh dread.

The slave bowed his head. "I am sorry, my lord. I've been told only to bring him."

Shianan gestured Luca back from the door. "With all respect to your mistress, I would like to know what will become of my slave."

"Oh, there's no harm to befall him, my lord. No ill treatment. Others have been called as well—Captain Torg, I know for one, and I believe General Septime for another."

Luca looked at Shianan. Those who knew Shianan best—those who might speak favorably of him, or who might protest his disappearance. Luca read the suspicion in Shianan's face. An order of silence and a considerable gift would be no ill treatment at all, but it would prevent the officers from asking too closely after the commander.

Shianan drew a slow breath. "And he must go immediately?"

"Yes, my lord. I am to bring him straightaway."

Luca tensed. "Master—"

Shianan's look cut him off. "Go on outside," he told the queen's servant. "He'll join you in a moment."

The slave bowed and left.

Luca looked at Shianan, feeling helpless. "What is it for?"

Shianan shook his head. "Holy One knows." He pushed at his hair again, looking over Luca's shoulder, avoiding Luca's eyes. "The only thing the king—he told me to keep out of the queen's path." His throat worked visibly. "If they try to do anything to you, to sell you off or imprison you or anything, you scream long and loud that you belong to Mage Hazelrig. Understand that?"

Luca nodded, not trusting his voice.

Shianan took another breath. "I've bid you farewell before," he said, "and it was not as final as expected. I pray this will be the same."

Luca reached for Shianan's arm. "Wait for me. When I return, I'll want to find you here."

Shianan gave him a sad smile. "Be careful, Luca."

Luca was brought to one of the small private rooms that lined the palace wings. There he was left to await Her Majesty's pleasure. It was not a prison cell, which gave him a glimpse of hope.

At first he paced restlessly, but finally he wore the edge from his nervous energy and sat in one of the several chairs. After a time, though, he began to fidget again, and he looked about the room for something to occupy him. But there was nothing. There was no reason to entertain a slave, who must wait upon their convenience. Indeed, it might be to their purpose to keep him wondering and fretful.

He wanted distraction. If only someone had left a book. Of course they would not assume he could read, and even if they knew him literate, they might not expect him to want the practice. What would they expect a slave to do, left to himself for hours?

Keep him idle, and he will long for freedom, quoted Luca to himself. *Keep him busy, and he will long for rest.* He took a deep breath and forced himself to release it in a long stream. He would play the typical slave, then, and see how he could best help Shianan in whatever might come.

The room had no windows, so he had no idea how much time had passed when the queen's slave finally found Luca drowsing on the couch. Luca sat up sharply, feeling vaguely guilty and greatly worried.

"You're wanted now."

Luca knew very little of the queen, other than her long hatred of Shianan Becknam and her late appreciation of his assistance to Prince Soren, and this new apparent reversal in seeing Shianan as a rival for her sons' security. The king had warned Shianan of her. It was best to assume she was hostile toward the bastard and to give as little offense as possible.

If there was one thing Luca had learned well, it was the appearance of base humility. He dropped to his knees the moment he entered the room where she waited, his eyes close on the floor.

"Come closer, Luca."

He rose, not quite straightening, and approached a few feet nearer before kneeling again.

"I will hardly be able to hear you from there. Come to the edge of this rug, if I must be specific."

Luca obeyed. "I am sorry, my lady. I did not wish to offend."

"Then you will answer my questions readily and honestly."

"Of course, my lady."

She paused. "By honest, I mean quite honest. More honest than a slave generally is, when answering questions regarding his master."

Luca's gut tensed. "I will endeavor to please, Your Majesty."

"I do not wish to be pleased by your answers—I wish to be pleased that they *are* your answers. You understand me?"

"Yes, Your Majesty."

"Your response is a bit too glib for my liking, but I suppose that is a slave's wont." She sighed. "Luca, nothing you say in this interview will be held against you. This is your moment to speak freely." She paused. "Bailaha said you were a freeman, once."

"So I was, my lady."

"How did you come to be enslaved?"

"I was sold for debt."

"Your own?"

"My father's." The less he said on that, the better.

"And you were sold to Bailaha?"

"No, my lady. I was fortunate enough to be tutor to a family."

"And you did not stay with them?"

"We were in Furmelle, my lady." There was little further explanation needed. Nearly every slave in Furmelle had been imprisoned, at least for a time.

"I see. You were one of the rebels?"

"I did not fight, my lady."

She gave a mild, ladylike snort. "I said you were to answer honestly, without fear of reprisal."

Luca did not respond.

"And after Furmelle?"

"I was sold with other prisoners, and I went to a tinker."

"Did you do well for him?"

"I did my best, my lady. I did menial chores with the draft work."

"How did you leave him?"

"He died, my lady; he'd been ill a long while. He died while we were in Davan, at the citadel of the Gehrn. The Gehrn kept me, and I served the high priest."

"The Gehrn?" Her voice held a note of distaste. "So you learned the love of war for war's sake, and brutality for the love of brutality. Did they teach you to fight?"

Luca nearly laughed at the absurdity of it, but his fear of the queen kept him sober. "Not I, my lady." He swallowed.

She shifted in her chair. "Did you know of the plot to disable the Shard and shield?"

Luca shook his head slowly. "I was... No, my lady, I did not."

"Speak plainly."

"I was the slave in the ritual that unmade the shield."

Queen Azalie's voice betrayed mild surprise. "Oh?"

"Had I known of it, my lady, I would have... I don't know. Perhaps I would have fled. Probably not, not then. But I may not have carried the implements so quietly into the cellar."

She considered this, and he wondered if she recalled his soft protest that he had not fought at Furmelle. She would believe him even less, now.

"How did you come to Shianan Becknam?"

"I was taken with Flamen Ande. Master Becknam took me from the prison."

A crooked smile colored the queen's voice. "And so you were grateful to him, and that colors your present testimony."

"No, my lady." Luca wished he could look at her, could see how she heard him. "He claimed me just as the Gehrn had done after the tinker had died. It was afterward—it was..." His voice faded uncertainly.

"Go on."

He licked his lips. "With great respect, my lady, I am not eager to share—"

"I have said I desire utmost honesty from you, slave Luca, and I mean to have it." Her voice was firm, but less menacing than the words it carried. "Again, you will not be punished for anything you relate here."

Luca sucked a breath. "And my master?"

She paused. "You mean to say that you would report a trespass on his part."

Luca remained silent.

"And you will not speak if you believe it will endanger him."

"A man should not suffer for kindness, my lady."

"Safely spoken without committing yourself or your master." She sighed. "I will grant a reasonable immunity if, as you obliquely suggest, his actions were rooted in kindness."

It was as promising an assurance as he was likely to receive, and she could demand more with less surety. Luca clenched his fists. "I was—wounded after the ritual, by its nature. It may not be unusual for a man to treat a new slave's injuries to make him useful, but it is less common for him to give that slave a chance to escape."

That startled her. "I had not expected that. And you did not flee?"

"My lady, I did not understand. I was too much a slave."

"And after that?"

"We—forgive me if this sounds presumptuous from a slave, my lady, but—we became friends. And... I have said Shianan Becknam remade me, restoring me after my service to the Gehrn and others. He went so far as to teach me to fight, though I was hardly an apt pupil and am no credit to him, so that I—became more myself. More than myself."

"And then he returned you to your brother."

Luca had not guessed that the queen knew this. "Yes, my lady."

"And what was your opinion of Bailaha?"

Luca blinked. "My lady?"

289

"Not now, as his slave, but when you went away with your brother and were free to carry your own opinion, what did you think of Bailaha?"

Luca cast his words into the chasm and hoped they would land well. "I intended to return to Chrenada as a freeman, to be near my friend."

"Sweet all." Queen Azalie turned and paced away, and Luca risked a glance upward. She was frowning.

After a moment, she faced him, her head raised again. "And your opinion now, as his slave?"

Luca swallowed. "I would be free if I had the choice, of course. But if I am not to be my own master, then I would commit that trust to a friend."

There was a long pause, and Luca wondered if he had spoken unwisely. Then the queen spoke. "You do know that I will not report your answers to your master? That he will not be gratified to hear of your praise?"

Luca clenched his fists. "It is not false praise, my lady. I answer honestly, as you instructed."

"Sweet, sweet all." She took a few steps. "And as you are so honest, now tell me your master's worst fault."

Luca was struck by the query, and for a moment he could think of nothing. He breathed in and out, working his fingers and considering. Shianan had intended to sacrifice himself for Ariana, stealing the Shard, but in the end had allowed another to be blamed for it. That treacherous secret, however, Luca could never betray, no matter what assurances had been given.

But his master had more than one fault. "He feels too keenly. That is, the world can be harsh, my lady, especially for slaves, and Shianan Becknam is the king's most loyal servant. He..." But he realized there was no way to complete that thought without venturing into criticism of the king.

"That was a very virtuous fault to report," the queen answered dryly, "to say your master is too attentive to the words of his liege."

Luca said nothing.

She moved away from him. "I have finished with you, Luca. Go back to your master, and tell him as much or as little of this as you think wise."

Luca, still kneeling, dipped his head lower, and then he silently backed from the room. There was no one waiting outside, and he started back toward the courtyard, gaining speed as he went.

CHAPTER 46

Luca had guessed the commander's door might be locked, but it seemed Shianan was under no illusions of defense, and the latch moved without resistance. His next thought was that the office was unlocked because Shianan had been taken while he was gone.

He pushed anxiously through the door. "Master Shianan?"

"Luca!" Shianan bolted from his chair as if he'd been perched on its edge all the hours Luca had been away. "What happened? Are you all right?"

"I'm fine," Luca assured him. "I waited an eternity, and then the queen asked me questions. That was all."

"That was all?" Shianan repeated. "What kind of questions?"

"About you, mostly," Luca answered bleakly. "A few others to be sure I was telling truth or to put me in the habit of answering, I think, but mostly about you."

Shianan stepped back, looking strained. "What could she want with... She already knows all she could want about me. More, even. What did she ask?"

"I think she wanted to hear what kind of man you are. Your character." Luca wished he could offer some explanation of her purpose. "She asked what I thought of you." He tried to smile. "I gave a good report."

Shianan did not respond to the sally. "She couldn't have called you for just that."

"She asked more than that. She asked how I came to your service, how I came to be a slave in the first place. She asked your worst fault."

Now Shianan did give a rueful smile. "'Soats. How did you pick one?" He paused, thoughtful, and when he spoke again it was in a curious, hesitant tone. "What did you tell her?"

"I told her, after a limping fashion, you were too careful of the king's opinion."

Shianan scowled. "There isn't much to be done with that. She knows it already, and it's hardly a fault to be mindful of the king."

"The queen said as much herself."

"What didn't you tell her, then?"

"Hm?"

"You wouldn't have said something so frail if you hadn't been scrambling for anything to hand. What was it you meant not to tell her?"

Luca hesitated. "It is not a slave's place to speak of his master's—"

"Don't you dare! Say it, Luca—what did you not tell her?"

Luca took a slow breath. "You let another man be blamed for your crime. It was a crime committed for just reason, but you let another be taken for it. More than one. You let men be tortured into confessing your crime."

Shianan stared at him. "Those men may not have stolen the Shard, but they were not innocent."

"No, of course they weren't. We are none of us innocent. And they had meant to kill you, so some would say it was right to let them fall for it, and yet—you knew they were not guilty of the crime for which they will die."

Shianan opened his mouth, checked himself, and then asked with great deliberation, "What are you accusing me of?"

"Nothing. I am no better; I know the truth, that Flamen Ande did not plot against the shield or intend to harm the Shard. But I've said nothing to defend him, and in fact I'm glad of where he is now." He shook his head. "I'm no better."

Shianan turned away. "Ande deserves—and he would never be held to account. Better the wrong crime than to go free."

"And what of our crimes that have gone unpunished? Should we be taken for something else?"

"What's your point?" Shianan demanded. "What do you want?"

"I don't know," Luca answered, and more uncertainty wavered in his voice than he had expected. "I don't know. I'm just a man, a slave. I can't pretend to judge."

"So you need another to do it for you? I know you go to the worship house at times—is it to hear judgment on what we have done?"

Luca was stung. "I prayed for you."

Shianan gave a disgusted snort. "You shouldn't have bothered. I tried for years, and not one of my prayers ever came true. Not one."

Luca did not reply.

"I would have thought you'd had enough of priests." Shianan cleared desk clutter savagely, occupying his hands.

"Ande was never that kind of priest," Luca answered. "And if he had been, he wouldn't have been that kind of priest."

"Heh." Shianan scuffed his toe at a long-dried spill of ink. "And it was your tale about the men who ambushed us being those who took the Shard, you'll remember."

"I said myself I was as guilty," Luca said more quietly. "We both lied. To save ourselves, and—for her. The woman he killed."

Shianan turned an outraged look on him. "You might pardon me not for my own sake, but for some nameless slave?"

"She had a name! That we did not know it makes her no less. You are a commander, a count, and even if you are the bastard, you could defend yourself. She couldn't. We lied to protect ourselves, but it also brought justice for her. That's all that kept us from being murderers, too."

"You make no sense," Shianan muttered. "And what will you do about it? Go and tell the truth, sacrifice the both of us so murdering bandits can be vindicated and a sadistic priest can be released? So the man you watched kill that woman can go free while we take his place?"

Luca set his jaw. "Would you tell Lady Ariana you let another man be tortured and killed for what you had done?"

Shianan kicked the heavy desk, shifting it a couple of squawking inches across the resisting stone.

Luca realized he had backed against the wall, unconsciously putting distance between himself and his master.

"Do not," snapped Shianan, still facing the desk, "ask me to regret what I have done. They were murderers for hire, and they would have killed both of us just for coin. If I could save Ariana and put away a criminal at the same time, that's work well done, isn't it?"

Luca said nothing.

Shianan braced his hands on the desk for a long moment. Finally he ran a hand over his face. "Pay no heed to me. I am only fretting about the queen and—everything else. It's a blister on my soul." He shook his head. "This conversation has gone all wrong. I'm sorry. I'm glad you're back, and well. You think what you want of me, Luca; Holy One knows you're entitled."

Luca did not answer. He began to move about the room, gathering up the items Shianan had scattered in his frantic straightening, occupying his own hands.

A knock at the door interrupted the heavy silence, and Luca turned gratefully to answer it. Outside waited a winded soldier, leaning with one arm against the frame and straightening as he caught sight of Shianan in the office. "Commander, there's been an attack."

"What sort of attack?" Shianan asked, coming forward and gesturing the man in.

"In Nalarbor. A runner just came, and we're going through—"

"What happened in Nalarbor?" demanded Shianan.

"An attack, sir. Ryuven attack. On civilians."

CHAPTER 47

Shianan bolted from his quarters and went to General Septime's office, pushing through the gathering crowd of soldiers waiting for news.

So Shianan was one of the first to hear, and as soon as the report was delivered, he excused himself, leaving General Septime to query for details. Shianan went directly to the palace, directly to the guest rooms where Tamaryl was staying, his pulse pounding in his ears.

He beat on the door with a fist, and the servant Fulke opened in a scramble. "My lord, what can—"

"Where is he?" Shianan demanded. He pushed past the slave. "Tamaryl! Where are you?"

Tamaryl came out from a rear room, looking startled. "My lord commander, I see something urgent has brought you here."

"You might say that." Without taking his eyes from Tamaryl, Shianan gestured Fulke toward the door. "Out."

Fulke did not even look to his temporary master for permission. He bolted.

Tamaryl's face darkened, though worry bled through his irritation. "What brings you here, commander?"

Shianan bit out the awful words. "There has been an attack. Ryuven destroyed a trading town to the northeast. Like Caftford."

Tamaryl opened his mouth, hesitated, and then said, "You would not jest about something like this."

"I would not."

Tamaryl stood rigid, his wings high, his eyes no longer seeing Shianan. "That can't be. That would negate the treaty, our peace, the trade, everything."

"It is the truth," Shianan said. "I had it from a military runner only minutes ago." Fury boiled in him as he looked at the treacherous Pairvyn. "More than forty civilians are dead, besides the military outpost. Grain and other stores were taken from the warehouses. It seems your willingness to trade for your wants lasted only as long as it took for us to let our guard down."

"No. No, we fought for this trade—for this peace."

He played it well. Staring at him, Shianan could almost believe it was a surprise to Tamaryl as well. "It was a Ryuven attack," he repeated. "You are the Ryuven emissary."

Tamaryl folded his arms, one hand to his mouth, his eyes on the floor between them. "It can't be. Unless—if Oniwe'aru sent me here while planning—but no, Oniwe'aru swore the oath, he couldn't betray the treaty—"

"An oath is only as good as the one who swears it," Shianan snarled.

"That oath cannot be lightly broken!" Tamaryl snapped, focusing again on Shianan. "The word he gave was binding, magically binding. If he knowingly betrayed it, there will be visible consequences. I must go and see him. I have to confirm if this was his doing."

"No," Shianan said firmly. "You are the Ryuven emissary, and you will remain to answer for Ryuven actions in Chrenada. You are here to oversee the new trade and to maintain peaceful relations, and you will be surety for both—and you will not flee when your people violate our treaty."

"We did not violate the treaty," Tamaryl said, though he seemed to be speaking to convince himself as much as Shianan. "I am here to keep the peace. We did not violate the treaty."

"You don't seem to be successful at keeping the peace, not with twenty-three dead soldiers and forty dead civilians."

Tamaryl flinched. "It might not have been Oniwe'aru. Perhaps it was a che acting on his own, raiding for his own gain and without the knowledge or permission—"

"A leader is responsible for his people," Shianan snapped. "If one of my soldiers kills someone in a village, it is the action of my unit and I will act accordingly. If your Oniwe cannot speak for his people, he is not a leader able to swear to a treaty."

"And as a commander, you would have the opportunity to see your unit and act," Tamaryl replied, but there was little strength to his voice. His eyes were unfocused again. "He could not have known," he repeated quietly, protestingly. "Surely he could not have known."

"You cannot flee," Shianan said. "The shield is being replaced immediately, to forestall future attacks, and to ensure you remain to answer what has happened." He had heard General Septime order the shield to guard the kingdom, but the latter reason was as logical, and a good warning to the potential agent who might consider further acts.

Tamaryl met Shianan's eyes. "I didn't do this. I had nothing to do with this, I didn't know anything about this. Please understand that."

"What I understand is that I pledged to guard the people of this kingdom and my soldiers who protect them," Shianan answered, "and that Ryuven treachery has killed them."

Tamaryl turned away with a groan. Shianan did not allow himself to be moved; there was no way to know if the Pairvyn was sincere. If he had known of the attack, he was a traitor, a liar, a murderer. If he had not known, then he was useless to keep the peace Shianan's soldiers needed.

Shianan turned and exited, slamming the door behind him as if the sound could underscore his warning to Tamaryl. He would see him held accountable for these deaths.

"Are you certain?" Ariana squeezed her interlocked fingers, wishing she had something else to do with her hands. She leaned over the man's sheaves of notes as if she could read them better herself, upside down. "Are you absolutely sure?"

He hissed through his teeth, irritated but also sympathetic. "I obviously haven't seen any of this for myself, my lady mage, but that is the report I have. Some of the merchants and business folk tried to defend the warehouses, and that's where most of the fighting happened. I have a list of names, no more details."

"I understand," Ariana said weakly. "Thank you."

"I'm sorry," said the man, more gently. "He was a friend of yours?"

"Of a sort," she said. "Kudo is the husband of my friend."

She had to tell Ranne. They would not know yet, not before the military and the Circle.

Word had ignited an immediate uproar in the Wheel. General Septime had ordered the shield to be raised, and the White Mage had assigned the complex preparations. All knew this was the end of the Ryuven treaty. The tentative peace had survived the prince-heir's dance on the edge of death, but it would not survive an open attack on a trading town.

But Ariana had seized on the name Nalarbor, remembering Ranne's complaints of missing her new husband. She had rushed to confirm the reported dead, and now she faced one of the most difficult tasks of a brutal year.

She almost wished she had not gone to ask. Then she would not be responsible for such news.

She sent a messenger to Bethia with a quick note that Ranne would need friends, but she did not specify the reason, in case something went wrong and she could not speak to Ranne first. It was not right somehow that others should know before her. Then Ariana started toward the baron's townhouse, on the far side of the market in a fashionable district.

She hated each step she took, but her feet moved without her direction, bearing her to a street she barely knew. She rang the bell at the door and resented the bright tone it gave.

"I need to see Ranne," she told the answering servant. "The younger Lady Kudo."

"She's just returned," the woman said. "Please come in."

Ranne was smiling when she saw Ariana. "Hello! I was just at the shop, Mama needed a hand—but you look terrible! What's wrong?"

Ariana took her hand and tugged her gently onto a couch. "Ranne—there was an attack. A Ryuven attack on Nalarbor."

Ranne went still, no sharp intake of breath or jerk of muscles, just a cessation of movement, as if she could halt time and prevent worse news. "If you came to tell me about it..."

"It was a bad attack."

"And you must be waiting for news. We're waiting to hear the casualties, waiting to hear how it was."

Ariana felt pressed between bindings, the air squeezed out of her. "We have a list of deaths." She choked. "Oh, Ranne—I am so sorry."

Ranne stared at her, closing the fingers of one hand over her chest as if to ward a blow. "You're certain?"

"I asked again and again. He—he's on the list."

For a moment Ranne did not move, did not breathe, did not twitch in Ariana's grasp. She stared ahead as if the words had not reached her. But Ariana could see the grief touch her, a ghost wrapping about her in an unshakable embrace. Ranne's eyes fell to their clasped hands, though she did not seem to see them. At last Ranne whispered, "Oh, Ariana."

"I am so, so sorry."

"Poor Connor," she breathed. "What will I do? What will I tell his father?"

Ariana pulled her close and held her as the first trembling gasps shook free of Ranne's chest.

But then words came, ragged and sharp. "He would never have gone to trade Ryuven goods if there weren't Ryuven traders here. They couldn't have come if the shield were still protecting us. We could have prevented this. Why is the shield gone while we invite murderers into our markets?"

"No," Ariana protested, though some part of her knew Ranne spoke only in grief. "No, we don't know what happened. The trade has been going so well—we don't know what happened."

"We know he's dead!" Ranne cried. "We know we let the Ryuven come and then they killed him!"

The door opened, and Bethia entered, her face full of concern. Ariana looked over Ranne's head and mouthed, *Connor's dead.*

Bethia's hands rushed to her mouth, her eyes wide, and she dashed across the room to envelope Ranne from the other side. "I am so sorry," she said, her voice cracking. "I am so very sorry."

Ranne, between them, began to sob.

CHAPTER 48

The council room was more crowded than usual, with the councilors, King Jerome and Prince Soren, Generals Septime and Kannan, much of the Great Circle, and the Ryuven emissary Tamaryl'sho. Shianan, standing in a corner because there were no chairs remaining, was grateful to have a place at all to observe.

He would be glad to watch Tamaryl forced to answer for his treachery.

Ariana stood on the far side of the room, also without a chair. Her stark black robes emphasized the striking change in her face. Even when she had been afraid in the cellar of the Wheel, held hostage by the Ryuven, or when she had fallen into the valley and begged him not to kill the boy Tam, or when she had hidden a treacherous Ryuven in her father's office, she had not looked like this. Shianan thought she looked...ashamed.

She had finally realized, then. She had finally realized what her optimistic insistence had done, lowering their guard against the Ryuven raiders and letting the Pairvyn ni'Ai into their palace. King's oats, was the royal family safe?

Shianan turned his attention to Tamaryl, seated at the crowded table but somehow alone. His eyes were on his hands, positioned curiously on the table's surface, fingers spread wide with the tips of the forefingers together. Was this some magical preparation, Shianan wondered? Or, with the White Mage and Silver Mage seated on either side of him, was this a sign that he prepared no magic?

"Let us begin," called Uilleam, Grand Chancellor of the Realm. He looked about the table and at those standing around the room. "You will note we have asked others to join our emergency session of the council today. We must set aside other matters for this most pressing, the recent invasion and massacre at Nalarbor."

Eyes all around the room shifted toward Tamaryl, who kept his eyes on his oddly positioned fingers.

"From our most current report, pending more information, we have heard of the complete devastation of our military outpost there, twenty-three soldiers and officers. In addition, we have confirmed the deaths of forty-five civilians, including two nobles pursuing trade." Uilleam lifted his head from his notes. "Our immediate responses have been to dispatch soldiers to dissuade bandit looters and to renew the shield over all of Chrenada to prevent further Ryuven incursions. This of course suspends all ongoing trade with Ryuven merchants, for dall sweetbud and for other goods."

Most of those present knew these details already, though the civilian death toll had climbed slightly in the most recent report.

"While we have many questions and many tasks facing us," continued Uilleam, "I am sure we are first most eager to hear from the Ryuven emissary, Tamaryl'sho."

All eyes in the room rested on the Ryuven. A heavy silence hung over them, thick with unspoken demand.

Tamaryl drew a slow breath and raised his head. "My lords and ladies," he began, "I regret I do not have anything satisfactory to say to you. I did not know of this incident until you did. I have heard nothing of it but what you have told me. I certainly was not privy to its coming. I can only express grief and dismay with you at the loss of life."

The councilors frowned, looked at the table or each other, folded or unfolded their hands.

"Tamaryl'sho," said Uilleam, "you have come here as the representative of the Ryuven people. If you do not have answers for us, we must assume the treaty is broken and—well, with open Ryuven attacks upon our people, we must again be at war."

"With respect, my lord, I think that assumption is premature."

The gathered councilors and others shifted and murmured.

"How many Ryuven died in the incident, Chancellor Uilleam?"

Uilleam checked his notes. "We have six bodies reported."

"Six," repeated Tamaryl. "That is about the size of an average trading party, I believe."

"Surely you are not suggesting that the town turned on six traders, and they in turn killed sixty-eight people."

"What we know is that seventy-four lives have been lost." Tamaryl looked around at them. "We have only the survivors' word that they were the attacked, and anyone who attacked a trading party would not be likely to admit it, especially if it went so poorly that it resulted in more human deaths."

"This is ridiculous!" burst General Kannan. "Our soldiers were there to keep the peace, not to attack traders."

"Perhaps they were not involved at the start," Tamaryl said. "They might have gotten in the middle of what had become a riot. I do not pretend to know what happened, my lords and ladies. I only say it is early to assume we are at war, before we have determined exactly what occurred and how."

"The report said the attack came in the night," General Kannan pressed. "That it was a surprise raid by Ryuven fighters, not traders. This could explain the disparity in casualties, six to sixty-eight."

"Or perhaps it was a raid, but perpetrated by fringe outlaws." Tamaryl's expression was strained. "I cannot believe it was a sanctioned attack. Oniwe'aru swore a binding oath, and there would be critical consequences to him if he ordered a raid after swearing to honor our treaty."

"Perhaps he might not order it," suggested Chancellor Washe, "but he might permit it."

"My friend is newly widowed," Ariana said in a weary, ragged voice from the far side of the room. The councilors and others turned to watch her. "She has been married only a few months, and now her husband is dead, killed in Nalarbor where he went to pursue new trade opportunities opened by this treaty. Can you tell us, Tamaryl'sho, who is responsible, so that we may demand justice and prevent further tragedy?"

She did not blame Tamaryl for the deaths, Shianan thought. But she blamed him for failing to prevent them, for deceiving her into believing the fighting had ended.

Tamaryl bowed his head. "I cannot, my lady mage. I am sorry. None of us here can say what happened, and we cannot commit the error of throwing away our treaty without knowing how it was violated."

"What about the bodies?"

All eyes turned now to General Septime. Chancellor Washe asked, "Which bodies, general?"

"It wouldn't be the first time bandits had tried to pass blame to the Ryuven. It seems improbable here—generally those mistakes are made by frightened farmers sending for aid and not in military reports—but we should at least be certain. Let's examine one or more of the bodies, and that will answer the question of whether or not the enemy was Ryuven and perhaps also whether they were merchants or warriors."

Others nodded. Kannon agreed, "It should be easy enough to differentiate the gear of a trader from that of a warrior, and it's not difficult to discern if a body has been redressed or altered, if the blood still adheres the clothing to the wounds and such. Let us have a proper report, or perhaps even some of these corpses, brought to sort and know the truth of the matter."

Some of the councilors grimaced in revulsion, but others nodded grimly. "It's best to know the truth of it," Chancellor Uilleam said. "My lord Tamaryl, do you agree?"

"I do," he responded, his voice even, if unenthusiastic.

"Good." Chancellor Uilleam looked about the room. "Commander Becknam, as you are familiar with the area and Ryuven raids, we charge you with this duty."

Shianan nodded. Going to investigate a massacre was an unenviable task, but it was better than remaining within the city walls, waiting for courtiers to debate fault and protocol. He would find what had happened and bring an undeniable demand for action. He kept his face neutral. "Yes, sir."

As the council filed from the room, muttering among themselves, Tamaryl remained in his seat, looking forward. If he stayed, he would not have to speak with them in the corridors and anterooms, and he would not have to support the frail defense he'd presented.

It was possible. It was possible the human traders had attempted to rob the Ai who carried the precious dall sweetbud. It was possible an assault had spread into a riot. It was possible that six Ryuven trained for trade rather than combat had successfully killed twenty-three trained human soldiers and twice as many civilians before succumbing.

He glanced down and saw the tips of his forefingers were touching. He pulled his hands apart.

The Silver Mage stood, exchanged a look with the White Mage, and then joined the stream out the door. Nearly everyone had gone before Ewan Hazelrig finally spoke to Tamaryl. "Do you think it was a rogue attack on Ryuven traders?"

Tamaryl did not want to answer the question. "It must have been."

"Because Oniwe'aru could not betray his oath?"

Tamaryl's heart convulsed in his chest. "Because if not, Oniwe'aru betrayed me." He looked at Hazelrig, keeping his voice low for his friend. "I did not see Oniwe'aru swear, so I cannot be certain that he swore a binding oath. If he did not, or if he did and then chose to take the consequences for breaking it, it means he set me up to take the fallout from the attack." He swallowed. "If it was an attack."

Ariana leaned over the table to see around her father, her face serious. "Do you think that's possible?"

"I don't know." Tamaryl could hear the faint quaver within his voice, the edge of a raised pitch, and though it shamed him he could not silence it. "I have been a headwind to Oniwe'aru for years. If he sent me here, in my weakened state, to be surety for the peace, and then ordered a raid—" He could not finish the sentence. He felt guilt at even suspecting the treachery—surely Oniwe'aru would not resort to subterfuge? He could have ordered Tamaryl's execution any number of times. He had even stopped it once.

But Tamaryl had frustrated him many times since then, and if Oniwe'aru did not wish to offend Edeiya'rika with killing Tamaryl directly, this might be an effective alternative.

He realized Shianan Becknam was still standing in his corner, watching them. He wondered how much the commander had heard. He wondered if it mattered.

"If Oniwe'aru has betrayed you," Mage Hazelrig said, "then that would also mean the peace is violated. It is not a case of whether or not the treaty is broken, it is whether or not Oniwe'aru was a part of it."

"Tell me about this binding oath," Shianan Becknam said from the wall.

Tamaryl glanced at him. The man had a right to know. It was his kingdom to defend, if the treaty ended. "Oniwe'aru swore—told us he swore—to honor the treaty with a binding oath. It places constraints upon the oath-maker, so that if he consciously violates his word, the magic returns upon him with wracking pain and disability."

"So it's possible to violate it," Becknam said. "If one wanted enough to do so."

"Or he may never have sworn it," Tamaryl admitted softly.

Ariana shook her head. "I was there. I felt magic when he swore. He used his own blood."

"But we do not know what magic it was," her father corrected gently.

Tamaryl nodded. "Blood would be required. But that might be only enough to give the look of the thing, without committing to the oath itself."

Essence, if he had been sent to be killed by the humans he meant to protect for violating the peace he meant to ensure—

"I need to walk," he said suddenly, pushing himself to his feet. "I have to move."

"You won't leave," Becknam said, not quite a warning.

Tamaryl faced him and snapped, "If I were to be stopped, it would be by either of the Mages Hazelrig."

Shianan Becknam returned his gaze with impassive dislike. This was it, Tamaryl realized. This was when Shianan Becknam won, winning Ariana's affection while Tamaryl became a traitor to the treaty he had given much of his life to create.

He fled out the council room door, not looking back at the mages behind him.

CHAPTER 49

Luca pressed close to the wall, staying well out of the way of the palace traffic. Outside the council room doors the corridor was full of scurrying servants, officious pages, several dismissive secretaries. One of these was scolding another, pushing back a sheaf of notes. "No, take this all back! They won't want this in an emergency session. The flamen is not a priority while the treaty is at stake."

Luca's ears caught the word and his stomach twisted upward. He glanced involuntarily toward them. They were only secretaries; dare he ask?

No, he had seen how royal secretaries disdained his master; they would not answer the bastard's slave's questions. But when the junior secretary left again with the stack of notes and the council secretary entered the council room, Luca hurried to the desk, looking about to see if any of the remaining pages were watching too closely, and checked the agenda items for the next regular session.

It was in the sixth line. *Upcoming sentencing for Flamen Manceps Ande, accused of sabotage and treason.*

Luca's heart twisted in his chest and for a moment he couldn't inhale. Then self-preservation prompted him back to his waiting place, out of traffic and sight, and he pulled long, deliberate breaths.

Ande's trial was nearly ended. Ande would be sentenced. Years of Luca's life, miserable years, would be avenged.

Would they?

Luca squatted in the corner, staring at the carpet with his mind spinning, until the council room doors opened and nobles, mages, generals, and others began spilling out. He jumped to his feet and pressed back until he saw Shianan near the end of the exodus. "What happened?"

"I'm off to collect the dead," Shianan said curtly. "And perhaps we're at war again, it's hard to say just yet. I need to pack."

✾

"Ariana! Over here!" Calissa waved, though Ariana had spotted her easily in the morning street. The bodyguard made her distinctive. "I am so glad to see you. I didn't want to arrive by myself."

Ariana slipped her arm about Calissa's elbow. "It's not so worrisome as that," she said. "Bethia can be a bit peevish when she's disappointed, but she also knows how to be a lady."

"Nothing against your friend," Calissa answered, "but she did seem standoffish at the ball. And it was my sister who was supposed to marry the prince she thought would marry her."

"And now your sister is returning safely to the Wakari Coast, and Prince Soren is on the market again, and Bethia won't lose a moment of charm," Ariana said with a smile.

"Well, eventually," Calissa said. "We won't be traveling while there are Ryuven raiders. We aren't used to that."

"Shianan could keep you safe," Ariana said loyally. "But whether you stay or go, Bethia's father is a duke, and she must keep her political nets open across Chrenada and the Wakari Coast and beyond. You caught her in the moment of watching her dream crash down—and, if I am cruelly honest, after years of political angling by her mother who, knowingly or unknowingly, misled her. She'll be more herself today."

"And then Ranne, whose husband just died. I'm so afraid I'll say something wrong."

"Oh, don't be," Ariana said quickly. "I think Ranne wants talk and noise and movement. This meeting was her idea, not Bethia's, so she wants to go out. She just doesn't want us coming to her in-laws' home, which I understand. It wouldn't be right."

"Of course," Calissa agreed. "Is this it?"

The duke's townhouse rose above them, bright and dignified with tasteful wealth. "Let's go in," Ariana said.

The bodyguard remained near the door as they were ushered into the sitting room. He would be taken to a servants' area and given hospitality.

Bethia welcomed them with subdued greetings. "I'm so glad you both could come. Your Highness, please, take a seat."

"I am merely Lady Calissa today," she said quickly. "I'm not here for a state visit, and I'm afraid of what my keepers would think if they believed I was. Ranne—I'm so sorry."

Ranne nodded. "Thank you. Please, let's sit down and—do anything."

They settled into Bethia's cushions and pillows and curled close to one another. Ranne began by questioning Calissa, a safe enough topic with wide range. "So you're staying in Alham? What will you do here?"

"I hope to separate myself from the marriage delegation and so to have no official capacity," Calissa admitted. "A hunting trip, except I'm hunting new friends." She grinned and then sobered. "That is what I told my lords Adoniram and Caza. But if I do establish relationships here, I might ask after becoming—don't laugh—an ambassador."

"Why would we laugh?" asked Ariana. "You'd make a wonderful ambassador."

"Thank you. It's just such a joke about surplus princesses, you know, married off to minor allies or noble houses—a sort of fourth-rate ambassador. Someone to secure good relations, if never useful again. But I'd like to be an actual emissary."

Bethia sat forward. "How are you going about it?"

"Oh, I have no idea," Calissa confessed. "So far I've only thought to get to know as many people as possible, get to know Alham, the court, all Chrenada. No one would take me seriously if I didn't know the land first."

"Ah." Bethia looked faintly disappointed. "I'd hoped you would have some royal insight. I, well, I too have been kind of thinking about diplomatic work."

"Really?" Ariana turned to her. "Oh, that would be perfect for you! You have a working knowledge of both trade and magic, you have the social standing, you have the training to move through courts—you should do it!"

Bethia's surprise broke through her hesitation. "You think so?"

"Of course! But don't ask me, ask Ranne."

"But I do want to ask you." Bethia fixed her eyes on Ariana. "I mean, I want to hear Ranne too, but you are the Black Mage, the heroine of Arakadamia, the—"

"The one who happened to be in the right place at the right time," Ariana said firmly. "Tamaryl'sho is the one who held the portal between worlds and carried the power to force the truce. Mage Callahan is the one who identified and promoted the—the dall sweetbud. I was alongside at the right moments."

"Because you trained hard and made the right choices," Ranne put in. "But Ariana is right, Bethia should absolutely be a diplomat. Look how she helped Connor and me to arrange our wedding."

For one terrible instant Ariana worried despite her assurance to Calissa that they would misspeak, that they would say something wrong and destroy the gathering with mention of the dead.

But Bethia swept in. "Of course—what else could I do? You two were perfect for each other. Any man who lies to his father that he's visiting a dockside whorehouse to cover his visits to a respectable merchant is someone you just have to assist. You can't help it."

Ranne laughed, so the rest of them could join her, and if she wiped tears from her eyes as she did, it was with fondness and joy as well as grief. Bethia leaned to embrace her, and Ariana mused that yes, Bethia usually had the right words when she wished. Diplomacy would be a good path for her.

"All right, enough of this," Ranne said, rubbing her hand across her eye. "I'll have plenty of time for crying tonight, and I want to think on happy things right now. I need to bring some things from the hall. Bethia, would you help me?"

"I'd be delighted."

"We'll be right back," Ranne said, sniffing and smiling, and they went out together.

"I wonder what that's about," Ariana said.

"It sounds like we won't wonder long." Calissa grinned and nudged Ariana with her elbow. "You know who would not be a good candidate for a career in diplomacy? You."

"What?"

"I'm thinking of the ball, where you took the king's offered boon and asked for Shianan Becknam."

Ariana flushed. Tamaryl's rebuke about bartering the bastard like a radish still stung, and then everything that had come of that had been wrong, the worst of wrong. She put her hands to the sides of her eyes, blocking out the room as she wished she could block out the memory. "That was a mistake. I am so sorry you saw it. That it happened."

"Oh, I'm sorry," Calissa soothed. "I meant it as a jest. Didn't it turn out well?"

Ariana stared at her. "You didn't—how could you not have heard?"

Calissa stared back, her eyes worried. "I never would have joked if I'd heard it ended badly! What I heard—Lord Adoniram was angry that Valetta's contract was delayed while they addressed the marriage of the bastard. I took that to mean..." She trailed off in growing horror. "I thought you were being kind about Ranne and weren't telling us the good news!"

Ariana shook her head. "Oh, no. No, the king wanted to marry me to someone else more suitable for a Mage of the Circle. I refused. And then—king's sweet oats, we were mad, but Shianan and I tried to marry. Right in the council room in front of the king."

Calissa gasped. "You didn't!"

"No," Ariana said, "we weren't able to finish. No handclasp. But we tried. And that angered the king even more, of course. I don't know what's going to come of it, in the end."

"Ariana, I'm so sorry. I wouldn't have said—I'm sorry."

"Oh, no, it wasn't your fault. I'm sure the king is working hard to make sure the details aren't known." She took a ragged breath. "But oh, Calissa, if you have any insight to offer... I feel I may have pushed things over the brink. Before we were not together, but there was a possibility, a hope that we might work things out. Now, I may have ruined that hope."

"Where is he now?"

"Shianan?" Ariana's heart twisted as she spoke what she'd been trying to avoid. "He's sent to Nalarbor. But I'm terrified the king will exile him or—something. Something terrible."

Before Calissa could answer, Bethia and Ranne returned, each with her arms full. "I have gifts," Ranne announced.

Ariana started up. "What? Why? Oh, Ranne, you didn't need to do—"

"Stop." Ranne looked embarrassed. "I needed to do something, something that wasn't choosing clothes for the burial, or holding my mother-in-law while she cried and suggested that maybe he wouldn't have gone himself to Nalarbor if he hadn't married a tradeswoman."

She paused to choke, and Bethia swiftly supplied, "The baroness has always been a snob."

Ranne shook her head. "No, she was coming to like me, I know she was. She's just upset."

"You're upset too," Ariana protested. "She has no ground to say such things to you while you're grieving with her."

"And they're not even a bit true," Calissa continued. "There were quite a few noble families trading in Nalarbor." When the others looked at her in surprise, she said, "I asked to see the reports. I am trying to understand Alham and the politics here. Connor Kudo was one of several venture traders from noble families."

Ranne nodded. "I know. It's not true, what she said. She's only upset. But anyway, I needed something to do while I was in my room. Our room."

She presented a leather case with two brass fasteners. She lifted the lid and fixed it into place to form a miniature work desk, with wide leather loops to hold vials, slots already full of creamy paper, and places for ink, for pens, for the minutiae of mage work. "This is for you, Ariana, to take on your field work."

"It's beautiful," Ariana gasped. "But I don't believe you made this in a day."

"You've caught me out," Ranne admitted. "I only finished it today. It was going to be a birthday present."

"When is your birthday?" asked Calissa.

"Not for months yet," Ariana said. "Ranne, really?"

"All right, it was to be for celebrating your rise to Indigo Mage," she confessed. "I thought it might come soon, with your return from the Ryuven world and Arakadamia and such. But then I finished it in one enormous blaze of work." She gave a small smile. "There's probably some salt still in the leather, but it will brush out."

She turned to the boxes in Bethia's arms. "And these are book boxes, for Bethia and Calissa. Not as detailed as a field desk, but I hope you like them."

"They're lovely!" Calissa exclaimed. "The colors are extraordinary!"

"These are my favorites. I'm glad you like them." Ranne opened a box to show the padded interior. "They'll accommodate several sizes."

"It's no wonder that you needed something to do, with your plague of a mother-in-law waiting to tell you that you were responsible for your husband's death," Ariana said fiercely. "That's inexcusable."

"No, please—it's important to me that you not blame her for what she said when she was upset." Ranne examined her fidgeting fingers, not looking at Ariana. "Because when I was upset, I think I said something terrible to you."

"What?"

"I sort of blamed you... I said Connor would not have been trading in Nalarbor if not for the treaty. And that might be true, but it's also true that if not for the treaty, the Ryuven might have been anywhere at all, or everywhere, not just Nalarbor. And no matter where they were or weren't, what you did was out of concern for everyone, and it did not cause the attack."

"Oh, Ranne." Ariana pulled her legs beneath her and faced her friend. "You were upset. I knew you were upset."

"But still." Ranne picked at her skirt. "I did not mean what I said. So I finished your field desk."

"You didn't have to do that," Ariana said. "But—I'm glad you did. It's gorgeous, like all your work."

Ranne smiled. "Thank you."

It was late when they finally left Bethia's townhouse. Calissa and Ariana walked on either side of Ranne, close enough that they bumped her as they walked. Behind them came Calissa's bodyguard, patiently ignoring the gestures she made for him to fall back.

"Thank you very much," Ariana said again.

"No, thanks to all of you," Ranne said. "This was wonderful."

Calissa put an arm through Ranne's. "Please come and visit me when you feel up to it. I have few friends here and no one at the palace, and I should be delighted to welcome you as my guest."

Ranne glanced at her. "At the palace?"

"Well, I can't come to a house of mourning for a visit, of course. And your mother-in-law will not dare to mutter around about her merchant daughter if that merchant daughter is a regular guest at the palace. Let me at least be of some use."

Ranne smiled. "I think I was unfair in telling you. She's not ordinarily so small-minded. It's only that she was casting about in her grief for something to blame. This was so senseless." She looked at Ariana. "She wasn't the only one."

Ariana put a finger on Ranne's lips. "And that's all that shall be said on that, ever again. When next you speak, it may only be to say how beautiful the stars are tonight."

Ranne tipped her head back. "You know, I believe they are. I'll miss them when they're clouded over, but they're beautiful tonight and they'll shine again another day."

Ariana dangled her field desk in one hand by its thick leather handle and slipped an arm about her friend.

Soren had not intended to meet the princesses in the gallery, but there was no way to gracefully retreat once he had entered. He put on a brave face and inclined his head to the women as they drew near. "Your Highnesses."

Princess Valetta made a courtesy. "We should thank you for your continued hospitality, my lord," she said, somewhat more coolly than the words suggested. "While the road is unsafe, it is good to have the walls of the Naziar."

"I am sorry your trip home has been delayed, but at least we have the continued pleasure of your company," Soren said. He glanced at Princess Calissa, a step behind her elder sister. "Perhaps it is a blessing of sorts, that we may continue to—"

"I might not call the stranding in a land plagued by Ryuven a blessing," Valetta observed, not charitably but not unfairly.

"Then perhaps the blessing is only my own," Soren said in what he hoped was a charming manner. He had not entirely surrendered the idea of regaining the Wakari favor, now that they had additional time granted by the Ryuven raid. They needed this alliance.

Princess Calissa chuckled. Soren worried she laughed at his attempt.

Valetta looked at her with something that wasn't quite disapproval. "I suppose you at least might be glad of our continued stay," she said.

"Of course you'd want to return home," Soren said quickly. "Anyone could see that. And we'll have you away as soon as we safely can."

Princess Valetta gave him a small smile. "I'm sorry. I didn't mean to sound churlish. I only...I never thought to be bound in a fortress with Ryuven circling outside."

"And we still aren't," Princess Calissa answered practically. "There's been only the single attack, quite a distance from here; they aren't raiding so near to the capital."

"We cannot stay in the capital if we mean to go home." Valetta straightened. "But complaining won't change anything. Thank you for accommodating us, Your Highness."

He bowed slightly, and she continued down the gallery.

Princess Calissa did not immediately follow. She tipped her head and regarded him. "My lord, may I ask you a question, not as Wakari to Chrenada, but just between ourselves?"

"Certainly you may, and I'll do my best to answer satisfactorily."

"My sister and our nobles are anxious to return home, but I feel no similar urgency. Once they have a safe window to depart, if I should wish to remain in Alham a while longer—could you recommend a suitable inn or guest house for a lady? I have found a friend here, but I hate to impose..." Her explanation continued unspoken, *or to involve another in the delicate political situation we've created.*

Soren wondered at her confidence that this Ryuven massacre was a mere inconvenience, soon to be resolved to send the royal party on their way. But then, she came from the Wakari Coast, where Ryuven were found more often in nighttime tales than in raids.

Still, she did not fear to stay where the monsters were real and threatening. Soren looked at her and made a decision. "My lady, please remain as our guest here in the Naziar. Our council and my royal father would be glad of a chance to make amends, and—I would be pleased if you would stay."

She smiled, a little embarrassed. "Thank you, my lord, very much. I would be glad to stay and learn more of Alham and her court."

"You're more than welcome. And I'm glad you have found at least one friend here so far."

She nodded. "Lady Ariana has been very kind and has taken me into her own circle. I'm seeing more of Chrenada than even I hoped."

"Lady Ariana Hazelrig?" Soren amended his assessment; if she was a friend of the Black Mage, she had no romantic illusions of the Ryuven threat.

Princess Calissa nodded. "We went last night to comfort another friend widowed by this latest raid. I think—it is not my country, but I can see how this treaty is necessary, and if indeed there has been treachery... I don't know how one negotiates with a faithless party."

No, she had no illusions of the Ryuven threat. Soren had always thought, when he'd bothered to think of it at all, the eastern lands counted themselves fortunate to have escaped most of the Ryuven threat and so looked upon the Chrenadan struggle as a bard's story. He might have been as ignorant as he assumed them to be.

"I know your time must be spent in addressing this renewed threat in what you thought was settled," she continued, "so I thank you for your hospitality and care."

"It is my pleasure," he said, and he found that he meant it.

"Are you sure you don't need me to come?"

Shianan tugged a strap against the buckle tongue. "Luca, we're going to dig up a half dozen corpses from a mass grave—if we're lucky and they weren't fed to the pigs. Trust me, you'll be happier here and minding the office."

Luca made a face. "I'll stay."

"Find something to do. Write to your brothers."

"I have." Luca's voice went quiet and flat. "I haven't heard back."

"How—" Shianan cut himself off. If Luca's worthless family had ignored his re-enslavement, if they held that against him...

"It might... It might be because I lost my inheritance."

"What?"

Luca looked away. "When I left, Thir gave me my share of the house. It was stolen when we were attacked. The thieves would have access through it to the house."

"But only to what was already yours," Shianan said, "so your brothers wouldn't be out any of their own. And surely they cannot resent you for being robbed."

"I would not have withdrawn all at once. If the thieves did, they could hobble the house finances. The money is never in coin, it's all investments and promises and deposits and loans, and pulling it out in coin would collapse the rest."

Shianan stared at him. "And you think they might refuse to answer you because they are angry over money."

Your own blood money. For your own blood.

Luca shrugged tightly. "Or they have not received my letter. That's possible, too."

Shianan shoved aside his dark anger. "Or, while I'm away," he continued, with a forced neutral tone, "you could see that the Heege border maps have been updated with the latest warlords' encampments. You could sleep an entire day. You could go to the market and buy yourself some new boots."

Luca shook his head. "I'll not be bored. I just... I didn't want..."

Shianan's hands stilled on his bag. "Go to Fhure, then."

Luca tensed behind him. "Could I?"

"I could send you on some errand or other. Enough for a quick visit, anyway." Shianan looked at him. "You can have friends, Luca."

"You're sending me off to visit Marla while you dig up old corpses."

"Look, you don't have to rub it in." Shianan went into the office and pulled a map from its pigeonhole behind his desk. "See, Fhure is not so far from the road to Nalarbor. You can wait for me on the way back to Alham here. Fedstone."

"That will be all right?"

"Of course."

CHAPTER 50

Shianan had done this before, so often that he could walk through the motions almost without thought, which would have been easier: Arrive too late to fight the Ryuven and instead face the resentful eyes of those who had expected better. Ask about the attack, observe the damages and losses, assure the survivors they were not forgotten and that their town would receive protection. Visit first the wounded and then the dead, a visible sign to the people that they mattered and a quiet, piercing reminder of what his own purpose was. And then, this time, ask about the remains of the Ryuven attackers.

The townspeople of Nalarbor had thrown the Ryuven dead into a shallow ditch outside the town, hidden by a hands-breadth of snow. Shianan ordered the bodies exhumed, while disrupted as little as possible. After the first two came up intact enough to travel, he went to negotiate the purchase of a cart from one of the local merchants.

Nalarbor, situated at the intersection of two trade routes, was grander than many raiding targets; the Ryuven must have been emboldened by their several short visits to trade in herbs and foodstuffs. They would have known exactly where to strike, given ample time to observe the market and warehouses. It seemed they had with their treaty not only invited the enemy within the gates, but shown him about the treasure house.

But the reports Shianan collected of the raid suggested they had made poor use of their knowledge. The fighting had not begun during a scheduled and overseen trade event, but in the evening as the market slowed and began to close, on a day when no Ryuven had come to sell or buy. That in itself was not surprising, but the consistent descriptions of the raiders floundering and fighting their way through the vendors and stalls made less sense. Given their new knowledge, why had they not simply appeared within the warehouse, taken what they wanted at their leisure, and then traveled home again, never even seen by human eyes?

It was as if they wanted to be observed breaking the treaty, Shianan thought. As if they wished to display their disregard for promises made to humans.

He would know why, if he had to demand it himself from Tamaryl.

Fedstone was a small village for its crossroads location, and the public room didn't seem to make any distinction between free and slave, as Luca could see both cuffed wrists and unweighted wrists at the crowded tables. He stepped close to Marla as a group pushed past them into the room and called to friends. "I suppose we had better find a table."

She nodded, and he threaded through the bustling room to a small table in the back, where they squeezed in to join three friends already eating. Luca braced himself for a warning snarl and even a cuff on the ear for daring to join them, but they only nodded curtly to the slaves and went on with their meal and conversation. Marla took a chair and looked away from them, toward the door.

Luca privately agreed with her hope that Shianan would not be long. This was the day they were to meet, but there was no telling how near Shianan was to Fedstone, or even if he had not been delayed on his mission. But the cold rain outside did not invite waiting at the public well. Luca hoped it would not turn to ice in the night, delaying Shianan and turning the roads treacherous.

It had been Marla's idea to accompany Luca here. They had gambled in Marla's coming from Fhure with Luca—she had suggested it would be good to remind Shianan of his people at Fhure, and she could convey the estate's good wishes to its master—but Shianan wouldn't be angry. He might be glad of having an aelipto to treat him tonight, or—Luca hardly dared to speculate—even in Alham. And if not, it was an easy walk back to Fhure in the morning.

Luca should have been a freeman, able to free her as well.

"We're losing our own pay to them," someone said at a table behind him. "I can't tell you how many I know who are willing to work, to do good work, but can't get hired because every farmer or sawyer has a slave for it instead. We've got to drive out these slaves if we want to be able to feed our children and be respectable."

Luca ducked his head, tightening his jaw. Beside him, Marla quietly shifted her hand to his forearm and squeezed, never turning toward him.

"Are you ordering tonight?" asked a serving maid, dusting her hands together so that her cuffs rubbed. "We've got fried vegetable cakes coming up fresh."

"That sounds grand," Marla said.

Luca nodded.

All day he had been drawing up his courage, but the walk had been fine and it had seemed a shame to spoil it with grave talk. He wanted to ask Marla's advice on his fledgling plan. He had one answer in his master, who had insisted on carrying the stolen Shard back to Alham and to the Court of the High Star, risking his own life. Luca would not risk his life, but he did not know if he was ready to risk less. Marla would listen, and she would give him good counsel.

At the door, a group of four men came in, laughing and slapping the wet from their sleeves. Luca glanced just long enough to register them—workmen earning a fair wage, happy, not looking to torment anyone, not immediately dangerous—and then drew a breath. "There's a trial—"

Marla's fingers clenched with sudden ferocity, and he looked from her to the happy men and then back. "What's wrong? What do you see?"

But Marla's face showed no alarm. Her eyes were wide, shining, full of a nascent joy. "It's Demario," she breathed. She rose from the table and rushed toward them, heedless of a slave's proper decorum. She caught a handsome man with curly white-blond hair by the upper arm and pulled him to face her. "Demario!"

Luca, watching them, saw the full sequence of his reaction, from his initial surprise at being accosted to a wide-eyed recognition and then finally revulsion. He jerked free of Marla's hands. "Don't grab at me!"

Marla stared, shocked. "But—I'm—but Demario! It is you!"

Most of the public room chattered on, unaware of the drama developing in their midst, but Demario's friends had stopped and were staring at him and the pretty young woman who had thrown herself at him. "Who's this? Another of your bad habits?"

"No one," Demario said, stepping away. "It's no one."

"I'm your wife!" Marla said, and some heads turned toward them. "Demario, I am your wife!"

Demario's mouth twisted into a mask of a smile, all false charm and handsome cheer. "No, my dear, that's not how it is, not now. We haven't been together for years."

"You promised we would find each other again!"

One of the workmen grinned. "Were you teasing a slave again? Or is she from your old days?"

Demario's mask grew fragile. "Marla, I never meant that. Don't make a scene over something so small. I only said something sweet to remember me by."

The last of Marla's joy drained out of her, leaving only a husk of hurt shock. "That's not true. You know it isn't."

Demario abandoned his smile. "Whatever it was or wasn't, it's the truth now."

Marla stared, her jaw hanging, her face pale in the public room's lamplight.

"Get off him," growled one of the laborer friends. "Go on and bother someone else." He gave Marla a little shove. Luca half rose in his seat, unsure of what he should do, and of what he could do against four freemen.

Demario gave a curt jerk of his head, signaling the friend to leave off, but he made no move toward Marla. "Look, it's over. I have a good place now, and that was nearly three years ago, and we've both moved on."

"I've waited for you all this time." Marla's voice wavered. "I asked for word of you everywhere, and I waited."

"Then you were a fool," Demario said, his tone gaining an edge. "I mean it, Marla—we're finished, we're done. I haven't been wasting my time pining for you. Don't hold your breath for me to come and get you."

He shook off her weak clasp and moved away with his friends. One said something below Luca's hearing, and Demario gave him a punch in the upper arm, and the others laughed.

Marla stood in the center of the public room, abandoned and unmoving. Luca rose and went to her, slipping his hand about her elbow, and tugged her toward the door. Around them voices rose, possibly calling encouragement or mockery or just unrelated jokes to friends, but Luca could not distinguish words over the empathetic shame and outrage rising in him.

Once outside, he drew Marla away from the door and around the corner into the narrow alley, tight enough to touch the walls with both elbows at once. Safe in the sheltered dark, pulled away from the rain dripping from the eaves, he drew her into an embrace, cupping her head against his shoulder. "I'm sorry. I'm so, so sorry."

Marla was rigid in his arms, not resisting but not yet grieving. "I don't... I don't understand. That was Demario, but that wasn't... He didn't mean that, he couldn't have meant that... It was my fault for surprising him in front of his friends. He was always sensitive to what others thought, and I should have known better than to—"

"Than to approach your husband directly?" demanded Luca. All the anger he had given up surged again in him, this time not for himself but for this innocent woman who had spent years waiting faithfully for the husband who had forgotten her in his success. "Marla, you cannot blame yourself for this. This was his choice, all of it."

"But why didn't he—?" Now Marla's voice finally broke, and with it the dam holding back her tears, and she trembled in Luca's grip as she began to sob. "Why didn't he want me?"

Because he is a hill-hog, not a man. Because he is too jealous of his status as a freeman to remind himself of his former slavery. Because he is a coward. Because he is a bully, striking at someone else to comfort himself with his own status.

Luca had no answer he could speak aloud, so he just held her.

At last Marla's tears slowed. "I'm sorry," she choked.

"Not to me," Luca said urgently. "Do not ever apologize to me for crying over betrayal."

Marla sniffed. "I suppose I can trust you most to understand." She pressed her forehead into his shoulder, convulsing a little as she fought to regain control. "Thank you for that."

Luca only squeezed her more tightly.

It was a long time later that they separated, wiped their eyes, and emerged from the alley. "I suppose that maid has given our cakes to other customers," Luca said, trying for a bit of joke.

Marla sniffed. "I'm not so hungry, anyway."

"Nor me, either."

Shianan left his soldiers at the inn's stable. They weren't pleased at standing watches on Ryuven corpses through the chilly damp night, but they had a sturdy roof and no real threats. None of the townspeople would be sneaking in to peek at the broad cart and its tarp-concealed cargo. A wet dog trotted into the stable, shaking water over the soldiers who groaned in real or feigned complaint.

Shianan should have been escorting the Wakari princess instead of dead Ryuven, but the Wakari contingent had delayed their departure upon the news of the massacre. Shianan wondered idly if Soren's intended bride might yet find a way to meet him in the delay. He wondered what that might matter in the great plans of royals.

He went into the public room and shook off the water clinging to his cloak. He waved to a server and then searched the room for Luca, who might be here instead of waiting somewhere in the evening mist. After a moment, he found him, but as he wove through the room to join him, the slave's dark expression worried him. "What's wrong?"

Luca seemed to come to himself, and he shook his head. "I'm sorry. I only—it's nothing that should concern us directly. But tonight, here in the public room, Marla's lost husband walked in."

There was a world of story behind that sentence, and Shianan had not been told it. "Marla lost a husband?"

"Demario. Let me explain: Marla came with me, here. She wanted to convey greetings from Fhure. But then she saw Demario. He and some others were sold away from Fhure when it was announced the estate would go to you, one last bit of profit for the interim steward. Marla has searched for him all this time, while it seems he was under no such burden."

"Ah." This was coming fast; Shianan tried to intuit the reason for Fhure's greetings and assess the discovery of a steward's embezzlement while listening to Luca relate the appearance of a man he'd never known.

"He's a freeman now, and he didn't look for her to redeem her—and she was in the Wakari Coast, he could have done it—and when she recognized him and went to him..." Luca's fingers tightened into fists on the table. "He humiliated her. Here in the public room."

Neither needed to say more about betrayal.

"Where is she now?" Shianan asked at last.

"In your room, upstairs. She didn't want to sit here, not where she could see him."

"He's still here?"

Luca nodded across the room. "That group of laborers, the one with the curly hair and the greased smile."

Shianan half turned and spotted him. "Can't say it looks like I suffered much with his loss. Though it would be an interesting legal question, if he earned his freedom but had been stolen beforehand..." And possibly a dangerous precedent for Luca.

Luca shook his head. "I don't want him back at Fhure. I don't think Marla wants him at Fhure, not now. I only wish I had a way to dull the pain of cutting him free."

The serving maid arrived at their table. "Sorry about your wait, it's lively tonight! We've got vegetable cakes frying up, and a nice dark ale to wash them down."

Shianan nodded approval and looked at Luca. "You've eaten?"

"Wasn't hungry."

"Then go upstairs and sit with her. I'll come after I've eaten."

He waited until the slave had gone, and then he smoothly switched seats so that he could look over the room and the table Luca had indicated. The maid brought his meal and ale, and he worked on both as he watched the men drink and laugh. The fried vegetable cakes were fresh and crisp, but he tasted nothing but the bitter tang at the back of his throat, staring at the man who had thrown away the love of a faithful woman.

At last they seemed to conclude their gathering, and the curly-haired man paid his bill and rose to leave. Shianan drained the last of his dark ale and left his empty dishes on the table.

Outside, the mist had increased to a drizzle, enough to annoy and chill those walking home. It wasn't long before the friends parted, and Shianan quietly followed the one Luca had indicated.

The rain and the dark made his approach easy. "Demario?" Shianan asked.

The man turned. "Yes?"

Shianan punched him squarely in the nose, knocking him backward.

Demario splashed in the muck of the street, one hand to his face, stunned and sodden in the filthy puddles. "What? What's wrong with you? Who are you?"

"You had that coming," Shianan snarled. "I won't send you back to your slavery, because she shouldn't be saddled with a latrine-lick like you. That's another debt you owe her."

Demario struggled upright, his eyes wide. "You can't—I'm a freeman, I earned my purchase, you can't send me back. Who are you?" He raised his hands, ready to fight.

Shianan punched him again. "I told you, I'm not interested in sending you back. I only want you to understand that you're a loathsome piece of garbage for what you did to her."

Demario stumbled and raised his fists defensively. He choked on blood from his nose. "She's everything I left behind!"

"She loved you when you were nothing. How much more would she have loved you when you stayed true to her?"

"I don't want a slave!"

Shianan hit him once more, ignoring the pretense at defense, and Demario staggered and splashed. "She didn't care if you were a slave."

Demario spat blood, diluted in the rain, and Shianan turned and walked away.

He washed his knuckles in the drizzle as he returned. He wasn't sure if his errand had made him feel better; initial consideration suggested it had not. It had done no one any good, not Luca, not Marla, and certainly not Demario. It had probably been wrong of him to do it.

It wasn't Demario he had punched. Well, Demario had taken the blows, and it was Demario's nose that would be misshapen, unless he had the courage to have it straightened. But it wasn't just Demario Shianan loathed.

Demario had abandoned the woman who had wanted him when he was nothing. He could have had her once and for all, safe in their freedom, and he had left behind the love Shianan couldn't have, discarded a precious thing as if it were rubbish.

She loved you when you were nothing. How much more would she have loved you when you stayed true to her?

He had lacked the courage to love Ariana openly and defiantly, so he had put aside the woman who had befriended him as the bastard. He had saved her life, but she would never know that, and he had repaid her honest friendship with rejection.

He wished he had the courage to love her.

He stopped at the stable to check on the cart of corpses. It was probably better that he was not escorting the Wakari princess.

CHAPTER 51

Luca balanced his tray, bearing his and Marla's breakfasts now that he'd left Shianan's inside, as he ducked through the child-sized door. He straightened, looked down the long balcony pasted onto the public house's roof, and froze.

Opposite him, Marla sat on the edge of the roof, one arm hooked around a weathered column supporting the balcony railing and the other extended. Her feet dangled over the edge and out of sight.

"Marla," Luca said, and it came out a whisper. "Marla, don't move. I mean, stay right there, so I can come to you."

She turned her head, and for just a moment her tear-streaked face looked puzzled. Then realization broke over her face. "Oh! Oh, no, no, it's not—it's nothing like that."

She wriggled backward, and Luca saw that she was straddling one of the railing supports, not sitting unprotected on the edge. His heart began to beat again, making up for lost time. The tray sagged in his grip.

Marla read it all in his face. "Oh, Luca, I'm sorry. I didn't mean—I wouldn't have frightened you like that."

He went to her and set the tray on the floor, shaking his hands loose. "I... Good."

Marla looked at the tray, looked at him, and then turned back to the sky. "You may stay only if you promise not to speak."

Luca nodded and sat beside her.

Before them, the sun rose over the wet town, coaxing life out of the townhouses and shops. Here and there columns of denser smoke marked the locations of bakeries, whose fires had not sunk overnight but had been stoked for early baking and morning sales.

"I wouldn't throw myself off a rooftop here," Marla said at last. "The Greater Asar River runs too near here, and I've heard ghosts cannot cross running water. I'd want to haunt and torment him all the remaining days of his miserable life."

Luca did not answer, guiltily grateful that she had forbidden him to speak.

Marla sighed. "Was I such a fool, as he said? We were slaves, we were separated, we had no expectation of finding one another again, much less of being reunited in any sort of sustainable marriage. Perhaps he was the realistic one, cutting free dead weight that could never be of value."

Luca kept his eyes on the yellow and orange of the sky. "Maybe he was more realistic. But that does not mean that you were a fool."

Marla's hand moved to his, closed about his palm, squeezed like a woman finding a rope in a whirlpool. "Thank you," she whispered.

They sat together in silence, and tears ran silently down Marla's cheeks. She did not wipe them away.

The sun burned away the orange and threw golden light over the city, and the sounds of the morning market rose to them, friendly greetings and urgent orders and good-natured bartering.

"I think," Marla said at last, "that by tradition, this is where I should be surrounded by female friends who all reassure me that he is a boot-licking pot of dysentery and that I am in fact glad to be relieved of the burden of him."

Luca smiled. "I am not a bevy of female friends, but I will do my best."

"I believe I owe you an apology," Marla continued. "A few months ago, you were suffering your own betrayal, and I told you to think on what had driven him to such action. I find now that I am wholly aware of the advantages of Demario's choices, and yet..."

Luca took a breath. "I never liked him anyway."

Marla looked at him and laughed. It was a bitter laugh, but it was at least a laugh.

They sat together for another few moments, watching the streets grow more active with morning business. At last Marla rocked her weight back and crossed her legs. "I think I'm not going to ask to come along to Alham."

Luca nodded. He had supposed as much. With her long-nurtured hopes dashed in callous rejection, Marla would want to be near her mother and friends in a familiar setting, not in a strange city with a master she hardly knew.

"But send us word when you can. Of the master's work and position, and of yourself." She squeezed the hand she still held.

"I'll try."

Shianan came out onto the balcony. "Am I missing something important?" He looked across the roofs and leaning windows. "Not the view, at least." He started to lean against the rail, thought better of it, and shifted against the wall beside the short door. "Marla, I didn't take the time to ask last night, but what brings you to Fedstone with Luca?"

His expression was neutral, but Luca thought he knew his master well enough to detect the too-neutral mask. Shianan was hoping—hoping for something.

Marla did not know him well enough to see it. "I'm sorry, my lord. I only wanted to bring you greetings from your house. We think of you."

"And you mean I should think of you, too."

Marla ducked her head. "They say you don't visit often, nor even write to Kraden."

"I suppose I don't."

When Shianan had returned last night, he had said little and had gone directly to bed, wrapping over and over in his blankets. Marla, unnaturally quiet since the scene with Demario, had followed his example in her own corner, leaving Luca to listen to the rain drumming on the slanted roof and wish he could do more.

Shianan waved a hand. "They're right. I've neglected the place."

"My lord, I don't mean to be—"

"You aren't; it's just another responsibility I've been shirking. I should thank you for the reminder." Shianan sighed. "And if that's settled, then let's be up and packing. I've got a cart of corpses to transport to Alham."

CHAPTER 52

A page walked through the halls with an over-sized bell, calling councilors, mages, and soldiers to the council room. Shianan followed the generals at a little distance.

The king and prince-heir attended as well. Chancellor Uilleam ascertained that all were present, and then he announced, "The bodies have been brought and laid out for our examination. I know this is not to the taste of all here, but I think we may agree it's important that we all observe, at least initially, to be sure there has been no misdirection. What decisions we make must be founded on our proper understanding of the facts."

No one looked pleased, but no one disagreed.

"Then let us go and see what awaits us at the midden."

"The midden?" someone repeated, before cutting off the word.

Shianan cleared his throat. "I brought the bodies this morning. But they have been dead for six days. They cannot be brought into the palace rooms."

No one answered, and after a moment Chancellor Uilleam gestured them out the door.

The six bodies were laid out on trestles, not at the midden proper but near it and well out of the public gardens of the Naziar. Shianan did not waste time looking at the covered forms as many of the councilors did—he had seen enough of them already—but instead watched Tamaryl as he approached, trying to divine the Pairvyn's thoughts.

The dead Ryuven smelled. It was not the worst of putrefaction; the bodies were only days old and the season was mercifully cold. But it was enough that they had been deliberately laid out for inspection in the open air. Many of the councilors had brought scented handkerchiefs or vials, which they held above their lips. Like the soldiers, Shianan noted, the mages of the Great Circle did not shield themselves from the scent of rot.

General Kannan took the initiative. "Let's get this over with." He went to the first corpse and pulled back the oiled tarp that enclosed it. Fluids ran out and onto the ground, and many of the observers shrank back.

The Ryuven was yellow-green with rot, bloated around the edges of the armor still strapped in place. He had died of an upward thrust to his torso, which had pierced the hardened leather and probably his heart or a lung. As Kannan examined and shifted the armor, the stained hole matched the wound. "Plenty of blood," Kannan observed. "This happened while he was alive. And armored, so not a trader."

The face was flaccid; the collapse of muscle had taken any last expression and blood had drained away from the upturned skin. The eyes were filmy white and marred with active insects. There was little left to speak of his motivation. All that remained was the armor and the wounds, both of which said plainly that it was a Ryuven warrior who had died at Nalarbor.

Tamaryl said nothing. His face, when Shianan glanced at him, was pale, like a fresher corpse himself.

Kannan pulled away the next tarp without ceremony or preparation. Several gasped and pulled their protective handkerchiefs to their faces. This one had died of an axe to his forehead.

"Not much to see here," Kannan muttered, dropping the tarp to the floor. He turned, leaving the body uncovered—Shianan suspected he enjoyed making the courtiers uncomfortable—and tugged back the covering on the next. "What about this one?"

This one had taken an arrow to the torso, which had bent the light armor into the wound. The others bore similar wounds and telltale marks. These had been warriors, dressed in their armor when they died.

"We have to be sure," protested Denys, his face screwed up in discomfort but his resolve firm. He was known to be a niggler for details, though whether this was conscientious or contentious depended on who spoke of him. "Were these Ryuven warriors who raided as in the past? Or were these merchants who donned armor because they suspected a threat? Can we be sure?"

Kannan sighed. "I think it is evident, my lord, when taken with the reports we have received, that these Ryuven were the attackers."

Denys held his handkerchief to his face but pressed on determinedly. "We cannot afford another Arakadamia without very good assurance, General Kannan. We must be certain."

Shianan stepped forward to the body who had died of the axe wound and, using a corner of the tarp to handle the slick skin, rolled it onto one shoulder. "Look here," he said, half lifting an arm. "You can tell the thickening of the skin where the arm regularly rubbed over the ridge of this leather piece." He glanced at General Kannan, who did not stop him, and then unbuckled the breastplate. "Look here, along the collarbone, and the neck. See how the skin has calloused? He did not wear this for a day. He trained routinely in this armor."

Shianan dropped the armor and released the body, which sagged back over a folded wing, arm flopping outward. The group was silent. With that revelation, the end of the treaty was certain. Peace was dead. It remained only to acknowledge it with words.

"Wait."

Tamaryl's voice was choked and thin, and his eyes were fixed on the body Shianan had released. He moved toward it, staring. "Look at his forearm."

Shianan did. There was a scar there—which seemed odd now that he thought about it, as Ryuven could heal themselves of minor injuries when they wished. Did he mean to suggest these were not Ryuven corpses? But the wings draping to the ground could not be manufactured so easily.

Tamaryl grasped the arm and turned the underside upward, exposing the scar. It was a series of small pricks of raised flesh, light and barely rising above the surrounding skin, forming two long lines slanting to a shared end, a narrow arrow like the flight of migrating birds. "Do you see this?"

They all did. But Shianan did not understand his agitation.

Tamaryl spun and tore open the thin sleeve of the next corpse. He looked and then dropped it. He moved around the bodies, checking each until he found another similar scar, made more visible once he buffed the failing outer skin. "Just two, but that is not surprising." He returned to the first body and jabbed his finger at the exposed forearm. "Look!"

"We see," Uilleam said. "But it means nothing to us."

Tamaryl looked wide-eyed around at them, an eerie grin growing on his face. He seemed almost giddy, and more than one courtier eased backward as he turned. "This is a mark of the Ientu. Not all choose it, but it is common among them, a mark of distinction and control over their own innate power." He pointed again at the long arrow. "These are not Ai. The treaty is not broken. The Ai have not broken the treaty."

Relief was nearly palpable in his voice, but Shianan did not understand. Neither did the councilors. "Are you saying these are not your warriors?"

"They are not," Tamaryl answered promptly. "You are in the habit of speaking merely of the Ryuven, because you have had dealings primarily with only one clan, and so the Ai and the Ryuven are the same to you. But we are many peoples, just as humans are many peoples. The Ai swore peace with you and offered trade. But these are the Ientu, and they would not be bound by our treaty any more than the Wakari Coast or Heege would consider themselves bound by an agreement made by Chrenada."

For a moment there was quiet, and then several people began to speak at once. Shianan stepped forward, holding his breath, to examine the mark. It was a series of raised scars, too neatly done and too similar on the separate bodies to be accidental.

"They do it with hot nails," Tamaryl said. Shianan jerked his head up, and the Ryuven grinned as if they were friends. "I never thought I would be so glad to see it."

"Tamaryl'sho," interrupted Mage Ewan Hazelrig, "are you saying to us, clearly and without hesitation, that these dead Ryuven are not Ryuven of your clan, but of another clan?"

"That is my assertion, yes." Tamaryl straightened from the bodies. "You have heard how the Ai have struggled for generations with a blight on our crops. Our supplementary food came from Chrenada—forgive me for speaking bluntly, it is no secret here. Other clans have warred with us, but we have defended ourselves, and none made so bold as to encroach upon our precious source of food.

"But now we have traders leaping back and forth between our worlds. Other clans will have observed by now that we are not sending raiding parties, but merchants. It is not unreasonable to believe that one of them—the Ientu, it seems—has ventured to extend their reach into Chrenada, assuming that if we are not making war here, it may be open to their own invasion."

"It is not." King Jerome spoke for the first time, from the rear furthest from the corpses. "Chrenada is a sole and independent kingdom, subject to itself, and not a field for harvest by the Ai, nor any other."

"No, of course not," Tamaryl assured him, turning to face the king. "The Ai value our equitable trade with Chrenada. That right to trade we will defend, and if it pleases my lord, I believe that desire for equitable trade is a possible solution to this unwanted incursion."

"I will not open trade with every invader who murders our people instead of extending an overture of diplomatic relations and trade negotiations," King Jerome said stiffly. "I will not reward death."

"I do not suggest you should," Tamaryl said. "But let me speak to Oniwe'aru and inform him what has happened here—as I am sure he is unaware of the actions of the Ientu, a clan that has not been friendly to us in a generation."

King Jerome frowned. "I do not see why Oniwe's opinions should have weight, now that you have said it is not his people who are killing mine."

Tamaryl inclined his head. "Consider, my lord, that Oniwe'aru was blamed initially for this attack upon your people. His honor has been assaulted as well as your own."

"It was not Oniwe's people who died in this attack," King Jerome retorted.

"With respect, my lord, I believe some were calling for the death of at least one of Oniwe'aru's subjects." Tamaryl kept his eyes steady on the king, not looking about the group. A few dropped their eyes to examine handkerchiefs or adjust sleeves.

"And what then do you propose, my lord Tamaryl?"

"I propose nothing as yet, Your Majesty. Give me leave to speak to my aru first, as you would have your councilors and generals inform and consult with you before acting."

"That would mean dropping the shield, which is the only protection we have against another such raid," King Jerome said. "And we have only your word that these Ryuven are not of your clan. Allowing you to return to your own world when there is doubt is not the first choice of a wise man."

"It may be the considered choice of a prudent man," Tamaryl answered evenly. "If I lie, and these Ryuven are Ai warriors, and you kill me, you have done nothing to stop the assaults and the raids will continue. Killing me accomplishes little but a brief indulgence of anger. If I speak the truth, and if these Ryuven are Ientu warriors, we might salvage our treaty and continue our trade. You stand to gain much more by continuing diplomatic relations."

"Gain what, exactly?"

Tamaryl turned his hands upward. "I must consult with Oniwe'aru. I do not speak as a ruler for the Ai. But most importantly, I

337

cannot speak for a ruler who is unaware of what is happening here. Oniwe'aru entered into this treaty for our mutual peace and he should be informed of any threats to that peace. I ask that you allow me to perform my duty to him and thus for you."

King Jerome frowned, and the council nodded. They understood the limits of ambassadors and emissaries. Beside him, Prince Soren looked unsettled, looking from his father to Tamaryl to the councilors and mages around them. Shianan felt conspicuous, standing beside the Ryuven, but it seemed more conspicuous to move away while everyone looked at them.

"We do not need to make a decision now," King Jerome announced. "Give us time to discuss this and consider what you have said."

It was all that Tamaryl could have expected, and he did not seem disappointed. He bowed. "Thank you, Your Majesty."

General Kannan flipped the tarp again on the nearest Ryuven body. "If these aren't yours, I don't suppose you'll be wanting them back."

"No," Tamaryl answered, "but it must be possible to dispose of them with a modicum of respect, as with any human soldiers who are not claimed by kin."

General Kannan scowled. "We don't generally carry back soldiers of the enemy. But we can find something."

"I'll see they're buried," Shianan said.

Tamaryl looked at him, and Shianan recalled the little farm where he and the boy Tam had buried bodies so, so long ago, a year before.

"Thank you, your lordship," Tamaryl said.

CHAPTER 53

Luca placed a half dozen notes on the desk. "These came while you were out," he said. "I think some are duplicate reports, but still."

Shianan fanned them on his desk. "But that's still four raiding parties." He clenched his fist on the desk. "King's sweet oats, when will we be free of Ryuven?" But it was hardly a question. He looked back at Luca. "Could you go to General Septime's office, please, and wait for whatever orders are being written? I'll want them directly."

"Of course."

"It's going to be multiple deployments, to address all these at once," Shianan mused.

He was correct.

Tamaryl strode into the Palace of Red Sands and nodded to the guard. She returned the nod with a sharp, clean movement. Tamaryl turned away then, blowing out air in a long stream. His arrival would be communicated to Oniwe'aru, who would admit him, anxious to hear how the new peace was faring in Chrenada and utterly unaware of any raids set to destroy the precious treaty. Certainly he was ignorant of the Ientu raiding party.

Certainly it was a Ientu raiding party.

When he was called, Tamaryl held himself to a respectable pace and entered Oniwe'aru's audience chamber, kneeling as if his heart and stomach were not throbbing together in exchanged places.

"Rise, Tamaryl'sho, and apprise us of the situation in the human world."

Tamaryl stood. Oniwe'aru looked well; did that mean he had not violated his oath?

Edeiya'rika was present, and another courtier, Akiri'sho. Was that good? If Tamaryl was right about the Ientu, it would be good. If he had been wrong, if Oniwe played a dark game, well, he did not know how an audience would influence the conversation.

"There is a problem, Oniwe'aru," Tamaryl said. A strong opening would demand Oniwe'aru's attention and set the tone.

"I am aware." The aru's mouth turned down. "A che died as he was departing for a trading visit and met that flame-cursed shield. Fortunately, the others had time to recognize his death and halt before they were affected. We called an end to all departures." He gave Tamaryl a narrow look. "We thought you might be dead, with the end of the treaty."

"The treaty may not be ended," Tamaryl said hurriedly. "I pleaded for the shield to be lowered so that I could come and speak with you. But first, I have a request." Tamaryl set his jaw. "Oniwe'aru, will you stand?"

"What?"

"Will you stand, and let me see you?"

Oniwe'aru rose from his stool, his head canted to one side. He raised his arms, palms to the ceiling, and spread his wings to half their span. Then he turned slowly in place. "Well?"

There were no dark, deep scores across his wings or other limbs. Tamaryl released the breath he was holding. It was possible the oath-wounds were hidden beneath his sleek garments, but...

"Thank you," Tamaryl breathed.

Edeiya'rika looked from Tamaryl to Oniwe'aru, her expression inscrutable.

"The trade had been progressing well, as I'm sure you've seen," he said. Oniwe'aru would have daily reports on the merchants' travels and sales.

"Good," Oniwe'aru said. He resumed his place on the stool. "Then what has raised the shield and brought you with such unexpected urgency?"

"The problem is with a raid on a merchant town, which killed over forty human traders, beside the soldiers. The Chrenadan council is understandably upset and is prepared to negate the treaty."

Oniwe'aru jerked upright in his low-backed chair. "What raid is this? A Ryuven incursion?" His face darkened. "Has one of our sho or che violated our word?"

A swell of relief rocked Tamaryl so that he actually shifted a wing to balance. Oniwe'aru was many things, but never a dissembler. He bore no oath-wounds; he had not known about the raid. He had not set Tamaryl to fall for a broken treaty.

Now the question was whether a rogue che or the Ientu had led the raid.

"Six Ryuven were killed in the raid," Tamaryl said, "and I had opportunity to see the bodies while pleading with the council not to nullify the treaty. Two of them bore a Ientu mark."

Oniwe relaxed. "Well, that is good to hear. It is not one of our own sho or che dishonoring my word."

"It would be good to affirm that with the Chrenadan king and council," Tamaryl said.

Oniwe'aru looked annoyed. "If they are Ientu warriors, that should be obvious."

"It is not obvious to them," Tamaryl said. "For generations, the Ai have raided the Chrenada stores and supplies. They have seen no other Ryuven, and they think of all Ryuven as Ai."

Akiri'sho sniggered. "How childish, to assume one clan is an entire race."

Tamaryl shook his head. "It is foolish from our view, of course. But as they cannot travel here, they see only those who come into their own land. And that has been Ai for as long as they can remember, and their grandparents, and their grandparents."

"How sad," Edeiya'rika murmured. "To lose details so easily."

"For them, the Ryuven are the Ai. It was difficult to convince them that another clan might be acting in their lands now."

"Then help their understanding," Oniwe'aru agreed. "We will trust you as our emissary to make it perfectly clear that the Ientu are not the Ai, that they are outside my influence, and that they, being outside our treaty, have not violated that treaty."

Tamaryl nodded. "Thank you. But I'm afraid that will not be enough."

"Not enough?"

"The king and council agreed to this treaty with us to end Ryuven raids. If Ryuven raids continue, they will see no advantage in the treaty."

"Well, we at least are not raiding them," said Oniwe'aru with a huff. "That is an advantage, certainly."

"Indeed. But it is difficult for them to understand why there have been no Ientu raids in all these years and suddenly, now that they have a treaty with the Ai, that has changed."

"Well, that should be obvious enough," Akiri'sho observed. "When we raided the human world, it was a precious resource to us, our own human-worked farms, and no one would have dared to challenge us for it. Now we are not raiding it, so it seems the fields are left unattended. The Ientu are greedy opportunists, so they will venture a few raids on humans to determine if that is profitable."

"On Chrenada," Tamaryl corrected mildly. "Not the entire race."

Oniwe'aru looked from Akiri'sho to Tamaryl, and his expression shifted to amusement. "Ah, Tamaryl'sho."

"I have to bring an answer to King Jerome and his council," Tamaryl said. "What can I say for you?"

"Just as I have said: the Ientu raiders have no part in our treaty and therefore do not violate it. Our treaty stands." Oniwe'aru gestured. "And as a gesture of good faith, we will lend our Pairvyn ni'Ai to their defense efforts."

Akiri'sho cut short his snort so quickly it might have been imagined. Edeiya'rika looked pained.

Tamaryl would not pass on the aru's words as they had been given; it was unlikely that King Jerome would recognize the disdain in the suggestion that the Pairvyn, a warlord for battles of conquest, would be needed in his defense, but Tamaryl would find another way to say it.

But he had been given permission to go out with the Chrenadan troops. That was good.

Philip was on Kuolema, guiding him through an arrangement of poles on the ground, and the young horse was picking his way delicately through. As Shianan reached the fence, he fought an irrational twinge of jealousy. Of course Philip was working with the horse; it was his task.

Kuolema's ears pricked toward the fence. At his next step he banged a foot against a pole, and for a moment he held his foot high, his ears flattened at the sting.

"Then you should pay attention," Philip admonished gently, rubbing the horse's neck. "All right, go on then." He loosened the reins, and the horse stretched his neck and walked to the fence, snuffling toward Shianan.

Shianan accepted the big head—horses were so unbelievably large, almost like the beasts of the mountains—and rubbed it. "Hello, there. You should be more careful."

"Take it as a flattery that he found you distracting," Philip said. "But he's done good work today."

Shianan combed his fingers through Kuolema's forelock, picking out a few bits of bedding and dust. He drew out a narrow apple core saved from his breakfast. "Of course he has. He's an excellent fellow." Immediately he felt foolish, as if he'd spoken gibbering baby talk in the market.

But Philip smiled. "I'm glad my lord likes him, too." He slid off the horse. "Would you like to take him around to cool him?"

Shianan climbed the fence and took the reins. There was no mounting block, and Philip stood close if Shianan needed a cupped hand, but Shianan gave a hop and caught the stirrup with his foot, swinging his right leg cleanly over the saddle and horse. He had brushed Kuolema only once while mounting, making the horse's ears flatten, and Philip's silent look of disappointment had been enough to ensure he did it properly thereafter.

He gathered the reins and they went off around the ring. Shianan avoided the poles; he didn't pretend to be able to teach the horse what he himself didn't know. But he could revel in the feel of riding and the partnership. Some, Philip said, rode a horse like directing a wagon, issuing orders to slaves and then hearing nothing. But others—and with his tone he invited Shianan to be one of these others—rode in unison with their horses, listening as much as speaking.

Shianan did not have long; he had stolen time from preparations to enjoy a few moments with the horse. At least he had escaped the long council debates weighing Tamaryl's insistence on another Ryuven clan as the perpetrator. In the end, they had agreed for now to repel these fresh raids—something Chrenada was well-prepared for, at any rate—and to allow the growing trade to continue. It fell to Shianan, of course, to lead one of the defense expeditions.

Too soon he turned toward the gate where Philip waited. He dismounted reluctantly.

Philip took the reins and loosened the girth. "If it's servant's work, then forgive my asking, but would my lord like to take him in?"

Shianan recognized the subtle compliment from the stablemaster, entrusting the invaluable horse to Shianan's even temporary care. He grinned his thanks and took back the reins.

"One moment, if you please," came a female voice.

Shianan and Philip turned together, both straightening as Queen Azalie approached. A maid followed her, but the queen's eyes were on them and the horse. "He looks very good, Philip. And he went well for you, commander."

"Thank you," Shianan murmured, awkward beneath her scrutiny and approval.

Kuolema extended his neck toward her, and she stroked the dark red head. "I am glad he's doing well. We're going to use him with my mare Ori."

Shianan nodded, noting Philip was not surprised by this announcement.

She looked to Philip. "Is Ori near ready? We'll have to do it soon, if it's to be done before the commander leaves."

Shianan smiled. "Your Majesty, I expect Kuolema can get the job done without my encouragement."

She laughed. "I'm sure he could. But he won't be here after you take him to the new front."

Shianan stared at her, struggling to form her words into meaning. It sounded like—but that couldn't be what she meant—

It was Philip who confirmed the queen's intent, with his startled and promptly-masked expression.

The queen smiled at the effect. "Commander, I understand in this deployment you are supposed to be partnering with a Ryuven officer."

"It's—Tamaryl'sho will be with Marshal Vanguilder's command."

"Nevertheless, a Ryuven officer will have great mobility on the field; you should as well. You'll need a fast horse to oversee a greater area. Kuolema is swift and has been practicing with you."

Shianan tried for a moment to suppress his reaction and then failed to an overpowering grin. "Your Majesty, I don't know what to say to this. I am—but I should decline. It's not to my usual style as a commander."

"Nor is working alongside a Ryuven. But I suppose we'll all have something new to try now." She gave Kuolema's neck a final pat. "Take good care of him, and may he take good care of you." She stepped back. "Send me word, Philip, about Ori."

CHAPTER 54

The bustle of military units preparing to march out filled the staging ground and spilled over into the surrounding streets. Shianan moved from captain to sergeant, answering questions, directing troops, solving or dismissing minor problems.

The mages had identified two sizable forces of Ryuven coming through the between-worlds, with barely time enough for soldiers to meet them. They would be pressing hard on the march to be ready for the Ryuven arrival.

It almost felt good to be back to the familiar defensiveness, and that worried Shianan faintly—why did fighting feel more comfortable than the peace they had wanted?—but he shook it away. There was no time to pick apart his vague emotions when they had a duty to fulfill.

He turned and saw Kuolema and Philip coming through the crowded courtyard. Kuolema tossed his head and flicked his ears in annoyance at the press but stayed steady beside the groom. Shianan was proud of him.

"Here he is, my lord," Philip said as they came near. "I've brought fodder for a supply wagon, and there's an extra hook pick in this saddle bag, in case he picks up a stone on the road. Now, you feel comfortable with him at night? You know to watch for that place on his withers where the sweat catches, to make sure it doesn't rub."

"I'll be very careful of him, I promise," Shianan assured him with a smile. "He'll tell you all about it when we return."

"I apologize, my lord. You've always done very well with him. It's just always something like sending a child out to his first work."

Shianan took the reins and stroked the horse. "I'm sure it is."

"Shianan!"

He turned and saw Ariana, gaping with one hand halfway to her mouth. Her eyes shone as she looked from him to Kuolema, realizing the horse was for him, and it was every ounce the glorious sensation he had imagined it would be.

He beckoned her closer. "This is Kuolema."

"He's beautiful." She reached a hand out tentatively. "May I?"

"Of course. He's more than friendly."

Philip smiled, recognizing Shianan's delighted pride, and took a step back.

"How?" Ariana breathed, spreading her fingers over the bay coat, reveling in the horse.

"He belongs to the queen," Shianan said.

Ariana looked wide-eyed at him, believing him but puzzled.

"She was grateful for the prince's recovery," Shianan said, "and this was her way of expressing that."

"Oh, Shianan, he's wonderful. I'm so happy for you." She turned on him. "And you never said anything!"

"So I could wait for this moment," Shianan admitted. "Your expression was worth a thousand omissions."

"You wretch. I'll never believe anything you don't say ever again." She grinned as Kuolema lipped at her forearm. "He's so gentle for his size! So you'll ride him into battle?"

"Oh, no. He's only here for his experience, and in case I should need more rapid observation or orders."

She nodded. "I'm so happy for you," she repeated. "He's wonderful."

He watched her stroke the horse, tugging a snarl from his dark mane and then scratching where Kuolema presented his chin, and he missed her. Missed her since the disastrous audience with the king, missed all the time he had not had with her since he had pushed her from his office, protesting that they could not be friends while he could not court her.

"Walk with me," he said, his voice softer and more urgent than he'd intended.

She looked up, startled, and nodded. Shianan looked to Philip, waiting at the end of the horse's lead, but the stablemaster was already gathering the line and speaking to the horse. He would see Kuolema's provisions packed and keep the horse settled in the busy yard.

Ariana fell into step beside Shianan and looked ahead as they walked, just another member of the Circle consulting with a military officer during preparations. "I've missed you," she said.

Her echo of his thoughts gave him a galvanizing rush. "I am so sorry," he started. "I should have—"

"Hush," she interrupted. "We have so little time together, and I don't want it filled with apologies and regrets. I want to talk with my excellent friend, and I want to pretend none of that, in that dreadful audience, happened. Will you do that for me? Just for now, at least?"

He nodded.

"But now I have to think of what I want to say first to the friend I haven't seen in so long." She gave a little laugh. "What news?"

"The high priest will be sentenced soon," Shianan said. "That's good news, anyway."

"It is. I am loath to admit how long I needed to realize you'd taken his slave—but then, I was otherwise occupied for most of that, and I haven't been to visit you very often." The back of her hand brushed his, an accident in her stride.

"That's Luca." It felt surreal to explain something so obvious and integral to his life. "You haven't had much chance to see him. He wasn't here after you—returned, either. I sent him home to his family on the Wakari Coast, but...he's back with me now."

"That must be a curious story," she said. "You'll have to tell me."

"He's my best friend," Shianan admitted softly. "The whole thing is curious."

She did not look stunned, or confused, or disappointed. She only smiled a little. "I knew you couldn't really think as you said at the Citadel."

But he had, as ashamed as he was to recall it now.

"Do you think I could hear the whole curious story?" she asked. "When this fighting is done, could we have dinner, like we used to?"

All the breath went out of him, and he kept his eyes across the yard, just another officer consulting with a mage of the Circle. "Yes, I would like that very much."

Her hand brushed across his knuckles again.

"Sir!" A voice drew his attention, but when he looked, two soldiers were hushing another, trying to avoid his gaze.

Shianan changed direction and went to the supply wagon they were loading. "What is it?"

"Sorry, sir, it's nothing that needs an officer," one of the men said. The woman beside him nodded, giving a sharp glance to the other man who had called. "Just a rusted latch. We'll get it done."

Shianan glanced down at the crate they were struggling with. Whether it had been stored improperly or had been purchased damaged, its latch was rusted in place. "You did well to notice this before loading it."

"Aldred and I have been caught on the road before," the woman answered. "No way am I going to load a crate of arrows I can't get into in a hurry. Just need to find a crowbar or something to break it before it goes in."

"Hands away, please," Ariana said, and there was a crackle of energy as something invisible slammed into the latch. The wood bowed and flakes of orange rust scattered. She gestured again, and again, and on the fourth magical blow the fatigued bolts gave way.

The woman lifted the lid, checking to make sure it moved smoothly, and nodded at the collection of barbed arrows within. "Thank you, my lady mage!"

"My pleasure...?" Ariana prompted.

"Nesta, my lady mage. This is Aldred, and here's Terrick."

"Nice to meet you all. Thanks for your efforts."

"Well, I can see my work here is finished," Shianan said, and they all grinned.

"Thank you, sir," said Terrick, the one who had called him to the others' chagrin.

As they walked away together, Shianan said to Ariana, "Thanks. I suppose it's different when you have magic at your disposal. Saves on walking for a crowbar." He grinned.

She snorted. "Magic doesn't solve every problem, you know."

"It has to help."

"Certainly it does. So does knowing how to swim, or knowing how to place a staff strike. It's all about the tool and the situation."

"Still." He looked at the empty grey sky. "What was the most powerful you've ever felt?"

The corners of Ariana's mouth turned up. "It's probably not what you think."

"Dropping out of the sky with the Pairvyn ni'Ai, blowing away an entire battle? That's my guess."

She shook her head. "Oh, no, I was too afraid to feel powerful. So much was at stake and I didn't know if I could wholly trust Tamaryl, which is ridiculous but things just then were bad, and I didn't have so much power, anyway—I was using the energy brought from the Ryuven world, which I barely had a grip on. So no, I didn't feel particularly powerful then."

They'd come to one of the tall wagons, tented for transporting the wounded through inclement weather. Shianan took the far side, away from most of the yard's eyes. "When, then, if not breaking up a battle?"

Her expression sobered. "When I first went to the Ryuven world, I was—ill. Their magic is dangerously strong, much more prevalent than here, a toxic atmosphere of power. Not toxic to them, but a human mage was never meant for such a thing. It kills most. All. All but me. I did not die, and I was given drugs to dull my senses and keep me safe but helpless and immobile."

He did not like to think of her so vulnerable in such a hostile environment, so he covered his discomfort with a small nudge and a jest. "And that's when you felt most powerful, drugged into a stupor?"

She didn't laugh. "One day, there was—they didn't think much of me, most Ryuven, because I was just a sleeper. Less than a sleeper. Only Maru, Tamaryl's retainer, thought of me as a conscious entity. So when he was attacked, she did not care that she did it in my room, because she didn't think of me as really present."

"Attacked?"

"It wasn't—she didn't try to stab him or cut him. She—she tried to force him. Was forcing him. And torturing him magically for resisting."

Shianan regretted his previous levity. "I—I'm so sorry. That must have been horrific, to be there while it happened."

"I couldn't face the magic," she said. "It hurt too much, and I knew it could burn me out as it had every previous prisoner. I never would have tried to channel it for myself. But Maru, who had saved Tamaryl and helped me, Maru was—it was awful. And so I took the magic and I used it, and it hurt and I was terrified, but then I was awake and strong and she ran from me. And holding that magic, knowing it could kill me, *should* kill me, was the most powerful I have ever been."

She looked at him and smiled, and that simple, unpretentious smile pierced him and coiled about his soul. He stopped and faced her earnestly. "That—that is why I love you. That you can face down your fear and risk yourself, and for someone else—that is your defining characteristic. It's what I admire in you and wish for."

She stared at him, her lips parted in wonder. "But—but Shianan, that is you."

He blinked at her.

Her hand slid up his arm, resting near his shoulder. "That is what you do every day. You do none of this for yourself—right now, you don't fight the Ryuven for your own benefit. You are brilliant at what you do, and you take some pleasure in doing it well, but it's not for glory or pleasure that you do these things. I have seen you step forward not just for the people you protect but for Luca, for me. You face the enemy soldier, you face the king, not for yourself but for those you care for." Her mouth tightened. "I know how hard it is. I know you must be afraid, and yet you do it. You are the bravest man I have ever met, and you inspire me to be brave."

Shianan stared at her, hearing her words and not quite daring to believe them. She couldn't know the depths of his fear, that was impossible, but even to say the milder truth of what she might think...

Ariana cupped his face in her hands, pulling him close. "You don't fight for yourself—but you are your strongest when you are protecting someone else. Think of how many people you are protecting today, Luca and me and the entire countryside and all the city-dwellers who rely on the farmers. Today you are saving all of us, Shianan, and that must make you nearly invincible." She leaned in and kissed him. "Go and be invincible."

She released him, smiling, and then moved away from the wagon and back into the yard where the troops were assembling. Shianan stared after her, the warm pressure of her lips still tingling through him. It was not the deepest or most passionate kiss, but it was one of the most important of his life.

She believed in him, drew inspiration from him, relied on him. In that moment he could not have failed her.

He shrugged his cloak into place and started toward his troops.

CHAPTER 55

The military exit from Alham looked far grander than usual, as it was two contingents leaving at the same time. They would take the same road at first, but eventually Shianan would cut northeast, with Captain Torg's and Captain Abbar's units, while Ariana would travel to the west with Marshal Vanguilder and Tamaryl'sho.

The general mood was of rising optimism. When the treaty was untrustworthy, when a lie of peace had been used to infiltrate and murder, there had been unrest and outrage. Now that the offenders were simply an enemy raiding party, all had settled into old routine. Raids were commonplace and understood; raids could be dealt with.

Shianan wished Ariana had been assigned to accompany his command, but that would have been too much to hope for. The generals knew, with everyone else, that the king had met with Ariana Hazelrig and Shianan Becknam after the ball, had ordered Becknam arrested but had not followed through, had later called Mage Hazelrig for a quieter second meeting. The generals had no wish to court trouble.

For this expedition, Vanguilder had the Black Mage, and Shianan had the Cobalt Mage.

Since the disastrous royal audience, Shianan had not seen Ariana but for their talk in the staging ground. He longed to sit with her, to talk with her—to finally speak aloud of the king's clandestine visit to his own office and test his reactions to that. But their most urgent words could not be shared before hundreds of soldiers.

On the evening of the first day, the mages attached to his command alerted him to an arrival through the between-worlds, and Shianan led a contingent to a hamlet targeted by a dozen Ryuven marauders. The fighting was quick and decisive; several Ryuven were dead within minutes of their arrival, and the rest fled into the sky and across the between-worlds once more.

It was all so familiar. It did not matter who the Ryuven raiders were; they were Ryuven raiders, and Shianan and his troops knew how to deal with them. It felt good to be able to at last make a quick and clear accomplishment.

In the morning, the trains prepared to split for their separate destinations. Shianan was in a bright mood as he groomed and saddled Kuolema. Apparently this new clan, whoever they were, lacked the Ai's accommodations to fighting humans over generations of practice, and they were not prepared to deal with human weaponry, human strength, and human magic. If this was how the new invaders would fight, this war would be far less brutal and far more brief than the last one.

And Shianan would be praised for his quick and efficient work, and then, just maybe, in the flush of his praise, he might ask—

His hand convulsed on the reins, and Kuolema threw his head in protest. Shianan closed his eyes against a sudden flush of self-loathing. How quickly he could fall once again into hoping he could win approbation, hoping he could use earned favor to purchase what he wanted. When would he learn?

Shianan tightened Kuolema's girth. The horse laced his ears flat to his neck, jerking his head, and Shianan frowned. He loosened the girth and ran his fingers along it.

"How are my two handsome fellows this morning?" Ariana extended a hand to Kuolema, who brightened and stretched his head for a scratch.

Shianan found a bit of hard grass stem caught in the girth's stitching. He pulled it free and flicked it away. "I never thought I should be jealous of a horse."

"So I cannot even acknowledge his beauty? So petty, you are."

Shianan tightened the girth again. It was strange and dizzying, flirting gently with Ariana Hazelrig, finally quietly acknowledging their desires, even if they were discreet and even if they knew it was only flirting. Dizzying and dangerous. "If you've finished sulking, my lady mage, please walk with me to the supply wagon."

"I was quite enjoying my sulk," she said, but she fell into stride on the other side of Kuolema. "Do you think the defense will go well?"

He glanced automatically at the sky. "As well as can be expected," he hedged. "To be honest, I expected more difficulty. I suppose these other Ryuven, whoever they are, aren't so practiced at fighting against human weapons and tactics."

"That makes sense." Ariana moved forward, so that she could peer around Kuolema's head at him. "So do you think it will look well for you, when we return?"

He wasn't sure he understood—not the question, which echoed his own, but the reason for asking it. "Well enough, anyway."

They stopped at the wagon and Ariana held Kuolema's reins while Shianan dug through the bound supplies for a fresh water-bag to replace his leaking one. Satisfied, he turned and mounted, gathering the reins. "Well, I should—"

"Shianan."

Her voice had a strange note, and it worried him. He looked down at her, searching for the trouble.

Ariana set her hands on Kuolema's dark red shoulder, just beside Shianan's knee. "I have been thinking. About returning to Alham, about the king, about...us."

Shianan went still, and for a moment he forgot to breathe. Kuolema flicked an ear rearward in concern.

Ariana moved one hand, cupping the back of his hand as he held the rein. Without thinking, he opened his fingers, gathering hers into his.

"Shianan," she said, so low that he could only just hear her, "what if we were married?"

Disappointment crashed over him. "But we tried—"

"What if we did not ask for a public wedding, for witnesses and ceremony? What if we simply were married?" She gazed at him, her eyes intense. "What if we returned to Alham married?"

It took the space of three rapid heartbeats for Shianan to realize her meaning. Like iron filings to a lodestone, his eyes dropped to their hands clasped together. They could bind their hands and hearts and lives, right where they stood.

She was waiting, mouth slightly open, worry and hope shining in her face. He would risk anything for that hope.

She saw his answer, and joy burst through her smile.

"Sir?" Captain Torg was approaching from the far side opposite Ariana, one hand shading his eyes from the sun. Shianan felt an irrational moment of panic, fearful of discovery, though Torg could not have heard.

Ariana gripped his hand more tightly. "Shianan Becknam, I take you as my lawfully wedded husband."

Shianan's heart soared. It was the simplest of vows, but it was all that was necessary by law and custom. He clutched her hand and swore his own. "Ariana Hazelrig, I take you as my lawfully wedded wife."

"Commander, we've got a problem with the fourth squad," Torg said. "They haven't—oh, excuse me. I didn't mean to interrupt."

He couldn't know. Their secret was secure.

"It's all right, captain," Ariana said with a final squeeze of her fingers to Shianan. Then she stepped back, pulling her hand free like drawing taffy. "He was just going."

"Sorry to bother you, sir, but we'd appreciate a word over there."

"I'm coming." Shianan nudged Kuolema forward, a bright golden bubble swelling within him. He did not fully understand what they had just done, did not know what it would bring to them—but he was glad to have done it.

After a few strides, he stopped and turned Kuolema. Ariana was still standing beside the wagon. Shianan trotted back to her.

Ariana, smiling, put one foot on the hub of the nearest wheel. As Shianan and Kuolema drew to a stop, she stepped up and leaned into the horse, her face upturned to Shianan.

He kissed her, and it was all the words they had never said, all the times they had never embraced, all the questions they had never asked, answered.

They separated, and Ariana's smile kindled a fire that would warm him for days. She stepped down, and Shianan rode away to rejoin Torg, who studiously looked ahead and asked nothing.

CHAPTER 56

City guards were not frequent visitors at the Wheel, but Mage Ewan Hazelrig was not too surprised to see this one. "You've come to say you're prepared for tonight?"

The man nodded. "Mostly prepared, my lord mage."

"Oh?"

"We've learned they've started recruiting grey mages."

"King's oats." Ewan put his pen down. "I'll speak to Mage Parma and Mage Odderman."

So it was that he and Elysia Parma were seated along one wall of a public room, pretending interest in an inferior stew, while Mage Odderman reclined in a corner with a half-filled tankard beside him. None were in their distinctive Circle robes, and Ewan had complimented Elysia on her lack of care. "You dirty down very well, it seems."

"Don't be small, Ewan. We'll do more harm than good if we look too respectable to be in this place."

The public room had done little to win her favor. The food, drink, and furnishings all catered to a client who cared more for the private rooms than quality of the offerings. Ewan suspected there might be more than clandestine business meetings in the rooms, but that was another day's pursuit for the city guard. Tonight, they were interested only in the group gathering for a joint venture.

"Though if I am perfectly honest," Elysia continued, "I must admit they have some ground to stand on."

"What?"

She shook her head. "Not to worry; I am here with you, on the side of the law. But I spent a long time watching for Ryuven, keeping them out of our markets and villages and warehouses. Every time I sense them coming across the between-worlds... It's a few minutes before my heart slows."

Ewan nodded. "I know. But if we could facilitate a peace so that the next generation of mages does not feel that spike of—"

"I know, I know. You needn't lecture me. I only say that I can empathize with their discomfort. Not, however, with its expression."

"Thank you."

"Hm?"

"For coming anyway. For helping to build a peace which is so uncomfortable."

She hesitated and then smiled crookedly. "Well, someone has to help your idealism along."

They poked at their greasy bowls, hiding bits of gristle beneath too-soft vegetables. Ewan mused that he might pick up a meat pie on the way home.

"Oh, no," Elysia murmured. "Not too quickly, but do you see who just entered?"

Ewan turned his head, straining to peer past the brim of his irritatingly slouchy tradesman's hat. "Ah."

Quince Ferrigam was a grey mage who had tested once for the Circle, before Ariana took the seat, and who was a fair candidate for a future opening. He went on regular assignments with military deployments, and Ewan liked him well enough. Elysia too, it seemed.

Quince stopped inside the door, looking around as if expecting to find someone or to be met.

"I think I need to visit the privy," Ewan said softly. "Keep an eye on things."

He adjusted his annoying hat and weaved through the cramped room, making his way by the door on his route to the rear. As he passed Quince he muttered, "Follow me, if you please."

Quince, clearly expecting to be met, did, and Ewan led him out the rear door and behind the low partition sheltering the privy ditch. At least, Ewan reflected with distaste, it was easy enough to tell they were alone.

He turned and faced the grey mage. "Quince Ferrigam, what are you doing here?"

Quince faltered and squinted. "Mage—Mage Hazelrig?"

"I don't know you so well, but this does not seem like your usual kind of place."

"If I may, my lord mage, I wouldn't have thought to have found you here, either." Quince brightened. "Are you connected with the work?"

"Leave my business for a moment. Did you come to drink alone, or to meet someone?"

"To meet. This, ah, is not my usual sort of place, as you say."

"And these friends, do you meet them regularly, or is this the first time?"

"I don't know most yet, just the one who asked me to come. They want mages, he said."

"Good, good. You have time to go on home, then."

"What? With respect, my lord mage, I need the work, and—"

"Not this work, you don't." Ewan jerked his head down the narrow alley. "Go on to another public house. You just mistook the name and went to the wrong one tonight."

Quince was struggling to keep up. "But he said the Goose and Bee—"

"Quince Ferrigam," Ewan said firmly, "take this advice from someone who knows your ambitions: go home."

Quince blinked and then nodded. "All right." He glanced up the alley and then went on alone.

Ewan heaved a sigh and went back inside. He slid into his seat across from Elysia. "He's out. Wasn't afraid to see me, was anxious to pick up a job here. Probably had little idea of what he was coming for. I sent him home."

She nodded approval.

A new group had taken the table beside theirs while he was away. It was only a few seconds before Ewan heard enough of their conversation to realize who they were.

"So there will be enough of us?"

"More than enough. We'll have to be quick; we can't let them get an alarm up. But it should be a swift entry."

There were four at the table, though by the reports there would be more before they went out tonight. These might have decided to have dinner as well as drinks for their bravado.

"We'll have a group at the front and the rear to keep—"

"Cesan!"

This came from a woman with grey-brown hair and a sun-lined face, approaching from the entrance. Her eyes were fixed on one of the young men at the next table. "Cesan, I've been trying to find you."

Cesan didn't look happy at having been found. "Mama," he said, and it was a protest at being embarrassed in front of his friends.

But his mother was undeterred. "I know what you're here for, Cesan. I'm no fool. Leave all this and come home."

Ewan, worried, sought Elysia's eyes. How would this play out? What of the raid?

"Mama, I can't believe you followed me all the way here. Go on, I know what I'm doing."

"Do you?" she demanded. "Because I don't. I don't see much of my son in this room."

"Leave him alone," growled another at the table. "A grown man doesn't need his mother running him like a goose girl."

Ewan tensed. If they would harm her, he would act, raid or no.

But Elysia's fingers rested on his arm, and she kept her eyes on the table. *Let this run out.*

"A man is grown when he takes on grown responsibility," the mother snapped. "And leaving his family and village to plant without him isn't the act of a grown man."

"I'm doing something else for the village," Cesan protested. "These people, we're ready for war. We're ready to protect ourselves, unlike the military, bringing Ryuven straight into our towns. I'm doing this for you, Mama. For you and for Papa."

"Your Papa would never—"

"He would, Mama. You know what he said before he died." Cesan looked around the table at his companions. "You all know my father died fighting the Ryuven. He was a soldier under Commander Becknam. He was injured and came home to die. So I know how the military cares more for their own priorities than for their soldiers."

"You lying barrow!" She pointed a finger. "What did your father say to you, as he lay on his deathbed? What did he say?"

"He said to do anything necessary to protect the family. By any means. And this is what is necessary, Mama. I'm doing this for Papa."

"Then why do you spit on his memory and lie through your teeth?" She slammed her hand on the table. "Your father said to do anything necessary to protect the family and to end the war. He said to end the Ryuven war by any means. And here you sit, spurning the end of it and planning to re-kindle the Ryuven fire by attacking your own countrymen."

"Shh!" Cesan hissed. "Mama!"

"Didn't I teach you never to do anything you couldn't speak aloud? Or have you forgotten that along with your father's dying wish?"

"I do this to protect you, Mama!"

"Protect me from what, exactly?"

"From seeing Ryuven in the main—"

"I've seen Ryuven, you mouthy turnip. I fought off a Ryuven raid when you were in swaddles and watched one crush your gran's shoulder. And now you want to *protect* me from seeing one standing calmly in the market, offering me coin for my grain? Is that the protection I'll have from you?"

Across from Ewan, Elysia suppressed a smile.

"I—"

"Your father gave his life to fight the war and breathed his last telling you to end it by any means necessary. And here you sit with your rutting friends all cowardly playing at being soldiers and squatting on his memory even as you take his name as your cause."

"We're not cowards, we're fighters!"

"Cowards, I said, and I'll hold to that. None of you are out facing what's really threatening us, those new raiders? And if you had half a nut in that gnawed-out shell, you would stand up to face what's unfamiliar. You'd walk into this new, frightening marketplace where we sell our grain instead of having it stolen. But you're all too afraid to face a Ryuven without a knife in your hand, even in the open market and even more with a ring of soldiers to protect you—so yes, coward I say." She slapped the table again. "Do whatever is necessary, he said, and yet you can't be bothered even to take a profit for your grain."

"There's more to life than profit," growled one of Cesan's companions.

"There certainly is," she retorted. "Much more. And none of it is helped by renewing a war." She turned on Cesan. "I'm asking you to come home. Your brother and your sisters want you home. I want you home. And I swear to you, if you come home, this will be the last word on all of this. But if you go on with these overgrown pox scars and leave Elston Field to the planting without you while you work against us, you've made your choice."

"It's not working against you, Mama."

"I'll remember you said that, as I dig rows myself and muse on how you'd rather have Ryuven raiding my fields than a safe market for me to sell in." She stepped back from the table. "Make your choice, Cesan." And, blinking hard but with her head high, she turned and went to the door.

The table of men shifted awkwardly. "Well, that wasn't what I expected tonight."

"No worries, Cesan," said one of the men. "Let it go. You're a long way from Elston Field."

Cesan, staring at the stained table, jerked his head in a nod. "Yes, I am." He pushed himself back from the shared bench. "Sorry, I'm out."

"What? You can't."

"I can. You go on. But she's right about the fields—if our farm was to be raided after we pushed against this treaty, then—"

"You'd rather have them come in without any resistance?"

"I'd rather try," he said curtly. "Like my father expected me to." He nodded to them, pulling a jacket over his arms. "Good luck, lads."

Ewan and Elysia busied themselves with their drinks as Cesan went out. Then Elysia raised a hand and waved her fingers, beckoning one of the youths who lounged by the door. "The man who just followed that woman out," she said softly, her words inaudible beneath the cursing of Cesan at the next table.

"The shrew and the sheep?" The boy grinned.

Elysia did not smile. "I'd like to know where they're staying tonight. Report back to me for a pia."

The generous amount ended his jests. "Right. I'll be back."

Ewan tipped his head. "Really, Elysia?"

"Come, Ewan, you got to save Quince. This one's mine."

He conceded.

At the next table, the men were gulping down the last of their stew. "After all that, we'd best get going," one urged with his mouth full. "Let's move."

They weren't the only table to shift. Little groups rose all around the public room, and more came from the back. All together Ewan thought they made two dozen.

Their informer had given them the gathering point for tonight, but he had not known the exact target. The city guards were to follow along and step in once the mischief started, and the mages were to act only if the grey mages allegedly among them moved against the guard. Ewan, Elysia, and Alan Odderman waited until the would-be fighters had left the house, and then they dropped coins for their own bills and went out after them.

The city guard stayed out of sight; Ewan would not have known they were also trailing the men from the pub. Finally they came to an herbalist's shop, and the group split into two, spreading around the front and rear of the shop.

Beside him, Elysia tensed, watching from the shadowed alley down the street.

"What do we do with traitors who buy from the Ryuven?" a man shouted, and the others cheered as they closed on the shop. There was the sound of breaking glass and a muffled cry from inside.

And then the city guard ringed the shop and its attackers, seizing men and pressing them to the ground. There was a flare of magic, but the three mages of the Circle shielded the guard members and then countered, dropping the two grey mages to the cobbled street.

"Hard to argue their innocence when they were taken with their hands inside the broken window," Mage Odderman observed.

"All a misunderstanding, surely," Elysia replied dryly.

When the guard had all in hand, including the grey mages, the three returned to the Goose and Bee, and the boy Elysia had sent after Cesan and his mother dashed up to her. "I've got the place you wanted," he said.

Elysia traded coin for information and gave Ewan and Alan an inviting smile. "Would you like to come with me?"

Mage Odderman opted to go home, but Ewan and Elysia returned to the Wheel. Now in their official robes, they went on to the inn where Cesan had joined his mother. Elysia pressed the innkeeper for the room and knocked on the door.

Cesan answered, startling at the sight of the Circle robes. "I—may I help you?"

"Your mother saved you tonight, Cesan," Elysia said without preamble.

"What?"

"The others are all prisoners now. You would have been among them."

"What?" he repeated, louder. His mother appeared behind him, her eyes wide. Then Cesan seemed to worry about denial. "What are you talking about?"

"Don't bother, Cesan, I was sitting two arms' lengths from you. I heard all of it, from your plans to attack the shop to your father's dying words. Going home with your mother tonight saved your freedom. Possibly your life."

"But..."

"She protected you from your friends—or the men you thought were your friends. Where were the Gehrn priests, Cesan?"

Cesan opened his mouth, hesitated, looked from Elysia to Ewan and back. "They were going to meet us after we took the shop."

"Hmm." Elysia raised an eyebrow.

Ewan stood to one side; he had little to add.

After a significant moment, Elysia turned her attention to the older woman behind him. "You did a great thing for your family tonight. He is fortunate to have a mother who cared enough to come for him."

Cesan's mother, shaken by his brush with danger, put her hands on him but kept herself from pulling him near. She nodded wordlessly.

"Good night to you both. Safe journey to Elston Field."

Cesan caught his breath at this final proof of her witness, as Elysia turned away and descended the stairs with Ewan.

"That was a nice touch, noting that the Gehrn weren't present for the arrests," Ewan told her.

"With any luck, that will get around to anyone he's close to in the novitiate," she said. "If they're going to play on suspicion and suggestions of conspiracy, they should be prepared to face the same."

"I wonder if it will be enough." They went out into the cool night, and Ewan continued, "Arresting those who commit crimes should discourage some of the rest, but they still went to the Gehrn."

"Or the Gehrn picked them like ripe berries from those already gathering in the market," Elysia countered.

"I wish we knew what this initiation was. I don't suppose you found anything on it in your reading?"

Elysia shook her head. "No, it's elite knowledge, recorded only in the writings kept personally by the high priests."

Ewan frowned. "We have someone who might know. Commander Becknam has the high priest's slave, Luca."

Elysia's expression darkened. "That's right."

"We know where to find him if we need him."

CHAPTER 57

"Commander! Sir!"

Shianan straightened as the scout ran toward him. "Yes?"

"We've found them, sir. Just over that hill, not even so far. They're tucked into a bit of cover but they're camped." The scout grinned. "I guess it's true they aren't the Ryuven we've been fighting. They're sitting and waiting for us."

"Well, it would be a shame to disappoint them." Shianan turned to Captain Torg. "Will you pass the word, please?"

"With pleasure."

Within minutes the wagons had been pulled aside, additional weapons distributed, armor secured, ranks re-formed. Shianan tethered Kuolema securely behind one of the taller wagons—no point to leaving the horse more easily visible—and took his place with the soldiers. He signaled to his officers, and they advanced quietly up the slope of dead grass.

The Ryuven were, as the scout had reported, encamped below, partially sheltered by the edge of the forest but not well-hidden. There were about thirty, he guessed, and confident in their conquest, hardly deigning to hide from the avenging army coming after them. Small barrels and crates were stacked in several piles; they were lingering to enjoy their spoils instead of escaping immediately to their own world. The arrogance of it fired Shianan's blood.

They looked like Ryuven. He would not have thought anything different of them, but with Tamaryl's explanations in mind, he could see small distinctions in armor and dress that suggested they were not the Ai he had always fought. At least they were wearing armor in camp, and not in complete disdain of Chrenada's defenders.

His soldiers and mages were in place, crouching low behind the crest of the hill and stretching to form long arms to close on the group below. The Ryuven would take to the air, of course, but with little time to arm themselves first.

Shianan raised his arm and signaled the attack.

The soldiers whooped and poured over the crest of the hill, descending upon the surprised Ryuven. The winged enemy leapt into the air, launching magical bolts at the front-runners, but the mages threw up shields that blocked the attacks and a few of the attackers, as they flew into the shields. Archers sent volleys of barbed arrows after the fleeing Ryuven.

The fighting was quick and efficient, and it was all over in twenty minutes or so. A dozen Ryuven lay dead on the field, and the others had fled across the sky or across the between-worlds.

Shianan walked among the dead, looking for the telltale signs Tamaryl had pointed out. But if the Pairvyn told the truth about the flying-birds marks being signs of another clan, then these were not the Ai.

And their inexperience with human soldiers had betrayed them here. They had expected frightened farmers and slow merchants; Shianan's troops had mowed them like wheat.

He had done well here. They had cleared the threat and done enough damage that these Ryuven would not soon return so brazenly. Now to clear the field, organize his wounded, and go home to Alham and to Ariana.

As a grey mage, Ariana had shared a tent while assigned to accompany the military. Now that she was a mage of the Circle, she had a tent of her own. It should have felt cramped and dark, narrow with the flaps closed, but with a single shielded candle and the gentle sound of wind outside, it was almost cozy.

Ariana suspected that had more to do with her state of mind than the tent's accommodations.

She had done it. They had done it. They had defied King Jerome's unreasonable prejudices and married. She had asked, and Shianan had trusted her, and they had done it.

Oh, how she hoped she would not betray that trust.

If she'd had someone else in the tent, she might have shared the bubbling joy she'd had to suppress most of the day. But she was not sure she could share; despite her pride in their defiance, there was real risk if the king learned before they had their precautions in place—whatever those precautions might be. But surely the triumphant return from a short and victorious campaign would be a good start; even the king would not want to publicly shame his war heroes.

Ariana pulled her blanket closer and smiled to herself. How did she want to share the news? She would bring Shianan to her home, one hand on his arm, and lead him in to dinner with her father. Shianan would feel awkward, she knew, so she should be the one to break it. Should she say it directly? "Papa, we're married." Or maybe, "Papa, you know Shianan, but now you may know him as your son."

She was sure she had read him correctly. He liked Shianan, respected him. He would miss the opportunity to celebrate her engagement and be present for the wedding itself, but he would understand their situation. He would help them, would advise on how to proceed with their clandestine marriage. Maybe Shianan could stay at their townhouse at times.

And they would announce their marriage to all; it would not be secret forever. King Jerome would see their success, would recognize Shianan's worth, and would acknowledge their union. It would be all right in the end, and worth the trouble.

Now there was only to quell the fresh raids and return victorious to break the news.

The slanting late winter sun was bright enough to invite a raised arm or a hat brim, but Shianan tipped his head back so that it shone full in his face. Returning victorious! This was a good day.

Beneath him, Kuolema danced a little on the road, as if to invite Shianan to share his delight in the pristine weather. He had done well in his first excursion, though of course he had not been subject to the fight itself. Still, Philip's training with dummies tossed into the sky and banners streaming over the young horse had done its part in inuring him to the concept of an airborne enemy. Even at the edge of the battle, as Ryuven fled over the wagons, he had been alert and agitated but not panicky. Shianan could hardly wait to report to Philip how well it all had gone.

He placed a hand on the red neck and stroked the flexed muscles there. Ahead of them, Torg's soldiers marched in rank, organized but relaxed, and called back and forth to one another. They too were pleased with the outcome of the previous day's battle. The few casualties rode with Captain Abbar, following a short distance behind. The first formal encounters with a Ryuven foe after the devastation of Arakadamia had been good for morale. Shianan's report would be a good one, citing success and anticipation of future success.

There was water ahead, a river or wide stream, shallow enough to be forded. It was no real challenge and had slowed them only slightly as they came this way previously, but the troops thinned into a narrow file to manage the ford. The water was not deep, but it was quick moving and cold, and there was no rush to crowd together.

As the soldiers drew together into lines and groups to wait their turn, Shianan moved Kuolema to the side and let him drink. He looked back over the soldiers, noting—or imagining—how many of them seemed to keep glancing at him astride Kuolema. He stroked the horse's neck again. He was glad he could finally be an officer they could be proud of.

The crackling bolt came out of nowhere, striking a group of soldiers relaxing a dozen paces back from the ford. Three dropped dead instantly. The magic ran through the others around them with arcane brutality.

Shianan gathered Kuolema's reins with a jerk, twisting in the saddle to see the source of the threat even as shouts went up all down the line. There was nothing in the sky. Where were the Ryuven attackers?

"There!"

But Shianan had already seen it, the only place they could be hidden. And as if that were a cue, a force of Ryuven surged from the copse of trees, raining magic upon the soldiers arranged in easy lines for their targeting.

The soldiers were not unarmed, most had swords or knives. But their polearms for staving off descending Ryuven or pinning one to the ground were on the supply wagons, as were their bows and the heavy arrows. They wore light armor, but not the specialized protective gear to guard from aerial attacks. They could never unload what they needed in time. They would be cut apart and cut down.

They had to have help. Shianan turned Kuolema and urged him into a gallop. Briefly he wondered if any of his soldiers would believe him to be fleeing, but he pushed the thought away. They needed reinforcements, and he could carry word faster than anyone on foot. Kuolema fell easily into a gallop and they barreled up the road, passing soldiers who were struggling to fall into formation as their sergeants called orders. Shianan barked a few commands, but they had been drilled well. He needed Captain Abbar's company, still in the hills behind them. They could help, if they hurried, but they had to be called.

He galloped around the soft slow curve of the road and up the rise that shielded Captain Abbar's company from view. "Ryuven ambush!" he called. "Ryuven ambush! Arm yourselves and come at once to defend!"

Immediately the sergeants began to organize the soldiers, and in a moment everything was deliberate chaos as they shared out armor and weapons. They would be along as fast as humanly possible. Now Shianan had to return to his own soldiers and lead them against the attackers until help could come.

He wheeled Kuolema and they set off on the road again at top speed. Shianan had barely ridden at this pace, and it was exhilarating and deadly and awful.

The fighting now was close and brutal. Human soldiers, packed too closely for efficient repulsion, tried to adjust as Ryuven after Ryuven dove and speared and threw concussive magic. In the river itself, a group of soldiers were pinned tightly together, swords and short spears outward and upward to guard against the Ryuven circling and diving at them. Shianan set Kuolema at the river, letting the horse choose his own pace and entry. The colt did not flinch at the fighting or the diving Ryuven but leapt into the water and plunged straight for the beleaguered soldiers without hesitation.

Shianan raised his sword to counter a diving attacker with a mace. The Ryuven screamed and faltered, but Kuolema only flattened his ears and jerked his head in fear. Shianan turned in the saddle to brace against a second attacker. There was movement from the front, a Ryuven in the stream.

The world went out from beneath Shianan and he flew through the air, reaching uselessly for anything solid before he slammed into the shallow water and the rocks beneath. The cold water shocked through him like a second blow, and for a moment he could not remember how to push up to reach the air. But he got his arms under him, and without releasing his grip on his sword, he shoved himself above the water and shook his eyes clear.

A Ryuven dove at him and by instinct he rolled, bringing his sword overhead to block as he went beneath the water again. The Ryuven's strike missed and Shianan completed his roll and surged upward, slipping on the uneven footing in the current but managing to cut a leg. The Ryuven jerked and flew away.

Another Ryuven, this one in the water—the same one as before? It didn't matter. Shianan saw him bringing his empty hands together for magic. Shianan slashed across the surface of the water, making the Ryuven flinch instinctively to protect his eyes from the spray, and charged into the gap it opened. The Ryuven went down to bleed into the current.

Shianan spun, shaking wet hair from his eyes without lowering his sword. All around him soldiers struggled against the Ryuven ambush. And there—there was Kuolema, squealing and thrashing on his side in the water, eyes and nostrils wide.

Shianan sloshed toward him, and then he saw the spear piercing Kuolema's chest, protruding again out his shoulder. His legs moved erratically and weakly, and his nostrils were already flecked heavily with blood.

No. No, no.

The horse fixed on Shianan and the white-rimmed eyes softened for just an instant. He made a mighty effort and rolled partly upright.

Shianan dove for the bridle. "No, no, stay—"

But the horse coughed, and blood flew, and he sagged again into the water.

Another attacker dove at Shianan, and he deflected the mace savagely. He tripped on a body in the water—the Ryuven he had just killed, the one who had braced a spear for Kuolema to run upon. He was already dead, so that Shianan could not kill him as he deserved.

He fought his way to the band of soldiers in the ford and together they pushed back toward the shore, to more secure footing and the aid of greater numbers. Then Shianan heard and saw Captain Abbar's troops arriving, and with the arrival of properly equipped fighters the Ryuven began to retreat.

Shianan lowered his sword and stared around him at the broken ranks and bleeding soldiers and the death of their easy victory. They had been baited, and they in their arrogance had laughed at the arrogant Ryuven who were found so easily and so vulnerable. With a rush it all fell upon him—the ceaselessness of it, the futility, the unending brutality.

He should go to oversee the gathering of the injured, their treatment, the collection of equipment and gear. But these were veterans, and their tasks were well-learned. He turned from the soldiers and staggered back to the stream.

Kuolema lay still, his head beneath the fast-running water and his flank like an island to mark his fall. Shianan dropped to his knees, resting one hand upon the pierced shoulder. "No," he breathed. "Please, no."

Kuolema—the affectionate nibbles, the nickers of greeting, the insistence on a scratch beneath the forelock. He was gone. And with his death, Shianan had to face Philip, had to report how Kuolema had died, had to—

Sweet Holy One, the queen. Shianan had let the queen's horse die. Her priceless young stallion, her generous token to honor him, destroyed with a company of soldiers, failure upon failure. For a moment, the horror of reporting Kuolema's death overwhelmed his sorrow for the horse, and at that a crushing wave of guilt rolled over him like the current burying the horse.

"Sir?"

Shianan could not answer.

"Sir? Will we move tonight?"

That would mean leaving Kuolema. But of course he could not bring back the horse like one of his fallen soldiers. But...

Shianan straightened and got to his feet, trembling in the cold water. "Yes. We can make a few miles yet. Let's go."

CHAPTER 58

The military line was formed into proper ranks as it wound into the gates of Alham, but to Shianan it still felt like they dragged into the city, as after Arakadamia. He walked along the soldiers, looking up and down for those who needed assistance or encouragement, avoiding the supply wagon that bore in one corner the saddle and bridle Kuolema had worn. Shianan did not know what the cost of the tack might be, and it seemed wiser to mitigate what losses he could.

But nothing could change that he had lost the horse entrusted to him.

Stay out of the queen's way.

Sweet oats, she had hated him all his life. He had been beyond foolish to think she had changed her opinion merely for meeting him face to face. What if she had sent the horse to battle with him as an excuse to punish and dispose of him?

He shifted his arm again, hoping to ease the strain on his shoulder. He had not noticed the injury until after the fighting—not too unusual, he'd learned, especially when it was not an open wound—when the breathless immediacy of battle faded and muscles began to stiffen and ache. His right shoulder had pained him and had, when he tried, constricted the reach of his arm. It was a result of his hard flip over Kuolema's head in the fall, he supposed, and he was fortunate it was only that. He had resisted putting the arm in a sling, when there were so many more seriously wounded, but as time wore on it sometimes grew more uncomfortable.

They had nearly reached the Naziar when he caught Luca's face in the street ahead. The slave came jogging toward him, his face bright and open, but as he neared he sobered. When he at last turned to match Shianan's weary pace, he was worried. "Welcome home, master."

Shianan nodded.

Luca looked up and down the line, and then he turned back to Shianan, his eyes wide. "Kuolema...?"

Shianan nodded again.

Luca's breath caught, and he turned his face away. Shianan was grateful he did not ask all the questions he must have had. But

Luca understood; Luca would be calculating the consequences. If owning a royal horse could bankrupt a man, what might killing one bring?

"I need a change of clothing," Shianan said quietly. "I will leave Captain Torg to oversee the arrival, and I must go to the queen immediately, before she has opportunity to hear from someone else."

Luca nodded, his face strained with neutrality, and then jogged up the street again.

Shianan did not know if Torg understood the full weight of the disaster, but he understood Shianan's silent distress, and he readily took responsibility for the soldiers' return, the arrangements for the wounded and the proper storage of the dead, the sorting of equipment for cleaning, repairs, and storage. Shianan pushed himself into a tired run for his office and quarters.

Luca had hot water and fresh clothing, a carefully-chosen outfit adequate for court wear but practical enough to suggest a soldier just returned from the front. There was little to help Shianan's predicament, but Luca was doing his best.

It was too early for Marshal Vanguilder's contingent—Ariana's—to have returned; they wouldn't be back for a day or two at earliest. But if the Ientu had laid one trap, they might have laid more. "Luca, if there's any word from the field—anything—I want to know. No delay."

Luca nodded.

Shianan wanted to stand with his hands submerged in the warm water all the rest of the day and the following night, putting off the awful task, but he forced himself to wash and dress, moving slowly to spare his shoulder. The dread in his gut coiled together and he sucked his breath, trying to control it. But it overpowered him and he convulsed, rushing to the basin to vomit.

Sweet Holy One, he was sick with fear. Again.

He spat and braced himself on stiff arms, trying to slow his pulse with controlled breaths. He realized Luca was standing silent beside him, with a cup of water and a fresh towel.

"'Soats, I am sorry," Shianan breathed.

Luca shook his head.

Shianan rinsed his mouth. "It's worse," he confided. "The queen hated me more than he ever did. But these past weeks—I thought, I thought she might feel differently toward me. She seemed grateful for my service to the prince, and kind enough to apologize for thinking poorly of me, and generous enough to lend a horse to honor me." He dipped his head, and the tense muscles across his neck and shoulders caught in protest. "And now I must go and disappoint her, turning all that kindness into hate and disdain once more."

Luca extended the towel, and Shianan wiped his face. He dropped it on the washstand, and it slipped to the floor. He shook his head. "I'm going."

The walk to the Naziar palace felt like climbing a mountain. He went in, somehow forced his request for audience through numb lips, waited in the dull hum of his anxiety. At last doors were opened and he was led into the queen's sitting room.

"Bailaha, welcome. I hope you bring a good report."

He folded to the floor, barely inside the door, and bent his head deeply over his knee. Behind him the door clicked shut.

"What are you doing all the way over there? Rise and come here, please."

Every fiber of Shianan's frame resisted approach, though her words could reach him no matter where he knelt. But he obeyed, straightening just enough to step forward and then kneel again.

When she spoke again, unseen before him, her voice had changed. "What is it? What is the meaning of this?"

He had thought and thought on the road, bending his thoughts on how to say the words, but each time his mind had recoiled just as fingers jerked away from a broken bone piercing the skin, unwilling and unable to probe or press it into working order. "Your Majesty," he managed. "I have something to report."

"What do you mean? Bailaha, I don't like this. You're frightening me."

He had not thought his muscles could tighten any further. "Your Majesty." His voice was unsteady, and he was not sure he could speak loudly enough to carry to her. "I regret to say—I am sorry to tell you—I have lost Kuolema."

His voice broke on the name, and he realized she couldn't have understood him. He cursed himself, his failure, his inability to speak, his stupid terror that he would hurt and disappoint her.

She rose from her chair. "Bailaha, what is it? What are you trying to tell me?'

King's sweet oats, he was going to break. "Kuolema," he managed. "I am so sorry."

She heard, at last. She gasped, and for a moment nothing in the room moved. Shianan squeezed his eyes shut and braced, ready for epithets, for blows, for anything.

"How?" she whispered.

He could not even swallow. "We were ambushed."

The blood rose in his ears, and he was not sure what she said next. It did not matter. It was better if he could not hear, better to coil into himself and wait until her fury had spent itself and he was released to lick his wounds—

Something touched him, and he jumped, pulling away despite himself. Her arms were on his neck now, and she would choke him, and—

She pulled him to her, folding him against her hair and dress and holding him tight, but not to hurt him. She was speaking again, and with her mouth so near his ear, he could understand. "Are you all right?"

He made his tongue form the only answer to any question she might ask. "I am sorry. I am so sorry. I know he was priceless. I know you—"

She jerked back, her eyes wide, and the horror of her expression lanced him so that he had to look down. He could not bear to see her shock and disappointment. He closed his mouth, biting off his words.

"Bailaha," she repeated, her voice soft and clear, "I asked if you were all right. Were you injured?"

He did not understand.

She put her hands on his face, one on each cheek, and he flinched from it. But she did not release him, lifting his head to face her. He resisted, averting his eyes, until at last she pinned him with her gaze. "Answer me."

"There was nothing I could do," he said in a hoarse whisper. "There was a pike. I went over his head as he fell. I killed the Ryuven, but I could not save him."

"But you—you're all right?" She held him in place. "Thank the Holy One."

Like a hint of music drifting into a dark room, a ray of understanding crept through his terror, and he understood. She did not ask how Kuolema could be dead while he lived unharmed—she asked if he was safe.

Everything in him contorted and he began to sob, abhorred at his body's betrayal but unable to even slow it.

Queen Azalie whispered something like a short, hot oath and she pulled him into an embrace, hugging him to her with both arms and enfolding him into a horrifying, excruciating, comforting trap. He gasped and clung to her, a drowning man thrown a line from a boat he had first imagined a sea monster.

He could not cling to the queen. He could not sob like a child in her presence, much less in her arms. He could not clutch her as she knelt on the floor beside him in his abased posture. "I'm sorry," he choked.

Her hand found his mouth, covering it as she pressed him close. "Hush," she whispered. "Don't you apologize for surviving."

He shook his head. "I'm sorry," he tried once more.

Her hand tightened. "Don't apologize for living," she repeated. "Not to me."

He stopped protesting, stopped trying to understand, stopped everything but crying. Her touch weakened him, broke his protective dams and secure walls, shattered his defenses and admitted not invaders, but aid.

After an interminable moment, his ragged sobs slowed, and now he could not move, could not face her across his humiliation. He rubbed at his face, and he wondered if he could bow and crawl away.

But as they drew apart she kept one hand on his shoulder, a featherweight restraint, and he could not flee.

"Oh, Shianan," she breathed, looking at him with a perplexing mixture of sympathy and sorrow. "Oh, Shianan, I am sorry."

Again, he did not understand. "No—I lost him. He died with me. I lost your horse, and I am so sorry—"

"Hush," she whispered. "Have I not said, what are a thousand horses against a son?"

He stared at her. "But His Highness..."

With fresh horror, he realized she was crying. Her sorrow was different, expressed in silent tears that bled down her cheeks, but she cried. He had brought the queen to tears. His heart stopped in his chest, squeezing out his breath.

She shook her head and pulled away, wiping at her eyes. "Now neither of us can be seen," she said. "I don't suppose you have a handkerchief?"

He did not. Of course he did not. He was a soldier and a bastard.

She rose and found one on a little table and dabbed at her face. She sniffed delicately and turned back to him. He bowed his head as a courtier, his inappropriate and humiliating tears turned to the floor.

"Shianan Becknam, please stand."

He did, though his legs threatened to betray him.

"Could you look at me?"

It put iron nails through his flesh, but he obeyed.

"I am so sorry to have lost Kuolema. But I do not blame you. It is a risk we take when we send any horse, or any person, to battle. As grieved as I am for his death, I am equally glad of your safety."

This was too much, and he looked down again, blinking furiously.

"I have said before that I was wrong, and it is true. I was very wrong. Now I see what I denied myself, and I regret what has been lost."

He could make no answer.

"I thank you for coming directly to tell me of Kuolema, And I am so sorry that it happened."

He nodded.

"Do you wish to stay to—"

He shook his head, too quickly, but he only wanted to flee. What had happened, what he thought had happened—it wasn't possible, and he could not bear to stay near it.

She hesitated, and for a moment he thought he had offended her, but then she nodded, "Of course. Do as you will."

He bowed deeply as she retreated to the door at the far end of the room. When she had gone, he scrubbed furiously at his face, wiping away the evidence of his shame before going out the door behind him.

CHAPTER 59

When Shianan moved the latch, Luca jerked the door open from inside. His worried eyes searched Shianan's face.

"It's all right," Shianan said wearily.

Luca did not look convinced.

Shianan rubbed his face self-consciously. He had scrubbed away the tears, but no doubt his eyes were still reddened. "It's all right," he repeated. "She was upset, but not angry."

Luca waited expectantly.

Shianan sighed. "She was grieved. Of course. But that was all." He rubbed a hand across his forehead. "I stopped at the stable. To tell Philip."

Luca reached to take his cloak. "I have some soup for you, kept warm."

"Thanks." Shianan hoped soup would soothe and settle his jagged nerves and rapid heart. Maybe he would have a drink as well, or several. He was exhausted, but terrified of not falling asleep, of seeing again all the losses they'd suffered. "No news of Vanguilder's unit?"

"No."

There was something off about Luca, he thought. He moved efficiently, but he avoided Shianan's eyes, or opened his mouth as if to speak and then said nothing.

Shianan went into his quarters, toed off his boots, and dropped into a chair. His shoulder hurt. The soup on the brazier was just at the edge of his reach, and the frustration of having to rise again was far too great to be reasonable. He stood just far enough to stretch, burned his hand on the stoneware, and cursed as he sloshed soup into the coals. He managed to reset the cup before it spilled further and sucked on his abused fingertips as he looked around for something to blunt the heat enough to handle. But Luca had left no laundry conveniently out of place, and after a moment he pulled off his own sock to retrieve the soup again.

Luca came from the office, looked at Shianan holding the cup with his sock, and went on to kneel beside the chest. He lifted a bottle and asked over his shoulder, "How strong do you want it?"

Shianan felt weighted in the chair, too heavy to move but not sleepy enough to escape. "Knock me out. I don't want to think of anything until tomorrow."

Luca traded bottles and then hesitated, looking down at the interior of the chest. "Are you sure?"

Irritation flared. "King's oats, Luca, haven't I had the day for it?"

Luca said nothing, but he rose and held out the bottle to Shianan, not making eye contact.

Shianan took it left-handed and unsealed it—what place did Luca have to criticize his drinking? Hadn't he offered it himself?—before tipping the bottle back to drink from it directly. 'Soats, he'd borne enough these past days. He'd earned one night of relief.

He tucked his bare foot beneath the other for warmth and alternated soup and liquor.

Ariana's breath throbbed in her side, but she could not pause to suck more air or brace against the sharp pain. More Ryuven swept toward them in a wide semi-circle, and though she had practiced endlessly against Ryuven fronts, she felt she was a step behind with every adjustment.

These Ryuven were strong. Unusually strong. No, that was not exactly it; their magic flowed differently than she expected. Each Ryuven attack she knew was an Ai attack, and these were not the Ai. Energies slid, splashed, snaked in unanticipated ways, and her every reaction was a heartbeat too slow.

She was vaguely grateful for the rush of battle that did not permit her thoughts to coalesce, keeping her from consciously acknowledging what she was seeing—that she was not prepared to defeat this enemy.

The Ryuven still fell to physical weapons, half healing themselves as they fought away from the soldiers attempting to finish them. At the far end of the field, Tamaryl'sho threw offensive magics against the attacking Ryuven, carving a gap for the Chrenadan archers. Here Ariana threw shield after shield overhead to protect the soldiers wielding mace and axe against the Ryuven they had managed to bring to the ground, but all her shields were less efficient than she expected.

A lull came, and Ariana wheezed, one arm across her stomach

as if it could support her.

"My lady mage," a soldier called, "are you hurt?"

She shook her head. It was only that this was so much more difficult, and that made no sense—

She turned, warned by some perception so subtle as to be nearly instinct, and raised her arm and a shield against the incoming bolt. She felt the magics collide, felt the bolt's impact, and then felt it press through her suddenly-viscous shield to reach the soldier below.

"No!" Ariana gasped as the soldier crumpled. She rushed to him, raising another shield as if it would be more useful than the last one. But the Ryuven was already swooping away from the archers targeting him.

The attack had penetrated her shield. Ariana remembered the hollow feeling of reaching for magic that did not answer—but this was powerlessness of a different kind, where she could act and yet it was simply not enough.

The soldier was not a mage; the magic took longer to kill him. Ariana trembled with the knowledge she could no longer pretend not to recognize. They were not prepared for this enemy.

"Mage Hazelrig!"

She spun on her knees and threw an inversion well over two polearm-wielding soldiers, a grey mage, and the screaming soldier on the ground reaching for where her hand had been. The assaulting energy flashed bright in Ariana's arcane sight and poured into the ground, leaving her breathless. Inversion wells were more efficient than shields, but more dangerous, especially with this unfamiliar magic. But there was no way to be careful, not here where her people were dying.

Down the line, Tamaryl's shields were holding, but he was only one.

Ariana struggled to her feet and gritted her teeth against the effort to breathe. She had not trained all her life to join the Great Circle in a time of peace. She was meant to protect their soldiers.

A Ryuven darted across the sky and lanced a bolt at her. She met it with an energy well, shrieking as it burned through her, and returned a volley of sharp blasts. The Ryuven swerved away, and Ariana started to turn toward the little cluster of soldiers. But four Ryuven came together, and she whirled back to face them.

Chapter 60

Luca half expected the guards to stop him, but they gave him barely a glance as he passed, probably assuming he was on an errand for someone important. Slaves did not loiter here, did not come here without cause.

It was early in the day, and the courtroom itself was mostly empty. The drama surrounding the shield's destruction had long been surpassed by Arakadamia, the treaty, the arrival of Ryuven themselves in the market plazas, the return yesterday of the defeated military expeditions. Few had come to watch the sentencing of the traitor Ande. If not for the palace servants' overheard exchange, Luca would never have known.

The room was not like the Court of the High Star, or at least what Luca remembered of it; he had been half-mad with fear and weariness that day. This was a mundane room, heavy with long implacability and judgment and relatively plain in its furnishings. Luca slipped onto a wooden bench.

He knew Flamen Manceps Ande more by his position in the front center of the room than by his face. The high priest was gaunt, bearded, and afraid, and he no longer wore the blue robes of his office but colorless prison garb. Luca could recognize the fear in him, the utter hopeless helplessness before callous power. Seeing it in the man who had taught it to him was disorienting.

"The Circle's mages have since confirmed, however," the presiding adjudicator was explaining, "there was no way to unwork the shield without the use of Ryuven blood. We must therefore conclude the destruction of the shield was deliberate and intentional."

"My lord," began Ande, with the dejected air of one who knows his effort is useless but must make the attempt once more, "I have sworn on my life there was no intent to harm the shield. I have told the court over and again the details of the ritual—"

"Quiet him," the adjudicator said wearily, and a guard stepped forward and seized Ande's hair. The high priest pulled away weakly but continued to protest, knowing it was his final chance. The guard delivered a practiced blow and Ande staggered, his shackled hands to his face.

"Given your willful and deliberate act of treason, then, we must—"

"My lord." Luca rose from his seat, hardly believing his own voice.

The adjudicator blinked at him. "What do you mean by interrupting here?" A guard was already coming toward him.

Luca gulped and spoke hurriedly, before his courage could fail. "My lord, I bring information regarding this trial and this prisoner. I must speak before sentencing."

The guard hesitated beside Luca and glanced at the adjudicators' platform, waiting for instruction. The presiding adjudicator frowned. "Who are you? Why have you come only now?"

"I was not permitted to testify when the shield first fell," Luca answered, trying to recall the words he had barely practiced. His knees were shaking, and he hoped no one could see. "I was the slave used in the ritual that unmade the shield."

There was a moment of quiet shock, and then the observers and adjudicators began whispering excitedly. The presiding adjudicator silenced them with a fierce word and then turned on Luca. "You'd better come here. Bring him."

The court guard put a heavy hand on Luca's shoulder, though he had spoken voluntarily. Luca moved numbly to the rail dividing those questioned from the adjudicators' massive table. It seemed the room shifted and moved about him strangely, tightening as if to entrap him.

He did not look at Ande.

The presiding adjudicator frowned dubiously down at him. "You are the slave, you say?"

"I was."

"And what is your position now?"

This would be precarious work. "I am servant to Commander Shianan Becknam, Count of Bailaha."

"Servant, you say? What is your status?"

The guard did not wait for Luca to answer but reached for his sleeve, pulling it back to expose the dull cuffs. "He's a slave, my lords."

Luca's stomach twisted, and he fought the urge to jerk free of the guard. *Speak quietly, give them just enough, get out...*

The presiding adjudicator's frown deepened. "You know that the word of a slave cannot be accepted in court, not without conditions of extraction."

Luca should never have come here, should never have attempted this, should never have dreamed of making a difference. He should have stayed safely in Shianan's quarters and let this end without him. "I—I know, my lord."

"Fortunately for you, we have all the evidence we need to convict without the dubious word of a slave," the adjudicator continued. "If it's revenge you're after, you'll have a taste in a moment. Now—"

"I beg your pardon, my lords," Luca said, and his voice cracked where he wished it would be firm. "I am sorry to interrupt, but I have not come to add my testimony to those condemning Flamen Ande. I've come to defend his innocence."

For a moment the room was silent. Luca wanted to look at Ande, to see the effect this statement might have, but he was terrified to take his eyes from the front edge of the long, massive desk where the adjudicators sat.

The silence was broken by the sigh of a man who has seen an unpleasant task, nearly finished, suddenly and unexpectedly prolonged. "You've come, at this late date, to defend a man who used your blood to commit treason?"

Luca swallowed and forced his tongue to work. "This man is not guilty of treason. The destruction of the shield was an accident, I can attest. He performed the ritual that unworked the magic, but he did not intend such a result and did not know it would happen."

The adjudicator scowled. "It has been established that only the application of Ryuven blood could have opened the spell holding the shield. We suspended this trial, by the Circle's request, so that this could be verified. Now, how do you say this was done? Do you deny the Great Circle's authority?"

Luca shook his head. "By no means, my lord. I do not presume to understand magic nor its workings. If the Great Circle has said it required Ryuven blood, then that must be so. And I say there was Ryuven blood in the ritual, my lord, though the high priest did not know it."

He could feel Ande's eyes on him, and he wanted to cringe, to turn on him and shout, to grovel, to flee. He felt also the eyes of the seated adjudicators, the few observers, the guards. He kept his gaze fixed firmly on the presiding adjudicator's carved and gilded desk.

"If you will permit me to explain, my lord—my former master and I went to the White Mage's office before the ritual. There were many items required, and we carried vials of oil and powders as well as the other implements necessary." Cord, and a whip. "These were set on a table in the White Mage's workroom while he and my master spoke." That was untrue; all had been in a covered basket, and Luca had not known its malicious contents until Ande had seized him in the cellar. But there was no reason for the adjudicators to doubt his explanation.

"When we were ready to go for the ritual, and the items were gathered up again, an extra vial was included by mistake," Luca continued. "I noticed and—and I tried to inform my master, but he did not wish to be interrupted by a slave." He could not resist this quick accusation, and if it made anyone present more tolerant with their own slaves, so much the better. "So I kept quiet, as instructed, until—until the ritual." Speaking of it was more difficult than expected. He fought the urge to rub at his throat, smoothing the feel of the constricting chain.

"And you believe that vial was Ryuven blood?"

"I think it must have been, my lord. It had the look of thickened blood. It would explain the great error, though my master had no intention of working against the shield."

"Hmm." The presiding adjudicator scowled. "What you say could save his life, if it is true."

Luca kept his eyes forward, away from Ande. "The destruction of the shield was an accident, my lord. I am certain of that." Unlike the destruction of Luca, which had been deliberate and malicious, but Ande was not on trial for that.

The adjudicator turned to Ande. "Do you recognize this man? Is he who he says he is?"

Ande turned, and Luca fixed his eyes firmly on the gilded desk. He could not look at him, not even now. But he heard the weakened voice, so different from what it had been. "Yes, he has been my slave for some time."

"Not yours any longer," Luca whispered, and then a fresh terror took him. What if the court recognized Ande's claim above Shianan's? What if, in sparing Ande's life, Luca put himself back with him?

The adjudicator laced his fingers and rested his chin on them, elbows on the high desk. "You were this prisoner's slave," he said flatly to Luca. "If what he has explained of this ritual is accurate, he bound you and flogged you to blood the Shard itself."

That and more, much more.

"Why do you come now to defend him?"

Luca swallowed, but the stone in his throat would not be moved. *Because he hurt me unjustly, and if I do the same I am no better,* he thought. *It's to prove that I am better.*

But that was a lie, as well. Even now he could not summon the strength to look at Ande, to take pride in his own superiority, his mercy, his morality. None of those had brought him here. His pride could not sustain him here.

The adjudicator frowned. "Well? Why do you interrupt us with this story to defend a man who did you harm?"

Luca took a breath. "Because it is the right thing to do."

The presiding adjudicator made a wry face. "The slave must show himself better than his master, eh?"

"No," Luca whispered. He could have never come, could have walked away without a shred of guilt, grateful that Ande could not pursue him. He didn't want to be here now. "No, not that." But it was difficult to explain, and more difficult before these dangerous, skeptical men and Ande himself.

Another adjudicator sighed with weariness. "Come, let's save time and trouble. What has he offered you? Or his fellows in the Gehrn cult? What have they paid you to testify on his behalf?"

Old emotions flashed through Luca and forged together into anger, giving him momentary strength and courage. "No one could offer money enough to help this man," he snarled with unfeigned disgust.

The presiding adjudicator blinked at the sudden ferocity and then seemed to accept Luca's statement. "That, at least, I believe," he allowed, and someone chuckled. "But I suppose we'll have to see if your posited defense will hold up once extracted for legal consideration."

The adjudicator to his left cleared his throat. "Reeve, it is the order of this court that you take this prisoner slave and deliver him to the duly appointed extractors in order that they may excavate the truth of his testimony from him. When they are satisfied of the truth, you will bring it and the prisoner slave to this court for our consideration in this matter."

"Yes, my lord!" barked the guard.

Luca's heart tumbled out of its place to flutter about in his stomach. "No," he tried. "I volunteered—I came of my own will—"

But it was useless, and the guard bore him with practiced strength out of the courtroom and into the narrow corridors.

"You know," said one man, shrugging out of his jacket, "when I joined up, this wasn't at all what I thought I'd be doing."

"Nor me neither," the other said. "I say, when they tell stories of boys joining up out of villages for the cause, it's a lot more about killing Ryuven and a lot less about beating slaves. This is going to sound something less glorious when I go home and they ask about my duties and service."

"My sister is one who doesn't much care for the institution. I can't tell her I've been a court excavator if I ever want to see my nephews and nieces again." He snorted. "Kind of funny, that I'm going to have to lie about getting the truth, don't you think?"

Luca couldn't see the humor of it just then. He was facedown on a forked wooden platform, his arms splayed and fastened at the wide end and his feet bound at the narrow base, and he was naked, shivering with cold and trepidation.

He had volunteered. He had volunteered his testimony to the Court of the High Star, and it had been all right; he had not been taken and beaten. It had been too much to hope it would work out the same way here.

I am surprised at the depth of your gratitude. Perhaps you hoped for minimal torture. A switch instead of a scourge, or maybe they would just twist a finger?

But he had not even done this to save the life of a man who had saved him. This had been blind trust in a greater justice, and it had been madness.

The two extractors charged with beating a confession out of him were scanning their tools. "I just don't feel like something with a lot of blood," the first said. "It's been a long few days, and I don't want to be facing up to that."

"We can't do anything permanent," the second said. "No crushing, no breaking anything important."

"What's important? And why not?"

"You know, a leg or arm versus a nose or finger or something. And it's because this one is still someone's slave, not a court-owned slave, and that means we have to give him back. It's no gamble whether whoever owns him will file a complaint if he's less capable, and you know how that will come down."

"I don't see how they can expect us to do our work without doing our work," the first grumbled. "So no machines, we'll have to sweat it ourselves. Guess we'll have some blood after all."

Luca licked his lips and tried twice to speak. "My lords, I'll give the witness directly. It need not be much effort for any of us."

The second man turned to Luca, rolling his eyes. "Don't you think more than a few prisoners sent down here offer to talk straightaway? But especially in the case of a slave, you should know we can't just accept that. Slaves lie; slaves have no honor or they wouldn't be slaves. The only thing that can be trusted is what's pried out of you."

Luca felt his frail dignity cracking, and his voice slipped close to pleading. "My lords, I volunteered to testify. I was not taken to be questioned, I brought my own witness to the court. I have no reason to hold anything back."

"Maybe that's so—though you said it at liberty, and not under pressure to speak true, so that's not certain." Here he gave a wink to emphasize the joke. "But whether that's true or it's not, however so, Dak and I have got to look like we earned our pay, and we can't do that if you look like a fresh-plucked daisy. So save your breath for getting through what's got to be done, and then we'll see what you have to say."

"Look, Gare, let's start with straps," the first one said. "They're heavy enough to do most of the work for us, and they won't make much mess. We can use the brads and save our arms."

Luca shifted on the stained wooden platform, but his bonds held firm. *Holy One, I only thought to do the right thing. Help me.*

The two men took up places on either side of him, each armed with a thick leather band the width of Luca's hand, punctuated with air holes and metal brads for weight and penetration. "Alfwin should be along in a moment to scribe, but let's get on with it."

There was the faintest *shh* of air through the holes, and then the first strap fell like heavy fire across Luca's bare back.

CHAPTER 61

"Is this true?" Elysia entered the White Mage's office without ceremony and held up the note Ewan had left on her desk. "Is the Pairvyn bringing another Ryuven to court?"

Ewan set down the jar in his hand; this would be a delicate conversation. "It is true. He has requested to bring another Ryuven courtier or officer to aid in negotiations."

"I don't see what is left to negotiate. We had a treaty with the Ryuven. We were attacked by Ryuven. For all that he says it was not their clan or tribe or what it may be, that is no reason for us to bring more Ryuven into our capital."

"Unless this one can offer a genuine solution to our Ryuven problem."

"The shield offered a genuine solution to our Ryuven problem," Elysia muttered. She seated herself at his table. "The only thing the mind fears more than damage and devastation is change and uncertainty, and sometimes change is the greater obstacle."

He sat across from her and folded his hands on the table.

"I have fought for the end of this war all my life. But I don't know if I can make the change and accept a new reality, now that it's here. If Ryuven in our capital, in the Naziar, is the price of ending the war... I give myself some small credit for being aware of my own mind in this, for consciously considering rather than just resisting. I'll claim a bit more for gritting my teeth against the sight of Ryuven in my markets and looking for the good they bring. I am not one of the disgruntled rowdies waiting with a cudgel and looking for an excuse. But to bring them, more of them, into the court—in the end, I don't know if I can do it."

Ewan nodded. "I understand." He looked at her and took a breath. "Elysia, I have waited twenty years. I have served twenty years as Grand Mage of the Great Circle, spent twenty years liaising with the generals and king, done twenty years of paperwork that you evaded by remaining the Silver Mage, so that now in this moment I can at last pull rank on you. Mage Parma, I order you to work with the Ryuven emissary."

It was perhaps the first time he had seen her truly speechless, and he wondered if he should make his escape before she recovered. It was too bad they were in his own office, making it more difficult to flee.

But Elysia waited a long moment, and when at last she spoke, her voice was level and thoughtful. "I did not want to be the White Mage because I did not believe it was possible to end this war, and I wanted someone who did believe to be in the position to end it. I wanted someone in that seat who believed what I could not."

Ewan gave her a careful smile. "You brought this upon yourself."

"I suppose I did." She sat back in the chair. "So I suppose I should trust your judgment—should trust in my own judgment in placing you here—and obey this order to work with the Ryuven in our midst."

Ewan cocked his head. "Placed me here? Was that an admission, at long last, that you tampered with the election to prevent your own ascendance?"

Elysia's mouth curled. "I refer only to my own vote for you, Ewan. But I trust to the decision I made that day."

"Thank you," Ewan said, and he meant it sincerely.

"So, you know something about this new emissary, I take it?"

"Very little, only a name and rank. But Tamaryl'sho seems to think it will be an important step in the stabilization of the treaty and relations."

"I hope you both are right."

Shianan entered his quarters and kicked the door shut behind him. He scowled at the paperwork on the desk and purposely turned his back on it. The military train was fully resettled, and that meant he should tackle the reports on his desk, but not yet.

The realization had crept up on him while he was distracted, a burr of a thought that had resolved into a memory of warm, tight fingers and a warm, urgent kiss. *He was married.* Sweet Holy One, he had married Ariana, despite everything. It sent alternating waves of heat and chills through him.

And he had not seen or heard of her since.

He went into the living quarters to find a chair that didn't face the stacked reports. There was another paper on his bed, out of place, and his first reaction was to ignore it as well. But then he considered that it was unlikely to have found its way past his office on its own; Luca must have placed it separately, out of the eyes of any soldiers or aides who came to his office. Perhaps it was a note from Ariana, kept safely out of others' eyes.

Shianan retrieved the sheet and read, and then read again.

I have gone to the trial of Flamen Ande to testify. If I do not return, please come for me.

King's runny oats, what had Luca done?

Shianan abandoned all thoughts of rest and bolted for the door.

It took him some time to learn which of the courtrooms was hosting Ande's trial—so different from his own—and to coax from the bailiff waiting outside the empty room the information that the court was recessed while the slave prisoner was questioned.

"There was no slave prisoner," Shianan snapped. "He came here of his own will."

"All slaves are prisoners here," the man replied, unflappable. "Slaves can't act of their own will, you know that."

Shianan resisted the urge to grab him by the open collar and shake him. "Where was he taken?"

A few minutes later, he rushed down the narrow corridor, lit poorly by too few lamps, to the grated door that led to the questioning cells. "Let me in!" he called. "Let me in!"

A guard appeared on the far side, looking annoyed at the noise. "Who are you and what authorization do you have?"

"I'm Commander Becknam, Count of Bailaha, and I'm here for my slave."

The guard frowned. "I'm sorry, my lord, but if your slave was seized for questioning, I can't just let you in to have him. All prisoners here are royal prisoners, and I need royal authorization for anything done with them."

"You took him back there quick enough on a court's order."

"These are royal courts, my lord. I would need something to overrule that."

Shianan would have punched his placid face if he hadn't been safely on the other side of the iron grill. "Open—this—door."

The guard looked alarmed and took a step back. "I'm sorry, my lord, I can't do that without authorization. If you will bring me such an order from the court or another royal authority, I will of course do—"

"I'll bring you an order," Shianan snarled, and he wheeled from the door. Was that screaming, coming faintly down the corridor? He couldn't be sure, couldn't be sure it was Luca. There were many prisoners, many criminals pressed here for implications against their fellow conspirators or thieves. He wasn't even sure he had heard cries at all.

He rushed from the justice building.

Shianan beat on the door without stop, heedless of who might see him. At last it opened, revealing Ethan with a more startled and perturbed expression than Shianan had ever seen on him. "My lord?" he asked, his tone somewhere between rebuke and concern.

"I need him. I need him now. It can't wait."

Ethan took a step back and held open the door. "Please enter, my lord, and I'll inform my master."

Shianan did not wait but followed Ethan through a warren of corridors. Soren got to his feet as they at last entered a rear room. "Shianan! What's wrong?"

"They have Luca. Please. I need your help."

"Who does?"

"The courts. They're torturing him for testimony."

Soren's face twisted. "I can't... I'll come."

Together they hurried across the Naziar, Soren in a concealing hood and limping as quickly as he could, and Shianan led the way to the iron-grill door. "Open up!" he shouted.

The guard returned. "Have you brought an appropriate order?"

Soren pushed his hood back. "Mine will suffice."

"My lord! Er, Your Highness!" The guard tried to jerk to attention and reach for the lock at the same time, with painfully awkward results.

At last the door was open, and Shianan stormed through. "Which way?"

"They took the slave prisoner to cell four, my lord. This way."

CHAPTER 62

The two extractors had set themselves on either side of Luca, one working over the length of his back and the other over his buttocks and thighs. Despite their initial protests of weary reluctance, they worked in quick, efficient strokes, and Luca's whole body throbbed and burned, fresh streaks of bright pain with each blow. His pride had been scoured away years before under Ande's cruel ministrations, and he grunted or cried with each fall of the strap.

"All right, let's do it again," said Dak. "Got the notes?"

The confessioner scribe straightened in his chair. "Go ahead."

Dak moved nearer Luca's head, facedown and his eyes squeezed closed in the only escape available to him. "Tell us how the Shard was tainted."

Luca drew a shuddering breath. "A vial of Ryuven blood was accidentally included. My master didn't want to hear my interruption. He didn't know it was Ryuven blood. The sabotage to the shield was an accident."

The scribe recorded this. "That matches. Once more should do it."

"King's own oats," grumbled Gare, and they started again. Luca tried to curl away from the straps but he was held fast to the table, exposing his swollen and bruised flesh to their brutal attentions. Pain and panic rose like a crushing wave, blurring perceptions.

When they paused again, Luca needed a moment to recognize that they were speaking to him. He dragged his head to the side. "Ryuven blood on the table. Took it by accident. All of it, accident. Please. It was an accident."

"Why was there a vial of Ryuven blood on the table?"

"I don't know."

"Why were the items for the ritual spread on the table?"

"I don't know."

Alfwin the scribe sighed. "Press him." As the men began strapping him again, he continued, "Weren't you his slave? Weren't you carrying the necessary items? Did you spill them on the table and collect them poorly?"

"No—!" Luca couldn't remember—it hadn't happened. Heavy blows fell, burning him. If he admitted clumsiness, would they hurt him more? "Please—it was an accident—I didn't mean it—please..."

Alfwin threw down his pen. "King's sweet oats, we were so close."

The extractors paused, leaving Luca shaking. "What's that?"

"Now he says he confused the vials, not prisoner Ande. That's a variation, and now we have to confirm the truth of it." He swore and bent to retrieve his pen. "And I had wanted to be finished early today."

"She'll wait," Dak said. "But 'soats. What do you want to do?"

"No," Luca gasped. "No, I didn't—that's not what I meant."

"Still have to give him back workable," Gare said. "So maybe let's burn him. That should sear up and leave him mostly whole."

"It'll take time to heat," grumbled Alfwin. "Can't you do something else?"

"I'm not risking a complaint from some shiny-panted noble that we cost him useful money just to get you to your girl a few minutes faster," Gare snapped.

"Don't see how anyone could complain. You're acting under royal authority in a treason case, and anyway he's clearly been flogged before, so it's not as if they could whine they preferred him pristine."

"Look, a couple years ago a fellow crippled a prisoner who wouldn't talk, got the answers out of him in the end, all looked good for the trial. But the prisoner was a slave for some duke or other and His Grace complained he'd been shorted the cost of him, and so they took the price out of the extractor's wages. I've got family to feed, and that's more important than your wick needing dipped, so sit down with your nice clean paper and ink and let us do our job, and then you can do yours."

Dak was already fussing with a brazier, blowing charcoal to light. The scribe bristled. "My duty isn't so fine as that. I have to sit through all this, too."

"Don't see you lifting a hand to help."

Luca squeezed his eyes shut, spent tears and spit cold against his skin. He had not imagined this. He had thought they would give him a few switches for the formality of it but would accept his volunteered testimony, rather than treating him as a recalcitrant who must be forced to confess. He throbbed and burned and more was coming, they would scorch him with irons, and he had not meant for any of this.

Please, help me.

There was a short knock at the door. Then a scuffle of feet, and a pounding at the door. "Open up! Open up in the name of the prince!"

Dak went to the door—locked against the unlikely escape of a prisoner—and fumbled with the keys. "Half a moment, I'm opening!"

Luca twisted, trying to see, hoping against hope for some royal reprieve.

Dak turned the bolt, and Shianan burst through the door, eyes wild and dangerous. "I want my slave."

Dak stepped back. "We're nearly done with him, my lord. Just finishing up the questions by order of the court—"

"I did not give him permission to testify," Shianan growled, "so the questioning is finished."

There was someone else in the doorway—Soren, the prince-heir.

"My lord, we are doing our duty as charged by—"

"I'll not have him broken up by you to save the life of a Gehrn who brought down the shield," Shianan snapped. "Unless you want to be responsible for the cost of him, you'll get him off that table and into his clothes."

Gare threw the confessioner scribe a darkly significant look and then moved to unbind Luca's wrists.

Humiliation and fear had flooded Luca when he had been stripped and bound, but now he felt icy hot shame as he rocked upright on the forked table, naked and streaked with his own tears and the extractors' work. Indignity was their tool as much as any other.

Dak shoved Luca's wadded clothing at him, and when Luca's hands shook, Dak swore and pushed his legs toward the under-braies himself. "Get dressed and get out of here," he muttered softly.

Luca didn't bother with anything beyond trousers and shirt, clutching the tunic and boots to his chest as he stumbled toward Shianan and the door.

"My lord, what do I report?" asked Alfwin the scribe. "I have to turn in an account and testimony to the court."

Shianan wheeled on him. "You can tell them that you lazed away your time here, as clearly these men have been working for some time and yet you haven't managed to ask your question."

The scribe stiffened. "My lord, I have taken a number of comparative statements and—"

"Then you have your report." Shianan's iron tone dared the man to raise protest again. He did not.

The two extractors said nothing, avoiding both Shianan's glare and the prince beyond him.

Unchallenged, Shianan snapped, "Then I will take my slave and go." He hooked a hand beneath Luca's upper arm, partly a possessive gesture for the watching men and partly support as he pushed him toward the door.

Dread had made the long, dim corridors even longer as Luca had entered; relief shortened them, and they were soon out into the open air, much nearer than Luca would have guessed in his bound terror. Shianan propelled him across the Naziar, taking long strides and not speaking. Luca was faintly aware of Soren trailing them, but the prince said nothing.

They reached the commander's office, and Shianan shoved Luca inside, drove them through to the living quarters, pushed him toward a chair. "Sit down," he said, his voice quavering dangerously, "and tell me what the hell you were doing."

Luca had been so caught up in relief that he had not realized Shianan's fury was not just for the extractors and the confessioner scribe. He stared at his master.

"You went to the trial," Shianan bit out, "where they could have seized you as his confiscated property. You went to his trial to testify—in his *defense*. Why?"

This wasn't fair. Luca could not face Shianan's anger so hard upon his own pain and terror. He reached for a blanket from his low mattress and pulled it about his hunched shoulders. "I hadn't thought they might consider me still his property. I've been sold multiple times since then, legally and illegally."

"Leave that. You went to speak for him! Why?"

Luca bit down his hot response and looked at his friend—really looked at him, for the first time since their escape. Behind the fury, there was fear in Shianan's eyes, deep fear fueling his rage. He had been afraid for Luca—and with reason. Shianan wanted to protect his friend from those who endangered him, even if that was Luca himself.

Luca closed his eyes, drew a breath, tried to think of words that could explain to Shianan what he could not fully explain to himself. "Do you remember, when the guards were taking you to find the Shard and we escaped, and I urged you to run? Do you remember telling me you would return the Shard, because it was necessary, even though it meant going back to face torture and even death?"

Shianan's fury had been checked, but he was not yet swayed. "The Shard would protect thousands of innocent people. You would save one despicable monster."

"He is innocent of the treason and sabotage he's accused of."

"He is not innocent by any other measure. Luca, what he did to you—I saw only a bit of it. I defended it to Ariana, because I had to, but... And what other—"

"Don't try to tell me what wrongs I've suffered," Luca snapped. "Don't catalog to me the full cargo of brutalities, indignities, violations, cruelties large and petty. I have a full accounting of them, I was there for all of them." The words tumbled out of him like grain down a chute, too plentiful and too fast to catch. "Bring him to trial for that, and I will testify in full and call upon the Holy One and the crown to crush him beneath the weight of his actions. I will speak and speak and speak, so that no dam may hold back my testimony. Bring him on that charge, and I will not defend him, but condemn him beyond doubt. So go, then, and tell the adjudicators that they have more charges to consider."

Shianan hesitated. "Luca... That's impossible. This was your only chance to see him put away. What he did to his own slave... He can't be brought up on that."

Luca leaned forward, the blanket slipping off his shoulders, his fingers clenched in the woolen folds so that fibers tore in his grip. His eyes locked onto Shianan's. "Then *make it illegal.*"

Shianan stared at him and then dropped his eyes, and when he spoke his voice was weak, helpless. "I know. I didn't—but now I see. I know. But I can't do that, Luca. I'm only a count, one with a hollow title, and that only because the council was too occupied to strip me of it. I don't have the ear of the council. There are so many things I would change in myself, Luca, and I wish I had the standing to sway the minds of men, but I am in the end an insignificant powerless bastard whom the court despises, and I can't."

Luca twisted the blanket in his fingers, hating Shianan's words and hating their truth. If Shianan protested slavery, it would be just one more potential political upset from the bastard. It had been frustration that had prompted Luca to speak, not expectation or hope.

In the corner of the room, near the door, Prince Soren cleared his throat.

Luca and Shianan jumped and turned, hot embarrassment jolting through them. "My lord," Shianan gasped. "I..."

Prince Soren smiled wryly. "It's not often, or ever, I'm wholly forgotten in a room. It was a new experience for me. Thank you."

Luca rose to his feet in mute horror. That they should have ignored the prince, argued before him, that Shianan should have been seen in such argument with a slave...

Soren made a dismissive wave and moved toward Shianan's bed. "May I take this seat?"

"I'll bring chairs from the office," Luca managed.

"You won't," Shianan said, regaining some firmness in his voice. "I'll bring them. You sit—after His Highness is seated, of course."

In a moment, three chairs were set at the points of a triangle. Soren sat in one, facing them. Shianan sank into a second, resting his face in his hands. "Sit down, Luca," he said wearily.

"I'd rather not."

"His Highness won't mind, not today."

Luca tugged the blanket about himself. "Still, Master Shianan, I'd rather not."

Shianan turned his head, and then his eyes widened with guilty realization. "Sweet runny oats," he breathed. "Luca, I'm sorry. 'Soats. Get that shirt off and let me see you."

Luca hesitated. "My lords..."

Soren had the grace to look embarrassed, and he rose. "I can bring a healer."

"It's bruising," Luca said tentatively, not wanting to correct him. "There's not much doctoring that can be done, I think."

"I've dealt with bruises," Shianan said. "And we'll want to stop the swelling before it gets worse. If only we had ice..."

"What can I do to help?" Soren asked.

"We need cold water," Shianan said. "I'll bring some from the fountain outside. We'll need to chill the bruises, to bring down the swelling."

"What about mage healing?"

Shianan shook his head. "Not for this kind of injury—it accelerates the body's own natural response, and in this case that would mean more swelling. But starflower or nettle leaf will help with the pain."

Luca remained still, freshly humiliated at the idea of exposing his degradation and injury, and not only to Shianan but to the prince. Shianan, caught up in his own convoluted anger and shame, scooped up a pitcher and went out through the office.

Luca stood with his head bowed, silent and ashamed.

Soren cleared his throat. "I might return to my own office. I have duties that might be missing me."

A prince's duties must take precedence over a slave's needs, Luca thought, before he realized that Soren was gently asking if Luca wanted him to go. The idea of a prince waiting upon a slave's answer boggled him, and he could not respond.

Then Soren leaned forward in his chair, so that he came into Luca's downcast vision, and he smiled ruefully but without making eye contact. "Not so long ago I was restricted to my bed, lying in my own filth until someone came to clean me like an infant and to treat my bedsores."

It wasn't the same, it wasn't like being exploited and shamed because of one's powerlessness, but Luca could see the attempt. He twisted his mouth upward, as was polite. "I am sorry to hear that, my lord. I am glad you're feeling better." That was true, at least.

"Use Becknam's bed. He won't mind. Where will I find his bandages?"

"I'll get them, my lord."

Shianan returned as Luca moved to the bed, facedown to expose his battered back. The skin was broken in places where the brads had caught or the edge of the strap had welted, or where swelling had torn open small fissures, but most of the damage was bruising. Shianan cursed the extractors, adjudicators, and Gehrn in a low, running stream as he worked.

"What are these scattered round marks?" Soren asked in a small voice.

"Punctures in the leather," Shianan answered. "So the strap falls faster and heavier."

Soren did not answer.

The prince, though plainly inexperienced, put forth his best effort. There was little expert work required; compresses needed to be chilled and placed over the bruising and then changed as they began to warm. Water ran from Luca's back and legs onto the bed. Luca lay with his face cradled in his arms, to expose his flanks as they had been exposed to the extractors and to hide the tears that ran silently into the bedclothes, as he lay helpless and exposed and every touch was kind.

CHAPTER 63

Shianan kept his eyes from Ariana's black door as he passed, refusing to think on how she was still in the field with Marshal Vanguilder and facing a new enemy, refusing to consider that the Black Mage's office would go to someone else if she did not return.

He knocked at the White Mage's door and waited, shifting with nervous energy.

"Your lordship." Ewan Hazelrig gave him a pleasant smile. "What can I do for you?"

"May I come in?"

The corridor was empty, but there was no reason to be unwary. There were laws.

"Of course, do come in."

Shianan followed him into the office. "You once had extra healing amulets," he said quietly. "I hoped you might have one now."

"Oh, no, I'm sorry," the elder Mage Hazelrig said. He gestured to a chair, which Shianan took. The White Mage turned another to face him and sat. "Are you injured?"

"It's not for me." The next words were more difficult, but he had to trust that Ewan Hazelrig already knew enough that they would be neither a surprise nor an offense. "It's for Luca."

Mage Hazelrig lifted his eyebrows. "Oh, no."

"I know the amulets shouldn't go to slaves, but I thought... He went to the Gehrn priest's trial. He offered to testify in Ande's defense, the idiot. And so they excavated the testimony from him, as the court requires."

Mage Hazelrig swore quietly.

"I know they're not good for bruising and swelling, not at first, but I thought perhaps for later... I've done what I can, but I hoped..."

Mage Hazelrig shook his head. "I had a few extras, as I said, from when Ariana and I were working together before she joined the Circle. But that was before Arakadamia. There's not an amulet in Alham, I would guess."

"None?"

"They take so long to make. Even with the batches already in progress before the battle, we won't have any for two months."

"Of course." Shianan nodded. "I'm sorry to have bothered you."

"If there's anything else I can offer?" Mage Hazelrig stood and turned to his tall cabinet of drawers. "You have willow bark?"

"He shouldn't have that for bruising."

"Ah, yes. Then I have lavender and cloves, and jackwort if you think that would be of use."

"I don't have lavender or jackwort at home."

"Then I'll send some with you. The market's closing soon, if it hasn't already."

Shianan nodded, grateful. "Thank you, my lord mage."

Mage Hazelrig looked at him with a question.

"I'm sorry. I'm just keenly aware I've interrupted the White Mage of the Circle to ask for illegal healing, to help a slave, hurt when he testified in defense of the man who brought down the Circle's shield. If I had any sense..."

"You have plenty of sense," Mage Hazelrig corrected. "Enough to know I would not balk at such a request." He crossed his arms. "I cannot say I want Flamen Ande to be released, but neither can I deny that his destruction was accomplished through ignorance and the concealment of cruelty, not through specific intention. I am surprised Luca chose to defend him, but I cannot condemn it—though I can hope he did not say much that might implicate us and our knowledge of Tamaryl. How much does he know?"

"Enough," Shianan admitted. "But he said he gave them a plausible explanation for the accident, vials from your office confused with the Gehrn's. He assured me they had no reason to suspect you or me."

Mage Hazelrig nodded. "Then please give him my best wishes for his recovery, and if you should need anything else, let me know."

"Thank you, my lord mage." Shianan took a step toward the door and then stopped. "You've heard nothing from Lady Ariana?"

He shook his head. "No."

"It is too early to expect word," Shianan told Mage Hazelrig and himself. "I only thought to ask. Thank you."

The darkness was a heavy, palpable thing as it oozed over Luca. It pressed him, smothered him, threatened to engulf him. It clogged his throat and lungs. It pinned him down.

Every night he had spent in Ande's citadel crept through that darkness to circle and stalk his low mattress, as his body burned and ached with fresh injury and old memory. He wanted to move, wanted to flee, wanted to pray, but his mind could not even form words. The rasp of his breath came through the remembered slap and crack of leather.

Then someone was moving in the dark, and Luca coiled as if he could escape into himself even as he knew, *knew* there was no escape. But light glowed into existence, and it was Shianan lighting a candle from an old ember.

He did not speak or look at Luca, only set water to warm. He opened the chest and withdrew the herbs he kept for his training injuries. Nettle went into the water, and starflower oil. Then lavender, to soothe inflammation and unrest, wafted through the room.

Shianan left the water to heat and came to squat beside Luca's low bed.

Heart racing, Luca wished he could feign sleep, but there was no escape in lies either. He pushed himself up from his bed, rising into the little hollow of safety the candle carved from the dark. It wasn't possible to sit back normally, so he hesitated on his knees, and that felt worse. He pulled his blanket around his shoulders, as if it might shield him—from memory, from shame, from being seen and known.

"I hate rainy nights," Shianan said without preamble, looking into the dark. "A bit, in the summer, but more in the winter. Icy nights are the worst of them. I toss and wake and wish for dawn until it ends."

Luca jerked his chin in a single nod. Was it raining? He couldn't hear drops against the roof through the hum in his ears.

Shianan turned and slid into the gap Luca had made on the low bed, leaning against the wall. He set the candle on the floor opposite them. "When I hear sleet beating on roof or window or tent, there isn't much I wouldn't give for blankets and a fire. None are ever quite warm enough, though."

Now Luca understood. He lowered his head, humiliated in his fear.

"But when it was raining in Fedstone—'soats, was that only a week ago?—with the rain hitting the window like soft little needles to my soul, it wasn't the same. You, and Marla, you were sleeping there, and it was such a small thing to make a difference—you're just as wet in a storm whether alone or with someone—but it did."

Luca's eyes burned.

"And now I wait for the king to learn what Ariana and I have done, and to respond to this disastrous deployment, and every time I close my eyes I see the littered field of that battle we—not even a battle, a rout, a slaughter. And I don't want to sit alone in the dark with that."

Luca moved his head, one short nod.

Shianan shifted, and the weight of his arm settled across Luca's shoulders—tentatively at first, testing for a flinch, and then settling like a thick woolen blanket. Luca exhaled, and the arm fell with his shoulders.

The candle sputtered and then gentled again. Luca sank lower, hesitating as he tried to ease weight onto bruising. He rocked to the side, bracing on one arm and leaning slightly into Shianan to ease the pressure.

Shianan looked across the room into the faint distant light of the brazier. "Why didn't you tell me? That you were going to do such a stupid thing?"

"I thought you would stop me." Luca's voice was thick. "I thought you would talk me out of it."

"I should have. That man—you did not owe him this. You did not owe him anything."

"I know." Luca heard an edge to his voice, and he tried to soften it. It wasn't Shianan he was angry with.

"Did the priests tell you to do this? At the temple, not the Gehrn—or if it was the Gehrn, if someone found you and—"

"No one told me to," Luca said. "It was—do you remember, when I said we survived because others took the blame for what we had done?"

"Other criminals. Murderers. Men who were punished for their crimes only because they were punished for ours."

"Still. There was so much..." Luca was grateful for the dark, for Shianan's fixed gaze across the room. "I don't regret what we did. What I said. But when I think about faith, or justice, about forgiveness and—"

"King's sweet oats, Luca, you aren't—you haven't forgiven him?" Shianan's body tensed, his arm rigid on Luca's shoulders.

"No!" Luca shook his head. "No, I don't think I'm that strong."

He felt Shianan's skepticism even through the dark.

"But I did not want him killed for treason he had not committed, not with my implicit lying to let it happen."

"You lied to save him," Shianan said quietly. "You could not have told the adjudicators the truth."

Luca had no answer.

"There's not much justice in this world. Maybe you should let it come where it can."

"Letting him be killed for something he had not done would not be justice."

Shianan blew out his breath. "I would like to see him pay for what he has done. I wish I could do that." He shook his head. "In Fedstone, I hit Demario."

"What?"

"I followed him out into the street, and I punched him. More than once." Shianan gave a tiny huff of humorless laughter. "I said he was a brute and a fool for disdaining her, but still I don't think he understood why."

Luca fought down a flame of vindictive satisfaction. "I shouldn't—but I'm glad to hear it. I wish I'd had the courage and the ability when he cut her in front of the whole public room."

"It was only the ability you lacked."

"What?" Luca shook his head. "I didn't—I didn't dare."

"Not starting a fight you knew would lead to more trouble for both of you wasn't a lack of courage, it was good sense. Two slaves cannot attack a freeman in a public room."

"But—"

"But you don't lack the courage, or you wouldn't have walked into that courtroom today."

Luca shook his head. "I couldn't feel my hands or feet. I could barely breathe. I couldn't look—I was terrified."

"Exactly. And yet you were there." Shianan looked across the room, and when he spoke again his voice was quiet and tight. "Can you explain it? Again?" He worked his fingers. "I thought you would hate him."

"I do hate him." Luca looked down, stretching the tight muscles and swollen skin on his shoulders. "I couldn't, not then, but since I've come back to Alham... I do hate him. I was pleased to know he was in jail and facing trial. I imagined what they would do to him."

Shianan shifted but remained quiet.

"Someone told me we choose our scars. Not that nothing can affect us, of course, but that we can choose what to keep. And I could not stop living that time while I hated him." It was easier to put into words, now he had done it. "The idea came to me that if I spoke for him—I could not speak for him in hate."

A long moment passed. At last Shianan asked, "Are you glad you did it?"

"Not just now," Luca answered honestly, the ghost of a bitter laugh in his tone. He shifted, trying unsuccessfully to ease the ache. "But I think I will be."

Shianan passed a hand over his face and through his hair.

Luca thought of Shianan carrying the Shard back to Alham and tried once more. "Haven't you done something solely because it was the right thing to do, and that right thing was the only difference you could make?"

"Yes," Shianan answered solemnly. "The day Ande was arrested. He had done so much—destroyed the shield, lost Ariana—and the only thing I could do to rectify any of it was to keep one bloody, mute Furmelle slave from becoming gambling money for the guards." His voice softened. "That was the best decision I've ever made."

Luca pressed his arms close against his torso and bowed his head. Warmth washed through him in gentle frothy waves, and he wished he had words grand enough to reply.

Shianan rocked to his feet, leaving a chill where his arm pulled away, and went to retrieve the warmed tea. He passed the earthenware mug to Luca. "Here. You'll want to blunt tomorrow; it's going to hurt."

It already did, but Luca knew it would worsen before it improved. He sipped the medicine.

At the chest, Shianan put away the herbs, and then he lifted a bottle. "Do you want something more?"

Luca's chest spasmed, and he thought of Renner, drinking through pain and letting both drive his cruelty, and of his father, eating mind-muddling viante to live his lie. He shook his head tightly.

Shianan put the bottle back. Then he went to his bed and pulled away the blankets, wrapping them about himself as he sat against the wall near Luca's low mattress.

"What are you doing?" Luca broke off the last word, ashamed of how he was glad for Shianan's presence, relieving the oppressive dark. "You can't sleep there."

"I can't sleep there either," Shianan said irritably, jerking his head toward his own bed. "The mattress is still wet with those compresses."

Luca's heart twisted with embarrassed gratitude. "But…"

"Quiet," Shianan growled. "I've slept in worse places than my own room. And didn't you just hear how much I hate cold wet nights? Shut up and let me sleep where I can."

An unfamiliar sensation swelled in Luca's torso and ran through him, and he hid his response in drinking the rest of the medicinal tea. Shianan closed his eyes and tipped his head back. Luca turned to lean his less-bruised shoulder against the wall.

Outside, the dark pressed against the high windows, but it could not reach Luca's low bed. Outside, Lady Ariana was away fighting an enemy more formidable than they had believed. But here they wrapped themselves in blankets and orange coal-light. They slouched against the wall, blankets drawn protectively against the cold dark, and let the candle burn down as they slid into sleep.

TO BE CONTINUED
Kin & Kind

GET A FREE STORY AND MORE

The website has everything from background research and inspiration to story glossaries and book club discussion guides, as well as an infrequent newsletter for events and releases. Go to **LauraVAB.com** to receive bonus stories and sneak peeks, special or advance offers, and release information.

Thank you for reading, and please be sure to review *Crown & Creed* at your favorite site. I read every review! and I'd love to hear from you.